FOR THEIR SINS

DI ALEC MCKAY BOOK 5

ALEX WALTERS

First published in 2021 by Bloodhound Books.

www.bloodhoundbooks.com

Print ISBN 978-1-913942-31-1

ALSO BY ALEX WALTERS

The Inspector McKay Series

Candles and Roses (Book 1)

Death Parts Us (Book 2)

Their Final Act (Book 3)

Expiry Date (Book 4)

Thriller

Winterman

1

There was something almost pagan about it. Not as explicitly so as some of the longer-established ceremonies around these strange isles, admittedly, and some of the God-fearing church types involved in tonight's event would be horrified at the mere suggestion. Even so, as Alec McKay stared at the masked figures and the bonfire topped with grotesque effigies, it felt as if they might be invoking something far from Christian.

'I hope you're not having regrets already?'

McKay turned to smile at Chrissie. 'I was just wondering why we didn't do it years ago.'

'Because we had good reasons for staying in town. Or we thought we did.'

'Remind me again what they were.'

'You liked to walk out to the pub of an evening.'

'I can still do that if I want to. But when did I last go to the pub? I'm getting too old for that kind of thing. I can barely drag myself out for something like this.'

They were standing in the darkness away from the fire itself, just yards from the sea. McKay peered out across the firth, seeing the string of lights from Ardersier doubled in the still waters. Behind him, the crowd was growing rowdier as the fire took hold. It was a cold clear midwinter night, the sky heavy with stars.

'I'm just worried it's going to be too quiet for you.'

'Doesn't seem quiet tonight, does it?'

McKay wasn't even sure why they'd come. This kind of community event wasn't really his scene. There was too much danger of running into someone you might feel obliged to talk to. But Chrissie was more sociable than he was, and she'd been keen to attend.

It had drawn an impressive crowd, especially in the circumstances. He could understand that. It had been like this for a few months now, despite the recurrent lockdowns. People were desperate to engage in some form of social life, taking any opportunity to meet other people. The tourists hadn't fully returned later in the summer, and the bars and restaurants had remained socially-distanced and unseasonably quiet. The locals had done their best to compensate, and that had continued into the autumn and winter.

This was the latest in a series of community events organised to boost the local economy and raise funds for good causes. McKay had attended one or two, usually when goaded by Chrissie, and – though he was reluctant to admit it – had generally enjoyed them. Even when socially-distanced, Chrissie could happily chat to some of their neighbours, while he was content to knock back a few glasses of cheap plonk or a plate of stovies.

Tonight's event was on a larger scale than most, and was the brainchild of a local writer. McKay had been concerned that, given the size of the event, he'd find it more difficult to be his usual unsociable self, but so far the darkness and the crowd had let him remain unobtrusively in the background, while Chrissie did enough blethering with neighbours and acquaintances for both of them. Chrissie had even volunteered to drive so he could enjoy a couple of local ales.

The bonfire was getting going now, and the crowd's excitement was rising. McKay hadn't bothered to check the schedule for the evening, but he knew it included music, fireworks and some other 'surprise events'. None of that appealed to McKay – especially the 'surprise events' – but he was happy to drink his beer and listen to the steady wash of the waters against the beach.

As if its owner had been reading those last thoughts, a voice said, 'Alec? I wouldn't have thought this was your sort of thing?'

He turned to find his boss, DCI Helena Grant, accompanied by a man he vaguely recognised behind his face-mask. 'Helena? Wasn't expecting to see you over here, either. Bit of a drive.'

'I couldn't really turn down an invitation from the organiser.' She gestured towards the man beside her.

McKay realised now where he'd seen the man before. His had been the face beaming amiably down from every noticeboard and shop window on the Black Isle for the past month. William Emsworth, best-selling author of crime fiction, and the driving force behind the evening's events. McKay allowed Emsworth a nod. 'Mr Emsworth. You've put on a good show.'

'Bill, please.' Emsworth held out his hand for shaking, then awkwardly withdrew it. 'Sorry. Keep forgetting we're not supposed to shake hands any more.' His accent was Scottish, but he sounded as if he'd spent a long time living elsewhere.

'Alec was never sociable enough to shake hands much in the first place,' Grant said.

'That's true enough,' McKay said. 'But I'm a real charmer below the surface. How do you come to know Helena, Bill?' McKay was mainly making his version of small talk, but he was also curious to know the answer. Helena had been a widow for a number of years. She'd made an ill-fated foray into online dating a year or so before, but recently, as far as McKay knew, had made no further attempts to reinvigorate her romantic life. Not, he conceded, that he'd necessarily be the first she'd rush to tell if she were back in a relationship.

Of course there was no reason for McKay to assume anything more than friendship between Helena and Emsworth. Except that something in Emsworth's expression suggested he might see things differently.

'It's a long story,' Emsworth said, in a tone that suggested he was only too keen to recount it.

'Bill contacted the comms team to see if there was anyone who could give him some advice on a book he was writing.' Grant smiled. 'For some reason, comms fobbed him off to me.'

'I'm very glad they did,' Emsworth said. 'You've really been most helpful, Helena. You've given me a lot of invaluable information.'

'If you're going to represent our work in your books,' she said, 'we might as well make it as accurate as we can.'

McKay wondered when all this had actually happened. 'Are we providing research services for crime writers now, then? Surprised we have the time.' He smiled to demonstrate he was joking, though his smile was hidden beneath his face-mask and, in truth, he wasn't entirely sure he was.

Emsworth nodded back. 'I hope it's all valuable PR for the force. I try not to depict you in a negative light, and I'm sure it must be helpful for the public to have a better idea of the valuable work you do. In any case, I was very careful not to waste any more of Helena's work time than I could help.'

'Is that right?'

'Bill was good enough to buy me a couple of excellent dinners in return for picking my brains,' Grant explained.

McKay bit back the first comment to enter his head. 'And now he's invited you here.'

'To be honest, I needed all the moral support I could get,' Emsworth said. 'It's been a fraught process getting this all together. Still, it looks like we'll all be locked down again after Christmas so I'm glad we made the effort.'

'Must have been a challenge.' McKay gestured to the crowd. 'But you seem to have attracted the numbers.'

'I'm very relieved. The biggest worry was the weather, along with all the usual social distancing concerns. People can wrap up against the cold, and it just helps sell the mulled wine. But if it pours with rain, it's a washout. We had a couple of marquees arranged as backup, but it would have cut the numbers dramatically. And people are still uncomfortable if they're crammed too close together.'

'I always was,' McKay said with feeling.

'Alec's generally keen to maintain the maximum possible distance from his fellow human beings,' Grant said.

'I suppose you see the worst of humankind in a job like yours,' Emsworth said. 'I have the luxury of only having to write about it.'

Chrissie had finished talking to the neighbour and rejoined them. She nodded a greeting to Helena Grant and looked with undisguised curiosity at Emsworth. Unlike McKay, she'd recognised him instantly.

McKay effected the introductions. 'Bill's apparently been taking lessons on policing from Helena.'

'I'm sure she's a much more appropriate tutor than Alec would be,' Chrissie said. 'He'd just tell you about the way he does things. Which isn't always in the police manual.'

'That sounds most intriguing,' Emsworth said. 'I'll have to pick your brains too at some point. You could give me some tips on the concept of the maverick cop.'

'Don't encourage him,' Grant said. 'He already makes my life hell.'

'Putting the hell into Helena, eh? Actually, Alec, I probably shouldn't tell you this, but she's very complimentary about you behind your back. She told me about some of your recent cases. Fascinating stuff.'

'Oh, God, don't tell him that.' Grant shook her head in mock despair. 'I'll never hear the last of it.'

'As long as you don't feature me in any of your books,' McKay said.

'I may be tempted to slip in a cameo.' Emsworth looked past them towards the rising flames of the bonfire. 'I'd better check that everything's on track. We're supposed to have a string quartet playing shortly and then we've got various local performers. Nothing too rowdy. Do you want to come along, Helena? I can introduce you to a few people.'

As soon as Emsworth and Grant had departed, Chrissie turned enthusiastically to McKay. 'Was that what I thought it was?'

'What?' McKay's face was a picture of innocence.

'Helena and Bill Emsworth. I had the sense they were an item.'

'I wouldn't know. Not really my territory.'

'Come off it, Alec. They were all over each other. Or they wanted to be.'

'You're the expert in that kind of thing.'

She shook her head. 'Well, I hope so. She deserves a bit of happiness after all she's been through.'

'You're not wrong about that. What did you make of him?'

'Emsworth? He seemed pleasant enough.'

'Bit smooth for my taste,' McKay said.

'Everyone's a bit smooth for your taste. Unless they're too rough.'

'Ach, well, you know my views on people.'

'You disapprove of them.'

'Present company excepted, obviously.'

'You were too slow there, Alec. But I'll take that as read.' She was staring past him into the orange glare of the bonfire. 'What's going on over there?'

Alec followed her gaze. He was expecting that some trouble might have broken out. That was always the risk of events like this. Most people were just out for a pleasant evening, but there were always one or two who downed too many pints and made a nuisance of themselves.

It didn't seem to be quite that, though. Some of the crowd were pointing into the fire, others were drawing back towards the water's edge. At first the mood was playful, but then there was a scream and the mood seemed to change almost immediately.

'Wait here.' McKay made his way through the crowd, incurring irritated responses from those he moved aside, some of them muttering darkly about his proximity. As he reached the far side of the bonfire, he saw that most of the crowd had retreated towards the water. A couple of young men were standing close to the flames, clearly troubled by the intense heat, pointing into the heart of the fire.

McKay was still some distance from the fire, but the heat was almost unbearable. 'What is it?'

One of the young men looked back at him, his face crimson from the heat. 'There's something in there. We're trying to see what it is exactly, but it's too bloody hot to get close enough.'

'What sort of something?'

The young man hesitated. 'This is going to sound stupid. But it looks like a body. A human body, I mean.'

McKay looked up at the summit of the large bonfire. Although it wasn't Bonfire Night, the organisers had positioned several effigies on top of the pyre. During the pandemic lockdown earlier in the year, residents had entertained themselves and others by positioning scarecrows around the Black Isle. Several of these had been donated to top the bonfire. It was almost as if people felt that, symbolically at least, burning the scarecrows would help finally to consign that period to history.

McKay gestured towards the scarecrows. 'Maybe one of those?'

'Could be. I don't know...'

McKay took another step forward, drawing as close as he could to the fire. It took him a moment to work out what the men had been looking at. Then he saw it, a dark shape in the centre of the flames.

He could see what the man meant. The object resembled the silhouette of a human body, stretched out in the stacked mass of wood. Whatever it was had become visible only as the wood had partially caved in to reveal the interior.

'You're probably right,' the young man said. 'Someone must have stuck one of the scarecrows in there for some reason.'

The more McKay stared into the flames, though, the less certain he became. There was something about the shape that didn't look like the scarecrows' crude approximations of the human shape. It was no doubt an illusion created by the layout of the wood and the movement of the flames, but McKay found himself growing uneasy.

There was little he could do in any case. The event had been well organised and there were no doubt fire extinguishers available, but those wouldn't be capable of extinguishing the whole bonfire. Any attempts to do so would soon be overtaken by the fire simply burning itself out. In any case, if that really was some poor bastard in the heart of the flames, it was far too late to do anything to help them.

The young men had accepted his explanation, and the rest of the crowd had lost interest in what was going on. A couple of stewards in high-visibility tabards were ushering the few lingering observers away from the fire.

McKay took the hint and made his way back to where Chrissie was waiting.

'What was it?' she said.

'Almost certainly nothing. Someone claiming they'd spotted a body in the bonfire. Maybe had a pint or two too many.'

'You mean a human body?'

'I could see what he meant actually. Just some trick of the light. How easy is a bush supposed a bear, and all that.'

'Creepy idea, though. I find those scarecrows disconcerting enough,' Chrissie said. 'I'm never keen on burning human effigies.'

They both fell silent as the first of the evening's fireworks whooshed into the air. The display was positioned so that the glitter of the fireworks would be reflected in the water. With the firth relatively still, the effect was spectacular.

On the temporary stage along the beach, a small classical ensemble had struck up what McKay, with his very limited musical knowledge, assumed must be Handel's 'Music for the Royal Fireworks'. 'Classy,' he said.

'I get the impression Emsworth's not one for half-measures,' Chrissie said. 'Even with the community funding this must have set him back a few bob.'

Leaving Chrissie watching the fireworks, McKay made his way to the pop-up bar on the edge of the crowd, buying a pint of Cromarty Happy Chappy for himself and a bottle of sparkling water for Chrissie.

'It's Inspector McKay, isn't it?'

He turned to see a young woman dressed in one of the steward's high-visibility jackets peering curiously at him. It took him a moment to place her behind her mask. 'It's Kelly, isn't it?' He was still struggling to recall her surname.

'Well remembered,' she said. 'But I suppose you have to have a good memory in your job.'

'It helps.' Kelly, a young student whose parents lived in the area, had become involved in a couple of his previous investigations. She'd seemed to have something of a nose for trouble, in a positive sense. 'Back from uni, are you?'

'Back for the Christmas vacation, yes. I wasn't sure they were going to allow it.'

'Must be your last year, isn't it? Not the best time to be graduating, I'm guessing?'

'Not really,' she said. 'The job market isn't exactly buoyant. I've applied to do an MLitt at Aberdeen for next year, so I'm just hoping that by the time I've finished things will have picked up a bit.'

'Good luck with it, anyway,' McKay said. 'It seems to be getting tougher for young people. I'm almost glad I'm getting old.'

'I didn't know you lived over here,' Kelly said.

'We moved here over the summer. Up near Culbokie. Looking for a quiet life, you know?'

'I'm usually looking for the opposite when I'm here. But I know what you mean.' She looked over her shoulder. 'I'd best go back. I'm supposed to be helping keep people away from each other as well as from the bonfire. People keep ignoring the barriers and warning signs.'

'They usually do,' McKay said. 'Try being a police officer.'

He made his way back to Chrissie, who in his absence had found yet another acquaintance. McKay nodded a greeting, handed over the bottle of water, and stood silently drinking his pint, watching as more fireworks scattered colours across the sky. He could take or leave fireworks, but he was always struck by their spellbinding effect on crowds. Everyone was staring in the air, transfixed at each new burst of exploding light.

McKay's attention was already wandering, and he looked back down at the bonfire. The scarecrows had been largely claimed by the flames by now, and the pyramid of stacked timber was collapsing in on itself. In the pale light from the flames, he could see a figure standing on the far side of the fire. Like McKay, the figure seemed uninterested by the fireworks and was staring into the heart of the fire. There was something about the silhouette – the stance, the shape of the body – that seemed oddly familiar even though it was too dark for him to make out the face. As McKay watched, the figure turned and disappeared into the crowd.

McKay took another sip of beer. He was almost beginning to enjoy himself, in a characteristically muted and unsocial manner. It occurred to him he was feeling at home here already.

It had been Chrissie's idea to move. She'd felt it would help them make a new start, put the past behind them. He accepted that Chrissie might well be right. But he'd felt uncomfortable at being uprooted from the house they'd occupied for the past fifteen years. More importantly, he'd wondered whether it was appropriate for them to leave the house where they'd brought up Lizzie. He'd worried they were cutting the final ties with her, already consigning her sadly brief life to the past.

For Chrissie, that had been precisely the point. Not that she wanted to forget Lizzie. But she wanted a way of coming to terms with their daughter's death. The memories would always be there, but they'd no longer be surrounding her.

McKay had eventually been persuaded by the house they'd found on the Black Isle. It was a new build, only a couple of years old, with spectacular views out over the Cromarty Firth, the summit of Ben Wyvis opposite. It was a pleasant place in a glorious location. More importantly it was a place without its own memories. It was a place where they could create their own, and that was what McKay was determined to do.

'You're very thoughtful tonight,' Chrissie said. 'Turning contemplative in your old age?'

'I was actually thinking that just at the moment I'm reasonably happy.'

'Well, there's a first. I won't ask in case I spoil the moment.'

'Probably wise. Do you want to get something to eat?' A couple of the local cafes had set up stalls selling barbecued meats and wood-fired pizzas.

'Why not? We might as well make an evening of it.'

They made their way to the barbecue stall and joined the short, well-dispersed queue.

'Seems to be going well,' Chrissie said.

'Your man Emsworth must be pleased,' McKay commented. 'He seemed nervous about it all.'

'Good for him for organising it. Doesn't take much for something like this to go wrong–' She stopped and stared at McKay. 'What the hell was that?'

At first, McKay had thought that the scream was just teenagers messing about, trying to scare one another. But there was an edge to the scream that indicated real emotion. It was momentarily choked off, then resumed louder, more terrified than ever.

'I'd better go and check.'

'I'd expect nothing else,' Chrissie said in a mock resigned tone. 'Ach, away with you. You're a bloody police officer before you're anything else. No one knows that better than I do.'

McKay smiled at her then hurried round to the far side of the bonfire. It was the same spot where he'd encountered the young men earlier, and he had a horrible feeling he knew already what he was going to find.

2

'Is this what happens whenever you go out, Alec?'

'What can I say? It's a gift.'

'Just remind me not to be in the vicinity next time.'

'Sorry if I ruined your evening, Helena.'

Grant stared at McKay as if daring him to say more. He gazed back amiably. It was nearly 11pm. The crowd had been dispersed as soon as it had become evident what had been found in the fire, although a few rubberneckers had hung around at the far end of the beach. Grant had summoned backup in the form of two squad cars, and the uniforms had helped seal off the scene. Grant had offered McKay a lift back later so Chrissie had headed off home. Emsworth was hanging around in the background, pacing up and down as if taking personal responsibility for what had happened.

'The only upside,' McKay said, 'is that we've also ruined Jock Henderson's evening.'

'You think Jock has a social life?'

'I've generally assumed he lies in his coffin awaiting our summons. But he looked a bit pissed off tonight.'

Jock Henderson was the lead scene of crime officer in the

region and, for reasons neither of them could clearly remember, a long-time antagonist of McKay. As McKay was speaking, Henderson emerged from the crime scene tent beside the remains of the bonfire. He made his way towards them, his movements as ever resembling those of an ungainly stork.

'You reckon you'd spotted this earlier in the evening?' he said to McKay in an accusatory tone.

'Not me. Some young guys. I went to see what they were looking at.'

'You didn't believe it was a body?'

McKay exchanged a glance with Grant, irritated that Henderson was trying to put him on the back foot. 'I don't know what kind of parties you go to, Jock, but I'm not accustomed to finding a corpse on the bonfire.'

'Tonight's your lucky night, then. Because that's exactly what you have. If you'd thought to have the fire extinguished earlier I might be able to tell you more about it.'

McKay had no intention of getting into a war of words with Henderson. In truth, McKay was kicking himself for not taking action immediately, even though his reasons had seemed sound enough at the time. But it was one thing to berate himself. It was another to have Jock Henderson doing it for him. 'So what *are* your limited skills able to tell us?'

Henderson's expression suggested he might be about to engage in a stand-up row. 'The body's very badly damaged by the fire so it's not possible to glean too much at this stage. We might be able to get more from forensics and the pathologist. All I can really tell you is that the body's male.'

'Is there no end to your powers, Jock?' McKay stared out across the firth, as if expecting the sea to provide him with more answers than Henderson had so far managed.

'What about cause of death?' Grant asked.

Henderson's face was expressionless. 'I'd need the doc to confirm, but I'd say he burned to death.'

McKay turned. 'You mean he was still alive in the fire?'

'Looks that way to me. From the way the body was contorted. Again, difficult to be sure but I'd say he'd been tightly restrained, maybe plastic ties. Whatever it was had disappeared into the flames, but it looks as if he'd been struggling to extricate himself.'

'Jesus,' Grant said. 'The poor bastard.'

'But how would you get a live body into the middle of a bonfire?' McKay asked.

'That's your territory,' Henderson said. 'I'm just telling you how it looks.'

'Nothing else you can tell us, Jock? Age, ethnicity.'

'I'd be struggling even to tell you his height. There are traces of clothing but difficult to tell what they might have been. I don't think that any usable ID is likely to have survived, except maybe anything metallic like keys, but we're still checking that. Not the easiest or the pleasantest of tasks as you might imagine.' He spoke with an apparent degree of relish. 'The one thing I've learned over the years is that the human body burns surprisingly well, if you give it half a chance.'

'Glad you've learned something, Jock,' McKay said. 'But it leaves us with the mystery of how anyone could plant a body in the middle of a public bonfire without anybody bloody noticing. Maybe we should have a word with your friend, Emsworth. He was presumably involved in setting up all this.'

'I'll leave you to it,' Henderson said. 'I'll see what else I can extract from the scene.'

'Don't push yourself, Jock. At least you spotted he'd been burnt. It'd be churlish of us to expect more.'

Henderson treated McKay to one of his trademark graveside

smiles. 'Has anyone ever told you you have a very juvenile sense of humour, Alec.'

'Only you, Jock. I always pitch my humour at the level of the recipient.'

Without offering a response, Henderson loped back over to the crime scene tent. Grant watched until he was out of earshot and then said, 'What is it with you and Jock?'

'Beats me,' McKay said. 'I always enjoy his company.'

Grant had beckoned Emsworth to join them. He looked exhausted and white-faced. 'It's an awful business.' He gestured towards the crime scene tent. 'Is it really...?'

Grant nodded. 'I'm afraid so.'

'But how? We tried to be so careful on the health and safety stuff. Somebody must have screwed up badly.'

Grant looked across at McKay. 'I'd ask you to keep this confidential for the moment, Bill. But we think he was put there deliberately.'

Emsworth blinked. 'You mean as a means of disposing of the body? But that would never have worked, surely? Someone was always going to spot it at some point.'

'You sound like an expert at disposing of bodies,' McKay commented. 'But then I suppose you are, in a manner of speaking.'

'I wouldn't exactly claim expertise,' Emsworth said. 'But it's the kind of thing I have to research from time to time. You should see my search history.'

'The thing is,' Grant went on, 'we don't think it was simply an attempt to dispose of the body. We think he died in the flames.'

'My God.' Emsworth stared at her. 'But how could that be possible?'

'We thought you might be able to help us with that,' McKay

said. 'Given you were involved in the setting up of the event, I mean.'

Emsworth looked horror-struck. 'Yes, of course. We built the bonfire over the last week or so to make sure it would be ready for this evening.'

'Who was involved in that?' Grant asked.

'Mainly our own volunteers. Some of the same people who were stewarding tonight and a few others. I can give you a list of names. It won't be absolutely definitive because we had people come and go fairly informally but it'll give you the majority. The wood was donated by various locals, and our team collected it by trailer and brought it back here.'

'When did you finish building it?' Grant asked.

'Couple of days ago. We were keen to get it done well before so that it would help promote the event.'

'So someone could have placed the body inside any time over that last couple of days?'

'I don't know how easy that would have been. The fire was well built. But I imagine you could have done it if you took a bit of time and care.'

'You didn't check it at any point?'

'Why would we? We kept an eye on it to make sure it wasn't vandalised, and we did a final safety check before we ignited it. But that was just to make sure that no children or pets had managed to hide themselves in the outer parts of the fire. It never occurred to me that someone might have planted anything – or anyone – right in the heart of it.' He stopped, as a thought had clearly struck him. 'My God. I lit the fire myself. Are you telling me I was actually responsible for burning someone to death?'

'Whoever put the body in there was responsible,' Grant said. 'You couldn't have known.'

'I know but– Well, it's a shock. You presumably don't have any idea who the victim is?'

'Not yet. To be honest, identification may be a challenge,' Grant said. 'We'll identify him in due course, one way or another, but it's likely to be a tricky one.'

'I make up this stuff for a living,' Emsworth said, 'but it's a whole different kettle of fish when it's for real.'

'That so?' McKay said. 'I sometimes think you writers don't realise how real this can be.'

Emsworth nodded. 'You're quite right, Alec. For me, crime's just a game, an entertainment. I understand that. Though I may know more about it than you realise.'

The comment seemed designed to pique McKay's curiosity, but he was in no mood to bite. 'Anything else you can tell us? Any suspicious behaviour among the volunteers? Strangers hanging around?'

'I can't imagine any of the volunteers being involved in something like this. They're just people who wanted to help out. It's been a tough year, and people just wanted to do their bit to keep things going over the winter. As for your second question, I'm not sure. We've had a few people hanging around I didn't recognise, but most of them just seemed interested in what we were doing. I can't say I noticed anyone acting suspiciously.'

'Seems most likely the body would have been placed in there overnight,' Grant said. 'I can't imagine how anyone could have done it in the daytime without being seen. That end of the beach isn't exactly overlooked, but we can see if anyone in the nearest houses saw any unusual activity.'

'I thought I had a lurid imagination,' Emsworth said. 'But I'm struggling to imagine why anyone would want to do something like this to another human being.'

'What motive would you give them?' McKay asked. 'If you were writing about this in one of your books, I mean.'

Emsworth gazed at McKay for a second as if suspecting he was being mocked. 'I don't know. I'm not keen on the lunatic serial killer trope so I try to give my killers at least a half-convincing motive. But I don't know why anyone would want to make the victim suffer in the way this poor soul has.'

'It's not unknown,' Grant said. 'This kind of stuff's often linked to organised crime. Revenge killings. Or a warning. Designed to be a deterrent. We don't get much of that stuff up here, but it happens occasionally.'

'But why here?' Emsworth said. 'Quiet little place like this.'

'That might be precisely why,' McKay said. 'Causes a stir. Gets attention from the media. It's easier to do the deed in somewhere out of the way than it would be in the city. Probably just a coincidence that they happened to choose this particular wee backwater.'

Emsworth nodded, then turned his attention to Helena Grant. 'Is there anything more you need from me tonight, Helena? To be honest, I'm absolutely bushed. I've been up since the crack of dawn getting this set up.'

'Yes, of course,' she said. 'I'm just sorry it didn't end up the way you'd hoped. Real shame after all the effort you and everyone else put in.'

'That's life.' Emsworth stopped, realising what he'd said. 'Or death in this case. The first part of the evening went well. It's just a pity we had to truncate it. But all that seems small beer compared to what's happened.'

'To answer your question,' Grant said, 'no, that's fine for tonight. We'll need to get a formal statement from you but that can wait till the morning. You don't need a lift home? I know it's not far but if you really are exhausted...'

'It's only at the top of the village. The walk'll do me good. Give me a chance to clear my head, come to terms with all this.'

He hesitated. 'I assume you're likely to be tied up here for a while yet?'

'I'm afraid so, Bill. I'm sorry we had to end the night like this.'

'There'll no doubt be plenty of other opportunities to compensate.'

'I'm sure there will, Bill. I'll be in touch.'

Emsworth looked as if he was on the point of saying something else, but instead he bade Grant and McKay goodnight and turned to walk back along the beach towards the village.

Grant turned back to McKay. 'As for you, Alec, don't you dare to say a word. Not a single bloody word.'

3

Kelly Armstrong manoeuvred her clapped-out car into a narrow parking space on the side road. She'd been driving for a couple of years now and was finally developing some confidence.

She'd begun this community work over the summer partly to help maintain her driving skills during the long vacation. Now, with the first semester of the year finished, she was supposed to be working hard towards her finals. But her parents had been able to raise no reasonable objections to her continuing the voluntary work over the Christmas break, and at least it took her out of the house for a couple of hours each day.

The scheme had started in the summer as a response to the coronavirus lockdown. A group of volunteers, with the local community group, had offered to deliver shopping to those unable or reluctant to leave the house.

The level of lockdown had varied over the autumn, but the volunteer scheme had continued for those who were housebound for one reason or another. Most of those who participated were not deprived or badly off – although there was also a parallel scheme linked to a local food bank – but simply lacked mobility. In Kelly's experience they also mostly lacked companionship. They could have ordered groceries for delivery from one of the local supermarkets, but in many cases they just wanted an opportunity for an extended chat.

That was fine by Kelly. She was in no particular rush, and she found some of the older folk interesting to talk to. The participants submitted a shopping list and made payment either by cheque or bank transfer, and then Kelly and others went to buy the goods either in the local shops or over in Dingwall before delivering them at an agreed time.

She climbed out of the car and lifted the bags of groceries from the rear. It was only 3pm but darkness was falling. They were only a couple of days past the solstice, the day before Christmas Eve, and the days were at their shortest. She looked around uneasily.

She'd been feeling nervous since the discovery in Rosemarkie a couple of days back. The case had gone quiet in the days since with no mention in the national or even local media. Either the discovery hadn't been what it had appeared to be, or, more likely, the police were keeping a lid on it.

She carried the shopping up the front garden path to Hamish's house. It was one of the older houses in the village, and he'd told her that parts of it were Georgian or even older. It had clearly been a fine villa in its day, though now it looked slightly neglected. Hamish had someone in to care for the garden, which offered a fine display in the summer but was now just a jumble of shadows that increased Kelly's discomfort.

Still, Hamish Forres was pleasant enough, a polite elderly widower who always seemed pleased at her presence. His shopping list was generally fairly short, and he was happy for her to purchase the items in the village store. She pressed the bell and waited.

After a moment, she heard bolts being drawn back as the door was opened. Hamish's face peered out at her, his expression uncharacteristically nervous. 'Kelly? I wasn't expecting you for a while.'

'It's when you asked me to come, wasn't it?' Kelly glanced at her watch. She was sure Hamish had asked for delivery around 3pm.

'Oh, yes. But the other young lady said you'd been delayed.'

'The other young lady?'

Hamish led her into the house. She followed him into the kitchen and placed the bags of groceries on the small kitchen table. 'Do you want me to help you put it all away?'

'If it's no trouble for you. Why don't you start doing that and I'll make us both a nice cup of tea. I could do with a brew.'

She suspected the offer of tea was just a ruse to delay her departure, but she had no problem with that. She had a couple more deliveries to make, but she allowed plenty of time between the deliveries for exactly this reason. A number of those she visited had few opportunities to talk to others during the week. Hamish's only son lived in Edinburgh and visited as often as he could, but Hamish had spent several months by himself during the previous summer's lockdown.

She began to put the groceries in the cupboards and fridge, while Hamish busied himself filling the kettle. 'So who is she?' he said.

'Who's who?'

'This other young woman.'

'I've no idea.' Kelly finally registered what Hamish had said previously. 'She said I'd been delayed?'

'She said it was some personal matter but you were hoping to get along later with the delivery.'

As far as Kelly was aware, there were no other volunteers making deliveries today. 'I don't understand. I wasn't delayed.'

'That's definitely what she said. She told me she'd come round to check I was okay and to see if I needed anything buying. I was surprised because I knew you were coming round with a delivery this afternoon anyway. I told her there must have been some mix-up, but she said you'd been delayed. That was why she'd called in to check that I was okay in the meantime.'

'What did she look like?'

Hamish dropped tea bags into two mugs and poured on the boiling water. 'About your age, I'd have said. Maybe a little older. Not as tall as you and – well, I'm not sure how to put this politely – but not as slim as you. Dark hair. Glasses. Very respectable looking. I thought she might have been one of the organisers.'

There were no 'organisers' as such, just a bunch of volunteers who helped each other out. A couple dealt mainly with the administrative side, taking the orders and organising the payments, while the rest focused on the buying and deliveries. Kelly couldn't immediately think of anyone who matched Hamish's description. The other women were much older than Kelly.

She put away the last of the groceries and gratefully accepted the mug of tea.

'Come into the living room and have a sit down,' he said. 'You're not in a hurry, are you?'

'I'm fine for fifteen minutes or so.'

'That's good. It's nice to get a bit of company.'

'What are you doing for Christmas, Hamish?'

'Gary's coming up tomorrow to take me down to spend it with them. That's why I mainly got tinned and packet stuff in the order. Just enough to keep me going when I get back after Christmas. They've got a wee girl now, you know, as well as the boy. Probably still too young to appreciate Christmas, but they'll no doubt spoil her rotten.'

'It's all about the children, really, isn't it?'

'What about you, Kelly? Spending it with your parents?'

'That's the plan. It'll be a fairly quiet one, given the restrictions.' Kelly would rather have been spending Christmas somewhere other than here. But there'd been nowhere else for her to go. She hadn't been in a serious relationship since she'd split up with her former boyfriend, Greg, a couple of years before, and her close friends were enjoying their own family Christmases. It wasn't that she disliked her parents or wouldn't enjoy Christmas with them. It was simply that she wanted a life of her own. The pandemic had limited her freedom even more than usual, and she was desperate for normality to return.

'Ah, well. I'm sure you'll enjoy it.'

'I'm sure I will.' She'd followed him into the large living room and sat on one of the armchairs opposite him, sipping her tea. 'I still haven't worked out who she was.'

'Who who was?'

'The woman who came here earlier. I can't think of anyone who fits that description. Or why she thought I'd been delayed.' She paused. 'Did you invite her in?'

'Yes, of course. Why wouldn't I?'

Kelly looked around the room. 'Did you leave her alone at all?'

'I invited her in here then went to make us both a cup of tea. She was very polite.'

'Where do you keep your wallet?' On her first visit, Hamish had wanted to pay her a little extra as a tip, but the volunteers had already agreed not to accept any gratuities. She knew he kept everything of importance in his old battered leather wallet.

'It's on the mantelpiece,' Hamish said. 'Why?'

Kelly half rose and peered towards the fireplace. 'I can't see it.'

'Behind the clock. That's where I always keep it.'

Kelly walked over and peered behind the old-fashioned carriage clock. 'It's not there, Hamish.'

'That's where I keep it–' He stopped. 'Oh, you don't mean... That wee girl.' Hamish was looking aghast. 'Why would anyone do something like that?'

'There are some unpleasant people in the world. I think you'd better call the bank and cancel your cards.'

Hamish sighed. 'I suppose so. I don't imagine I'll need them over the Christmas break anyway. I still can't believe it.'

'I think I should call the police, too,' Kelly said. 'I don't want this woman to be able to pull this scam with anyone else.'

'Do you really have to?' Hamish said. 'I feel pretty stupid about it.'

'You weren't stupid. I'm sure she was very plausible. We'd better put something up on the local social media pages too. It makes me so angry.'

She helped Hamish find the number for his bank. While he was calling the security line, she called the police enquiry number to report the theft. Slightly to her surprise, the call handler took her report seriously, promising an officer would call on Hamish to take details later in the afternoon. 'I'll see if we can issue a statement warning people in the local area too,' the call handler said. 'Does Mr Forres know if anything else was taken?'

'He doesn't think so. We'll double-check before I leave.'

She ended the call and turned back to Hamish, who had completed his call to the bank. 'I'm glad I called them,' she said. 'They've had a couple of similar incidents around Inverness in recent weeks but this is the first one on the Black Isle. What did the bank say?'

'Looks like we were in time. No unauthorised deductions against either of the cards.'

'What else was in your wallet? Anything important?'

'Not much. A bit of cash, but not a fortune. My driving licence, not that I use that much these days. A couple of loyalty cards.' He smiled, wistfully. 'I don't use those much these days either. So, no, nothing of importance.'

'That's something,' Kelly said. 'And you don't think anything else has been taken?'

Hamish gazed around the room. 'I don't think so.'

'Not a terribly successful scam, then. Just inconvenient for you.'

'Ach, it could be worse.'

'That's the thing about you, Hamish. You take everything in your stride.'

'When you get to my age, you don't have a lot of choice. I'm kicking myself though. I'll be more careful next time.'

Kelly looked at her watch. 'I'd better get on. You sure you'll be all right?'

'I'll be fine. I've learned my lesson. I'll even make sure that police officer shows me his ID when he comes.'

'Quite right. I'll see you after Christmas, then. Hope you have a good one.'

'And you, Kelly. Thanks for helping me out with this.'

'I didn't do much. And I felt partly responsible, given that she was pretending to be part of our team. We'll have to have a think about how we prevent that happening again. We didn't think it would be an issue because we all know each other, but we hadn't envisaged someone might pull that sort of scam.'

'Ach, well, it certainly wasn't your fault, Kelly.'

She knew rationally that was true, but couldn't help feeling a degree of guilt that, however inadvertently, she'd exposed Hamish to this. She felt oddly violated herself. It was almost as if the woman had impersonated her.

As she stepped out into the late afternoon's gloom she felt an unexpected chill of fear. She looked around, as if expecting the woman still to be lurking in the shadows. That was the strangest part, she thought. This was nothing more than a mundane scam perpetrated on a vulnerable elderly man. But it felt more than that. It felt as if something evil had entered the neighbourhood. Something with far more serious consequences than a stolen wallet.

4

'Hell of a time to kick off a major investigation,' DS Ginny Horton said.

'That's the trouble with murderers,' Alec McKay said. 'They never think what's convenient for us.'

'I wasn't exactly thinking about my own convenience,' Horton said. 'More the challenge of getting together the resources we're going to need. It's tough enough at the best of times. Two days before Christmas definitely isn't the best of times.'

'Real Scots don't celebrate Christmas anyway.' McKay was pacing up and down the room, his demeanour reminiscent of a caged animal desperate to return to the wild. 'They wait to get properly pissed at Hogmanay.'

'You haven't seen the massed array of Christmas lights on the houses round our way. You can't move for flashing snowmen and twinkly reindeer.'

'They must all be bloody incomers like you.'

Horton was English. Or rather – as even McKay was forced to acknowledge after the truth had emerged in one of their previous cases – she was Scottish but sounded and looked quintessentially English. Which, in his view, just meant that people were likely to underestimate her.

'Times are changing, Alec. I mean, even you're changing. I never expected you to be moving house at your age.'

'Less of the "your age", thanks very much.' McKay finally ceased prowling and took a seat at the table. They were in the room that had been designated the major incident room for the investigation. For the moment, it hardly looked like a hive of industry, but that was mainly because most of the team allocated to the enquiry were already out working on their various duties. 'How are we doing, anyway? Helena is pulling as many strings as she can to get additional resources, but it's a bit of a tightrope. Given half a sniff those buggers down south will want to take over the whole case.'

'Maybe Christmas is a blessing, then. Might discourage them from venturing north.'

'Flurry of snow in the Cairngorms, Edinburgh cut off. You might be right.' McKay pulled out his trademark pack of gum, offered it half-heartedly to Horton, and then painstakingly unwrapped a stick to chew himself. It was a habit he'd started to help give up smoking. Now it was just a habit. 'With a bit of luck, they might also be put off because it looks like a tricky one. They prefer the cut-and-dried cases where they can just waltz in, arrest the obvious perpetrator, and then waltz out again, with another notch on their bedposts.'

'And your razor-like investigative powers are telling you this one isn't going to be like that?'

'Just a hunch. Maybe the fact that we don't yet even have a clue who the victim is.' He shook his head. 'We might get the identity through DNA or dental records, which would be a huge step forward. Jock confirmed there was no ID on the body – or if there was it had been consumed by the fire. Fingerprints destroyed. Clothing pretty much gone.'

'You think that was the intention?'

'Maybe. Partly, anyway. Though if that was the only reason for doing it, they could have killed him more humanely. My guess is they wanted him to suffer. It's not as if the body was just dumped in there. They must have gone to some trouble.'

'So who'd commit a murder like that? Some gangland thing?'

'I've had a brief chat with the intelligence guys to see if we've had word of any new developments on the gang scene up here. There's definitely been a bit of coming and going, ironically partly due to the sad departure of Archie Donaldson.' This had been one of the outcomes of a recent investigation. Donaldson had been a local businessman, involved in a range of illegal activities.

'Do we know who?'

'You know those intelligence buggers. They play it close to their chests. Knowledge is power. But there are a few names in the frame, apparently. They're supposedly sending me all the info. I'll give them twenty-four hours and then stick a rocket up their collective arses. It could easily be that our chappie is collateral damage in their pathetic turf wars. Maybe warning someone off?'

'What about Donaldson's daughter? Didn't we think she had designs on his business?'

'The mysterious so-called Ruby Jewell? She's disappeared off the face of the earth. Although she struck me as the type who wouldn't stay disappeared for long.' McKay eased himself back in the office chair, staring at the ceiling as if hoping for some inspiration to emerge from that direction. 'It's a thought, isn't it?' he said, finally. 'From what we saw, she's more than capable of engineering something like this. She wouldn't do it herself. She's not one to get her hands dirty. But it's possible she's behind it. She's certainly a ruthless wee bastard.'

'Doesn't get us very far if we don't know where she is, though,' Horton pointed out.

McKay sat upright, with the air of a cat spotting a mouse. 'It's a good thought, though. Worth keeping in mind when we see what gems intelligence unearth for us.' He grinned. 'Sometimes you're not entirely a waste of space, Horton.'

'Bugger off, Alec. You'd be nothing without me, as you know very well.'

'Aye, well, I need you and Helena to keep me on the straight and narrow.'

'The day you stay on the straight and narrow will be the day you're finally ready for the knacker's yard. Which, for the avoidance of doubt, may not be far off.'

'Don't push it. I was beginning to warm to you.'

'I don't want us ever to become too cosy,' Horton laughed. 'I wouldn't want us to lose that unique edge of mutual suspicion and loathing.'

'It's been my life's work.'

'So I've noticed. So what else have we got?'

McKay shook his head. 'Three fifths of bugger all. Doc Green's promised to prioritise the post-mortem so I'm hoping we'll get that today. But I don't know what it's going to tell us that we don't already know. What about mispers?'

'I've got someone trawling through all the local missing persons. Don't seem to be any likely candidates among the recent cases.'

McKay sighed. 'Until we identify the victim we're going to struggle to make much progress. I'm not putting much faith in the house-to-house stuff.'

'You never know.'

'You never do, but you can often guess. Still, we'll see. We're a nosy bunch over in the Black Isle.'

'You'll fit in well then. How are you finding it over there? Must be a change from the big city.'

'Or even from Inverness. I've lived there before, you know.'

'I remember. That poky little place in Rosemarkie. This sounds a bit different.'

'Well, it's still just a bungalow. But, aye, it's the kind of place Chrissie's always wanted. View of the sea, or at least the firth. Mountains. Nice new kitchen. Decent sized garden. She's in heaven.'

'And you?'

'Aye, me too. It's quieter than I'm used to, but that's fine. I can see what you and Helena mean about putting the job right behind you when you get home. I've never quite done that. Always been too much on the doorstep.'

'Let's hope for Chrissie's sake you develop some better habits, then. More work-life balance.'

'Now may not be the best time to start though.' He shrugged. 'But it never is, is it?'

'Another Christmas spoiled for Chrissie, then?'

'Another Christmas improved because I won't be under her feet. She's got her sister, Fiona, coming up today.'

'How is she?'

'Growing accustomed to life without Kevin, I think. But still not quite come to terms with everything that came out.' McKay's brother-in-law had also been part of the investigation that had resulted in Archie Donaldson's removal from the local business scene. 'She'll be glad of time to blether with Chrissie. I'll make sure I spend Christmas Day with them, barring any dramatic developments here, and that'll be more than enough for Chrissie, trust me.'

'Oh, I'm happy to trust you on that.'

'What about you? Quiet Christmas?'

'We never have anything else. Isla's only too keen to lock the outside doors and keep the world at bay, while we stuff ourselves with turkey.'

'Sounds perfect.' McKay pushed his way to his feet. 'Right, I'd better go and track down Helena. I said I'd give her a quick debrief after today's meeting, though there won't be much to report.'

'Is it true about her and this writer guy?'

'Ginny, you should know better than to try to pump me for office gossip.'

'Yes, but is it?'

'Judging by the way they were behaving the other night, I'd have said so. Mind you, coming across a burned-alive corpse might have put a dampener on their romantic aspirations.'

'I hope not. Not permanently anyway. She deserves a few moments of happiness.'

'You reckon?' McKay was already at the door. 'I'd have thought she got more than enough of those working with us.'

5

Crawford stood at the window of his office, staring out over the loch. It was almost noon, but the sun still remained low in the southern sky, as if it could barely trouble itself to rise above the horizon. It was a clear bright midwinter day, and the trees around the water threw long shadows. *The kind of day when you might almost expect the monster to manifest itself*, he thought.

His ex-wife was the reason he'd ended up here. It wouldn't have been his choice. At the time he'd have preferred somewhere livelier, somewhere in the city. Left to his own devices, he'd have ended up living in Edinburgh or Glasgow. That was where the action was, not to mention most of his business. He'd spent far too much time flogging up and down on the inadequate train service.

And yet his ex-wife was long gone and here he still was. Partly just inertia. He'd spent enough time living a semi-nomadic lifestyle. Moving here had been settling down. Just because she was no longer here to share his more settled life didn't mean he had to change those plans. She was the one who'd become restless, but that had been predictable and, by the time she went, had seemed no great loss.

The truth was he'd fallen in love with the place. He didn't know quite how or when it had happened, but at some point he'd realised this was where he wanted to be. All the fuss with the pandemic had only reinforced his views. During those months, he'd been unable to travel and was forced to conduct his business remotely. To his slight surprise, it had worked well. Though he missed some of the face-to-face opportunities to influence, he'd encountered very few problems.

Since then, he'd made some changes to his lifestyle. Even now the restrictions had been lifted, he'd continued to conduct most of his business from home. He still travelled to the central belt or to London once or twice a month. He had more freedom, more spare time, and his productivity was greater than it had ever been.

His major discovery from the weeks of lockdown had been that he'd never felt lonely. However much he'd justified them in business terms, his previous repeated trips south had been partly driven by a search for companionship. He'd been worried that, stuck up here with only his own company, he'd have felt isolated. But when the solitude was forced upon him, he'd found he actually rather enjoyed it. A relaxed dinner by himself, washed down with a few glasses of wine, was a more relaxed and pleasurable experience than eating in some fancy restaurant with a tedious client.

Of course, he still saw people. He had friends locally he'd visit from time to time. He met up with people when he made his trips to the big cities. He had a cleaner and a gardener who came in periodically and whom he'd come to think of as friends. But the majority of the time he was by himself and it turned out that was fine.

He'd just finished the last of the morning's video conferences. There were one or two clients who still insisted on seeing him face-to-face, but the majority had accepted that the world had changed. He suspected that many of them had discovered they preferred to work remotely, just as he had. The few who preferred a hands-on service were mostly those whose egos needed cosseting. But they weren't generally the bigger players. Most were more than happy to operate at arm's length, revealing only what was necessary to get business done. It suited the nature of their business, of course. These were people accustomed to operating beneath the radar, taking care to avoid attracting too much attention from the authorities. Even if most of what they did wasn't strictly illegal, they were happy not to attract too much scrutiny. Even if they trusted Crawford – and he sincerely hoped they all did – they'd see no harm in keeping him at a distance.

He stood for another few moments enjoying the wintery view across the loch, and then made his way down to the kitchen. He was intending to make himself a coffee and a sandwich and have a quick online skim through the *Financial Times* and other newspapers. He focused mainly on the financial and business news, but also kept an eye on national and global politics. It was one of the factors that kept him a step or two ahead of the competition.

It didn't take him long to prepare the sandwich. That was another thing about working from home. In the old days, he'd have been out on the road much of the time, and either lunching at some overpriced restaurant with a client or grabbing some unhealthy takeaway as he rushed for a train or a flight. But Crawford was a man of simple, if refined, tastes. Here at home he was content with some decent bread filled with locally-produced cheese and ham, with a decent cup of coffee.

He was sitting down to eat when his mobile buzzed on the kitchen surface beside him. He glanced at the screen, wondering if it was worth delaying his lunch to take the call. The question was answered by the name on the screen. Gordon Prebble, one of his major local clients and not a man to be kept waiting, even at the end of a phone line.

Crawford thumbed the call button. 'Gordon. How are you?'

'I was wondering if you could pay me a visit, Simon, just to discuss one or two issues.' Prebble never wasted time on pleasantries. 'In the next day or two.'

If the caller had been anyone other than Gordon Prebble, Crawford would have pointed out that the next day was Christmas Eve, and that there was still supposed to be no mixing of households up here. But he suspected that both the pandemic and the Christmas holiday barely registered on Prebble's mental radar. 'I'd be delighted to fit you in tomorrow some time, Gordon.'

'Eleven o'clock, then.' It wasn't a question. Prebble had zero interest in anyone else's convenience, and never even pretended he had. If he'd been a less substantial client, Crawford would have dropped him years ago. As it was, he was worth the hassle. 'Eleven's fine,' Crawford said. As a mild gesture of resistance, he added, 'I'll need to be away by twelve thirty, though.'

Prebble didn't even acknowledge Crawford's words. 'I can spare you an hour.'

Before Crawford could respond, the call was ended. Crawford stared at the phone for a moment, then – having first made sure the call really had been cut – he said, 'And a merry fucking Christmas to you, Gordon.'

6

'So what have we got?' Helena Grant watched wearily as McKay prowled slowly round her office. Even after all these years, she still hadn't decided whether his habitual restlessness was an act or an involuntary habit. She'd gradually trained herself to ignore it. McKay liked nothing more than to provoke a reaction, and she tried hard to deny him that pleasure. 'Jacquie come up with the goods then?'

Jacquie 'Doc' Green was the pathologist who worked most closely with the police locally. She was well-respected and generally well-liked, as well as being one of Grant's closest friends.

'Some of them, anyway.' McKay halted for a moment by the window, peering out into the darkness of the late afternoon as if seeking some external sign. 'Fair play to her, she's pulled out all the stops to get us something before the whole world grinds to its annual Christmas stop.' He paused. 'Except for us, obviously. We keep buggering on.'

'If you say so, Alec. So what is it she's got for us?'

'Not a lot, but that's not really her fault.'

'I'm more inclined to blame whoever stuck the body in that bloody great bonfire,' Grant said.

'I assume that was the intention. If they hadn't managed to pull the body at least a little way clear of the flames at the end, we'd have had nothing but a set of badly charred bones.'

'And as it is?'

'Not much more than that, to be honest. But a fair bit of the flesh hadn't been entirely barbecued. So we can be certain that the victim was white. Doc confirmed Jock's suspicion that the fire was almost certainly the cause of death.'

'I'd hoped that idea was just a product of Jock's fevered imagination.'

'Not sure even Jock's imagination is quite that fevered. She thinks Jock's assessment was spot on. That the victim was heavily restrained, probably sedated at least initially. The only blessing, if you can call it that, is that asphyxiation would probably have got him before the flames. But according to the doc, the twisting of the body suggests he was fully aware of what was happening.'

'We really need to get the bastard who did this, Alec.'

'We've had a few bastards to deal with,' McKay agreed, 'but this one beats them all. There's one other thing. Looks as if the victim was middle-aged. Doc reckoned that the state of the bones suggested someone in their thirties or forties.'

'So not some young gang-war type?'

'Not some spotty teenager, anyway.'

'What about DNA?'

'We've got samples which we've had checked against the database – that was another favour I had to call in – but nothing.'

'So not a villain?'

'Not one we've caught and convicted, anyway,' McKay said, 'but I'm guessing that doesn't cover them all.'

'Doesn't get us very far, though.'

'Not unless we find some other match, no. We've had a look at missing persons in the appropriate age group. One or two possible candidates nationally, but no one local. We're looking into all the possibles, but none of them looks like a strong candidate. No one who seems likely to have ended up in the middle of a bonfire.' He shrugged. 'Though I suppose looks can be deceiving.'

'No one would ever guess you were a pussycat with a heart of gold, Alec.'

'Which proves my point. Anyway, we don't have a lot else. One of the hands was relatively undamaged, and Doc reckoned there might be a possibility of a partial fingerprint, but I'm not building my hopes up. There were a few scraps of clothing left which might offer us some forensic insights, but again I'm not optimistic.'

'What about reconstructing the likeness of the face from the skull? Aren't we supposed to be able to do that kind of stuff with computers these days?'

'They can do anything with computers these days,' McKay said. 'If we've got the money for it. And the time. I don't imagine that would be the easiest thing to organise over Christmas. Anyway, they never look like real people. Not even people from round here.'

'So what next?'

'Doc's noted the state of the teeth. Fortunately, our man still had most of them, with only a couple missing at the rear of the mouth. A couple of fillings. So dental records might be an option, but that's not going to be an easy task over Christmas.'

'Nothing's going to be an easy task over Christmas.' Grant sighed. 'What's the plan on that?'

'We're going to continue everything we can with those who are willing to work, as long as you're willing to sign off the overtime bill. But it'll limit the house-to-house stuff. I'm planning to take Christmas Day off, just to reduce the chances of Chrissie ritually disembowelling me but I'll be in contact if anything breaks. Ginny's formally on call too. I don't want to lose momentum, but there's not much else we can do.'

Grant nodded. 'I was hoping to take a couple of days off this year for once.' As a widow without children, Grant had been happy to work through the last few Christmases, allowing others the time off.

'Don't see why you shouldn't,' McKay said. 'It's not like you contribute much anyway.' He held up his hand. 'Joke. Seriously, you deserve it. Like you say, you've done your bit for the last few years. If need be, I'll come in.'

'I sometimes wonder who's actually in charge here.' Grant smiled. 'But, thanks, Alec. That's appreciated.'

McKay finally ceased pacing and lowered himself into the chair opposite Grant's desk. 'Any particular plans?'

'Plans?'

'For Christmas. Just wondered if you had any particular reason for taking the time off this year?'

'Ah. So that's the reason you were being so gracious. You're just after the gossip.'

'Never crossed my mind.' McKay paused. 'So is there gossip?'

'I imagine there's plenty round the office. For what it's worth, and if you must know, I've been invited to spend Christmas with Bill.'

'Emsworth? Well, that's nice. I hope it proves very enjoyable.' McKay's expression suggested he was genuinely pleased to hear the news.

Probably he was, Grant thought. They'd known each other a long time and, for all their bantering, were genuinely fond of one another. There'd been a couple of moments over the years – particularly when McKay had briefly separated from Chrissie –

when she'd wondered whether that fondness might blossom into something more serious. But McKay was happily back with Chrissie, and for the last year or more Grant had been seeking a way of restarting her life.

'And if you're wondering,' she added after a moment, 'yes, Bill and I are in what I believe people call a relationship.'

McKay looked surprised. Less at the news itself, she suspected, than at the fact that she'd volunteered the information. Maybe that had been a mistake, but speculation was no doubt already rife among the team so it was probably better to be open. There was no surer way of disseminating the news efficiently around the office than telling Alec McKay. He could be discreet enough when it suited him, but mostly it didn't.

'That's good to hear,' McKay said. 'Seriously. I'm very pleased for you.'

'It's early days so I'm not investing all my hopes in it, but we get on well and he's a nice guy. He knows about stuff that's new to me.'

'That so?' McKay raised an eyebrow.

'Books and films and plays, Alec. Culture. You wouldn't understand.'

'Aye, we didn't have any culture in Dundee when I was a bairn. We couldn't afford it. Maybe he'll open up new vistas for you.'

'Only you could make that sound like an innuendo. Anyway, that's the story. A quiet Christmas at Bill's. Just the two of us.'

'Very cosy.'

'We're both in the same boat. Bill's divorced. His parents are both dead, and he doesn't really have any other close relatives. He's generally headed for a holiday overseas at Christmas, but this year we thought we'd spend it at home. His home, to be specific.'

'Sounds idyllic,' McKay said, with apparent sincerity.

'There's even some snow forecast, so you might get a white Christmas. And if it doesn't work out, you can always tell him you've got a murder enquiry to be getting back to.'

'You really know how to set the mood, Alec. But you're right. We've a murder enquiry to be getting on with, so let's get on with it, shall we?'

7

Gary Forres pulled his car carefully into the closest parking space he could find to the house. This was a quaint little village and he could understand why his dad had chosen to retire up here, but it had some pretty major disadvantages, at least from Gary's point of view.

For a start, it was miles from anywhere. Even from most other parts of Scotland, including Gary's home in Edinburgh. The long trek up the A9 was a pleasant enough drive in the summer, when you could appreciate the spectacular landscapes of the Cairngorms National Park, but it was less attractive at this time of the year. Gary had set off early so he could arrive here in daylight, but by the time he got his dad sorted and ready to go they'd be making most of the return journey after dark. At least the threatened snow wasn't forecast to arrive until the following day. He wouldn't be surprised if the road was closed at some point over the holiday.

He climbed out of the car and stood for a second looking at the proximity of the two vehicles on each side of it. That was the second problem with the village. There was never anywhere to park. Or, if there was, it was usually at least two streets away from his dad's house. It would be easier if he had a smaller car but that wasn't a price Gary was prepared to pay. These days his dad drove a small Ford which was parked in its usual place immediately outside the house. Gary wondered how often the old man actually used the car these days.

They'd had their strained moments in the past, but now Gary generally enjoyed time spent in his dad's company. Not that they had too many opportunities other than over the phone. That was another result of Hamish's decision to move up here. He'd always said he didn't want to be under the feet of Gary and his family, but Gary suspected that it was Hamish who wanted the solitude.

Gary wondered how well that mindset had survived the pandemic lockdown. After all, Hamish wasn't getting any younger. He'd always been fiercely independent, continuing to drive, to make his weekly trip into Dingwall for shopping, and heading out to one of the local pubs a couple of times a week. All that had come to an end with the lockdown. He'd been well looked after by the local volunteers, but in their twice-weekly phone conversations Gary had detected a new tone in his father's voice – not quite sadness or regret, but perhaps just a wish that things were different. He'd told Gary how much he welcomed the weekly visits from the volunteers delivering his shopping. It was the first time Gary could recall his father sounding actively enthusiastic about the prospect of others entering his house.

Gary made his way along the narrow street and turned into his father's front garden. The house was looking a little neglected, he thought. That had been another example of his father's stubbornness. When he'd announced he wanted to move back up here, they'd tried to persuade him to buy somewhere low-maintenance. Maybe a small bungalow on one of the new estates.

But that, of course, was not Hamish's style. He had the money to buy the kind of place he wanted, and the kind of place he wanted was somewhere like this. A period character house, as the estate agents would say. As his father had grown older it had become harder for him to look after the place. There'd been talk of getting the exterior of the house redecorated in the spring, and in the bleak midwinter sunshine it looked as if that would be needed.

Gary pressed the bell and waited. He had a set of keys and could have let himself in but that was yet another area where Hamish still preferred to assert his independence. In Gary's mind, that raised another question. How long would his father be safe living here all alone?

For the moment, he was in decent physical health and he certainly had all his wits about him. But Gary had been disturbed by the theft of his father's wallet, which Hamish had mentioned, apparently casually, in their telephone conversation the previous evening. The theft itself was unimportant, and it sounded as if his dad had taken the necessary action before any serious consequences resulted. But the incident had made Gary aware of his father's increasing vulnerability. He'd never thought of the old man as someone who might be susceptible to that kind of scam.

There was still no sign of movement from within the house. Gary pressed the bell again. After another few moments, he pulled out his mobile and dialled his father's number. There were extensions upstairs and down, and he knew his dad could hear the trill of the phone from out in the garden.

He could hear the phone ringing inside, but it remained unanswered. Gary frowned. His father had known roughly when to expect him, and had mentioned nothing about leaving the house. In any case, his father had largely continued to self-isolate even after the formal lockdown had been lifted, recognising that his age rendered him relatively vulnerable to the effects of the virus. He was unlikely to have chosen now to pop out to the supermarket.

Gary dug into his pockets and found his set of keys to the house. He unlocked the front door and stepped into the gloom of the hallway. The phone was still ringing, still unanswered. Gary ended the call.

The silence that followed seemed almost eerie. 'Dad!' Gary peered into the living room. It was empty, although there were signs – a paperback spread-eagled on the table, a coffee mug – that Hamish had been in there relatively recently.

Gary continued through to the kitchen. Again, it was empty with the same signs of recent occupancy – an empty cereal bowl and another mug by the sink. Gary tried the back door, but it was locked.

Worried now, Gary hurried back through the house checking the remaining ground floor rooms. There was a room which Hamish had semi-jokingly designated the 'library', with the old man's extensive collection of books set out on built-in shelves. There was a small downstairs lavatory, and a utility room beyond the kitchen containing a washing machine and tumble dryer. All the rooms were empty.

Gary continued upstairs. There were four rooms up here – his father's bedroom, two other bedrooms furnished as guest rooms but now used only by Gary and the family on their occasional trips up here. At the top of the stairs was a large bathroom.

He looked in each room in turn, increasingly baffled. There was no sign of Hamish. His bed was still unmade and had clearly been slept in. Where the hell was he?

Gary made his way back downstairs and rechecked all the rooms, as if he might somehow have overlooked his father's presence. Perhaps the old man had popped out to see one of his neighbours for some reason. Maybe to let them know he was going to be away over Christmas. It was possible, though uncharacteristic of Hamish, who tended to remain on distant if cordial terms with his immediate neighbours.

His father had a mobile phone but Gary had already noticed it sitting on the kitchen table. Maybe that was another indication that Hamish had only popped out for a few minutes.

Gary returned to the kitchen and filled the kettle. There wasn't much he could do except wait. If Hamish hadn't returned in half an hour or so, Gary could try visiting the immediate neighbours. He was almost certainly worrying about nothing. Hamish had mentioned leaving a set of keys with one of the neighbours – though he hadn't said which one – in case there was any problem while he was away. Most likely, that's where he was.

Gary sat himself down at the kitchen table to wait. Actually, he thought, although it might be unusual for the old man to visit his neighbours, this wasn't entirely untypical. Whenever Gary had travelled here to bring Hamish back south, he'd always had difficulty prising the old man out of the house. There was always some task that needed to be completed, some issue with the packing that delayed their departure. Gary was never certain whether this was a deliberate strategy on Hamish's part, or simply an unconscious resistance to stepping outside his normal routine.

It seemed his father had found a new way of delaying their departure. All Gary could do was sit down, relax and enjoy his coffee, while doing his utmost to quell the nagging unease he was still feeling. He wouldn't have to wait long, he told himself. At any moment, he'd hear the scrape of the old man's key in the front door.

Any moment now.

8

Ginny Horton took the left fork from the main road above Rosemarkie, trying to spot the house name she'd been given.

McKay had called her a few minutes earlier to break the news about Helena Grant and Bill Emsworth. 'You understand I'm not just calling to spread trivial office gossip.'

'The thought never entered my head, Alec.'

'I just thought you ought to know. Before you speak to him.'

'Does this complicate Helena's role in the investigation?' Horton asked.

'It's a good question. I didn't think it was the moment to raise that, but it's something she'll need to think about.'

'Knowing Helena,' Horton said, 'she'll already be thinking about it.'

'Aye, I imagine so. No flies on our Hel. And it's probably okay. I'm the SIO, and I don't think we're seriously considering Emsworth as anything but a witness.'

'I suppose he's a possible suspect, but no more than anyone else with access to the bonfire. Which is pretty much anyone on the Black Isle or surrounding areas. Or further if they drove here especially to provide us with a body.'

'The whole event was his idea,' McKay pointed out. 'I presume the bonfire was his idea too. That's something for you to explore with him. But it doesn't mean much.'

'I'll check what the background to the event was, and how widely it was publicised. The bonfire could have just been used opportunistically as a way of disposing of the body.'

'It's possible,' McKay said. 'Worth exploring, anyway.'

'Anyway, give my love to Helena. She deserves a bit of good news on the relationship front. Presumably I shouldn't say anything to Emsworth?'

'Probably best not. Helena's only just told me, and I'd hate her to think I was just itching to spread the news around the office.'

'Heaven forbid. Okay, I'll play it straight unless he says something. I'll let you know how it goes.'

She'd ended the call with McKay before turning onto the single-track road that she'd been told led to Emsworth's house. After another fifty metres, she spotted the house sign he'd described to her when she'd set up the meeting.

The house was an imposing place set high above the village, with a spectacular outlook over Rosemarkie Bay. Below, she could see the pale strip of the beach, the Moray Firth stretched out before her. On a bright winter's day, with the sun low in the sky, the waters were a rich blue.

The front door of the house was already open, Emsworth waiting for her in the doorway. 'DS Horton, I presume? I heard you arriving.'

He was a tall, slim man, probably in his forties, with a neatly trimmed beard and an impressive mop of greying hair that, to Horton's inexpert eye, looked expensively styled. *He's a good-*

looking man, Horton thought, *for those who liked that kind of thing.* 'Mr Emsworth. Good to meet you.'

'Please call me Bill. Everyone does.'

Horton smiled. 'Thank you, though it's probably better if we keep things on a formal footing.'

'Take your point. I'm used to dealing with the police in less formal contexts. Anyway, do come in.'

He led her into the hallway. Horton had been unsure about the age of the house. The frontage looked as if it might be nineteenth century or older, but the house had clearly been substantially extended at the rear. Emsworth led them through into a large airy living room with a vaulted ceiling and large windows looking out onto a small but well-maintained courtyard garden.

Emsworth – or someone working for Emsworth – had made a considerable effort with Christmas decorations. There was a large Christmas tree, tastefully adorned with colour co-ordinated baubles and tinsel, and a range of other Victorian-style decorations around the room. Horton wondered whether this was Emsworth's customary practice, or whether he'd gone to additional trouble in honour of Helena Grant's stay.

'Can I get you some coffee?' Emsworth said, adding with a smile, 'Or would that be too informal?'

'I'd love a coffee if it's no trouble.'

'No trouble at all. Like most writers, I live on the stuff. Take a seat and I'll be back in a second.'

Horton took a seat and looked around. She presumed Emsworth worked elsewhere in the house. The only indication of his profession here were the bookshelves lining one of the walls, containing a substantial number of volumes. It was an attractive room, and one that she suspected reflected Emsworth's character in its slight fussiness and attention to detail. She felt nothing in the room – the furniture, the décor, the pictures on the wall – had been chosen or positioned casually.

Emsworth returned bearing a tray with a cafetiere, two mugs, milk and sugar, which he placed on the low table between them. 'Please do help yourself.'

She did so and pushed the tray towards Emsworth who had taken a seat on the sofa opposite her. 'How long have you lived here, Mr Emsworth?'

'About eighteen months. Before that I'd led a very peripatetic existence. A few years in the US, a few years in Manchester, too long in London. It all seemed a good idea at the time.'

'What brought you here?'

'It's a question of what brought me back,' Emsworth said. 'I'm a local lad. Well, local-ish. Born in Dingwall. But my parents moved to England for work when I was still small, so I've no real memories of it. But the link was enough to bring me up for holidays for many years. I'd been vaguely thinking about the idea of buying a small place I could use for writing, but which I could also let to holidaymakers. Then I thought why not go the whole way and actually move up here. There was nothing keeping me down south. I can write anywhere, and I can do all the business with my agent and publishers remotely.' He laughed. 'Of course, now they're all working remotely.'

Horton was forming the impression that Emsworth was keen on the sound of his own voice. It was quite an impressive voice, a mellifluous mix of Scots and American she could imagine working well at public readings. 'You must be settled in now, then?' For the moment, she was keeping the conversation light, wanting to build up a rapport with Emsworth before she moved on to the more challenging topics.

'I must say, I kept myself to myself for a few months because I was head down working to a deadline. And then of course there was the lockdown. But over the last few months everybody's been very welcoming. I'm starting to feel part of the community now. People are pleased I've moved here permanently rather than buying a property as a holiday home.'

Horton took a sip of her coffee. 'That's good to hear. I've been here a good few years now but it's been my experience too.' She paused. 'I don't want to take up any more of your time than I have to, but I need to check out the background to the solstice event and the bonfire. We haven't yet succeeded in identifying the body, so we need to collect as much information as we can.'

'Take as much time as you need. I'm fascinated to be in the middle of the real thing after writing about it for so long. I did speak briefly to DCI Grant and DI McKay on the night, but you're presumably aware of that?'

'I've seen a note of those discussions. I may go over some of the same ground. You might recall something now that didn't occur to you in the immediate aftermath of the discovery.'

'That might well be true,' Emsworth agreed. 'I wasn't thinking very clearly on the night. I was just in shock really.'

'Understandably. It might be helpful to go back to the beginning. Can I ask about the inspiration behind the solstice event?'

Emsworth shrugged. 'Inspiration's a big word for it. It was one of those wheezes that a few people came up with over a few pints. A lot of people round here had a tough time over the summer because of the lockdown. The tourist season just didn't happen, and even when things began to open up, there was nothing like the volume of visitors you'd normally expect. They've tried in various ways to extend the season and there's been an effort to keep things going, as far as possible, over the winter. The solstice thing was just intended to support that effort. Another attempt to bring in visitors and create a sense of something going on even during the dark months. It was part of a series of December events we put on. Generally they went pretty well. A lot of the local traders were involved, and we brought more people into the restaurants and cafes, so we were pleased with that. The solstice event was supposed to be the climax of it. Even more so after they'd announced we were going to be locked down again after Christmas. Big bonfire, music, stalls with the various local hospitality businesses represented. It was going well. Pity it ended like it did.' He shook his head, his expression suggesting he was visualising what had been found in the bonfire.

'Who was involved in setting it up?'

'A group of us. All locals. I can't even remember how I first got involved. Just got chatting to someone in the shop or the pub, I imagine. We had a small steering committee, but there was a wider group of volunteers who did the legwork. Mostly people from the village or the surrounding area. I'm struggling to imagine that any of them would have been involved in something like this.'

'We can't disregard any possibility,' Horton said, 'but it's also possible they might have talked about the bonfire to friends, family or others from outside the village.'

'That's true, and we also publicised it in the local media during the weeks beforehand, so anyone could have been aware of it. Concealing the body wouldn't have required any particular inside knowledge.'

Horton was silent for a moment as she thought about how to phrase what she was about to say. Emsworth already knew the body had been burned alive, but she didn't know how that had affected his own emotions about what had happened. 'Except of course that the body must have been placed in the fire not too long before the event.' The nights had been below freezing for the last couple of weeks, and Doc Green's view had been that an immobile individual would have quickly succumbed to hypothermia.

Emsworth frowned. 'Oh, yes, of course. Presumably you think he wouldn't have been able to survive longer at this time of the year.'

'I'm afraid that's the way it looks.'

'I'm still struggling to come to terms with the fact that I killed him. I lit the fire and that poor bastard was still alive.'

'I'm sorry,' Horton said. 'The whole thing's awful. But you're not to blame for it.'

'Rationally I can see that. But I've spent years writing about this stuff. Not really taking it seriously. For me, it's just been the basis for writing what I hope are entertaining books. This has brought home just how real it can be.'

'All too real, I'm afraid.' Horton could see Emsworth was making an effort to think rationally about what had happened.

'I assume you're talking to the residents in the houses closest to the beach?' he said. 'They might have seen something.'

'Yes, we're following up with all of those.'

'I don't know that I can tell you much more. I had a look at the fire in the afternoon before the event, but I didn't go peering inside it. I didn't notice any signs it had been disturbed, so whoever did it must have gone to some trouble.'

'How difficult do you think it would have been?'

Emsworth thought for a moment. 'It would certainly have taken some time to do it properly. We'd stacked the bonfire carefully. There was a lot of straight firewood but we'd bulked it out with any wood people were happy to get rid of – bits of broken furniture, old pallets, all kinds of things. It needed some care to ensure it was stable. So you'd need to take some care in ensuring you kept it all in place and then even more care in putting it back so the disturbance wouldn't be noticed.'

'You didn't see anyone hanging around while you were building the bonfire?'

'I've been racking my brains about what I might have seen, but I still can't think of anything out of the ordinary. We had a few people stop and chat to us while we were building the fire, but they just seemed like your ordinary visitors. Most of them were more interested in finding out about the event generally rather than paying any real attention to the bonfire. I don't remember anything that seemed suspicious. I've asked some of the other volunteers, but their recollections are the same.'

'If anything does occur to you, then just let us know.' Horton handed over one of her business cards. 'Sometimes memories do pop unexpectedly into your mind after the event. Often when you stop trying to remember them.'

'I've learnt that in writing my books,' Emsworth said. 'If you're stuck with the plot, there's no point in trying to force it. Sometimes the solution just comes, usually in the middle of the night. I'm sorry I've not been more help. I want to do anything I can to bring to justice whoever was behind this.' He paused. 'Especially in the circumstances.'

'I'm very grateful for your time, Mr Emsworth. I'll leave you to get on with your work.'

'I've not exactly been productive over the last day or two. It all seems very frivolous compared to something like this.'

'We don't tend to see the worst of it up here, but it's amazing how ruthless people can be. This could well be some sort of gangland or underworld killing, designed to send a message.'

'Underworld?'

'It's a possibility. We're not immune to that stuff up here. It's mostly small-fry operators, even compared to Edinburgh or Glasgow, but there are tensions. We made a breakthrough with one of the bigger players earlier in the year, so there's been some jockeying for position since then. This might be fallout from that.'

'Sounds an unpleasant business.'

'It can be.' She pushed herself to her feet. 'Thanks again for your time, Mr Emsworth. It's been most helpful.'

'I doubt it has,' Emsworth said. 'But I'll do anything I can to help. If anything else occurs to me, I'll be in touch.'

9

There was a sudden rattling at the front door. Gary looked up, assuming the sound was his father finally returning home. Gary looked at his watch, feeling a mix of relief and irritation. He'd been sitting here for the best part of an hour, idly surfing the internet on his phone, waiting for his father to return. It was always the same. No matter how much effort he put into ensuring his father would be ready to leave, there was always this kind of delay.

'Welcome back, Dad,' he called. 'About time.' He rose and peered out into the hallway. There was no sign of his father. Just a couple of envelopes lying on the doormat, Christmas cards addressed to his father. The rattle had been the letterbox.

So where the hell was his father?

He'd been wondering how long he should sit here before trying to track his father down. He looked at his watch again. Time was getting on. Even when Hamish reappeared, Gary knew there'd be another hour or so of faffing before they could get away. They'd end up travelling back even later than planned, the threat of snow still in the air.

Cursing, he found a scrap of paper and scribbled a terse note for his father, which he left in the centre of the kitchen table. He made his way out of the house, ensuring he'd taken the keys with him. He hesitated then walked to the road, wondering where to start. He spent a moment peering into the interior of Hamish's car, but that provided no clue to its owner's whereabouts.

The closest neighbouring house was on the right. His father's detached house pre-dated the rest of the street and was set back in its own garden. The remainder of the houses were terraced cottages, white-painted and attractive in the midwinter sun.

Gary pressed the doorbell of the first house, mentally rehearsing what he was going to say. After a few moments, the door opened and a youngish man, probably in his mid-twenties, stared out suspiciously at him. 'Yes?'

'I'm sorry to bother you. I'm Gary Forres. My dad's Hamish Forres who lives next door.'

The man had clearly assumed he was about to be subject to a doorstep sales or charity collection pitch, and now relaxed visibly. 'Good to meet you. What can I do for you?'

'I just wondered if you'd seen my dad today. I'm picking him up to take him down to ours for Christmas, but he seems to be out. His car's still there so I'm assuming he hasn't gone far.'

'I haven't seen him today. Did he know what time you were coming?'

'We'd arranged all that last night. I thought he might have just popped out somewhere, so I let myself in to wait for him. But he's been over an hour now.' Gary had persuaded himself not to worry but now, as he recounted the details, he felt his anxiety growing. His dad could be thoughtless sometimes, but he surely wouldn't have just disappeared for so long without at least leaving an explanatory message.

'Like I say, I've not seen him today. But I don't see that much of him anyway,' the man said. 'He doesn't seem to go out a lot these days.'

'That's Dad,' Gary agreed. 'He'll only stop telling you he's independent when they're carrying him out in a box. But the pandemic's cramped his style a bit.'

'Tell me about it,' the man said. 'Not sure what to suggest about your dad. You could try asking some of the other neighbours. They're probably a bit closer to him than I am.' Now it was clear he couldn't offer any help, the man seemed keen to bring the conversation to an end.

'Thanks. I'll try them.'

'They'll probably be more help than me. I can't say I know your dad well. I've only been here a short time. Sorry.'

'No, that's fine. You've been very helpful.'

'Hope you track him down without too much difficulty. I can't imagine anything's happened to him. You can't sneeze in a place like this without everyone knowing.'

'He'll no doubt turn up when it suits him. Thanks again.'

The next house was another whitewashed terrace, with a selection of knick-knacks visible in front of the net curtains that suggested a more elderly occupier. Gary pressed the bell and waited. After a lengthy pause he heard movements from inside. The door opened on a chain and a wrinkled face peered out. 'Yes?'

'I'm really sorry to bother you. I'm Gary Forres. Hamish Forres's son. I'm just trying to track down my dad and I wondered if you'd seen him by any chance?'

'Track him down?'

'I'd arranged to pick him up today to take him to our house for Christmas so he wouldn't be on his own. But he doesn't seem to be at home. I just wondered if you had any idea where he might be?'

'You're his son?'

'Gary. I'm not sure if we've met before...'

The door reopened with the chain removed. The woman peered out at him, scrutinising him carefully. 'I've seen you with Hamish once or twice.'

'Good to meet you, Mrs...?'

'Jane Brown,' she said. 'And you, Mr Forres.'

'Gary, please. I just wondered if you had any idea where my father might be. I'm getting slightly worried.'

'You'd best come in,' she said. 'It's cold out there.'

He hesitated, knowing he wasn't supposed to enter the house. But she was right about the cold, and he didn't want to make her stand on the doorstep to talk. He reluctantly stepped inside. It was the house he expected, that of an elderly woman living by herself. Tidy and well maintained, but with old-fashioned décor, the shelves laden with ornaments and souvenirs.

'I don't know if I can really help you,' she said. 'I've been trying to think where he might be. He does pop over here now and again, but only if there's a reason. He leaves a set of keys with me in case there's any need to access the house when he's away. You have been able to get into the house?'

'Yes. I've checked the house. His car's still outside, so he can't have gone far.'

'There are a couple of other neighbours I can phone who might have seen him. We used to see Hamish out and about all the time, but the lockdown changed all that.'

'It certainly affected Dad. He always used to go and do his own shopping and he liked going for walks around the village. But he was wary of leaving the house in the pandemic.'

'We all were,' Jane said. 'The oldies, I mean. I didn't really leave the house for months.'

'How did you manage?'

'It wasn't so bad. We had a local volunteer group who used to bring in shopping for us. I'm as independent as your dad, but I was grateful for that. Grateful for the company too. That was the worst thing. You don't realise how much you want to have a blether with folks in the street or in the shops until you can't do it any more. I phone my daughter every couple of days so it's not too bad.'

'Dad would never have admitted to feeling lonely, but it's been getting to him. I could tell by the way he talked over the phone.' Gary shrugged. 'I thought he'd be keen for us to take him back for Christmas for once. Typical of him to disappear.'

Jane laughed. 'Hamish always does what he wants, I think. Could he have gone to do some shopping?'

'Anything's possible.'

'Let me check with the neighbours,' Jane said. 'We're a bunch of curtain-twitchers here, so someone might have seen him go out.'

She disappeared into the hall and he heard her talking earnestly on the phone, but couldn't hear what was being said. After a few moments, she returned. 'That's a little odd.'

'What is?'

'Was Hamish expecting any other visitors today?'

'Not as far as I'm aware. Why?'

'I was just talking to Ellen who lives round the corner. She tends to be up and about early – well, we all do at our age. From her kitchen she can see Hamish's front garden. There was a car pulled up in front of it this morning. About nine she said.'

Gary looked puzzled. 'A car?'

'Pulled up right in front of your dad's house. She noticed it because it was double-parked outside the gate. Something fairly big, she said, though she knows as much about cars as I do.'

'She's sure it was visiting my dad's?'

'She said two people got out and went to your father's door.'

'He didn't tell me he was expecting anyone.'

'She's not sure what happened after that. She was looking

out of the kitchen window and one of the visitors turned and stared at her, so she felt a bit embarrassed. She went back into the living room so didn't see if your father answered the door. When she went back, the car was gone.'

'My dad didn't get many visitors. I'm sure he'd have mentioned it if he was expecting someone.'

'I'm afraid none of the other people I spoke to had seen any sign of him today. I tried the village shop just in case he'd walked up there. They know him in there because he usually goes in to buy his daily newspaper, but they hadn't seen him today.'

'I just can't think where else he could have gone to. I'd better get back to Dad's house, just in case the cantankerous old so-and-so has got back and decided not to bother phoning me. I wouldn't put it past him. Thanks for your help.'

'I'm sure it'll be fine. He'll come strolling in at any minute.'

Outside, the day was already growing darker, the low sun disappearing behind the surrounding houses. The sky remained a clear blue and the temperature had dropped even further. Gary waved the woman farewell, and trudged back to his father's house.

Nothing had changed in his absence. Gary walked through into the kitchen. He'd been here over two hours now. Where the hell was Hamish?

On an impulse he picked up his father's phone. It was an old-fashioned model rather than a smartphone and, typically of his father, it was switched off. Gary switched it on, knowing his father never kept the phone locked. It had occurred to Gary, as a long shot, that the list of contacts in the phone might provide ideas for other individuals his father might be visiting.

He found the list of contacts and scrolled down, but nothing caught his eye. There were a few names he recognised, but none of them local. There were other names that meant nothing to

Gary, but none of the numbers carried the dialling code for the village. He found a handful of shops and businesses, but the closest of those seemed to be in Inverness.

He closed the contact list and idly opened the list of texts received. His father had always been scathing about the act of texting, so Gary wasn't expecting to find anything of significance.

There was one text received earlier that morning, timed just before 9am. It read simply, 'We're here as promised. Now it is the end.'

Gary stared at the message, trying to make sense of it. *Now it is the end. The end of what?*

He dialled the number from which the text had been sent but received only a 'line unavailable' message. He exited the list of texts and opened the 'calls received' log. There was an inbound call from the same number late the previous evening. The call was timed at 11.30pm and had lasted a little over a minute. Gary could imagine his father giving any caller the shortest of shrift at that time of night.

Now it is the end.

What the hell did that mean? He felt a chill of unease, an indefinable sense that something was wrong.

He hesitated a moment longer, then picked up his own phone and dialled 101.

10

McKay turned right onto the road leading down to the seafront. Even coming back here had stirred uncomfortable memories of the period, a couple of years before, when he and Chrissie were going through some difficulties. He'd rented a small bungalow, enduring a solitary and rather bleak existence here. He'd even briefly been suspended from his job as a possible suspect in the murders they were investigating. It was a time he wanted to put behind him, one of the reasons he'd initially been uncertain about the decision to move over to the Black Isle.

But, as always, Chrissie had been right. They needed a new start, and this was the right place to do it. Almost as soon as they'd moved into the new place he'd felt better, as if he'd finally cast off a weight from his shoulders. Some of that burden would never completely go of course, and he didn't want it to. He couldn't simply forget about or ignore the death of their own daughter, or the wedge it had driven between him and Chrissie. But he was coming to terms with it, and he and Chrissie had both learned not to offload their guilt onto the other.

If he was honest with himself, his return here tonight was

another part of that exorcism of the past. The couples' therapist that he and Chrissie had been seeing would use some phrase like 'facing up to your demons'. For McKay, this wasn't exactly a demon – or if it was it was a very passive one – but it felt like a ghost from the past.

He'd expected that being here at the solstice event would have the same effect, but in with all the crowds and the noise it had felt different. Then, at the shocking end of the evening, he'd had too many other things to think about.

So he'd wanted to come back alone, when the place was quiet, just to absorb the feel of it. He wanted to remember, and then try to forget, the man he'd been a couple of years before. Another step towards the future.

He hadn't admitted any of that to himself. Not till he'd actually arrived here. He'd told himself it was just a working visit. He was simply making a short detour on his way home so he could get a better feel for where the body had been found. The last time he'd been here, on the day after the solstice event, the scene had been cordoned off, the examiners still carrying out their work. They'd been surrounded by clusters of curious onlookers, peering to see what was going on and whether the rumours and gossip were true.

McKay left his car at the far end of the seafront and climbed out into the darkness, pulling his heavy coat tightly around him. As he walked, he was struck by a blast of chill wind off the firth.

It was still only early evening, but the sun had set hours before and, other than the pale glow of the street lights and a few lights showing in the houses on the front, it was fully dark. McKay could taste snow in the bitterly cold air.

Head down, he trudged out towards the beach. This place held other memories, too. A struggle in the rising tides that had nearly led to Ginny Horton's death. That had been only a few years before, but it felt as if it had happened in a different life.

He continued along the beach to the point where the bonfire had been positioned. The last remains of it had been removed now and the site tidied up, but he could make out where it had been. He stared at the charred area as if expecting it to reveal some new evidence about the case. Then he looked up and gazed around him.

How difficult would it have been to have brought the victim here and placed him in the stacked bonfire? *Pretty bloody difficult*, he thought. If you knew or had checked out the area, you'd be able to drive a vehicle fairly close to the edge of the beach. Assuming the victim had been fully restrained or unconscious – and McKay couldn't imagine that anyone would otherwise submit to being placed in the centre of a bonfire – you'd then have had to carry him at least a hundred metres or so.

That was before you started unpacking some of the stacked wood without bringing the whole damned edifice down on your head. This far down the beach the light was poor. It was some distance from the nearest street light, and there was no other illumination. They'd have been working with flashlights, no doubt, but it still wouldn't have been an easy task, particularly if you were trying to work without attracting attention. Even in the early morning, any bright lights out here on the beach could still have caught the eye of any onlooker in the houses on the hill above the beach.

All of which raised the question of why the body was brought here in the first place. If you wanted to kill someone painfully, there would be easier ways to do it. If you were primarily concerned with the discreet disposal of the body, there would certainly be simpler and more reliable options. In his discussions with Helena and Ginny, they'd talked about the killing being intended to communicate a message or warning. If so, it would have been a pretty graphic one to the intended recipient. But again it felt to McKay as if there would have been more straightforward ways of achieving the same result.

The question nagging at him was whether there was any significance in the method chosen. Something about the location, the fire, the individuals involved in the event, or even the timing.

A fire sacrifice on the night of the winter solstice.

It was the first time the idea had occurred to him, and he felt a chill run down his spine. Was he just being fanciful, falling prey to imaginary ghosts summoned by the windy darkness of a midwinter night? He looked around him, suddenly feeling exposed.

The beach was empty. A cold wind blew in from the sea, carrying the scent and taste of salt-water. The sky above remained clear, filled with stars, but there were clouds gathering on the horizon. Snow had been forecast before morning.

A fire sacrifice.

There'd been something in the publicity for the event, he recalled now. A piece written by Bill Emsworth for the local magazine, the *Black Isle Chatterbox*. Chrissie had shown it to him. It was a humorous piece about how they were using some of the scarecrows local residents had made during the pandemic lockdown. McKay had been baffled at first because the whole scarecrow phenomenon had largely passed him by. It had happened shortly before they'd finally completed their move out here once the full lockdown began to be lifted.

Chrissie, on the other hand, had made a point of keeping in touch with events in the area they were moving to. She'd explained to him that some of the volunteers at the local museum of Pictish life, Groam House, had promoted the idea as a light-hearted response to the lockdown. Residents had been encouraged to build the scarecrows and leave them in conspicuous places. Some had been destroyed as lockdown was lifted, but others had remained in place or been stored away. McKay had found the remaining ones slightly unnerving. He'd occasionally spot the lifeless figures in unexpected places, their slowly decaying figures haunting the fields, hedgerows and gardens.

Emsworth's idea had been to ask for donations of scarecrows to the event, where they'd be placed on the bonfire as a 'sacrifice' to drive away the troubles of the past year and bring on the start of the new. 'A symbolic healing process,' he'd jokingly written.

It was light-hearted nonsense, bulked out by pseudo-scholarly references to Frazer's *The Golden Bough*, Celtic magic and all kinds of other mythological stuff. Emsworth was clearly skilled at drumming up publicity, and the idea of the 'fire sacrifice' had been picked up by a couple of the local newspapers. Emsworth had been very careful to position the whole thing as a joke. He'd said he had no wish to offend anyone's religious beliefs, and he hoped that everyone would participate in the spirit he'd intended.

That was why until now McKay hadn't made any connection between Emsworth's jokey initiative and their grotesque discovery. But now the thought made him feel uneasy. Was it conceivable that someone had taken Emsworth's idea more seriously? That someone had taken the opportunity to perform a genuine human sacrifice?

McKay pulled up his coat collar, his head ducked against the rising wind, and began to trudge back along the beach towards the seafront. It was still relatively early, but there was no one else in sight. The only other signs of human life were the lights showing in some of the houses.

As he reached the road, McKay stopped and looked back across the beach. The place felt different somehow, as if his own grisly idea had tainted the landscape. Was it really possible?

That an actual human sacrifice had been performed in this place just days before?

A second thought struck him. If a human sacrifice had really been performed here then, at least in the most literal sense, the act had been carried out by Bill Emsworth himself.

Could that also be significant? Emsworth himself had been unaware of the significance of his action, but was it possible that someone, for whatever reason, had intended him to perform the act?

McKay was conscious he was drifting into the realm of fantasy, his imagination overexcited by the darkness and the wind and his own endless pondering on the investigation.

'That's what happens when you come out of the big city,' he muttered to himself as he climbed back into the car. 'If you don't watch yourself, you start to turn into one of the credulous locals.'

11

'I understand your anxiety, Mr Forres, but there's no need for you to worry just yet. Most likely, there's some straightforward explanation and your father's perfectly safe.' PC Billy McCann was glad that his face-mask partly concealed his sceptical expression. He was a conscientious young officer, but he felt he had drawn the short straw here. It was a call that normally wouldn't have justified an immediate visit, but he had happened to be in the vicinity.

He could see Forres was genuinely worried, but, as far as McCann could understand, the father had been missing for only a couple of hours. Forres had acknowledged that, although his father was less mobile than he used to be, he was still capable of walking around the village and had all his wits about him. In McCann's view, the most likely explanation was that Hamish Forres had popped out to visit a friend and had lost track of the time.

But now he was here, McCann had no choice but to take the case seriously. 'Perhaps the best thing would be if I take some details, and then we can decide how best to proceed.'

Gary Forres had been pacing up and down the living room

in a manner that made McCann feel slightly dizzy. Now he finally stopped and took a seat on the sofa. 'Of course, you're right. I'm just struggling to think straight.'

'Let's just take this step by step. What time would your father have been expecting you this morning?'

'I told him between about ten and eleven. I did try to call him on the hands-free when I was a few miles away to let him know I was almost there, but the phone just rang out. That didn't worry me particularly, because Dad's not keen on mobile phones. For a start, he won't acknowledge that they're mobile.' He gestured to the phone lying on the table. 'As you can see.'

'But you'd have expected him to be here to meet you at that time?'

Forres hesitated. 'The thing about Dad is he always does what he wants. Don't get me wrong. He's always very pleasant and, well, a decent bloke. But at the end of the day he does things on his terms. It's always a struggle to prise him out of the house when I come to pick him up.'

'So what you're saying,' McCann offered cautiously, 'is that he wouldn't necessarily have let the fact you were coming prevent him from going out?'

'If you put it like that, maybe not. But I wouldn't have expected him to stay out this long.' Forres was beginning to look uncomfortable, as if realising he might have dragged McCann over here unnecessarily. 'I'm just trying to be honest with you.'

'He knew you had a set of keys?' McCann asked, pointedly.

'Yes. He'd have known I could get into the house.'

'You say you've spoken to the neighbours?'

'I spoke to Jane Brown who lives next door, and she phoned all the people she could think of who might know Dad. It was one of those who told us about the car.'

'Car?' McCann looked up. So far the conversation hadn't touched on this topic.

'Sorry, yes. I told you I wasn't thinking straight. The neighbour told Jane she'd been looking out of her kitchen at about nine. She saw a car pull up outside here, and then a couple of people apparently visiting my dad. She didn't see whether Dad answered the door to them.'

'Your father wasn't expecting anyone, as far as you know?'

'He didn't say anything. He's not exactly been overwhelmed with visitors up here, especially since the lockdown, so I'd have thought he'd have mentioned it.'

'Could be anything, of course,' McCann said.

'Yes, but then there's this.' Forres picked up his father's phone and fumbled with the keys before handing it to McCann. 'He received this text about the same time.'

'You've no idea what this means?'

'None at all. But it can't be a coincidence, surely? He received a call from the same number late last night.'

'After you'd spoken to him?'

'Much later. I spoke to him early evening. This was late at night. You can see it in the logged calls. It was just a short call. Couple of minutes.'

McCann hesitated. 'This does seem to put a slightly different complexion on things, though I'm not sure how to interpret it. Is it possible that these were friends of your father's who've taken him out somewhere?' Even to his own ears, it sounded an unlikely explanation.

'If he knew he was going to do that, he'd have let me know, surely? He could have phoned me while I was driving up. He can be thoughtless, but not to that extent.'

'He's not prone to be forgetful?'

'Sharp as a tack, still.' Forres paused. 'Although there is one other thing.'

'Yes?'

'You'll no doubt have this on record. The police, I mean. He was robbed, just yesterday. Some young scam artist.'

McCann looked up, his brain making a connection. 'Is this the young woman who claimed to be from the local volunteer group? A stolen wallet?'

'That's the one.'

'I'm sorry, Mr Forres. I hadn't made the connection. I saw the case on the log, but I hadn't registered the name.' He hesitated. 'I'm not sure how to put this, Mr Forres. But is it possible that your father's faculties might have deteriorated more than you'd realised? Elderly people are sometimes good at concealing these issues from their loved ones.'

'I don't think so. I mean, it's possible he's less on the ball than he was. There'd have been a time when I wouldn't have given any scam artist a chance against him. But I talk to him regularly and I've seen no sign of any deterioration in the way he talks or thinks. He used to be in business, and he still understands that world inside out.'

McCann was beginning to feel out of his depth. He still felt that there was some straightforward explanation for Hamish Forres's absence, but the text message gave him pause for thought. There was something disturbing about the wording. Then there was the theft of the wallet. Were the two incidents somehow linked?

All he could do was play it by the book, take down the details and make a risk assessment to determine how the case should be handled. On the face of it, this would be a low priority investigation. There was no strong evidence that Hamish Forres was particularly vulnerable, despite his advanced age. He was physically mobile, albeit within limits. His cognitive abilities seemed to be undiminished. He had been missing only for a few hours, and there was no reason to assume he had come to any harm. It was possible he might have suffered an accident or illness, but in a small town the news would surely soon get back here.

'You'll appreciate there's only a limited amount we can do at this stage, Mr Forres. I'll have a chat with some of your neighbours, though I don't know if they'll be able to tell me any more than you've discovered already. I can check the local hospitals and whether there've been any emergency calls that might have related to your father this morning, in case he went out and was taken ill or had an accident. It's also possible he might have been taken in by someone locally. If that's the case, I imagine we'll hear soon enough.' McCann shrugged apologetically. 'Beyond that, there's not much more we can do at this stage. If your father doesn't turn up within a reasonable timeframe...'

Gary Forres was pacing around the room again. 'So you're basically telling me you can't do anything until it might be too late?'

'I appreciate your concern, Mr Forres, but at present we've no real reason to believe your father might have come to any harm. He's an adult with all his faculties, and he's only been absent for a short time.' McCann stopped, trying to think what further practical help he could offer. 'I take it you've searched the house thoroughly?'

'Yes, of course. But have a look for yourself. I'm not thinking entirely clearly, so I might have missed something.'

'What about outdoor clothing? If your father did go out somewhere, do you know what he would have been likely to wear?'

Forres stopped pacing for a moment. 'I hadn't thought about that. Hang on...' He walked out into the hall, and McCann heard him open a cupboard door. McCann rose and followed him.

Gary Forres was standing beside a large cupboard next to the front door. 'He's got a couple of overcoats. One's more of a raincoat, the other's a heavy tweed-type thing that he'd normally wear on a day like today. Both of them are still in here.' He gestured towards the cupboard. 'His boots are here too. He wouldn't go out walking in winter without wearing the boots. He always goes on about how sturdy they are and what good grip they have.'

'Would he wear something different if he was travelling in a car?'

'I told you. His car's still here. He can't have driven anywhere.'

'I was thinking as a passenger. What would he wear when he was driving back with you today, for example?'

'Pretty much the same, to be honest. That's Dad. He'd clamber into the car wearing his big heavy coat and those big boots and then complain that he was too hot. He wouldn't travel light at this time of the year.'

'You don't think there's any possibility he could have bought a new coat or boots since you last saw him?'

'He'd have told me. There's not much happens in Dad's life these days. If he buys anything new, he always makes a point of telling me. Even something as mundane as a new coat or a pair of shoes.'

'So you're saying he left the house without putting on any outdoor clothes.'

'He just wouldn't do that. He's a stubborn old so-and-so. He'd never leave the house in winter without dressing for it. Or in most of summer for that matter. He wouldn't even do it if he was popping to the shop in the car.'

McCann led them back into the living room. 'So how do you explain what's happened?'

'I can't. Unless–'

'Unless he didn't leave the house voluntarily?'

'When you say it like that it sounds absurd. Who'd make

him leave the house against his will? I mean, Dad's an old man. Long retired.'

'This is a slightly awkward question, but is your father a wealthy man? This is quite an impressive house.' Even up here, McCann thought, a house of this age and character wouldn't have come cheap. This kind of house rarely came on the local market.

'It depends what you mean by wealthy. He was a successful businessman, and he's certainly comfortably off. He's always been a bit cagey about it, making jokes about my inheritance. My impression is that he's got a decent sum squirrelled away, but I don't know much more than that. You don't think...' Forres trailed off, as if reluctant to contemplate what McCann might be thinking.

'I'm just trying to understand the situation,' McCann said. 'If you're suggesting that somehow your father was taken away against his will, there'd have to be a reason for that. It sounds far-fetched, but in the circumstances I don't think we can entirely discount the possibility.'

'So you're suggesting what? That he might have been kidnapped. That they're looking for a ransom?'

'I've no idea. That kind of thing's extremely uncommon in this country. And on the face of it your father wouldn't seem to be an obvious candidate. Normally, I'd be telling you to sit tight and give it another few hours. But the text message and the car do seem odd. You've no idea what they might have meant by "the end"? The end of what?'

'I haven't a clue. And Dad's not prone to getting texts or even calls on his mobile.'

'Okay,' McCann said after a pause. 'I'm going to escalate it. What are your own plans?'

Forres looked at his watch. 'That's one of the issues. I was expecting to have set off back by now. But I don't feel as if I can in case he turns up.'

'It has to be your choice, Mr Forres. You could leave a message for your father asking him to phone you as soon as he returns.'

Forres looked hesitant. 'I suppose. But I'd be worrying all the way back. I think I'm better staying here till we've a better idea what's going on. I'll phone my wife and let her know.'

'I'm sorry,' McCann said. 'It's the last thing you need just before Christmas. I still think there's some straightforward explanation and he'll turn up before too long.'

'I hope you're right. None of it makes sense. Dad can be irritating sometimes, but he doesn't normally do anything like this.'

McCann felt eager now to get something moving. If Hamish Forres walked through the door in the next hour with some sheepish explanation for his absence, McCann would end up looking a numpty for taking it so seriously. But if Forres was safe, that wouldn't matter. And if he wasn't, McCann was definitely making the right decision. 'Okay, Mr Forres. I'll go and take another look around. Why don't you make yourself a coffee and try to relax.'

12

'Helena!' Emsworth's greeting on opening the door was effusive.

'I hope you weren't expecting anyone else,' Grant smiled. 'You do know we're not allowed to mix with other households?'

'Certainly not. I was just delighted as always to see you. Luckily we can be each other's support bubble.'

'You know how to say the right things, Bill. I'm delighted to be here.'

'You'd better come in.' Emsworth peered past her into the darkness. 'Smells like snow out there.'

'They've forecast some overnight. Just a sprinkling, I think.'

'Enough to give us a white Christmas, I hope. Can't remember the last time we had one.'

'Not for a few years, even up here,' she agreed. 'Usually seems to wait till January, just to add to the misery.' She followed him into the spacious hallway. He'd pulled out all the stops to get the place ready for Christmas. 'It's looking very Christmassy.'

'Well, that's the idea. This place isn't really Victorian or even Edwardian, but I've taken a few liberties with the period style.'

'It looks marvellous,' she said. 'Very cosy.'

'I'm aiming for a cosy Christmas,' he said. 'Just the two of us. One of the few benefits of social distancing.'

'Sounds idyllic. Better than most of my recent Christmases by quite a long way.'

'I'm sorry to hear that,' Emsworth said. 'Though I'll do my best to make this one a success.'

'I've usually just been working,' she explained. 'That's how I was able to justify taking tomorrow off as well as Christmas Day and Boxing Day. They owe me several.'

'I'm very glad to hear it. It means we can have a proper little holiday together. I hope the ship stays on course in your absence.'

From their first meeting, she'd been amused by his manner of speaking. The slightly florid and self-conscious language, the sense that he was always partly giving a performance. If it had been more exaggerated, it might have been irritating, but he seemed to know how to keep it under control. At first, she'd assumed the verbal style would be echoed in his writing, but she'd read a number of his books now and his written style was almost the opposite – simple, unadorned and plain. Perhaps he allowed what he took out of his writing to flow into the way he spoke.

'It'll be fine,' she said. 'Alec McKay will deputise very ably. He'll probably rub a few people up the wrong way, but he'll have it all under control. The main issue's clearly the murder investigation.' She'd followed him into the living room, and was now gazing with admiration at the ornately decorated Christmas tree, stretching up into the vaulted roof space. 'I don't think anything new's likely to break over Christmas, though obviously the investigation's continuing. Mind you, I should warn you that, if anything major does happen, I might still need to go in.'

'Let's hope it doesn't, then,' Emsworth said. 'Keen as I am for you to bring the perpetrators to justice.' He gestured towards the tree. 'What do you think? All my own work.'

'You're a man of hidden talents, Mr Emsworth.' She leaned over and kissed him on the lips. It wasn't the first time, but she still felt slightly awkward with the intimacy.

'You wait,' he said. 'Now, would you like a coffee or something stronger?'

She looked at her watch. It was still only just after 6pm, though as she'd driven here through the darkness, it had felt much later. 'Coffee for the moment. We can move on to the harder stuff later.'

'Very wise. Don't want us falling asleep before supper. I have a haunch of local venison ready to roast.'

'Goodness. As I say, hidden talents.'

'I'm pushing the boat out this Christmas,' he said. 'In celebration.'

'Of what?'

He was already disappearing out of the door on his way to the kitchen, but he stopped and looked back. 'Of us, of course. What else?'

Grant remained slightly unsure if this really was a good idea. She'd been hoping for a new relationship, a serious relationship, for a couple of years now, but it had increasingly felt out of reach. Then, out of the blue, Bill Emsworth turned up. They'd got on well, bonding during Bill's so-called research sessions, in which he'd plied her with questions about police procedure in exchange for excellent dinners in Rocpool and the Mustard Seed. They'd discovered they had plenty in common, and the 'research sessions' had gradually transformed into genuine dates. It had happened more quickly than she'd expected, and she was worried she might be rushing into things.

On the other hand, neither she nor Bill were getting any

younger. This might be the one chance they had to start something new, so why not give it a try? So far she was enjoying it.

She sat herself on the plush sofa and looked around the room. She'd been here a couple of times already, and she liked the house. It felt like Bill himself – just a little ostentatious in its style but comfortable and welcoming. Despite its high vaulted ceiling, the living room felt cosy against the chill of the winter night. She was already beginning to think she could feel at home here.

Emsworth returned bearing two mugs of coffee. 'Hope I've remembered correctly. Milk and no sugar?'

'Exactly right,' she said, as he seated himself beside her.

He sat back on the sofa, watching her. 'I hope I don't prove too boring over the next few days,' he said. 'I do tend to live a quiet life these days.'

'Exactly what I want. I get plenty of excitement and stress at work.'

'I had a visit from one of your people today. DS Horton?'

'Ginny? I hope she was gentle with you.'

'The very model of professionalism. I'm not sure I could help much, though.'

Grant nodded. 'I don't want to seem difficult, Bill, but it's probably better if we don't talk shop. I'm skating on slightly thin ice anyway given our relationship. It really wouldn't be appropriate for me to discuss the case. Sorry.' She shifted awkwardly, wondering if she'd already managed to offend him.

Emsworth smiled. 'No, you're quite right. I've no desire to put you in a difficult position. I fully appreciate the sensitivities.' His smile widened. 'Anyway, it gives me an excuse to talk about me instead. My favourite subject.'

'There we go then,' she said. 'We're all winners. Anyway, it's about time. I've given you all that inside knowledge about policing. Now you can tell me the secrets of writing.'

'I wish I knew what they were,' he said. 'I've written twenty novels, and it seems harder each time. I keep thinking eventually I'll discover the trick, but it hasn't happened yet.'

'Are you working on something at the moment?' They'd never really discussed Emsworth's work, except in relation to his questions about policing.

'I'm always working on something. Quite often more than one thing. At the moment, I'm editing one book and trying to write another.'

'That must be confusing.'

'It can be. Especially if you work in the chaotic way I do. It's only a matter of time before I insert the wrong character into a book.'

'Do you enjoy it?' she asked, unsure if it was a stupid question. 'The writing, I mean.'

'Well, I wouldn't do it if I didn't, I suppose. Nobody forced me to take up this profession. Mind you, if you were to ask me when I'm in the middle of trying to make a plot work, I might tell you differently. It can feel like hard work sometimes, but it's not exactly digging ditches.'

'You've obviously done quite well from it,' she said, looking around the room.

'Don't let the house fool you. I'm making a decent living from the writing these days, but it's not exactly made me rich. Not yet, anyway. This place is the result of being able to buy a small house in London in the days when I had proper jobs. Bought it for what seems like peanuts now – though it didn't then – and sold it for enough money to buy this place. But I do okay, as long as I keep writing.'

'I supposed I'd assumed you'd always written,' Grant said. 'I didn't realise you'd had other jobs. That was just naïve of me.'

'It's what people always assume if they don't know how it works,' Emsworth said. 'I mean, I have always written. It just took me a long time to get published. And even longer to start making any money from it. I almost gave up a few times. I did various other jobs, but ended up running my own business, which was pretty all-consuming in itself, so I was struggling to find time to write. But I realised it was what I really wanted to do. In the end, I sold the business – for less than I should have done, looking back, but it gave me enough to tide me over – and carried on doing consultancy work for them. That gave me some savings, a bit of an income, and enough time to take the writing seriously. Luckily it worked.'

'I hadn't realised it was like that,' Grant said. 'I'd never really thought about it.'

'People tend to assume we're all J. K. Rowling and the money just comes flowing in, but it's not like that, except for a fortunate few. You have to want to do it.' He stood up, collecting the now empty coffee mugs. 'I'll go and get the food going. And return with a drink for you. Any preferences? Wine? G&T?'

'Wine's fine. Whatever's going.'

'Red okay?'

'Anything, honestly. I'm very unfussy.'

'Well, you've already agreed to spend time with me.' He smiled. 'Make yourself at home. I won't be long.'

While she waited for him to return, she busied herself exploring the room. Not in a nosy way, she told herself, but just to get a better sense of who Bill Emsworth might be. There was a low cabinet along one wall, which held a selection of ornaments and photographs. Most of them were unrevealing, though Grant assumed some of them had particular sentimental significance for Bill.

She moved around the room and peered at the tightly packed bookshelves. She was an enthusiastic reader herself, but in no sense a collector of books. She tended to read a book once and then donate it to one of the charity shops in Inverness, and increasingly she was buying e-books to save herself the trouble of disposing of them.

Bill was clearly a very different kind of reader. He'd told her these bookshelves were only part of an extensive book collection located around the house, with the majority in the room that he used to write in. The books here were mostly crime novels, including some impressive old hardback editions of famous writers whose names she recognised. Agatha Christie. Dorothy L. Sayers. Margery Allingham. Ngaio Marsh. Other shelves including American writers such as Raymond Chandler, Dashiell Hammett and James Ellroy. Many of the other names meant nothing to her, but she assumed they were similarly renowned crime writers. The books were organised thematically rather than alphabetically, though she had no idea of the significance of some of the clusters.

The second shelf was devoted largely to books on true crime, ranging from serious scholarly studies of famous murders or murderers to more sensationalist accounts. Some of the books she recognised from her own studies in criminology – Ludovic Kennedy's book on John Christie, Gordon Burn's books about Peter Sutcliffe and Fred and Rosemary West, and various others. She supposed that kind of reading was as essential to Bill's work as, in its way, it had been to her own training. The more sensationalist accounts of true crimes had never appealed to her, but again she imagined they would be useful in feeding Bill's plot lines.

'I see you've discovered the Black Library.' Emsworth had re-entered the room without her hearing, and his voice just behind her ear made her start. She turned to see him smiling at her. 'Sorry,' he said. 'Didn't mean to make you jump. Thought you'd heard me come in.'

'I was engrossed in looking at the books,' she said. 'It's a fascinating collection.'

'This is just a small part of it. There's all kinds of stuff scattered about the house.'

'I'd have thought you'd have kept the crime stuff in your work room?'

'I do. These are just overflow shelves, really. Wait till you see how much stuff I've got up there.' He gestured towards the true crime section. 'That's what I call the Black Library. My little joke. Like the old Black Museum in Scotland Yard.'

'It's still there, I think,' Grant said. 'In New Scotland Yard, that is. They just call it the Crime Museum these days.'

'Of course they do. Political correctness gone mad and all that. By the way, I've brought wine as promised.' He gestured towards two glasses sitting on the low table beside the sofa.

She wondered how he'd managed to enter the room and place the glasses on the table without her hearing. She had been focused on the bookshelves, as she'd said, but even so he must have moved very quietly. For a moment, the thought made her uneasy, as if he'd deliberately crept up on her.

It was nonsense, of course. If you're trying to sneak up on someone, you don't stop to place two glasses of wine on the table first. It was probably a sign of how tired and stressed she was that the idea had even occurred to her. She needed this Christmas break. 'How's the food going?' she asked.

'All under control. Roast potatoes in and cooking. I don't want to put the venison in too early in case it overcooks.'

'You sound quite the expert.'

'Hardly. But I enjoy cooking. Even when it's just for myself. But it's more fun when it's for someone else. Especially when that someone else is you.' He raised his glass and clinked it against hers. 'Cheers. And a very merry Christmas to both of us.'

'Thank you,' she said. 'I think I needed this more than I realised.'

13

As forecast, there had been a fall of snow overnight. Not a particularly heavy one, Crawford had been relieved to see, but enough to make him grateful for his four-by-four. No matter how much snow had fallen overnight, Gordon Prebble would have been deeply dissatisfied if Crawford had wanted to postpone their meeting. It was never a good idea to leave Prebble dissatisfied.

There was almost certainly no reason why they couldn't have discussed whatever Prebble wanted to talk about over the phone. But that wasn't how Prebble worked. If Prebble summoned you, you went, no matter how inconvenient it might be.

Prebble lived in a characteristically imposing Victorian house just outside Strathpeffer. He'd once told Crawford the history of the building, but Crawford, nodding politely, had taken none of it in. Some Victorian entrepreneur who'd spent a fortune building the place and then almost immediately gone bust as a result of his technology being superseded by a cheaper or better alternative. Crawford had forgotten the details, but he recalled Prebble's finger-wagging conclusion. 'That's the lesson,

Simon. You have to stay one step ahead of the game. Take your eye off the ball, and the plates will stop spinning. You'll be up shit creek without a paddle.' Prebble tended to talk in clichéd mixed metaphors.

The majority of the drive over had been unproblematic. The main roads had been cleared of snow, and it was only on this final stretch, as Crawford turned off onto the single-track road that led to Prebble's place, that the route became more treacherous. The vehicle would cope with these conditions easily enough, but Crawford still drove with caution. He had no desire to fall victim to Prebble's wilfulness.

At the top of the hill, the landscape opened up before him. Prebble's house commanded a view out over the Black Isle and the surrounding countryside. After the overnight snow, the morning was clear and bright, and the view was spectacular, with the hillsides white-coated and the silvery stretches of the Cromarty and Moray Firths visible in the far distance. It was another of those days – increasingly frequent of late – when Crawford felt inclined simply to continue driving, head off somewhere by himself rather than wasting time with an arsehole like Prebble.

Maybe that day would come. It was what he was planning for, after all. It was why he wasted his time on arseholes like Prebble. It was only a matter of time.

After another mile, he turned onto the lengthy track to Prebble's house. The track was unmetalled and rough. Prebble didn't lack the money to improve it, but Crawford suspected he preferred it this way. It discouraged unwanted or casual visitors. More importantly, perhaps, it slowed any vehicles down sufficiently to enable Prebble to be aware of their approach. He didn't like to be taken by surprise. Crawford assumed that there would also be CCTV cameras scanning the track, but he'd never been able to spot them.

Prebble's house loomed ahead of him, gothic and slightly sinister in the winter sunlight. Crawford had never been sure why Prebble had chosen to live up here. The house was impressive enough and there was no question that Prebble preferred his privacy, but Crawford couldn't believe that entirely compensated for the inconvenience of this remote location. There must be days, in the very depths of winter, when this place became inaccessible. Presumably that was how Prebble liked it.

A hundred metres or so from the house the tough track broadened into a well-maintained gravelled driveway. The contrast was stark enough to confirm that the state of the track was a deliberate choice. Crawford pulled his four-by-four in beside Prebble's own BMW X-drive, and climbed out into the chilly morning. As he walked towards the house, the large oak front door opened and Gordon Prebble appeared, staring out at him accusingly. 'You're late.'

Crawford looked at his watch. It was two minutes past eleven. He was momentarily tempted simply to return to his car and drive away. Instead he said, 'Sorry, Gordon. Roads a bit tricky this morning.'

'Time's money, you know, Simon. And money counts.'

Thanks for that nugget of wisdom, Gordon, Crawford said to himself. 'We'd better get down to it then, Gordon. Whatever it is.'

Prebble ushered him inside and led him down the hall to the office. It was an imposing room, lined with oak panelling and with a large bay window that commanded a view across the hills to the open sea.

Crawford wasn't expecting to be offered coffee, but for once Prebble surprised him. He had a fancy new espresso machine which he was clearly keen to show off. 'Espresso?' Crawford assumed that Prebble hadn't yet worked out how to use the steamer.

'Why not?' Crawford watched as Prebble placed a cup on the machine and pressed the button to prepare a double espresso. The machine went through its grinding routine before depositing a thick black coffee into the cup.

'Clever, isn't it?' Prebble handed Crawford the coffee. 'My new toy.'

'Impressive.' Crawford took a sip. 'Very nice.'

'Ought to be, given what it cost.' Prebble made himself a drink then gestured for Crawford to take a seat at the large table that dominated the room. 'Right. Business.'

Crawford sat down and took his notebook out of his briefcase. 'What can I do for you, Gordon?' *And why is it so bloody urgent*, he wanted to add.

'I'm selling up, Simon.'

Crawford looked up, surprised. Whatever he'd been expecting, it wasn't that. Prebble had, until now, struck him as one of those who would always be there. Some of them went into this to make a quick buck – or a quick several million bucks – with an exit strategy to retire to the sun. But those were the exception rather than the rule. Most of them were addicted to it. Addicted to making money. Even when they were wealthy enough not to need to work again, they couldn't help themselves. They'd keep on plugging away until they were carried out of the office in a coffin. Crawford had always seen Prebble as one of those. 'Selling up? How do you mean?'

'Exactly what I say. I'm selling up. Everything. Taking a clean break.'

Crawford raised an eyebrow. 'That's... quite a surprise. What's prompted this?'

Prebble shrugged. 'It just felt like the right time. I'm getting too old for all this.'

That was another surprise. Prebble was a fitness addict, who had installed a well-appointed gym in the cellar here. He was slim and muscular, and looked much younger than his sixty-five years. He retained an impressive thatch of hair, although Crawford assumed Prebble had been dyeing it for some years now. Even so, he wasn't the kind of man who would normally acknowledge his age, much less offer it as a reason for retirement.

'It's a big step,' Crawford pointed out. 'You're sure about this?'

For a moment, Crawford thought Prebble would lose his temper. He didn't like to be offered even the mildest of challenges. 'Yes, Simon, I'm sure about it. Though frankly that's none of your fucking business anyway.'

Crawford held up his hands. 'No, of course not. Like I say, I was just surprised.'

'I like to surprise people, Simon.'

That was true enough. Prebble preferred to keep people on the back foot. 'Well, I wish you well, Gordon. What is it you're looking for from me?'

'I'd have thought that was fucking obvious.'

No doubt it is to you, Crawford thought, *but I don't possess your gift of fucking telepathy.* 'In detail, I mean. What exactly are you looking for?'

Prebble sighed in theatrical exasperation. 'Okay, Simon. Let me spell it out. First of all, there's my investments. You know, those very large sums of money you're supposedly looking after for me. It's not been a great year for them, has it?'

'It's not been a great year for anyone,' Crawford pointed out. 'There was a global economic crash as a result of the pandemic.' *Just in case you hadn't noticed*, he added silently to himself. 'If your investments had been with anyone else, you'd have done far worse. As it is, you've more than held your own.' Whatever else he might be, Prebble was no fool, and Crawford knew that Prebble was well aware of how well his investments had done in the circumstances. Some of the techniques Crawford had used were on, or even beyond, the limits of strict legality and the nature of some of the investments was questionable. But Prebble knew that too.

'I just want to make sure everything's as secure as it can be.'

'Do you want me to move some of it into lower exposure areas?' Crawford already knew what the answer would be. 'I can do that if you like, but obviously the returns would be less. Probably significantly less.'

'I just want you to keep a fucking close eye on it all. That's your job, Simon. I don't want any toerag salting it away from under my nose.'

Was that what this was all about? Did Prebble think Crawford was somehow feathering his own nest at Prebble's expense? Crawford had sometimes been tempted to do that, particularly since he was well aware that he could probably do so without most of his clients even noticing. But it wasn't worth the risk. He made enough of a turnout of this as it was. If any of his clients were ever to catch him not playing straight, his reputation would be destroyed. 'No one's going to do that, Gordon. Not on my watch. I know what I'm doing.'

Prebble's mood seemed to soften slightly. 'That's why I'm prepared to trust you with this stuff, Simon. I just want you to be crystal clear that if you ever fuck me about – well, you won't do it twice and you'll live just about long enough to regret you did it the first time.'

'I'm not going to fuck you about, Gordon,' Crawford said calmly. 'That's not the way I work. You know that.' He had the sense that Prebble was genuinely rattled by something. All the familiar bluster was there, but there was a new uncertainty beneath it.

'Aye, well, some people seem to be trying to. So take this as a shot across your own bows.' He smiled. 'Remember what happened to Bruce Dennis.'

Dennis had been Crawford's first employer and mentor, the main reason why Crawford was in this business. He'd been killed in a drive-by shooting many years before, apparently the victim of internecine rivalry. 'Bit below the belt, Gordon,' Crawford said. 'Trust me, I'm on your side. I'll keep everything under control. That's what you pay me for. Whatever the circumstances.'

'If you sense anything out of the ordinary, I want you to give me the heads-up straight away.'

'What kind of thing?'

'That's your job.'

Crawford really had no idea what Prebble was talking about, but he saw no point in taking the discussion further. He was unlikely to gain any further clarity and would probably succeed only in antagonising Prebble. 'I hear what you're saying, Gordon. What else?'

'That's only the start. I want to liquidise everything.'

Crawford blinked. 'Everything? How do you mean?'

'What I say. All the business. All the assets. Everything.'

'That's not really my area of expertise, Gordon. But I can recommend people, depending on what you're looking for.'

'That may be useful. I've got some of my own contacts, but I want to make sure everything's done properly. I want to squeeze as much as I can out of this.'

Crawford hesitated. 'I'm not quite sure how to ask this, Gordon. But are you having problems with the business? I mean, is this intended to forestall some more formal action?' He was conscious Prebble might not even understand what he was asking, but he also knew that he couldn't straightforwardly ask Prebble if he was going bust. Not if he wanted to leave the house in good health.

Prebble stared at him for a moment. 'We're not in trouble, if that's what you mean.'

'I just thought that, well, with everything that's happened this year...'

'This year's been good for us, Simon. It's like wartime. That kind of crisis always creates lots of opportunities. That's not what this is all about. I'm just looking for something new.'

Like hell you are, Crawford thought. None of this rang true to him. He had no idea what was really motivating Prebble to take this step, but it was something more than just a desire for a life-change. Something was troubling Prebble, and Crawford couldn't imagine what that might be. Whatever Crawford might think of Prebble, he'd never struck Crawford as someone who would be easily intimidated. 'So what do you want me to do exactly?'

'I've already got people disposing of various assets. Some of them won't be easy to liquidate, as you can probably imagine.'

Crawford could easily imagine, knowing the dubious nature of Prebble's enterprises. 'I can maybe suggest one or two reliable people who can help you with that. Discreetly, obviously.'

'I assumed you'd know some of the right people. I'll let you know where I'm having difficulties. But the main thing I want from you is to make sure that all the proceeds are suitably invested.'

'And by suitably, you again mean discreetly? As well as safely and untraceably.'

'You know me well enough, Simon. You know what I'm looking for.'

'I think I do after all these years. And of course you want a lucrative return.'

'I take that for granted.'

Of course you do, and you've no interest in the lengths I go to or the risks I take to achieve those returns. 'You know I'm the best, Gordon.'

'Aye, so you keep telling me. Okay, that's it. I just wanted to tell you what was happening, and to put you on alert that your services will be needed. I'll be looking at the assets, and I'll let you know if we need more specialist help with the disposal. I prefer to work with people I know, but I assume your associates will be trustworthy.'

'I wouldn't work with anyone who wasn't, Gordon. Okay, I'll wait to hear from you.' It was clear that, as far as Prebble was concerned, the meeting was over. Crawford pushed himself to his feet. 'Have a good Christmas, Gordon.'

'I doubt I'll notice it,' Prebble grunted. 'I'll call you in the next few days once I know how things are panning out.'

You do that, Crawford thought, *and no doubt you'll drag me out here yet again for a conversation which could easily have happened over the phone.* Except, of course, Prebble didn't trust phones. He didn't trust anything much, but his reluctance to discuss anything of significance over the phone was legendary.

'You can see yourself out,' Prebble said. It wasn't a question. 'And one other thing, Simon.'

'Sure.'

'I assume this goes without saying but not a word to anyone about what I'm doing.'

'You know me, Gordon. Soul of discretion.'

'I hope so, Simon. For your sake.'

'I'll wait to hear from you, Gordon.' Without allowing Prebble any opportunity to respond, Crawford walked out of the room, heading for the front door. Prebble had been a lucrative client and, whatever was going on here, it seemed as if he was about to become an even more lucrative one. That thought helped Crawford to keep a lid on the anger he always felt when having to deal with Prebble directly. Prebble might be an arsehole, but he was an arsehole who paid well.

He pulled open the front door and stepped back out into the daylight. It was still a bright day, although the sky was clouding over again. More snow was forecast overnight, so it looked as if it was going to be a white Christmas, for those who cared about such things. Crawford mainly cared only about getting back home and being able to relax for a couple of days without having to think about the likes of Gordon Prebble.

He climbed back into his car and sat for a moment staring at the view, trying to absorb what he'd heard. Something was going on here, and Crawford had no idea what it might be, except that it was far more serious than Prebble suddenly opting for an early retirement. It struck Crawford again how exposed Prebble potentially was up here. No doubt the security was tight, and Prebble was as streetwise as they came. But Prebble had never allowed anyone to get close to him, and, as far as Crawford was aware, there were no live-in staff up here. That had been how Prebble preferred it. Crawford wondered whether Prebble might be coming to regret that now.

As Crawford set off back along the rough trackway towards the road he was struck by a sudden intuition that, despite everything that been said in his meeting with Prebble, this would be the last time he would drive up here. *Something is about to happen*, he thought. *Something bad.*

14

'If you want to get off soon, I can hold the fort.'

'What's wrong with you, Alec? Are you on the verge of turning into a half-decent human being?'

'Aye, well, don't let on to that lot, will you?' McKay gestured out towards the still-busy incident room. 'Or they'll all want a slice.'

Ginny Horton looked at her watch. 'It's barely afternoon. I can't slip off yet.'

'It's Christmas Eve,' McKay pointed out. 'Even in our game, we can exercise the odd bit of flexibility. Anyway, the offer's there. It may be your only chance to take advantage of my largesse.'

'That's true enough,' Horton said. 'Okay, I might take you up on it and get away a bit early. Isla's got the day off and is doing the prep for Christmas lunch so it's not too stressful tomorrow. Be good to give her a bit of a hand.'

'Well, there you go, then. Never say that your Uncle Alec doesn't give you anything. Besides, it doesn't look as if anything new's going to break today. I'm just hoping it stays quiet for tomorrow so I can enjoy an uninterrupted day with

Chrissie. Not to mention Fiona.' He shook his head. 'Suspect it won't be fun for Fiona. It's bound to bring back memories of last year.'

Horton nodded. 'This time last year she was still happily married without a care in the world.'

'Or at least only the same kind of cares as the rest of us. It's a shock to see how quickly that can all fall apart. She seems okay so far, but Chrissie's worried that it might hit her suddenly.'

'Hope you manage to have a decent Christmas, anyway. And that nothing new blows up here.'

McKay shrugged. 'Depends what it is. If we get a sudden breakthrough, I'll be delighted even if it means foregoing the turkey. But I'd be surprised if we get much new over Christmas. Everybody's plugging away but there are limits to what you can do.'

'By the way,' Horton said, 'there has been one mildly interesting development this morning, but I don't think it's likely to be relevant to us.'

'I could do with something interesting,' McKay said. 'Go on.'

'It's just that I asked for us to be updated with any new missing persons reports, in case any of them turned out to be our man. There've been a couple across the region, but nothing that fits in terms of age or sex. Then we had one this morning that at first I thought might be more promising. Man in Cromarty.'

'Fits the bill,' McKay agreed.

'Except that unfortunately he doesn't. When I read the report, it turned out that he'd actually gone missing yesterday morning. His son arrived to pick him up because he was due to spend Christmas with the family in Edinburgh, but no sign of the father. Too old, too.'

'How do they know when he went missing?'

'The son had spoken to him on the phone the evening

before. Just confirming when he was likely to arrive. So he was safe and sound then.'

'Definitely not our man, then,' McKay said, glumly. 'Unless he'd managed to rise from the dead.'

'Seems not. It's an odd one, though.'

'Why odd?'

'I noticed on the log that the PC who'd dealt with it was Billy McCann. I got to know him a bit because he was helpful when I had all those issues with my stepfather.'

'I remember. McCann was the poor wee bugger you kept calling out.'

'He was the officer who happened to be on duty when I called for support,' Horton corrected. 'Anyway, he's a decent cop. I gave him a call just to double-check the report and make sure that this definitely wasn't our man. Whole story seems a bit odd. Son turns up. No sign of the father. Son assumes the old man must have popped out for some reason, though that's apparently out of character. Son waits around for an hour or so and gets anxious, so goes to talk to various neighbours. Nobody's seen the father but one of them saw a car turning up outside the father's house early that morning.'

'Maybe the father got a better offer for Christmas?'

'By all accounts he's not the most sociable type. Anyway, the son eventually calls the police and Billy gets the short straw. At first, Billy's not too concerned, and assumes that there's probably some straightforward explanation for the father's absence. Then the son shows him the father's mobile, which has been left in the house, and which shows receipt of an odd text message at around the time the car was seen outside the house.'

'What sort of odd text?'

'Something about it being the end. McCann reckoned he found the message slightly threatening, though it's hard to know how to interpret it. The other odd thing is that the father seems to have left the house without any outdoor clothes, which again the son reckons is untypical, especially in the depths of winter. That was why Billy decided to escalate it, even though the old man had only been missing for a few hours and there are no other immediate grounds for concern.'

'The father wasn't suffering from dementia or anything like that?'

'No. Sound in mind and fairly sound in body, according to the son. Not as mobile as he used to be, but able to get around.'

'Sounds an interesting one.' McKay's tone suggested his own interest was limited. 'Just a pity he wasn't considerate enough to go missing a few days ago so we could claim him as our victim.'

'You're all heart, Alec. There is one other interesting thing about this one, though.'

'I hope this is as interesting as the previous stuff,' McKay said. 'I could do with a nap.'

'The missing old man is Hamish Forres.'

McKay sat up. 'That actually is interesting.'

Hamish Forres had come onto their radar from time to time during investigations into various people trafficking and money laundering activities in the region. Most recently, following the death of Archie Donaldson, one of the major local operators, they'd been working with the Revenue and the National Crime Agency to identify his potential associates. Forres had had a background as a supposedly legitimate businessman, who'd spent his career working in the import/export industry.

In Forres's case, as in others, they'd concluded there was no mileage in investigating further. Forres himself was now retired and, although there'd been various rumours during his career, the police had never uncovered any substantive evidence of criminal activity in his businesses. If they'd had the resources to launch a full-scale investigation, they might well have found something, but neither the police nor the partner agencies had identified sufficient justification for doing so.

'What was your view of Forres?' Horton knew McKay's views were often out of step with the official positions adopted by his more senior colleagues.

'If you want my considered and thoughtful opinion, he was up to his oxters in it.'

'In what exactly?'

'In his case, fraud and money laundering mainly. In his heyday Forres was a dab hand at extracting money from the public purse and trousering it himself. Any development grant that was going. He knew the right people and he greased the right palms. But there was money coming in from other dubious sources too, winding its way through the labyrinth of Forres's businesses until it popped out the other end as clean as a whistle.'

'Very poetic. So why wasn't he investigated further?'

'You tell me. Friends in high places? Funny handshakes? Who knows? In fairness, conducting an investigation into someone like Forres is always tricky. You need a lot of resource and expertise to make it stick, and there's always a risk of embarrassing someone senior even if you succeed. It's easier to turn a blind eye.'

'Forgive me, Alec. I said you were in danger of turning into a half-decent human being, but I see you're the same old cynical curmudgeon you always were.'

'I wouldn't want to let any of you down.'

'From what Billy McCann told me, your assessment of Forres's character would come as a complete shock to his neighbours and friends. And maybe even to his son.'

'Oh, aye?'

'They all reported that he was a perfectly pleasant old man.

A quiet sort, who kept himself to himself, but was always amiable towards his neighbours. Friendly chap.'

'I daresay his neighbours would have said the same about Sawney Bean, if they'd known he was there.'

'But you think Forres was a crook?'

'I'm sure of it. We'd have had a hell of a time trying to prove it, though. And by the time we linked him to Archie Donaldson, he was well retired so that was another reason not to pursue it. There are plenty of new villains for us to worry out, without wasting time on the superannuated ones.'

'I guess. Is Forres wealthy? Billy reckoned the house was impressive, but not exactly billionaires' row.'

'Don't know,' McKay said. 'If you'd asked me a few years back when Forres was at the top of his game, I'd have said he was rolling in it. But from what the grapevine tells me, he's lived a quiet and abstemious life since retiring. I mean, Cromarty for Christ's sake. It's nice enough, but not exactly Monte Carlo or Nice. So either he'd spent it, which doesn't seem likely from his circumstances, or he's somehow managed to lose it. Which would be careless. Or...' McKay paused for a theatrical moment, then continued, 'He's squirrelled it away. For what reason, who knows? To fund a retirement somewhere warmer than this godforsaken country? To leave to the son who was good enough to take him home for Christmas? Or because it's just what misers do? They're good at amassing wealth, but don't know how to spend it. I've always been the opposite.' He paused, thinking. 'Interesting that he's gone missing, though. I assume he's not gone gaga, or anything like that?'

'Billy said he'd checked that out with the son, who reckoned he was in full possession of his faculties. The neighbours thought the same.'

'Intriguing, then. Especially the car and the text.'

'What are you thinking? That he might have been kidnapped?'

'You don't normally phone kidnap victims in advance,' McKay pointed out. 'And it seems unlikely up here in the wilderness that is Highland Scotland. More likely, there's some straightforward explanation that no one's thought of. Either that, or the old bastard's fallen down a hole somewhere. I assume your PC friend is aware of his background?'

'He wasn't, but he is now. Anyway, whatever the reasons, Forres has been missing overnight now. Which doesn't bode well for someone of his age, especially at this time of the year. The son's frantic with worry.'

'I'm sure he is. I would be in his shoes. Especially with our lot on the case.' McKay leaned back in his chair, a contented expression on his face. 'Luckily for us, it's not one we have to worry about. Not unless he pops up dead from something other than natural causes. Which, in the case of our Mr Forres, is not impossible.' He paused, thinking. 'Although if your young PC friend has no objections, I might send Josh Carlisle over there to stick his nose in when they next speak to the son. Coincidences make me uneasy. Forres clearly isn't our victim, but another disappearance, especially one with Forres's background, rings alarm bells for me.'

'I'll check with Billy McCann, but I'm sure I can talk him into it.'

'I'm sure you can. I've been on the end of your influencing skills often enough.'

'I'll see what I can do.' Horton hesitated. 'Going back to our victim, are you serious about this fire-sacrifice idea?'

McKay had already shared his thought of the previous day with Horton. He'd expected her to laugh, but to his surprise she actually appeared to take it at least semi-seriously. 'I don't know.'

For once, McKay looked almost embarrassed. 'It was just an idea.'

'It's certainly an idea. It gives me the creeps.'

'Not a nice thought, is it? But I guess we can't entirely write it off as a possibility.' He grinned. 'Especially over on the Black Isle. They have some funny ways.'

'You're one of them now, Alec. You've gone over to the dark side.'

'That's what worries me. Before you know it, you'll find me at the Clootie Well sacrificing a goat at the full moon to ward off the coronavirus.'

'Might have worked better than some of the stuff that was done.' Horton looked around at the papers scattered across her desk. 'You really reckon you can manage without me?'

McKay looked around as if checking how much resource was available to him. 'I reckon we can just about cope.'

'In that case, I'll take you up on your very generous offer and push off for Christmas.'

'You do that. I'll do my best not to disturb you.'

'Don't hesitate if anything breaks. Isla knows the score as well as I do.'

McKay smiled at her. 'How long have you known me, Ginny? Do you think I'd hesitate for a second?'

15

Gary Forres woke early, initially baffled by his surroundings. It took him a few moments to engage his brain and recall the events of the previous day. It was still pitch-black outside and at first he thought it was still the small hours. In fact, it was nearly seven and he already knew he'd be unable to sleep longer.

He'd felt he had no alternative but to stay here overnight, on the off-chance that his father should either reappear or be tracked down. He'd called home to break the news, and Barbara had supported his decision. She'd still believed there would be some straightforward explanation and Hamish would eventually come walking back in. 'It's what he's like,' she'd said. 'You know that. Always Mr Charming, but never gives a thought for anyone else.' Gary's first instinct had been to defend his father, but he couldn't really disagree.

So she'd been fine with him staying over, but he could tell that the children were disappointed. They'd been looking forward to spending uninterrupted time with their father over the Christmas break and were keen to have him back home. The children's relationship with Hamish had always been more distant, but they were still fond of their grandfather and had been eager to see him. Barbara hadn't told them anything about what had happened, only that Gary and Hamish had been delayed.

Gary's anxiety had further increased overnight. The chances of his father simply returning had receded by the minute. He'd dug out an instant dinner from Hamish's freezer and had a miserable solitary evening, the television playing silently in front of him. Eventually, he'd forced himself to go to bed. He hadn't expected to sleep, but in the end he'd somehow managed a reasonable night's rest.

Now, mid-morning, he sat in his father's kitchen, wondering how long he should wait before seeking further information from the police. They'd almost certainly have nothing more to tell him. The young PC had promised to call him with an update later in the afternoon, but had said he'd phone immediately if there were any developments, positive or negative.

Gary spent the morning trying to decide what to do next. He eventually decided that, if there was no further news by mid-afternoon, he'd have to drive home anyway. There was little he could do up here. The police were following up all the relevant contacts, and there was nothing he could add to that process. Whatever might have happened to Hamish, it seemed increasingly unlikely he would now simply turn up. When he was eventually tracked down, whatever the circumstances, Gary could return immediately.

In the meantime, he found a can of soup in his father's kitchen cupboards and made himself some lunch. He'd had a walk over to the village shop earlier and bought himself a newspaper and some snacks for the journey home, mainly just to get a breath of air and help pass the time. He had a superstitious hope that his brief absence from the house might somehow prompt Hamish's return, but he knew as soon as he stepped back into the hallway that the house remained empty.

There wasn't much more he could do here. He'd wait until PC McCann had called with his update and then head home. He was preparing to take one last look round the house, in the vain hope he'd spot something he'd missed on his previous searches, when the front doorbell rang.

Gary jumped to his feet. It took him a second to realise that whatever else his father might do on his return he was unlikely to ring the doorbell. This was more likely to be news and quite possibly bad news. He hurried down the hallway and opened the door.

Billy McCann and another man were standing on the doorstep. McCann was in uniform as usual, but the man beside him was dressed in a heavy waterproof jacket over an open-necked shirt.

'Nothing new, I'm afraid, Mr Forres. But it's early days and we're following up all the avenues we discussed. I just wondered if we could have a word and gather a little more information. This is my colleague, DS Carlisle.'

Gary turned his attention to the other man, a fresh-faced individual who looked too young for his role. 'CID?'

'Yes, sir. I've been asked to assist PC McCann on this.'

Gary had initially been both impressed and surprised at how seriously the police were taking the search for this father. From Gary's perspective, that was both reassuring and concerning. He led them through the house into the living room and invited them to take a seat. 'What can I do for you?'

Both men were looking uncomfortable. Eventually, McCann broke the silence. 'This is slightly awkward and I'm not sure how to put it...'

Carlisle interrupted, 'Perhaps it would be better if I explained. We'd like to ask you a few questions about your father.'

Gary was baffled by the exchange. 'Yes, of course. Anything I can do to help.'

'Do you know much about your father's former business?'

'Not really,' Gary said. 'Dad kept the business very much to himself. Why do you ask? Do you think it might be relevant in some way?'

'We're keeping an open mind at the moment,' Carlisle said. 'But it's the reason why I've become involved.'

'But Dad's retired. Why would this involve his business?'

Carlisle was silent for a moment, his expression suggesting he was trying to decide how to frame his next words. 'The thing is, sir, we had reason to look at your father's former business as part of an enquiry earlier this year.'

'What sort of enquiry?'

'I'm not at liberty to say too much. But it was an enquiry into a local businessman who was engaged in various illicit activities. It was a joint investigation with HMRC and other agencies. In the course of the investigation, we had reason to look at various business associates of the individual in question. One of the companies that came up was your father's.'

'Dad's business? He wouldn't have been involved in anything illicit.'

Carlisle held up his hand. 'Nobody's suggesting he was, sir. I should add that no further investigation into your father's business was conducted. We had no reason to believe that your father was involved in anything untoward, and, particularly given that your father had retired, no reason to proceed any further.'

'So why are you here?' Gary could feel his irritation increasing. His father was missing, and this man seemed to be interested only in some tenuous links with a past enquiry.

'The reason I'm here,' Carlisle said slowly, 'is that our investigation earlier in the year involved some serious criminality and some very unpleasant individuals.' He paused. 'It was a murder enquiry. A multiple murder enquiry.'

Gary felt a clutch of fear in his stomach. He had no real idea what the man was even talking about, but it was clear he wasn't here to bring any reassurance. 'I still don't understand. What does this have to do with my father?'

'Quite probably nothing.' This was McCann, who seemed to be regarding his colleague with some annoyance. 'We don't want to give you the wrong impression, Mr Forres. But we do need to pursue any possible leads.'

Carlisle appeared to be equally irritated by McCann's intervention. 'As my colleague has said, we don't want to concern you unnecessarily, Mr Forres. I'm sure that your father's business operations were entirely above board, but we do have evidence that, for whatever reasons, he had dealt with the individual we were investigating.'

'What are you saying?' Gary was staring at the two men. 'That my dad was picked up yesterday by some kind of mafia hit squad? If you think anything like that is even a possibility, you don't know my dad. It's absurd.'

'We're not suggesting anything, sir,' Carlisle said. 'The individual we're talking about had a number of perfectly legal business interests as well. That's often how these people work. Laundering their criminal proceeds through otherwise legitimate businesses. Your father was no doubt involved with them perfectly innocently. But it's a connection we have to consider.'

'Even if Dad had somehow inadvertently become involved in something, how could that affect him now? He's retired. Sold up the business.'

'Do you know anything about the sale of the business?'

'Not really. Like I say, Dad kept that stuff pretty much to himself. He'd just decided that he'd had enough. From what he said, he wasn't looking to make a fortune. He'd been winding down the business, and he was just looking to sell the assets and goodwill for a fair price. I honestly don't know what he made from it.' He looked up at the two police officers. 'I suppose I stand to inherit his estate, but I've honestly no idea what it's worth.'

'You've never discussed that with your father?'

'It's not something that interests me. I've no desire for anything to happen to Dad. When it eventually does, and assuming I outlive him, then, yes, I'll inherit. If there's some money there, I can't pretend I'll turn it down. But it's not something I've any expectation of. Who knows what might happen? Dad might end up having to go into care and live to a hundred, in which case the money will probably be largely gone. I've just always made a point of not even thinking about it.' Gary took a breath. 'I'm sorry, but I really can't see where this is going. Even if my dad did go off in that car yesterday, there's no reason to think that's anything to do with his business past.'

'Do you have any idea who might have visited your father?' Carlisle asked. 'There are no other members of the family who might have visited, taken him off somewhere?'

'Not that I can think of. I'm an only child and so was my dad, so there's very little immediate family. My late mum had a sister, and I've a couple of cousins on that side, but they wouldn't have turned up here out of the blue. I don't think he's seen my aunt for years.'

'Nevertheless, it would be useful if you could let us have contact details, just so we can check,' McCann said.

'I'll dig them out for you.'

'What about other friends?' Carlisle asked. 'People he

worked with, or old friends from the past? Anyone who might have made a visit unexpectedly. Perhaps just because they were in the area, if they'd come up here for Christmas or Hogmanay?'

'I don't know,' Gary said. 'I mean, of course it's possible that Dad had friends I wasn't aware of. But he never talked about anyone. I had the sense he was lonely up here, though he'd never admit it. We kept trying to persuade him to move south, but he was adamant he wanted to stay. And when Dad makes up his mind, it takes a lot to change it.'

McCann exchanged a glance with Carlisle. 'I don't want to seem unduly pessimistic, Mr Forres, and there's still plenty of time for your father to be found safe and well, but we are increasingly concerned about his welfare. We've checked the local hospitals and any emergency calls made yesterday. We've spoken to the immediate neighbours and to other people in the village who were suggested as possible contacts. There are other steps we can take such as checking the various CCTV cameras to see if there were any sightings of him–'

'What about the car?' Gary asked. 'Can you track the car that visited. That might have been caught on CCTV.'

'We're looking at that too,' McCann said. 'Because the village is relatively quiet at this time of year, it should be identifiable.'

'I don't understand this,' Gary said. 'Someone like my dad can't just disappear.'

'People do,' Carlisle said. 'At least temporarily. There could be countless explanations, and there's still every possibility your father will be found safely.'

'But with every hour that passes, that becomes less likely,' Gary said. 'I'm not stupid. I can work out the implications of an elderly man being outdoors overnight at this time of the year. Even if he just had a fall somewhere and hasn't been found yet…' He trailed off. 'But I still think he went off in that car. I've no idea why or who the visitors were, and I've no idea why Dad wouldn't have been in touch since. But that surely seems the most likely explanation.'

McCann nodded. 'But it raises as many questions as it answers. We'd like to issue an appeal to the local media, if that's okay with you. I'm afraid it's not the best time to be making an appeal of that kind. There'll be no newspapers tomorrow, and the local TV and radio news will be limited over the holiday. But we can also get it out through the force's social media channels. People are usually keen to share missing persons appeals, so that's likely to reach a substantial audience.'

'That sounds a good idea.'

'Do you have a good quality recent photograph of your father?'

'I'll have something on my phone. Hang on.' Gary flicked through the images on his phone until he found a full-face image of his father. 'How's that? I can text it across to you.'

'Perfect,' McCann said. 'What about you, Mr Forres? What are your plans now?'

'I don't know. Part of me desperately wants to stay in case he walks in. But rationally there's not much I can do here, and I've two young children who are keen their dad should be home for Christmas. We haven't told them anything about what's happened.'

'I'd suggest you head home, Mr Forres. If there are any developments, we'll contact you immediately. You can leave a note for your father, and we can keep an eye on the place too.' He shook his head. 'I appreciate it won't be much of a Christmas as things stand, but at least you can be with your children.'

'I just feel as if I'm abandoning him.'

'You've done everything you can. Leave it in our hands now.'

Gary stared at the young officer for a moment. He knew

McCann was being sincere. But he was sure, just as he presumed McCann was, that the chances of a ‘positive outcome’ were becoming increasingly slim.

16

McKay finally arrived home later than he'd intended on Christmas Eve. It was always the same before any break, however short. People would remember at the very last minute that they needed to talk to you about some long-standing enquiry, or they'd urgently need your signature on a document they'd been sitting on for three weeks. That tendency was worst at Christmas, particularly among those taking off the full period from Christmas to the Hogmanay hangover holidays. They behaved as if the world would be ending over the holiday, and their tasks had to be completed before the coming apocalypse. It was all the more frustrating given that McKay himself would be back at his desk in thirty-six hours or so.

He turned off the A9 towards Culbokie. The main roads were fully clear of snow now, though there was still a partial covering on some of the back roads. More had been forecast overnight, so it looked as if they were set for a genuine white Christmas, the first McKay could remember for many years. As far as he was concerned, snow was mainly a nuisance, but he knew that the prospect would please Chrissie and Fiona.

In the dark, the snow-covered fields looked pale and eerie.

He passed through Culbokie, with its village shop and pub, now both closed for the Christmas break. The village was looking festive, decorations blinking rhythmically in the darkness. His own place lay a half mile or so beyond the village, just to the left of the road in a setting that overlooked Cromarty Firth. He turned into the short track and then turned again into their driveway, pulling up behind Chrissie's and Fiona's cars.

He was glad now they'd bought this place. His only doubt had been the move from the bustle of the city centre to the relative silence and isolation of this place. He'd always seen himself as a city boy, but he'd grudgingly come to recognise that he enjoyed it here.

In any case, the solitude was partly illusory. Their nearest neighbours were close by, and they could walk from here into the village. But he'd come to appreciate the fact that, just as Ginny and Helena had told him, he could leave the office, come up here and, at least for a short while, put the pressures of work behind him.

He climbed out of the car, enjoying the silence of the winter's night. On a clear night, the sky here was relatively unaffected by any nearby lights and would be heavy with stars. Tonight it was clouded over. The first flakes of fresh snow were already beginning to fall. *Merry Christmas*, he thought.

He entered the house to be greeted by the sounds of Chrissie and Fiona chatting in the kitchen. He poked his head round the kitchen door. 'Evening, all.'

'About time,' Chrissie said. 'I thought supper would spoil.'

McKay assumed this wasn't true. He'd phoned to update her at the end of the afternoon and had told her what time he expected to be home and he was ten minutes earlier than he'd said. But Chrissie would never miss the opportunity to remind him that, though she tolerated the vagaries of his working life, she wasn't entirely ignoring them. There'd have been a time when that would have irritated him and he'd have responded with some sharp and unhelpful retort. But their couple's counselling sessions had helped him recognise that Chrissie wasn't being unreasonable. She was happy to support him in his work, but she wanted him to acknowledge her own sacrifices. 'You should have had yours without me,' he said. 'I wouldn't have minded.'

'Ach, no, it's Christmas. You have to eat together.'

'Have I got time to get changed?'

'Five minutes, so be quick. We've done a fish pie. Thought we wouldn't want anything too heavy ahead of tomorrow's festivities.'

'Sounds good. I'll be right back.'

McKay made his way through to their bedroom, and quickly climbed out of his work suit, pulling on some old tracksuit trousers, a T-shirt and a sweater. He was old – and old-fashioned – enough to think he ought to wear a suit to work, though many of his younger plain-clothes colleagues had abandoned the idea. But he was always glad to remove it as soon as he arrived home. It felt as if he was shedding the cares of the job and allowing himself to relax.

By the time he returned to the kitchen, Chrissie was already doling out the fish pie. Their Christmas lunch tomorrow would be the full sit-down affair, but tonight they were in the mood for something less formal. McKay took his food and sat down in the living room, balancing the plate on his knee. Fiona, Chrissie's sister, came and sat opposite him. 'Busy at work?' she said.

McKay always enjoyed Fiona's company, even though her current visit, on the near-anniversary of her husband's death, had had its uncomfortable moments. Given the circumstances of her husband's death, he was reluctant to mention his current major enquiry. 'We're always busy,' he said. 'Doesn't even seem to quieten down for Christmas. I'm just hoping I can get through tomorrow without being disturbed.'

'I saw on the news about that body in Rosemarkie,' she said, dispelling his hopes that she might have been unaware of the story. 'You'll be working on that, presumably?'

'Aye. Among other things.'

'I'd never really thought much about what you do,' she said. 'Not till – well, what happened last year with Kevin. That brought it home to me. I don't know how you do it.'

Chrissie had joined them, taking a seat on the sofa next to Fiona. 'He thrives on it. Don't let him tell you otherwise.'

'Even so, it must be wearing to be dealing with that stuff all the time.'

McKay waved his fork in the air, looking for a way to change the subject. He never felt comfortable talking about his work. This was partly for reasons of confidentiality, but mainly because he felt as if he was exposing something of his innermost self. Middle-aged Dundonian males just didn't do that. 'Nice fish pie,' he said.

'It's fish from that wee man who comes down in his van from Scrabster,' Chrissie said, clearly playing along with him. 'I got some smoked salmon for tomorrow's lunch too.'

Fiona smiled. 'I get the message. Shut up, Fiona.'

'Ach, that's not–'

'No, you're right, Alec. The last thing you want is to be talking shop tonight. I was just blethering on.'

'No worries,' McKay said. 'But you're right. I'm looking forward to a break. Even a short one.'

'Let's hope you get one,' Chrissie said. 'It doesn't happen often. I sometimes think you prearrange some signal for you to be called in as soon as you start getting restless at home.'

'You know,' McKay said, thoughtfully, 'that idea had never occurred to me...'

Fiona laughed. 'You're incorrigible, Alec McKay.'

'People keep telling me that,' he said. 'I don't even know what it means.'

The rest of the evening passed pleasantly. After they'd eaten, McKay produced a bottle of a local single malt and they had a dram as a nightcap. Both McKay and Chrissie had been drinkers in their day, but these days consumed little more than the occasional shared bottle of wine and a few drinks at Christmas and Hogmanay. McKay sipped the whisky, enjoying the burn at the back of his throat.

They sat, chatting about not very much, until Fiona gave a stage yawn. 'I think I'll call it a night. What's the drill for the morning?'

McKay remembered the days when their daughter, Lizzie, had been small and they'd invariably been dragged out of bed far too early so she could get at her presents. They were all a little old for that now. 'Don't think we have much of a drill these days.'

'Get up when you're ready,' Chrissie said. 'We'll do a bit of breakfast then aim for Christmas lunch early afternoon.'

'Sounds good to me,' Fiona said. 'As long as I'm allowed to do my bit.'

'You'll be allowed,' Chrissie confirmed.

'Which is more than I ever am,' McKay said. 'Chrissie won't let me anywhere near the kitchen when she's cooking.'

'That's because you get in the way. I reckon it's a deliberate strategy.'

'I'm just trying to be a new man. Do my bit on the domestic front.'

'That'll be the day,' Chrissie said.

'I'll leave you two to argue that out,' Fiona said. 'Goodnight, both of you.'

After Fiona had departed, McKay rose and pulled back the

curtains. In the daytime, the room enjoyed a view out over the Cromarty Firth to the summit of Ben Wyvis. On a clear evening, the lights of Dingwall were visible at the far end of the firth. Tonight, though, the night seemed pitch-black. McKay pressed his face closer to the window. 'Snow's still coming down,' he said. 'If it carries on like this it should be thick by morning.'

'Just like the ones we used to know, eh?' Chrissie said. 'Not that I can remember many. Every year, Lizzie used to long for a white Christmas but we hardly ever seemed to get it.' Their daughter had died in what remained largely unexplained circumstances a few years before, one of the factors that had strained their marriage almost to breaking point. They'd made considerable progress in dealing with their respective emotions about what had happened, but McKay didn't know whether either of them had yet fully come to terms with the loss.

'I seem to think that my childhood was full of white Christmases,' McKay said. 'But I'm sure it wasn't. Memory plays tricks.'

'I dare say.' Chrissie's face was expressionless, and McKay had no idea what she might be thinking. 'Right, I'm heading to bed too. You going to be long?'

It was still relatively early, but McKay suddenly felt exhausted, as if all the strains of the last few days were catching up with him. 'I might just have another wee dram and then I'll join you.'

'You take care,' she said. 'You're not used to drinking these days.'

'I reckon I'll survive two whiskies at Christmas, don't you?'

'On your head be it. Literally.' She came to stand beside him at the window, kissing him softly on the cheek. 'If you're not too long, you might even find I'm still awake.'

That was something, he thought after she'd left the room. They'd neither of them ever been ones for grand romantic gestures, but there'd been a period, when their marriage had been at its lowest point, when they barely even seemed to come close to each other. It hadn't been anything conscious on McKay's part, and he assumed the same was true of Chrissie. It had just been as if, without their realising, their relationship had slipped down several gears. Now, finally, the old affection, the old love, seemed to be returning.

McKay poured himself the smallest of drams and walked back through the hallway to the front door. He pulled it open, immediately struck by a blast of chill air.

The snow was still falling heavily, the thick flakes swirling in the cold night. McKay wasn't enticed by the prospect of a white Christmas, but something about the sight of the drifting snow stirred a childish excitement in him. Maybe Chrissie was right. At heart, he was nothing but a big kid.

He stood for a moment longer, sipping the last of his whisky, then stepped back to close and lock the door. He placed the empty glass in the dishwasher in the kitchen and made his way to bed.

Despite what Chrissie had said, she was already deeply asleep. He smiled, kissed her gently on the forehead, and then undressed and slipped into bed beside her, finally turning off his bedside light.

He was woken, after what felt like only minutes, by the loud buzzing of his phone on the bedside table. Still only half awake, he fumbled for it and looked at the time. Already nearly 7am. The screen showed the calling number as restricted which was likely to mean only one thing. He thumbed the call button. 'Morning.'

'Is that DI McKay?' The voice at the other end of the line sounded puzzled, an effect McKay often had on people.

'Speaking.' McKay was waking up now, preparing himself for what he was about to hear.

'It's Colin Harcourt here, sir. From the Area Control Room.

I'm sorry to bother you so early but we had instructions to contact you if there were any relevant developments–'

'Aye, I know. It was me that gave you the instruction. So what's happened?'

'We've had an incident called in.'

'Go on.' McKay knew he had a reputation in the force. This poor lad was probably terrified out of his wits at the prospect of having to disturb the dreaded Alec McKay at sparrow fart on Christmas morning. There was a lesson there. If McKay could learn to be gentler with people, maybe they'd get to the point more quickly.

'It's a body, sir. Found in Cromarty.'

'Suspicious circumstances?' In practice, the circumstances surrounding any dead body were always treated as suspicious until proved otherwise. At the same time, McKay wasn't keen to be dragged out of bed on Christmas morning to attend the body of some drunk who'd died of hypothermia.

There was a short silence at the other end of the phone. Finally, Harcourt said, 'It looks to be a hanging.'

'A hanging? You mean a suicide?' For a moment, McKay was on the point of backtracking on his commitment, only a few seconds old, to adopt a gentler approach with his colleagues.

'Not really.'

'Not really?'

'We're still getting the details, but my understanding is that the circumstances don't indicate a suicide.' There was another pause. 'I understand it looks like murder.'

'Okay,' McKay said wearily. 'Give me the details and I'll get over there.' His mouth still tasted metallic from the previous night's whisky, and the last thing he wanted, on this Christmas morning, was to drag himself out of bed and force himself into the freezing cold.

He finished the call and turned over to look at Chrissie. As he'd expected, she was already wide awake. She gave him a rueful smile. 'Was that it, then? The prearranged call?'

'No, of course–'

'I'm joking, Alec. It sounded important so you'd better get yourself out there.' She shook her head, still smiling. 'Mind you, if you're not back in time, this time we really will be eating without you.'

17

'Coffee?'

Helena Grant opened her eyes, and wondered where she was and who the hell was standing beside her. It had been the same the previous morning. Clearly, she wasn't yet accustomed to having company. Not this kind of company, anyway.

Her head cleared and she pushed herself up to a sitting position in the bed. 'Goodness. What time is it?'

'About eight thirty. I hope that's not too early for you on Christmas Day.'

She was sitting up now, the duvet pulled closely around her body. That seemed a little superfluous given what had happened in the bed on the previous two nights, but she was still feeling self-conscious. 'Not at all. I think yesterday was the first time I'd slept beyond seven for years.'

Bill Emsworth was standing by the bed, fully dressed in jeans and an open neck shirt, bearing two mugs of coffee. He placed his own on the bedside table and then sat down on the bed beside her before carefully handing her the second mug. 'Sleep well?'

'Must have done. I don't remember anything after...' She trailed off. 'Well, you know.'

'Well, that was quite memorable. For me, anyway.'

'And for me,' she said. 'Though this is all taking a bit of getting used to. I'm rather out of practice.'

'I'd no complaints.'

She felt herself colouring. 'Not with that. Well, I am with that too. But I was thinking more of the whole relationship thing.'

'It does take a bit of getting used to, doesn't it? But I think we're beginning to get there.'

'Yes, I think we are.'

'Anyway,' he said, 'Merry Christmas. We even have snow.' He reached down beside the bed and produced a package wrapped in glistening silver paper. 'I didn't know what to get you, but thought I ought to get something.'

'You really shouldn't have.'

'You can say that more sincerely when you've opened it.'

'I doubt it. I was in the same position. Had no idea what to get you either. So I played safe. I tucked it away over there behind my case.'

While he walked over to fetch her present, she pulled opened the wrapping on his. Inside was a neat box inscribed with the name of an Inverness jewellers. She opened it and peered inside. She'd had a momentary fear that Bill might have misjudged the moment and that the box would contain an engagement ring. But she should have known that he was more sensitive than that.

The box contained a simple but elegant silver pendant. 'It's lovely,' she said. 'Though you really shouldn't have.'

'Why shouldn't I?' he said. 'It's not as if I've anyone else to buy presents for.'

'Well, it's lovely. Thank you. I'm afraid my present's very dull by comparison.'

He was pulling off the wrapping. 'I wouldn't say that. It's my favourite.' He held up a bottle of Ardbeg Corryvreckan.

'I remember you saying. Quite distinctive, you said, if I recall.'

'A bit of an understatement on my part, but well remembered. We'll have to have a celebratory dram later.'

She took a sip of her coffee. 'So what's the plan for today?' They'd spent the previous day happily doing not very much together. They'd been for a long walk along the beach to Chanonry Point, and sat for an hour or so hoping in vain to spot the dolphins. Other than that, they'd largely sat chatting in Emsworth's house. From Grant's perspective, the whole day had felt effortless, with none of the struggling for small talk that she'd experienced in past attempts at establishing relationships.

'I assumed we'd have another strenuous day,' he said. 'I was planning to make us a light breakfast. How does eggs royale sound?'

'Eggs royale? Is that the one with smoked salmon? Sounds perfect.'

'Excellent. Perhaps with a glass of Christmas champagne, if that's not too decadent?'

'I'm not used to this kind of life,' she said. 'But why not?'

'Then I've got a goose for Christmas lunch. I say lunch, but I was thinking mid-afternoon.'

'Ideal. Can I help?'

'No, the cooking's my job. Your job's to sit and enjoy yourself.'

'I'm not used to that. I'll start getting twitchy.'

'If you do, I can give you some tasks. Tasting the food. Opening and checking the wine. That kind of thing.'

'I can probably manage that.'

'Okay. I'll go and start things downstairs? Do you want a bath or shower before you get dressed?'

'Just a shower. Wake myself up. Then I'll be down.'

'No rush. We've got the whole day ahead of us. See you shortly.'

She lay there for a few minutes longer, still holding the pendant. It was lovely, she thought, and just perfect. Something beautiful, a little intimate, but nothing that was too presumptuous about their relationship.

Why did that matter to her? She supposed because she was still reluctant to be rushed into anything, not that Bill had shown any signs of wanting to do that. That didn't mean she didn't want a new relationship. But she'd enough bad experiences to know how easy it might be to make a mistake. So far, everything with Bill seemed idyllic, and their intimacy over these few days would be a good test of that.

After a moment, she climbed out of bed and pulled on the dressing gown she'd left on the end of the bed. She walked over and pulled open the curtains.

As Bill had said, it was a white Christmas, a rare enough event even in these parts. The hillside and clustered houses below were coated white with snow. Perhaps that was an omen, she thought, a positive sign. The snow had stopped falling for the moment, although the sky was still heavy with cloud and the morning remained dark. The trees were bending before the strong wind blowing in from the sea, and the deep reddening of the clouds above the bay indicated sunrise was imminent. They were on the verge of a new year, a new start. There was plenty for her to be concerned about, both for herself and for the country and world at large. But for the moment she realised, slightly to her surprise, that she was happy.

18

As he emerged from the car McKay was caught by the chill wind off the sea. They were at the very end of the Cromarty Firth here, the waters sheltered by the twin headlands of the Sutors to create a natural harbour. Beyond the firth, there was nothing but the open North Sea.

McKay ducked his head against the wind and peered around. The body had been discovered on the grassed area by the waterfront beside Cromarty Lighthouse. Fifty metres away, he could see a marked car parked on the grass. A group of men with flashlights were standing beside it. Presumably his destination.

He'd had a fairly hairy journey over here. The snow had continued to fall overnight, and as yet there'd been no opportunity to clear the roads. McKay's car was an all-terrain vehicle which he'd bought for precisely this kind of circumstance, but there'd been a few moments when he could feel the wheels sliding beneath him.

Fortunately, the snow had ceased some hours earlier, though the heavy clouds suggested more might be coming. The sun had not yet fully risen and, despite the crimson streaks in the south-eastern sky, McKay suspected it would have only limited impact on the day's pervading gloom.

Pulling his coat more tightly around him, he trudged across to the group, peering to see if he could recognise anyone. There were a couple of uniforms who were unfamiliar to him. As he approached, one turned, clearly with the intention of sending him away.

'Don't waste your time getting up my nose, son.' McKay waved his warrant card. 'I'm supposed to be here. DI McKay.'

McKay could see the PC exchange a look with his colleague. As so often, it seemed McKay's reputation preceded him. 'Sorry, sir. Didn't realise.'

'No need for the "sir", son. I'll take your deference as read. What's the story?'

The PC pointed towards one of the trees. 'That's the story.'

McKay's gaze followed the pointing finger and he gave a low whistle. 'Quite a story.'

The body was hanging, apparently by a makeshift noose, from a bough of one of the trees that lay between the grassed area and the street above McKay had had an idea what to expect from the description given to him by Colin Harcourt, but the reality was still shocking. He pulled his flashlight from the pocket of his coat and walked forward, shining the beam up into the tree.

The body was hanging about ten feet above him. Its lifeless face was stark and angular, the blank eyes staring down as if in admonishment. The body was dressed incongruously in a casual shirt and trousers. It appeared to be shoeless. McKay moved the light back up to the face.

It took him a moment to be sure. He didn't want to get too close and risk disturbing the area beneath the body. As so often, death had changed the features to be almost unrecognisable. The passing of life often softened the deceased's face, but here the opposite was true. This victim had not gone gentle into the good night. *Well, bully for you, pal*, McKay thought. Whatever the background, this was not a way that anyone wanted to die.

McKay turned back to the PCs. 'I know who it is. A guy called Hamish Forres. He was reported missing a couple of days ago. Who found the body?'

'There were two of them,' the first PC said. 'Over there.' He gestured to a man and woman standing awkwardly a short distance away. 'I thought you'd want to talk to them.'

'Two of them?' McKay said. 'What the hell were they doing out here on Christmas bloody morning?' But his question was already answered by the large Labrador sitting quietly beside the man. 'Of course. It's always the bloody dog walkers.' He walked over to the couple and introduced himself. 'Not the ideal start to Christmas for you.'

'Aye,' the man said. 'A bit of a shock right enough.'

'Do you mind answering a few questions.'

The man pointedly stamped his feet as if to remind McKay how cold it was. 'Do we have a choice?'

'Since you ask, sir, not really. We'll need to take a formal statement from you in due course, but for now I'd just like to get your impressions while it's fresh in your minds.'

'It's certainly that,' the woman said. 'It'll be a while before I forget it.'

McKay had begun to take notes. 'Can I ask your names?'

'Alastair Farlowe,' the man said. He was a tall, skinny man with a face almost as chiselled as the corpse's. 'This is my sister-in-law, Becky Delaney.' The woman was, by contrast, relatively short, perhaps slightly overweight. She gazed at McKay through thick spectacles with an expression that he guessed would normally have been cheerful.

'I take it you were out walking the dog?'

'I was,' Farlowe said. 'Becky just tagged along for the ride, as it were.'

'I'm staying with Alastair and his family for Christmas,' Delaney explained. 'I'm not the best sleeper, and I'd woken up early this morning. I was sitting in the kitchen drinking a cup of tea, so when Al appeared to walk the dog, I thought I might as well tag along. Bracing morning for a stroll.'

'It's certainly that,' McKay said. 'So how did you happen to stumble across our friend over there?'

'It was the dog,' Farlowe said.

Of course it was, McKay thought. *It's always the bloody dog.* Still, in this case it had at least prevented the body being discovered by someone who might have been more traumatised by it. Kids out for a Christmas morning walk, for example. 'What happened?'

'We'd just come down here for a walk along the front,' Farlowe went on. 'We'd reached this point when the dog started barking and raced over to the tree. Had no idea what was going on. We'd got torches with us but at first I couldn't see anything. Then, well, I looked up...'

'Not a pretty sight.'

'Aye, you might say that. I've never seen anything quite like it. And I'd rather not see anything like it again, if I'm honest. We called you lot straight away. That's about all I can tell you.'

There was no reason not to take the story at face value, and it was very likely the couple would have nothing more useful to tell him. 'You didn't see anyone else around?'

'Not a soul,' Farlowe said. 'Only us daft enough to be out at this time on Christmas Day. Especially one as bloody cold as this one.'

McKay decided it was time to take the hint. 'Okay. If you give me your addresses, we can let you get back into the warm. We'll be in touch to get formal statements but we can leave you undisturbed for today.'

McKay took their addresses and bade them good morning. He'd considered asking them to treat their find as confidential for the moment, but decided there was little point. Whatever these two might do, news of the find would be all round the town and beyond within a few hours. At least there was no sign that Farlowe had recognised the hanging man as a fellow local resident.

He turned back to the two PCs. 'I assume the examiners have been called?'

'On their way, apparently.'

'We'll no doubt be waiting a while for them to drag themselves out of bed. In the meantime, I'll see what other resources I can get out here.' He looked around, peering through the half-light. 'We'll need to seal off a large area. We can't disturb the scene so we'll have to leave our friend up there for the moment. But I don't want anyone else stumbling across it unexpectedly. If you two can start that, I'll keep an eye on things for the moment.'

The first PC was still staring at the suspended body. 'Funny kind of suicide, isn't it?'

'I'd have said so,' McKay agreed. 'For a start, how the hell did he get himself up there?'

'If you want my opinion,' the second PC said, 'the only way that could have been done is if someone put the noose round his neck, threw the rope over the branch and secured it before pushing the poor bugger off the road.'

McKay wasn't sure he did want the PC's opinion, but the man was probably right. The snow beneath the body was largely undisturbed, other than the tracks left by Farlowe's dog. What they were looking at was almost certainly murder. The only real question was whether Forres had died as a result of the hanging or had been dead already. Either way, it wouldn't have been an easy task to get the body up there, which meant the PC's guess about the body being dropped from the road was probably correct.

Whatever the precise sequence of events, McKay couldn't envisage why anyone might go to this trouble. If you wanted to kill someone, there were easier ways to do it. And why leave the body displayed like this?

While the two PCs busied themselves sealing off the scene, he got on the phone back to the operations room. Trying to drum up resources on Christmas morning was a challenge, but McKay was as persuasive as ever. Fifteen minutes later, he'd organised a decent response, including various members of his own team. It would take them a while to get out here, but he wasn't planning to go anywhere. He'd hesitated over whether to call Ginny or Helena. He was keen that both should enjoy a rare break today, and he knew that they'd want to come out. At the same time, Helena Grant in particular would be angry if she wasn't kept informed.

In the end, he felt he had little option but to call Helena. The phone rang briefly before she answered. 'Alec?'

'Aye. Sorry to bother you.'

'This better be good.'

'It is,' he said. 'Or rather bad.'

He heard her sigh. 'Go on.'

'We've another body. Hamish Forres.'

'Where?'

'Cromarty.' It took him only a few seconds to update her on the discovery.

'You're saying it doesn't look like suicide?'

'Not remotely. I don't know much more because the examiners aren't here yet.'

'Do you want me to come over?'

'No. It's all in hand. You need a break.'

He expected her to argue, but instead she said, 'You're sure?'

'Don't you trust me to look after things, Helena?'

'Since you ask, not entirely. Or at least I trust you to look after things in the way that suits you. But, yes, you know what you're doing, Alec.'

'I do.'

'Okay. I won't interfere. But if there are any issues you'll let me know straight away?'

'Of course. But if you don't hear anything, assume everything's all right. Get a proper break. You deserve it.' As he spoke, McKay was watching a white van turning onto the grassed area. 'I'd better go. The examiners have just turned up in their clown car. Don't want to keep them waiting. I assume it's warm and cosy where you are?'

'Very,' she said. 'Good luck, Alec.'

He finished the call and turned to greet the white van heading slowly across the grass. 'Right,' he said to himself, 'let's send in the clowns.'

19

The van pulled to a halt and after a few seconds Jock Henderson unfolded his ungainly body from the car. His movements reminded McKay of someone struggling to erect a deckchair. 'Morning, Jock. Looks like the old band are back together again.'

Henderson regarded him with apparent bafflement, as if he were unsure why McKay's presence was merited. 'Always the old buggers like us who draw the short straw on public holidays, isn't it?'

'I'd say so,' McKay said. 'Let the youngsters enjoy a day with the kids.'

'I'm told this is an interesting one.'

'There's our body.' McKay gestured towards the tree.

The morning was growing lighter, though it was still gloomy under the heavy clouds. Henderson peered where McKay was pointing and raised his eyebrows. 'Bloody hell.'

'Quite.'

'That's going to take some getting down.'

'I imagine it took some getting up, too. Story of your life, Jock.'

Henderson ignored him. 'I take it you've called for backup?'

'Cavalry's on its way. Though may take a while. I assumed you'd want to do your stuff on the scene before it's disturbed getting the body down.'

Henderson regarded McKay for a moment. 'You know, Alec, if you stay in this job long enough you might finally learn how to do it. You're showing real promise.'

'Trailing in your wake, Jock.'

'Okay.' Henderson sighed. 'I've got Pete Carrick coming out to assist, but I can make a start while we wait for him.'

'You are spoiling us,' McKay said. 'Laurel *and* Hardy. We're honoured.'

'Bugger off, Alec.'

Satisfied he'd finally got a rise out of Henderson, McKay allowed the other man to get on with his work. He'd no doubt wait till Carrick and other support arrived before doing any of the heavy lifting in terms of erecting the crime scene tent. For the moment, Henderson was contenting himself with photographing the body and the surrounding area.

Despite their long-standing and semi-serious antagonism, McKay regarded Henderson with respect. The man was undoubtedly good at his job, with years of experience and an almost obsessive attention to detail. Henderson had almost no imagination, but that was probably a strength in the role. McKay had seen plenty of unpleasant things in the course of his career, but rarely had to really get up close and personal with any of that. McKay was never sure how the examiners dealt with what they witnessed, but they seemed to fall into two broad categories. Some, like Jock Henderson, were dour and gloomy. Others – and Pete Carrick was a perfect example – were jovial and apparently light-hearted, responding to their experiences with a distinctive graveyard humour.

McKay turned and stared out at the sea. He assumed the sun

was fully risen now, but other than a slight lightening of the clouds there were no obvious signs of it. It was still bloody cold, a biting wind sweeping in from the firth. He could taste the snow in the air, and knew there'd be a further fall in the course of the day. That would make their job here even harder.

McKay had little doubt how difficult the job would be in any case. In any murder case, the priority was to kick off the investigation as quickly as possible, make best use of the hours before the evidence decayed and witnesses' memories grew less reliable. The opportunities to do that on Christmas Day would be limited, even if he could accrue sufficient resources to get things moving.

More cars were arriving behind him. Another marked car and a civilian vehicle had pulled up by Henderson's van. McKay walked back, preparing to greet the new arrivals. The marked cars contained two more uniformed PCs, whom McKay directed to helping seal off the crime scene. The second car belonged to Josh Carlisle.

'Morning, Josh. Thought you'd be opening your presents.'

'Can't say I was all that popular with Katy this morning.' It took McKay a moment to recall that Katy was Carlisle's girlfriend. 'Luckily I'd bought her a decent present or two this year, so I'm not completely in the doghouse.'

McKay could never quite imagine Carlisle in a relationship. He couldn't even quite shake off the idea that Carlisle was still a schoolboy who'd somehow managed to sneak into an adult job. 'Buggers don't seem to give any thought for me or you when they get themselves murdered. Mind you, don't know how much we'll be able to get done today.'

Carlisle's attention had clearly been caught finally by the sight of the murder victim. 'Holy shit,' he said. 'Is that him?'

'No, Josh,' McKay said wearily. 'That's a spare corpse we brought along just in case we were short. Of course that's him.

Can you hold the fort here for a few minutes? I want to make a few phone calls.'

'Anything particular you want me to do?'

'Not for the moment. Just help the uniforms to keep the scene secure. Stop any curious locals from poking their noses in. I'm surprised we haven't had more dog walkers already. I'd have thought that a place like this would be crawling with them, even on Christmas morning.'

He left Carlisle gazing in wonder at Forres's body and made his way back to his car. His main task was to get someone working on getting things set up back in the office. One question was whether they should set this up as a new enquiry or link it to the existing murder investigation. Ultimately, that decision was above his pay grade, but it might affect the decisions he made today.

On the face of it, there was nothing to connect the two killings, other than that they'd taken place a few miles from one another. The circumstances were different, as were the nature of the killings. But the similarities troubled McKay. Both murders were bizarre, and in both cases the killers had gone to unnecessary lengths. McKay's gut was telling him not to treat the two cases as distinct, but he had no real evidence to support that view.

There was one further task he needed to carry out before getting started on the administrative stuff. It was perhaps time that he disturbed Ginny Horton after all. He dialled her number.

'Morning, Ginny.'

'Morning, Alec. I'm guessing this isn't good news.'

'Not really. But I'm not asking you to disturb your day off. Well, not much anyway.'

'Go on.'

He told her about the discovery of Hamish Forres's body, and the grotesque nature of Forres's death. 'Not ideal for Christmas morning,' he concluded.

'That's one way of putting it. You're sure it's Forres?'

'Pretty sure. Obviously, it's hard to do a formal identification when the body's suspended ten feet up in a tree. But I don't have much doubt it's him.'

'Christ. I'd assumed we were past the point where he would turn up safe and sound, but I didn't quite envisage he'd be found like that.'

'I don't think anyone would have expected that, Ginny.'

'Do you want me to come over?'

'No, I want you to take the rest of the day off as planned. There's only going to be a limited amount we can do today, so you might as well get your break. But there is one thing you could do for me.'

'Happy to help.'

'I'm going to arrange for someone to break the news to Forres's son. I'll do it through Edinburgh so they can see him face-to-face. Again, not exactly what anyone wants on Christmas Day, but there's no alternative. It occurred to me someone ought to tell Billy McCann too. I know what it's like when you're working a missing persons case and it ends up like this – although admittedly not many end up quite like this. I'd rather he heard the news from a friendly voice than just off the log or through formal channels.'

'This must be the new sensitive Alec McKay I keep hearing about,' Horton said. 'Okay, I'll track down Billy and let him know. Don't know if he was scheduled to be on duty today but the ops room will have his number.'

'Thanks. It'll come better from you.'

'If you say so. You sure you don't want me to come out?'

'No. I'll get what I can moving today and we can take it from there.'

'I take it you've told Helena.'

'Oh, aye, and I told her not to come out as well.'

'How did she feel about taking orders from you?'

'Funnily enough, on this occasion she seemed happy to accept it.'

'How did she sound?' Horton asked.

'It's not a concept I really understand, but otherwise I'd say she sounded happy.'

'Well, that's good. We should all be happy at Christmas.'

'I'll remember that as I sit here at the edge of the world staring at a dangling corpse while having my arse frozen off by gale-force winds from the North Sea.'

'You have to get your kicks where you can, Alec. You love this kind of thing. It's what you live for.'

'I just like to do my job. Speaking of which...'

'Okay. I'll break the news to McCann. And you've got to let me know if you need me to come in.'

'Enjoy your Christmas, Ginny. All the best to Isla.'

He ended the call before she could respond. Across the waterfront, a couple more marked cars were arriving, disgorging uniformed PCs. A year or so before, he'd have been nervous about leaving Josh Carlisle to deal with them, but the young lad had matured considerably since then, partly because of some of the professional challenges he'd faced.

McKay dialled back to headquarters and began setting up the infrastructure needed to deal with this new investigation. He'd decided that for the moment he'd treat it as part of the ongoing enquiry, if only because that meant much of what was required was already in place. He could discuss it with Helena when she returned and they might ultimately conclude differently, but for now he was inclined to make best use of the limited resources available.

Once he was satisfied that everything was under way, he

climbed out of the car and stood watching the activity ahead of him. A second examiner's van had arrived and a group of PCs were erecting the crime scene tent. Jock Henderson had been joined by Pete Carrick, and they were working on the area beneath the tree from which the body was still hanging.

McKay approached Josh Carlisle. 'How's it going?'

'Not so bad, considering. This bunch seem to have an idea what they're doing. Henderson and Carrick are just finishing what they can do with the immediate site before we start trying to get the body down.'

'That should be entertaining.'

'We were wondering about involving the fire brigade. It might be needed, but they're going to give it a go themselves first. Jock Henderson's keen that we should do as little damage as possible to the body or even the rope.'

'I bet he is. I bet he's not offered to give you a hand either. Not that I'm offering either. Benefits of rank.' He looked past Carlisle at another car pulling up. A stooped figure climbed out and regarded the scene gloomily. 'Looks like the cavalry's arrived. Our friend, Willy Ingram.'

Ingram was one of the crime scene managers, a DS with countless years' experience of organising scenes of this nature. Although even Ingram wouldn't previously have encountered one of quite this nature, McKay had asked for Ingram specifically, partly because he knew Ingram was one of the safest pairs of hands and partly because he couldn't imagine Ingram would have had much else on, even on Christmas morning. He was a man largely devoid of social skills. Rumour had it that he was married, but no one had met his wife, and McKay had occasionally suspected she might be fictitious. Ingram seemed primarily married to the job. McKay guessed that if Ingram's wife was now spending Christmas Day alone, she might be glad of the lightening of the mood.

'Willy,' he said. 'You're a welcome sight.'

Ingram nodded acknowledgement. 'Alec.' He offered no further response.

'Interesting one, this, Willy.'

'Aye?' Ingram sounded as if the concept was unknown to him. 'Well, I'm sure I can keep it all under control.'

'I'll leave it in your safe hands. I'm heading back to HQ. Give me a call when you've got things sorted so I can plan next steps.'

Ingram nodded vaguely and walked over to consult with the examiners. McKay turned to Carlisle. 'Reckon you might as well bugger off for the moment, Josh. Go and enjoy Christmas with Katy. There's not much more we can do here for the moment.'

'Sure you don't want me to give you a hand?'

'Are you not keen on spending time with Katy, son? If so you probably ought to break the news to her sooner rather than later.'

Carlisle looked affronted. 'Of course I am. Just trying to be helpful.'

McKay grinned. 'I'm only joking. But, seriously, you've caught me on one of my rare good days. Take advantage of it and bugger off. And a Merry Christmas to one and all.'

20

For once, Crawford had slept late. It was an indulgence he allowed himself only very rarely. Most days he was awake no later than 6am. Even in the depths of winter, he'd make his way down to the gym he'd had built in the cellar, spend forty-five minutes working out, and grab a shower before eating a light breakfast. He'd be at his desk and working by 8am at the latest. Since he'd been working largely from home, he'd become a creature of routine, recognising it would be too easy to allow his usual discipline to slide.

Today, though, he'd decided he was allowed a break. He hadn't set an alarm and, when he'd woken naturally in the early morning, had forced himself to turn over and return to sleep. He'd next been woken by the dim daylight filtering through the uncurtained window. He looked at his watch and saw that it was past nine thirty.

He could tell from the quality of the light that, as forecast, there'd been a fall of snow overnight. He wasn't exactly the romantic type, but the thought of a white Christmas didn't displease him. It would help reinforce his determination to make the day feel special.

He'd contemplated having some friends to stay for the Christmas holidays, as far as the restrictions allowed. But by the time the idea had occurred to him all those he'd spoken to had made other plans.

He hadn't minded too much. He spent much of his time in solitude these days, and he'd no particular issue with doing the same at Christmas. He'd just make sure that, in a quiet way, he enjoyed himself. He'd try to avoid doing any work today and just relax.

He contemplated doing his usual workout, which he generally found energising, if not exactly relaxing. After a moment, he decided that today even that was too much like hard work. Instead, he set a bath running and made his way downstairs to prepare himself a coffee.

The kitchen, like the living room, had a view out over the loch. Despite the gloom of the day, the landscape was spectacular, the grey waters caught in the middle of the newly whitened setting. Clouds were thickening on the horizon, and more snow would fall before evening. That was fine by him. He had nowhere to go, plenty of food in the house, and for once had the time to appreciate the beauty of his surroundings.

He carried the coffee back upstairs, finished running the bath and climbed in, preparing to enjoy a lengthy relaxing soak.

His mobile rang almost as soon as he'd entered the water.

He could hear it buzzing away on the table in his bedroom and forced himself to ignore it. But that went against the grain. He very much prided himself on being always available to his clients, the only exception being when he was already in a client meeting or taking a client call. Even then, he always phoned back as soon as he could. It was a small point and largely cosmetic. But Crawford knew his clients appreciated it. It was one of those details that enhanced your reputation.

But today was, after all, Christmas Day. He ought to be

allowed at least one day without concern for what his clients might be wanting. He closed his eyes until the phone ceased ringing, and then smiled with relief.

Almost immediately, the phone rang again.

This time, he ducked his head under water, holding his breath to block out the insistent sound of the phone. When he finally emerged, the phone had fallen silent.

Almost immediately, it rang again.

Shit, he thought. Either it was something genuinely urgent or it was Gordon Prebble being even more demanding than usual. Cursing, Crawford hoisted himself out of the bath and wrapped a towel around himself. He sat down on the side of the bed before picking up the phone.

Prebble. It was Gordon bloody Prebble. Of course it was. Who else would it be at this time on Christmas Day?

Crawford was tempted to let it ring a fourth time, but he knew then he'd have to deal with Prebble in an even worse temper. Sighing, he pressed the call button and took the call. 'Gordon?'

'That you, Crawford?'

Of course it's me, Crawford said to himself. *You've just phoned me. Who the hell else would it be?* Out loud, he said, with just a touch of weariness. 'It's me, Gordon. What can I do for you? By the way, you do know it's Christmas Day?'

'So I've been told,' Prebble said. 'Unfortunately, Santa didn't bring me what I wanted.'

'Gordon?'

'Have you seen the news?'

No, Gordon, Crawford wanted to say. *I haven't seen the news, Gordon. In fact, I've only just got up and I was just about to enjoy a long relaxing bath.* 'What news?'

'I saw it online. Local press. Forres has gone missing.'

'Forres?'

'Oh, for Christ's sake. Hamish Forres. How many bloody Forreses do you know?'

'Okay but – missing? What do you mean?'

'I mean just that. He's vanished. Off the face of the earth in a puff of white bloody smoke.'

The image was rather more imaginative than anything Crawford expected from Prebble. He was sounding more anxious than Crawford would have expected him too, talking frenetically and too fast. There'd been a trace of that in their conversation the previous day, but now it sounded more pronounced.

'I don't understand,' Crawford said. 'How does someone like Hamish Forres disappear?'

'I'm guessing,' Prebble said, 'either because he wanted to disappear or someone else wanted him to.'

'I'm sorry, Gordon. I'm being a little dense this morning. Just talk me through what's happened.'

'Just what I say. Forres has disappeared. It's up on the local news sites this morning. Police are making an appeal for anyone who's seen him.'

'That's very interesting, Gordon. I'm not sure what it's got to do with me.'

'He's one of yours, isn't he? Another client, I mean.'

'You can't expect me to answer that, Gordon.'

'Don't fuck me about. I know he's a client of yours.'

Crawford suppressed a sigh. 'Gordon, would you want me to confirm that you're one of my clients to anyone who asked?'

There was a moment's silence while Prebble absorbed this. 'Okay, but I know he is.'

'I'm still not sure what this is all about, Gordon. Let's accept that I know exactly who Hamish Forres is and, yes, I've had some dealings with him over the years. I'm still not sure why I should be concerned about whatever's happened to him.' This wasn't entirely true. Crawford had no particular interest in what might have happened to Forres, but he was another valued client. Not as lucrative as Prebble himself, but a decent earner.

'What we talked about yesterday,' Prebble said. 'I'm pressing on with it urgently now.'

'Is something wrong?'

'What do you think?'

In truth, Crawford didn't know what to think. It had been clear the previous day that Prebble was rattled in a way that Crawford had never previously seen. Now, he sounded even more jittery. If it had been anyone but Gordon Prebble, Crawford would have said he sounded almost afraid. 'Are you saying you think something's happened to Forres?'

'I keep telling you. He's *disappeared*.'

'He's getting on a bit,' Crawford pointed out. 'Maybe he's just gone walkabout.'

'Forres was sharp as a tack last time I spoke to him.'

'I don't know, then,' Crawford said. 'I've no idea what's happened to him.' He was increasingly bored with this conversation. Whatever might be troubling Prebble, in other respects he was being his usual tiresome self. Phoning out of the blue when it suited him. Oblivious to the fact that he was intruding on your life. Talking in riddles and assuming you knew exactly what he was blethering about. 'Is there anything specific I can do for you today, Gordon?'

'Just another heads-up. That's all. And you might want to watch your own back.'

'My back?'

'You're not on the front line. But your hands aren't clean.'

Crawford had no idea what Prebble was talking about. Front line? What did he think he was? A bloody solider in the trenches? 'I'll be careful, Gordon.'

'You do that,' Prebble said. 'You might want to think about getting out yourself.'

Crawford was about to respond when he realised that Prebble had already ended the call. *And a very Merry Christmas to you*, he thought. *What the hell was that all about?*

Crawford gave up on the idea of a bath, and instead took a quick shower before dressing. He'd had various plans for breakfast but his conversation with Prebble had dampened his enthusiasm for anything too ambitious. He fried a couple of rashers of bacon to make a sandwich, prepared another coffee, and sat down at his laptop.

Despite himself, he'd been intrigued by what Prebble had said. Forres had been one of Crawford's clients for a long time. He had been retired a while now and his need for Crawford's services had been diminishing, but the loss of his business would be a blow. On the other hand, his death might create some immediate opportunities. No one understood Forres's tangled financial affairs quite as well as Crawford did.

He clicked on the website of one of the regional newspapers and found the story about Hamish Forres. Police were appealing for anyone who might have spotted the elderly man to contact them. Beside the story, a large full-face image of Forres stared out of the screen.

There wasn't much to the story itself. A statement from Forres's son echoing the police request for any sightings, and a short account of the circumstances of Forres's disappearance. The only intriguing element of the story was a suggestion that Forres might have left the house as a passenger in someone's car.

So what did Prebble think had happened to Forres? That he'd been kidnapped? It didn't seem likely. Forres had a bob or two – probably rather more than his neighbours or even his family knew – but he was hardly in billionaire territory. He was retired and no longer any threat to anyone.

The most likely explanation was that the old man was more confused than anyone had realised. Crawford knew from dealing with his own late father that it was quite possible for an intelligent individual to conceal the onset of dementia. Crawford's father had been a widower, living alone, and had found ways of dealing with his increasing forgetfulness and confusion. It had only been as his health deteriorated to the point where he was becoming confused about where he lived that Crawford had realised his father wasn't fit to be living alone.

It could easily be the same with Forres. If the son lived in Edinburgh and saw his father only occasionally, any decline might not have been obvious. Maybe Forres had become confused, wandered off by himself. Mostly likely, his body would eventually turn up. It was tragic, but that was how these things tended to go.

Crawford finished his coffee and sandwich, and stacked the crockery neatly in the dishwasher. The day already felt spoiled for him. He'd had plans for nothing much more than unadulterated laziness, but somehow Prebble's call had disrupted that. He was even wondering if he ought to check his files on Forres. Of course, the real stuff wasn't written down on paper and any key documents were held in encrypted electronic files. But it might be worth checking that everything was in order before anyone started delving into Forres's affairs.

He cursed himself for his own thoroughness. But, again, it was what his clients paid him for. He checked and double-checked all the details, leaving nothing to chance. So that was now how he'd spend the rest of Christmas Day, working his way through Forres's documents to make sure nothing had been missed.

He sighed and made himself another mug of coffee, staring out of the kitchen at the snow-covered landscape. The gloom of the day had thickened still further, and the few houses visible across the firth were already showing lights. It had already started to snow, an occasional snowflake glittering in the light from the house. It was only a light new sprinkling so far, but more was forecast for later in the afternoon.

For a moment, Crawford felt inexplicably vulnerable. It was the same feeling as he'd felt on leaving Prebble's house the previous day. As if the prospect of living in isolation was no longer quite as enticing as he'd once found it.

The snow was coming down harder now, thick flakes dancing in the air, occasionally drifting as they were struck by the buffeting winds. He could still make out the loch, but visibility was reducing by the minute. Soon, the house would be lost in the centre of another blizzard.

21

McKay had been back to headquarters to check everything was being set up as he'd requested, and to offer some moral support to the skeleton team working the holiday. He'd then headed home for a late and not particularly leisurely Christmas lunch with Chrissie and Fiona, before finally setting off back to Cromarty to see how the examiners were getting on.

The weather was closing in again and the roads were even more treacherous than earlier in the day. It was only mid-afternoon but already almost dark. As he approached Cromarty, out on the firth to his left McKay could see the orange lights of the oil platforms stored in the waters at Nigg. There'd been more of them than usual this year, to the point where the locals – who were generally relatively sanguine about the proximity of these metal behemoths to their attractive little town – had begun to complain about the sheer numbers. Today, in the snow and fading light, they looked eerie, mysterious angular creatures keeping watch over the town.

He drove along the front past the Royal Hotel, and followed the track past the harbour to the grassed area. The massed vehicles were still there – several marked cars, the two examiners' vans and various others. He pulled up behind them and climbed out, ducking his head against the falling snow.

A further tent had been erected beside that over the scene, allowing some space for working in the relative dry and warmth. As he approached, one of the PCs walked over to greet him. He looked familiar, and it took McKay a moment to recognise him as Billy McCann.

'Afternoon, son. Shame it's ended up like this.'

McCann nodded. 'I'm not entirely surprised. I mean, I didn't exactly expect it to turn out like this, but I'd assumed we wouldn't get good news. Can you thank Ginny again for letting me know personally? It was better hearing it that way.'

'I hope you were on duty anyway?' McKay said. 'You didn't come in specially?'

'No, I was on duty. My partner's a nurse so we usually both come in over Christmas and take the time off when it suits us. I'd already got the summons to come up here, though I didn't know what it was all about. It's a weird one, isn't it? I just thought he'd have had a fall or been taken ill somewhere. I never imagined anything like this.'

'I don't think any of us could have imagined anything like this. I see they've managed to get the body down.'

'Eventually,' McCann said. 'It was getting a bit Keystone Cops in a grotesque way. They were contemplating getting the fire service out here with a cherry picker, but in the end they managed to manoeuvre the body back onto the road up there. The examiners were concerned it might have got damaged in the process but everybody seems happy in the end.'

'Everybody except poor Hamish Forres,' McKay said.

'It's a horrible way to die.'

'Have we had that confirmed?' McKay said. 'I mean, that he wasn't already dead before – well, this was done?'

'I'm not sure, to be honest. I was a bit too shocked by it all to think clearly.'

'I'll go and talk to the examiners and see what pearls of wisdom they can share with me.' He turned back. 'Don't blame yourself, son. You did everything you possibly could to find him.'

'If I'd found him before this happened...'

'I don't know how or why this happened to him,' McKay said. 'But my guess is it was unavoidable from the moment he went missing.'

'But why would someone do this to an old man?'

'Forres was an old man with secrets, son. More than his family realised, I think.'

McCann nodded wearily. 'This will have been a hell of a shock for his son. I'm glad I didn't have to break the news to him.'

'He's got more shocks to come, if he was unaware of his old man's background.' McKay smiled at McCann. 'Keep going, son. It's just part of the job.'

He made his way across to where Pete Carrick was standing outside the crime scene tent, drinking from a bottle of water. The snow was still falling thickly, a strong wind whipping in from the water. 'Perfect day for it, Pete.'

'Isn't it always?' Carrick said. 'One way or another.'

'How's it going?'

'We're just examining the body now we've finally managed to get it down. There's not much doubt that it was death by hanging.'

'Shit,' McKay said. 'So he was alive.'

'Until he was pushed off the road. Looks like it.'

'Poor bastard. Even Hamish Forres didn't deserve that.'

'Who is this Forres guy anyway? I've heard the name but I don't know anything about him.'

'He's largely managed to stay off our radar. Or, more accurately, he came up on our radar more than once but we never actually managed to pin anything on him. One of our local legitimate businessmen.'

'Oh, right. One of them.'

'Up to his neck in all kinds of things. Money laundering. Smuggling. And worse, I imagine. But he was smart. He kept his hands clean. The respectable face.'

'Looks like it caught up with him in the end, though.' Carrick took a deep swig of his water. 'Someone went to some trouble with this.'

'That's what intrigues me,' McKay said. 'Why would anyone go to this much effort? Particularly people who might have an interest in killing Forres. If they wanted to take him out, I'd have expected a more straightforward approach.' He shook his head. 'The whole thing's baffling. I don't know why anyone would want to take him out anyway. He wasn't even in business any more. Anything else useful you can give me at this stage?'

'Not much, I'm afraid. He was dressed casually and wasn't wearing any outdoor clothes. There's nothing on the body that suggests he'd been expecting to leave the house. There's no evidence of any damage to the body before death. The rope that was used was some sort of plastic fibre. Probably just some proprietary product, but we'll get it checked out.'

'The other question,' McKay said, speaking half to himself, 'is where he's been since he disappeared yesterday.'

'Somewhere indoors, I'd say, if that's any help. The clothing was damp but only consistent with being out in last night's snowfall.'

'Any idea on time of death?'

'Not really. The body was cold but given the overnight temperatures that doesn't tell us much. Pathologist will be able to give you a better idea, but I suspect it's going to be difficult to be precise. The only clue to that is that the snow up on the road seemed to be undisturbed so the deed must have been done before it started falling. I don't know what time that would have been here.'

'We can find out,' McKay said. 'Thanks, Pete. That's very helpful.'

'Wish I could give you more. But there's not a lot to say that's not pretty obvious. We might get more from forensics.'

'Let's hope so.' McKay paused. 'I'm not sure how to break this to you, but we ought to be looking at Forres's house as a potential crime scene. It sounds as if he might well not have left it voluntarily.'

'You want to break that news to Jock or would you like me to?'

'I'll let you have the pleasure.'

'Thanks for that.'

'Think of it as my Christmas gift to you. I'll have a word with Willy Ingram and get him to have the site sealed off.'

'He's over there somewhere,' Carrick said, 'helping to keep the crowds at bay.'

'Have we had many rubberneckers?'

'A few. Mainly just people out for a walk and the like. Willy and the lads have done a decent job of sending them on their way.'

'Thanks, again, Pete. I'll let you get back to Jock. Wouldn't want him to have to cope on his own for too long.'

McKay made his way over to where Ingram was standing talking to one of the PCs. 'You coping, Willy?'

'Seem to be managing. Been pretty quiet.'

'That's Christmas Day for you. People have better things to do than gawp at a corpse. I've just been thinking about Forres's house.'

'As part of the crime scene? I'm ahead of you,' Ingram said. 'Already sent a team up there to get it sealed off.'

'I've just broken the news to our examiner friends. If you speak to Billy McCann over there, he can give you the lay of the land. He was dealing with Forres as a missing persons case.'

'Already spoken to him,' Ingram said. 'He told us one of the neighbours has the keys.'

'Telepathy's obviously improving, Willy. Don't know how you do it. You manage to not even sound smug about it.'

Ingram shrugged. As both he and McKay knew, he was just good at his job. He'd have been thinking about exactly what was needed here, and how best to manage the limited resource available. 'My biggest worry's the weather.' Ingram gazed up at the swirling snow. 'If this continues the roads will be closed and we'll end up with a team stuck out here.'

He had a point. McKay tended to be fairly sanguine about the weather. You had to be if you lived up here. Snow was rarely much of a problem, and the roads were generally cleared fairly quickly, one way or another. But the forecast was for the current snow to continue for some hours yet, and it would be difficult to get any additional support over the holiday. 'I'll leave that to your good judgement, Willy. Do what you think's best but err on the side of caution.'

'I always do,' Ingram said. 'If we can get finished here, I'll call it a night. Make sure Forres's house is properly secured and then get away.'

There wasn't much more McKay could do down here. Leaving Ingram to his work, he walked round and up onto the road from which Forres had been pushed. He'd decided not to approach any of the householders here earlier, knowing he was bound to interrupt their Christmas lunch. That was still possible – McKay's recent Christmas Days had stuck to no particular routine, and he had no idea about what was the norm for others – but he hoped that most would have finished by now. He hoped he'd interrupt nothing more than a post-prandial nap.

He'd contemplated not disturbing them at all for today, knowing he'd be kicking off extensive door-to-doors once resources were available. But it was possible that someone as close as this had seen something useful the previous night. He pressed the doorbell on the house closest to where the body had been found. There were lights showing inside so he assumed someone was in there.

After a few minutes, the door opened and a man's face stared out at him suspiciously. 'Yes?'

'Police,' McKay said. 'I'm really sorry to bother you today, but I just wondered if you could answer a few brief questions?'

The man peered over McKay's shoulder as if expecting that McKay might be accompanied by a horde of other officers. 'This about what's going on down there?'

McKay gazed up at the falling snow meaningfully. 'Do you mind if I come in?'

'Aye, sorry. Wasn't thinking.' The man led McKay into the hallway. 'We're a bit of a mess. Recovering from Christmas dinner.'

'I'll only keep you a few minutes,' McKay said. 'I don't want to interrupt your Christmas.'

'No worries. It's you or the Christmas telly. Come through.'

McKay followed him into a sizeable living-dining room. Despite what the man had said, the room was tidy enough, although the remains of a Christmas dinner including the half-stripped carcass of a turkey were spread out on the table. The other occupants of the room were a woman of roughly the same age as the man, and an elderly man. 'Police,' the man explained to the others.

'We wondered if you'd come to talk to us,' the woman said. 'We've been watching what's been going on down there.'

That was a good sign, McKay thought. Curtain-twitching nosy neighbours. 'I'm sorry to have to trouble you.'

'I'm Frank Cameron,' the man said. 'This is my wife, Kerry, and my dad. He's over for Christmas. He lives on his own, so we're his support bubble,' Cameron added defensively, as if daring McKay to challenge him.

McKay nodded. 'That's fine. We'll probably need to talk to you in more detail in due course, but I just wanted a word straight away in case you've any immediate knowledge that might help us.'

'What sort of knowledge?'

'A body was found out there this morning–'

'I saw it,' Cameron said bluntly. 'Why would someone do that to themselves? And in a place where it might be found by bairns.'

That partly answered McKay's intended questions. Cameron had clearly assumed that the death was a suicide, presumably without stopping to ask himself how someone might have got himself up there in the first place. That suggested he and the others hadn't witnessed anything during the preceding night.

'We're still ascertaining the circumstances of the death,' McKay replied neutrally. 'I don't suppose any of you witnessed anything unusual in the course of last night. The body was found this morning, so we're assuming the death occurred overnight.'

Cameron shook his head. 'We went to bed fairly early. We had supper, a few drinks. Watched a bit of TV. We were in bed by ten.'

'I saw something,' the father said, unexpectedly.

McKay turned to him. 'When was this?'

'I'm not sure exactly. I got up to, well, spend a penny. I can't get through the night these days. As I was going back to bed, I had a look out of the landing window at the front. Was wondering whether it had started snowing, because they'd forecast it overnight–'

'What did you see?'

'There was a car parked out there, with its engine running and its headlights still on. I watched for a few minutes, wondering who it might be. Not that I really know anyone along here, other than Frank. I'm up from Perth–'

'What happened?'

'Nothing, really. After a few minutes the engine stopped and they turned the lights out. I assumed it was just one of the neighbours getting back late from some Christmas thing, so I didn't really think much about it. But it would have been just where the body was.'

'Did you notice the make of car?'

'Sorry. It was fairly dark and they weren't near any of the street lights. Something large, I'd have said. One of those people carrier things.'

That was potentially helpful, McKay thought. A distinctive vehicle travelling in the early hours of Christmas Day should be identifiable on some of the traffic cameras in the area. Even the A9 would have been largely empty.

But that raised another question. Why would anyone take the risk of committing this kind of murder so openly? Admittedly, the chances of being interrupted on that particular night were relatively low, but they weren't entirely negligible. If the father here had peered out the window a few minutes later or had been more curious about what was going on, he might have witnessed them carrying out that appalling act. If another of the neighbours had been similarly awake in the small hours or had been disturbed by the sound of the car, they might have looked out at the wrong moment. Why would anyone take that risk?

If they did manage to identify the car, it would most likely turn out to have fake plates. If Forres had been killed by one of his rivals, the murder would have been professionally orchestrated, so attention would have been paid to that kind of detail.

But that just made the risks involved here seem even stranger. 'You didn't see anyone leave the car?'

'Not while I was watching. But that was only a few minutes.'

'And you don't know what time that might have been? Even roughly.'

The father thought for a few moments. 'I suppose I usually get up between two and three. Don't imagine last night was much different.'

'That's helpful,' McKay said. 'I presume it wasn't snowing at that point?'

The father shook his head. 'No, the road was still clear.'

'That might help us pinpoint the time.'

'I don't understand,' Cameron said. 'If that poor so-and-so took his own life, what's this car got to do with it?'

'As I say, sir, we're still investigating the circumstances of the death,' McKay said blandly. 'We're looking for anyone who might have witnessed the incident or the individual concerned.'

'Someone local, is it?' Cameron asked.

'I'm not at liberty to reveal the identity at this stage. I'm sure you'll understand that.'

'Aye, of course. Sorry. It was just a bit of a shock. Christmas morning, too. Not what you expect.'

'And nobody else witnessed anything overnight?' McKay looked around at the others. 'In that case, I'll leave you to enjoy the rest of your Christmas. I'm sorry again for having to disturb you today. You're likely to be visited again by one of the investigating team, but that will just be routine.'

Cameron led him back to the front door. As he opened it, he said, 'I've been trying not to alarm the others, but that didn't look like a suicide to me.'

So Cameron was more perspicacious than he'd seemed. McKay said, 'As I said, we're still investigating the circumstances of the death.'

'Aye, I suppose you have to say that. Well, I won't worry the family.'

'Thanks again for your time, sir.'

McKay stepped out into the still falling snow. There was already another inch or two on the ground. He could see below that the crime scene team were beginning to disperse. They'd got an ambulance up to take the body, and were dismantling the tents. They were departing more quickly than would normally have been the case, but Willy Ingram would have weighed up the risks and benefits. With the falling snow, they wouldn't get much more from the scene in any case.

McKay walked further along the street and surveyed the neighbouring houses. Those on either side of the Camerons were in darkness, the owners away for Christmas. It was time for him to cut his own losses and get himself home while he still could. He gazed across the grassland towards the sea. He was certain that this and the bonfire murder were linked. Two bizarre murders that had involved effort and risk on the part of the perpetrators. Two killings designed to attract attention.

If he was right, then maybe they'd taken a step forward. At least they knew the identity of the second victim and had somewhere to start, which is more than they had with the first. *That's right, Alec*, he told himself, *you look on the bright side.*

His head bent against the wind and falling snow, he trudged back to his car.

22

'How's it going?' Helena Grant asked.

'All under control, or at least I think it is. I'll be with you in a few minutes.'

'Sure there's nothing I can do? Peel sprouts or something?'

'The whole point is to spoil you rotten. And I enjoy cooking.'

'I'm not going to argue strongly.'

Bill Emsworth did look as if he was in his element. He was even wearing a professional-looking white apron, and it wasn't difficult to imagine him donning a chef's hat. Grant's late husband had been a decent cook, but always left the kitchen in a state of utter chaos. By contrast, Bill cleared up as we went. He worked tidily, carefully chopping and preparing each ingredient before cooking.

'You could pour me another beer, if you really wanted to make a contribution.'

'I can just about manage that.' She opened the fridge and took out a bottle of one of the local ales. She was on red wine, trying to pace herself. She wasn't accustomed to drinking so early in the day, even at Christmas.

While she poured the beer, he said, 'Once I've done this, I can leave it to itself for a while and come to sit with you.'

'That would be nice,' she said sincerely. She'd had a quiet but enjoyable day so far. They'd had a leisurely breakfast, then braved the snow for another walk on the beach. There were a handful of other people around – dog walkers, families with kids enjoying the snow, one or two other couples like themselves.

She'd liked that. Thinking of the two of them as a couple, as an item. It was a long while since she'd been in that position. She was still being cautious, but it was feeling right. Even the gloomy weather hadn't dampened her spirits, though the icy wind eventually forced them to abandon their walk and return to the house.

Bill had originally intended to cook the Christmas dinner in mid-afternoon, but they'd been distracted by their chatting and he'd started later than planned. She didn't mind. She wasn't particularly hungry yet, and the only danger was that she might get mildly drunk before they ate.

She enjoyed talking to him very much. She'd worried they wouldn't have much in common, and that that would make conversation awkward. She'd been partly right in the first assumption, but the second hadn't followed. Their backgrounds were very different. Bill's was steeped in books and literature, though he'd done a huge diversity of jobs in his younger days, including establishing and running various businesses.

Grant herself was a graduate, but her degree had been in psychology and she'd followed that with a masters in criminology. Bill asked, 'That was what led you into the police?'

'Not directly. I'd had a very vague idea of wanting to do something in criminal justice, but hadn't seriously considered the police. I was looking more at things like prison psychologist or something in probation. But it was all a bit half-baked. Then I saw an advert for graduate recruitment into the police and I thought why not.'

'Any regrets?'

'Who knows? Sometimes I wonder about other routes I might have chosen. But not really. I've mostly enjoyed it so far. It's not always easy. No, I'll put it another way. Sometimes it's bloody difficult. Not so much the investigatory stuff, though that can be challenging, but everything that goes with it. All the sensitivities, the public exposure, the internal politicking. The endless admin. We spend more time on that than we do on catching criminals or preventing crime.'

'It goes with the territory in any high-profile job these days,' Bill pointed out.

'Doesn't make it any less of a pain in the backside, though.'

For her part, she'd quizzed Bill on his writing process and all the minutiae of producing a book. She'd never been a great reader, but she usually read a chapter or two of a crime novel or thriller before going to sleep. She'd never really thought about the books as anything other than a finished artefact, a product delivered as if by magic into her hands. She'd never considered how much work had actually gone into producing that artefact – the writing and re-writing, the editing and proofreading, the design of the cover, the printing of the finished article. It had never occurred to her to wonder how the author had come up with that plot, or how they'd managed to make it work.

'It must be a hell of a job,' she said.

'I've done harder ones,' he responded. 'I can't pretend that it's like working at the coal-face or hammering in rivets in a shipyard. I sit on my backside and churn out words. But there are times when it feels almost impossible.'

'Writer's block?'

'I've never really suffered from that. Touch wood.' He enacted the words by reaching out to press his fingers on the surface of the coffee table. 'But there are days when it's just not coming. When you sit staring at a blank screen wondering why you thought it was a good idea to take up this writing lark.'

'How do you deal with that?'

'There's no point in trying to force it. I get up, go for a walk, try to do something different. Eventually something pops into my head – usually when I'm least expecting it – and I get on with it. The whole process is a mystery to me.'

They'd spent the majority of the day blethering like this. He'd placed the goose in the oven of the Aga earlier, so that was well underway. 'I've been very organised,' he said. 'Prepared a lot of it in advance so won't need much effort today.'

'I'm impressed.'

She left him completing his various tasks in the kitchen and returned to the living room. The curtains were still open though it was already dark outside and the snow was falling thickly. She contemplated calling McKay to check how everything was going, but managed to stop herself. McKay would be coping just fine, and she didn't want to do anything that might disrupt how she was currently feeling.

She closed the curtains and turned back to survey the room. Bill had lit the wood stove earlier, giving the room a welcoming and cosy feel. She lowered herself onto the sofa and took a sip of her wine, enjoying the rich warmth in her mouth. She knew almost nothing about wine, other than what affordable wines she liked best in the local supermarket, but she guessed this was something pricy.

She'd been meaning to ask him to give her a proper tour of the house. It was hardly a mansion but it was a sizeable place and so far she'd really only seen this room, the kitchen and the bedroom. She was particularly intrigued to see the room where Bill worked, which was upstairs with a view out over the bay. He'd told her not to expect much, that it was not much more than an office, but she still had an urge to see the environment in which he worked his particular form of magic. Still, that could wait until tomorrow.

She sat back, her head already slightly woozy from the wine. She needed to be careful not to drink too much. It wouldn't do to be semi-comatose by the time Bill served the food.

The living room door was half open and she heard Bill's voice from the hallway. She sat up, assuming he was calling for her. Then she realised he was talking to someone else, presumably on the phone. She couldn't hear what he was saying, though he sounded slightly agitated at least by his own usual tranquil standards. None of her business, anyway.

After a few minutes, his voice fell silent and he entered the room, brandishing his glass of beer. 'There,' he said, 'I can leave it to look after itself for a while.'

'All okay?' she said. 'I thought I heard you talking to someone.'

'An old mate who phoned supposedly to wish me a happy Christmas. Think he'd already knocked back a few too many sweet sherries.'

'Haven't we all?' Grant took another sip of her wine as if to demonstrate.

'Heard any more from your colleague about this body?'

She'd felt she had to break the news to him about McKay's call in case it had ended with her having to head into work after all. 'I'm assuming that no news is good news, at least as far as my involvement's concerned. Alec's more than capable of looking after everything.'

'Do you think this is likely to be connected to the previous killing?'

'It's too early to say. I don't really know the circumstances of this latest case. I don't know if it's even an unlawful killing.' It sounded as if she was fobbing him off, which she supposed she was, but she was also telling the truth. McKay had been able to give her no more than the bare bones of an account, although he'd seemed in little doubt that they were dealing with another murder.

'Yes, of course. And I appreciate you can't really talk about it to me. It's just my writerly curiosity. Always on the lookout for plot ideas.'

'I hope that's not all you see in me,' Grant laughed. 'A source of plot ideas.'

'I can't deny you give me ideas. Not much to do with writing, though.'

She leaned her head against his shoulder and allowed him to put his arm around her shoulders. 'It's going well, isn't it?'

'The dinner?'

'No, idiot. This. Us. It's going much better than I'd feared.' It was perhaps partly the wine talking, or at least disinhibiting her, but she wanted to say it.

'Did you think it was going to be a disaster?'

'Of course not.' She paused, picking her words carefully. 'But I was wary. It's been a long time since I was seriously involved with anyone. I didn't want to allow myself to believe this could work.'

'It is, though, isn't it? Working, I mean.'

'It is for me. I hope it is for you.'

'Of course it is.' He laughed. 'All we need now is a successful Christmas dinner to make it perfect.'

'I think that's in safe hands. And so am I.'

'I hope so.' He took a mouthful of beer. 'Speaking of which, I probably just better check that nothing's burning. That would never do.'

23

McKay woke early on Boxing Day, grabbing his clothes and stumbling out to the kitchen wearing his dressing gown, so he could leave Chrissie sleeping. He'd have a shower and a coffee and then head into the office, assuming that the road conditions would allow it.

They'd had an enjoyable enough Christmas night, once he'd finally returned from duty. They'd enjoyed the usual ritual exchange of presents, mostly items that each knew the others wanted. To McKay's slight surprise, Fiona's present to him had turned out to be an unscale-looking Swiss Army knife.

'I didn't know what else to get you,' she'd said, apologetically. 'I thought it might come in useful.'

'I'm sure it will,' McKay had responded. 'You never know when you might need to get a boy scout out of a horse's hoof. Seriously, Fiona, it's grand.'

It didn't much matter. Chrissie and Fiona were already several drinks ahead of him, regaling each other with increasingly raucous anecdotes from their childhood. McKay had been happy to leave them to it, helping himself to a light supper from the cheese and crackers Chrissie had brought out after lunch.

He'd limited himself to a couple of beers, knowing he'd be up early in the morning. His head was still buzzing with speculation about Hamish Forres's death, and his overactive brain wouldn't allow him to sleep late.

In the kitchen, showered and dressed, he peered out through the window. It was only a little after 7am and still pitch-black outside. The snow had stopped falling but the garden was thickly coated with white. As he sipped his coffee, he took out his phone and checked the status of the local roads. All the main roads had been cleared overnight, but the B and C roads were much more variable. That, and the short resources over the holiday period, was likely to constrain the extent of the follow-up work.

All he could do was do his best to get into the office and to play things by ear. At least the forecast predicted no further snow. He swallowed his coffee and made his way out of the house.

The first challenge was to clear the track up to the main road. It wasn't far but the snow had drifted and several sections were under a substantial depth. McKay trudged up to check the state of the road itself. There would be no point in clearing the track if the road was impassable anyway.

Although the road was still covered with snow, he could see that several cars had already passed by. He returned to the house, dug out a spade from the shed, and spent fifteen minutes clearing the snow to the edge of the track. Finally, he cleared the snow from the car itself, ready to begin the journey into the office.

For the most part, it was easier than he'd feared. He drove with caution until he reached the A9, from where the roads were largely clear of snow until he reached Inverness. There were few vehicles on the road, other than the odd lorry. McKay had no idea whether the Cairngorm stretch of the A9 further south was open – the highest sections were usually among the first to close in poor weather – and the roadside illuminated signs offered no information.

Police HQ was equally quiet. Again, that wasn't surprising. Boxing Day had fallen on the Saturday this year, so it was a holiday weekend. Most people would be off for a few days leaving only those on shift and a few conscientious souls like McKay to keep the place going. Even some of those would have been prevented from travelling by the weather conditions.

Ginny Horton was already sitting at her desk, tapping away at her computer.

'Just you and me then?' he said.

She looked around as if to check the truth of his assertion. 'So far, anyway. But it's early.'

McKay looked at his watch. 'I suppose it is. Surprised to see you in already.'

'When was I ever in late?'

He sat himself down in front of her desk. 'How were the roads out your way?'

'Better than I'd feared. That's one reason I was in so early.'

'One reason?'

'The other reason was that I couldn't sleep. Kept thinking about what you told me about Forres's death. Nasty way to go.'

'I suppose it would have been quick in the end. But if he was aware of what was happening...' McKay stopped. 'Not quite as bad as knowing you were about to be burned to death, but unpleasant.'

'Are we treating the two killings as linked?'

'I'm working on that basis. For the moment, anyway.'

'One of Forres's business associates?'

'Maybe. One of my tasks for this morning is to check who else we looked at when we were trawling through dodgy local business types back in the spring.'

'Surely if it was someone like that, they'd have been reported missing?'

'Some of these people aren't always keen to involve the police. It might also depend on who's left behind to care about their disappearance.'

'At least Forres had a son to care about him.'

'A son whose world is shortly to be turned upside down, I suspect,' McKay said. 'Forres seems to have kept his real business under wraps.'

As they'd been talking, a few more members of the team had been arriving. McKay's plan was to hold a morning briefing meeting with whoever managed to get in and then consider how best to allocate resources. Most of the team already had tasks allocated in respect of the bonfire murder. McKay's inclination was to allow them to continue with those rather than spreading the resource too thinly. There were some practical steps he could take, though, particularly in trying to track the vehicle that had been witnessed at the time of the hanging.

'I've just been looking through Billy McCann's notes of his interviews with Forres's son,' Horton said, breaking into his thoughts. 'I suspect you're right. He doesn't seem to have much idea at all about his father's former working life. Mind you, most of the neighbours saw him as a kindly old codger who kept himself to himself.'

'I bet they did,' McKay said.

'One thing, though,' Horton went on. 'It looks as if Forres was robbed the day before he went missing.'

'Robbed?'

'Some sort of scam. Fake visitor who got into the house and took his wallet. Pretended to be one of the volunteers delivering food.'

'Interesting coincidence. Hard to see how it might connect to his disappearance, though. Nothing else taken?'

'Forres said not. I suppose we can't be sure now.'

'Who are these local volunteers?' McKay said. 'Might be worth talking to whoever visited Forres normally in case they can add anything.'

'I've just been looking them up,' Horton said. 'Just seems to be a small local group. Here.' She swung her screen round to show McKay. 'There's a list of the people involved and phone numbers.'

McKay scanned down the list. 'Well, well. Kelly Armstrong. She gets everywhere.'

'Kelly Armstrong? That name rings a bell.'

'It should do. We keep bumping into her.'

'Oh, right. She was working in that bar in Fortrose...'

'And she's stumbled across at least one dead body,' McKay said. 'If she wasn't such a nice wee thing, I might get suspicious.' He paused, thinking. 'Come to think of it, I ran into her on the night of the bonfire too. She was working as a steward at the event.'

'She does seem to have a knack of being in the wrong place at the wrong time.'

'It's a small place,' McKay said. 'And she tends to involve herself in things. That doesn't make her a murderer.'

'I'm not suggesting it does. But her proximity to both these killings is interesting. If it was someone we didn't know, it might make us look twice.'

'If we didn't know her, we wouldn't know she had any link to both killings,' McKay pointed out. 'And it's a tenuous one. We don't know she was the volunteer who visited Forres, and there were a dozen or more stewards at the bonfire event. But it might be worth talking to her. She's a smart kid. She might be able to tell us something.'

'I'll give the group a call,' Horton said. 'See if they can tell me who visited Forres. Whoever it was is probably worth speaking to. If nothing else, they can tell us what frame of mind Forres was in.'

'Have we had any other similar scams reported in the area?'

'There doesn't seem to be anything in Cromarty. There are a few instances of similar scams in other parts of the Black Isle over the past few months, but no more than we usually get. When we do get reports, there's usually a spate of them in the same area – people going door-to-door on some pretext till they find someone who falls for it. It's odd that Forres's should have been a one-off.'

'Also interesting that they should have specifically referenced the volunteer group,' McKay said. 'Most of these toerags are opportunistic, trotting out the usual bollocks about being there to check the electricity meter or whatever. This one must have done a bit of background research.' He pushed himself to his feet. 'Right. I can't sit here listening to you blethering on all day. I've got work to do.'

Horton clearly had no intention of rising to the bait. 'We all have, Alec.'

'I'll go and try to whip this lot into some sort of shape.' He looked over his shoulder at the half dozen team members now dotted across the large open-plan office. 'Not exactly heaving, is it?'

24

Simon Crawford had allowed himself to sleep late again on Boxing Day. Strictly speaking, he supposed it was a working day. Christmas Day had fallen on a Friday this year so the Boxing Day holiday was on Monday. Today was just another Saturday and Crawford expected to work on Saturdays. His decision this year to force himself to rest over Christmas had been a conscious effort to break his workaholic routine, but he was already beginning to regret it.

He wasn't cut out for resting. It made him tense and irritable. He needed to feel he was doing something. If he was honest with himself, he needed to feel he was making money.

He climbed out of bed, showered, dressed and headed downstairs. More snow had fallen overnight, and the main road was still largely covered, although a handful of tyre tracks indicated that some vehicles had passed that morning. He had no plans to go anywhere today and, if necessary, didn't need to leave the house for several days at least.

As he made coffee, he checked his phone and groaned. Three more missed calls from Gordon fucking Prebble, along with a voicemail. He clicked the voicemail and listened. 'Where the hell are you, Crawford? I expect more prompt service than this.'

Expect away, then, Crawford thought. He was gradually coming to the conclusion that Prebble was more trouble than he was worth, particularly if he was on the way out in any case.

'Further change of plan since we spoke,' Prebble went on. 'I want to stick a rocket up everything, get it fucking moving. I want all this sorted PDQ. Call back.'

Fuck that, Crawford thought. *Fuck that for a fucking game of fucking soldiers.* He prided himself on the quality and promptness of service he provided to his clients. Sometimes, especially when dealing with the likes of Gordon Prebble, he wondered why he bothered. It wasn't as if they could go anywhere else to obtain the services he provided. And there were limits, which Gordon Prebble managed to exceed on almost every occasion. Crawford was damned if he was going to jump at Prebble's say-so to cater to whatever whim might have suddenly popped into his head.

He was tempted simply to ignore Prebble's calls, but he knew Prebble would just keep on calling. Crawford took a preparatory sip of his coffee and called Prebble's number, but it rang out to voicemail. 'Gordon, it's Simon Crawford here. Sorry I missed you earlier. Call me back when you're able.'

Despite his original intention of taking the day off, Crawford spent much of the morning working. At around 1pm, he broke for lunch and tried Prebble again. Prebble would at least see that Crawford had made an effort to get hold of him, even if Crawford was reaching the point where he didn't much care what Prebble thought. Again, the call cut to voicemail. This time, Crawford didn't bother leaving a message. Most likely, for all the supposed urgency of his earlier message, Prebble's attention had already moved on to something else.

Crawford made his way downstairs with the intention of

making himself a light lunch. He had a pan of soup simmering on the cooker and was halfway through making a cheese and pickle sandwich when the front doorbell rang.

He had very few visitors here at any time, other than the occasional client or friend who came by prior arrangement. Puzzled, he made his way to the front door and peered through the spyhole. He'd long been cautious about security up here. Even based on his legitimate income, Crawford was a wealthy man who lived in a well-appointed but remote house.

There was a figure standing on the doorstep, standing too close to the spyhole for Crawford to be able to make out any details. He couldn't even tell whether the figure was male or female.

The doorbell rang again. He couldn't really even pretend not to be at home. He had lights on in several of the ground floor rooms as well as in his office upstairs, all shining out through uncurtained windows.

Even so, there was no reason to answer the door, he told himself. Whoever the visitor was, it was unlikely to be anyone he wanted to see. It probably was some passer-by – someone who'd broken down or become stuck in the snow. If so, that was unfortunate but it wasn't his problem. He had work to do and didn't need to be disturbed.

The doorbell rang for a third time, and then the figure knocked on the door beside Crawford, startling him. The doorbell rang once more. Almost immediately, Crawford was startled a second time, this time by a single buzz from the phone in his pocket. He pulled it out and stared at the screen. A text. It read: 'It's me, Jo. I'm outside. Are you going to let me in. It's bloody freezing out here.'

Jo? Who the hell was Jo? He didn't know anyone called Jo. Certainly not anyone he knew well enough for them to turn up unannounced on his doorstep. He racked his brains for any friends or acquaintances or business associates called Jo, but could think of no one.

The only possibility was that this mysterious Jo had come to the wrong house. He couldn't immediately think of anywhere else in the area that might fit the bill instead. There was no other house for a mile or so in either direction, and there was nowhere that remotely resembled this place. Even so, it seemed the only plausible explanation.

Except, of course, it didn't explain how this person had his mobile number.

He pressed his eye to the spyhole again, hoping the figure might have moved, but all he could see was a fuzzy greyness, as if the figure was standing immediately next to the lens.

The phone buzzed again. Another text. 'FFS, Simon. I know you're in there. Stop buggering about and let me in. It's bloody freezing.'

Whoever Jo was, she was behaving as if she knew him well. Was it possible he knew her by a different name?

There was another hammering at the door, much louder and more vehement. He could hear someone shouting outside, though the door was too thick for him to hear what was being said.

He didn't have any choice. Checking that the heavy chain was securely in place, he unlocked the deadlock and slowly eased it open, peering out into the daylight.

His unexpected visitor was a young woman, probably barely out of her teens.

'About bloody time. What the hell are you playing at, Simon?'

He stared at her. 'I'm sorry...?'

'For Christ's sake, just let me in. It feels like I've been standing here for hours.'

'I'm sorry. I'm afraid I don't know–'

'Stop pissing about, Simon. I don't know if you think this is funny, but I really am freezing to death.'

His brain was frantically trying to place her. Her face maybe looked vaguely familiar, he thought, but he couldn't work out where he might have seen it before. He had a vague idea that she'd had a different look – different hair or different glasses, perhaps. Today she looked like a serious student, with dark brown hair tied back and a pair of heavy-framed glasses through which she stared at him impatiently. She did look cold, he thought. She was dressed only in a thin jacket over a T-shirt and jeans, her arms wrapped around her body.

Whoever she might turn out to be, he couldn't just leave her out there. The best bet was to get her inside, give her a coffee, and then come clean about not having a clue who she was. 'You'd better come in.'

'You don't have to be like that, Simon. I know you weren't expecting me today, but I thought you'd be pleased to see me.'

He couldn't think of an immediate response. He closed the door sufficiently to allow him to remove the chain and then opened it to admit her.

He never knew what happened after that. The door was forced inwards and he was thrown back into the hallway, stumbling before losing his footing. Something was thrown over his head and he felt a cord pulled tightly around his neck. He struggled briefly, kicking out with his feet, but felt something being pressed down on his face cutting off his breath.

He knew it was already too late. The person holding him down was too strong for him, and he could feel his consciousness slipping away. He kicked out once more, his foot connecting with nothing, and then, moments later, he was still.

25

The wind whipped from the sea, and Helena Grant had her head down as they trudged along the beach. They'd planned to do something different today – a drive north to Dornoch or west over to Ullapool. But when they'd woken to find a thick blanket of snow on the ground, they'd shelved those plans and stayed closer to home.

Grant would have been happy just to stay inside but Bill had been keen to get a breath of air. They'd headed down to the waterfront with the intention of walking at least part of the way towards Chanonry Point.

'I'm not sure how far we'll get,' Bill said. 'It is bloody cold. More than I'd thought.'

She couldn't disagree with him, even though they'd both dressed in anticipation of the freezing weather. 'Let's see how we do. It's certainly blowing the cobwebs away.'

A handful of others had braved the weather to come walking down here, most of them striding purposefully along the beach as if in pursuit of some specific objective. In the garden of one of the houses on the seafront, a father was enthusiastically building a snowman with a couple of small children. The sky was still heavy with clouds and the day had remained gloomy, although no more snow was forecast.

'How long do I have you for?' Bill said, as they made their way along the beach. 'This weekend, I mean.'

'How long do you want me?'

'As far as I'm concerned, you can stay here permanently,' Bill said. 'But I imagine you might have other things to do.'

That certainly sounded like an offer of some kind, she thought. 'I imagine they'll want me back at work at some point. But I'm okay till Monday, if that's not outstaying my welcome.'

'Of course not. I'd love you to stay as long as you can.' He paused. 'It seems to be working, doesn't it?' He sounded tentative, as if broaching a potentially controversial topic.

'It is for me,' she said. 'I hope it is for you.'

'Couldn't be better. More so than I'd dared hope, to be honest.'

'You wait till you start discovering all my bad habits.'

'They couldn't be worse than mine. We can live with that, can't we?'

'I imagine so.'

'Right, Monday it is, then. I can start planning what else to cook for you.'

She'd never really encountered anyone like Bill who enjoyed cooking for its own sake. He'd told her, when she'd offered to give him some help, that he actually found his time in the kitchen relaxing. 'It's creative, just like writing,' he'd said. 'But I use different skills, a different part of my mind. I don't really even have to think what I'm doing a lot of the time.'

'Whatever you cook, it's bound to be lovely,' she said. 'Everything you've served me so far has been.'

'You say the nicest things. Even if you don't mean them.'

'Oh, I mean it, all right. You don't know what my normal culinary diet is like.'

'In that case, thank you for your kind words.'

'And thank you for the delicious food.'

They'd ended up at the water's edge. It was heading towards low tide, and the waves were lapping at Bill's solid walking boots. Beyond, the firth was topped with whitecaps, the cry of the gulls incessant. 'I'm glad you can stay longer,' Bill said. 'Any more news from Alec McKay?'

'I gave him a call for a quick debrief this morning while you were cooking breakfast. Nothing much new to report. There should be something on the news tonight.' She didn't want to say any more and hoped he wouldn't press her.

'It'll cause a bit of a stir locally.'

'You think so?' She looked at him with curiosity. None of the detail had been revealed, including the manner of Forres's death, and she wondered whether Bill had picked up some inside information. She didn't imagine she was his only connection in the force.

'Two murders in a small place like this within a few days. And of course people will assume the two killings are in some way connected.'

'We're keeping an open mind on that at this stage. It's something I'll need to explore with Alec when I get back in.'

'Glad everything's under control with it, anyway. Means you can stay on here with a clear conscience.'

'Alec knows what he's doing. He has his own idiosyncratic way of doing it, but he's very capable. I can relax at least for the next day or two.'

'Shall we walk on a bit and then head back for a bite to eat?'

'Why not? I'm not entirely freezing yet.'

'When we get back, I'll make you hot chocolate, maybe enhanced with something stronger.'

'Sounds like a deal.'

They walked on, watching the waves slowly receding down the shoreline. Ahead of them through the gloomy afternoon they could see the curve of Chanonry Point, the squat lighthouse. Despite the weather, Grant could make out a cluster of people on the point, no doubt looking for any sign of the dolphins.

As they turned back, Bill's mobile rang. 'Bugger,' he said. 'I'd better take this. You carry on. I'll catch you up. I'll just be a few minutes.'

'I can wait if you like.'

'You go on. It's too cold to be standing around. I won't be long.'

Reluctantly, she continued walking along the beach. Behind her she heard Bill taking the call. She paused for a moment to allow a woman apparently being taken for a walk by her dog to cross her path, the dog chasing down to the sea. Grant glanced back. Bill was still talking on the phone. She turned, watching as the woman struggled to prevent the dog from dragging her into the sea, and then continued walking, as slowly as she could reasonably manage.

It was another few minutes before she heard hurried footsteps behind her. 'Sorry about that,' Bill called.

'Problems?' she asked as he drew level with her.

'Just publishing stuff. It'll get sorted.'

She was on the point of asking more, but something about his manner had indicated he didn't want to discuss it. It seemed odd to her that someone should phone him about a publishing issue over the holiday, but she didn't know anything about that kind of business. 'I'm looking forward to that hot chocolate,' she said.

'I'll see what I can rustle up.' He still seemed distracted, his mind elsewhere. 'Dash of brandy, maybe. We'll need something to warm us up.'

'Brandy sounds excellent,' she said. 'Right, let's get back. I think my fingers are considering detaching themselves from my hands.'

26

By the afternoon, the main roads were largely passable and McKay dispatched the small team of available officers to conduct initial door-to-doors near the murder scene. He wasn't optimistic of discovering anything new. If anyone really had witnessed the killing, they'd have been in touch by now. At most, they might find another witness who'd seen the car. It was just part of the process they needed to go through.

There was plenty of continuing activity relating to the bonfire killing, but McKay's feeling was that they were treading water. They'd struggle to make progress until they at least knew the victim's identity.

The Forres case was a different matter. They had known contacts to be interviewing, and at least a possible motive for his killing, and they had the means to check out his business and finances. There were countless unanswered questions, but they had some idea of where to start.

So for the moment McKay had decided to throw the majority of resource he had – which in the circumstances was pitifully small – at the Forres case in the hope that something might stick. *Let no one ever tell you you're not optimistic, Alec old pal.*

It was later in the afternoon that his optimism was partially rewarded. He'd had one of the team working on the traffic cameras. It would normally have been a thankless task, but McKay had reasoned that there would be very few cars on the road in the early hours of Christmas Day. That assumption had been correct. After around 1am, the volume of vehicles was very low indeed, particularly away from the main A9.

The officer in question, a young DC called Ben Connor, had entered the office in some excitement. 'Guv?'

The youngsters liked calling McKay 'guv'. It made them sound like they were in some 1970s TV police drama. That was fine by McKay. At least it was better than 'sir', and it showed him some of the respect he deserved. 'Son?'

'Think we might have something.'

'As long as it's not contagious. Sit down. You're making the place look untidy.'

'Guv.' Connor sat and slid across some printouts from a plastic wallet. 'Several sightings of this vehicle at around 2.30am on Christmas Day. The first couple from cameras on the A9. That first one's on the Kessock Bridge, and the second's at the Munlochy junction. We've got a temporary speed camera there because of the collision record. Then we've got a third one on a temporary camera on the B9169. Looks like they took the north road out along the Black Isle, presumably because it was less conspicuous than going through Fortrose and Rosemarkie.'

'What you're saying is that they came right past my house. Pity I wasn't up having a piss or I might have spotted them.'

'Guv?'

'A wee joke, son. As it were. Any sightings of it coming back?'

'We've got one from the camera on the back road. Bit over an hour later. Timings are on the photos.'

McKay nodded, taking this in. 'Where's the camera sited?'

'At the junction just after Culbokie.'

'It's a reasonable drive from there to Cromarty. Twenty-five minutes or so. If this is our vehicle, it suggests they didn't bugger about long doing the deed. Ten, fifteen minutes.' He paused, still thinking. 'Not the easiest task. So they must have had it well prepared. They must have scoped out the location in advance.'

'Looks that way, doesn't it?'

'What's the vehicle?'

Connor said, 'It's an MPV, which is what we were looking for–'

'That's a very good start, son.'

Connor blinked at him for a second. 'It's a Volkswagen Sharan. Looks dark colour from the cameras, though it's hard to make out.'

'Registration?'

'The plates are fake. Relate to a BMW 5-Series with a keeper in the south of England somewhere.'

'Of course they do,' said McKay. 'Still, at least that seems to confirm that this is our vehicle. So it takes us a small step forward. Next thing is to check whether there are any sightings of it further afield. If it was caught north of the Kessock Bridge that must mean Inverness or beyond.'

'Do you want me to move on to that next?'

'You might as well. It's something we can usefully do while most of the world is still nursing its post-Christmas hangover. And this gives us a better idea of timing. Suggests they'd have been in Cromarty around 3am, which fits. The snow didn't start coming down till around 3.30 or so. Maybe another reason they weren't keen to hang around.'

Connor nodded. 'I'll see what I can find.'

'The other question,' McKay continued, 'is whether this was the same vehicle that was sighted outside Forres's house when he disappeared. The witness said something large and dark, but didn't have much of a clue beyond that. We can show her some images of the relevant type of vehicle and see if they ring any bells, though that's probably unduly optimistic. Be interesting to see if the same vehicle is spotted more than once over the last couple of days. It's a quiet wee place at this time of the year, so someone might have noticed an unfamiliar vehicle if it appeared more than once.'

McKay was largely talking to himself now, though happy to treat Connor as a captive audience. The next question, he supposed, was whether the vehicle might have visited the town at an earlier point if these people had wanted to scope out the location before carrying out the killing. That might have been done at any time. 'Sorry, son. Just mulling it all over. Hard thinking doesn't come naturally to me. Good work with the car.'

'Don't know if it really gets us very far,' Connor said, ruefully.

'It's more than we had. This gives us confirmation of timings. Likely confirmation that whoever did this isn't local to the Black Isle. It gives us a model of car to look out for and to reference in any media appeals. Even if these people ditch the car, which I guess is likely, someone's bound to spot it and that'll give us more to work on. It's a step forward, son.' This was the kind of speech that, in his own career, he'd always found deeply uninspiring, though it was obviously true as far as it went. But it was the bollocks you were apparently obliged to spout in a line-management role. He could tell Connor was unimpressed.

'I guess so.'

Ginny Horton waited till Connor had left the room before crossing over to McKay's desk. 'He looked a bit shell-shocked. What did you do to him?'

'Just congratulated him. Bit of a motivational talk.'

'Ah. Poor wee thing.'

'He's got some good stuff.' He slid the printouts across the desk towards her. 'Looks like our car. Fake plates. Places the time of death around 3am.'

'Makes sense.'

'I'll have a word with comms. We can reference the car in any appeals for information. Young Connor's going to check for sightings in the previous days.'

'Meanwhile,' Horton said, 'I've been contacted by Forres's son.'

'Forres's son?'

'A couple of the Edinburgh lot went round to break the news to him. Five o'clock on Christmas Day, would you believe? Family had just sat down to Christmas dinner.'

'You can't win with that kind of thing. If they'd waited, family might have complained about not being told straightaway. Must have been a hell of a shock, though.'

'He seemed okay in the circumstances. I suspect he'd already realised the outcome was unlikely to be positive.'

'And then he called you?'

'I'm not quite sure why. Obviously, we needed to speak to him, but I hadn't envisaged he'd be able to tell us very much we didn't already know. But he told the Edinburgh officers he was keen to talk to someone involved in the investigation, so eventually he ended up talking to me.'

'Impressions?'

'Still in a state of shock about it all, I thought. A bit guilt-ridden.'

McKay tipped back in his chair to what looked like a dangerous angle, and stared at the ceiling. 'You think he might have something to be guilty about?'

'Just generic generational guilt – I should have done more to help him, I should have come up here earlier, I should have realised how vulnerable he really was. That stuff.'

'We've all been through that,' McKay said. 'Even me. So why was he so desperate to beat a path to our door?'

'Apparently because he wants to tell us about his dad. The real Hamish Forres.'

'Does he have a clue about the real Hamish Forres?'

'Who knows? He was keen to speak face-to-face. He's driving up tomorrow. He's keen to get back into his father's house. Partly just for sentimental reasons but also to make sure it's secure and safe, given that it's likely to be unoccupied for some time.'

'Don't know if the examiners have finished there yet,' McKay said. 'But we can't stop him once we open it up. And if he's up here we can get the ID confirmed and get anything we can from him.'

'I don't know how much he'll have to tell us,' Horton said. 'But he might know more than his father realised. That's sometimes the way with children. They absorb stuff without even knowing they're doing it. Osmosis.'

'Bless you.' McKay grinned and pushed himself to his feet. 'Right, I can't sit here blethering to you all day. Some of us have got work to do. And I can't even contemplate that awful prospect without another coffee.'

27

Sacha had thought she'd be unable to get up here today. They had a long-standing regular arrangement. It was sometimes disrupted by external factors – or more often by Gordon's unpredictable whims – but it had continued this way for several years now.

She usually came up here twice a week to carry out the various duties that Gordon had allocated to her. Those duties included some cleaning, the preparation of some meals to be frozen or chilled for the subsequent days, and – as Gordon required – more personal services.

She'd begun to wonder whether it was appropriate for her to continue to perform the last of those. But there were problems in changing their long-standing arrangements. The first was that Gordon wasn't the kind of man to take no for an answer. The second was that she couldn't ignore what Gordon had done for her. He'd no doubt done it for his own selfish reasons, but that wasn't the point. Without him, her life would be very different and far, far worse. Gordon himself never let her forget it, but she didn't need him to remind her. She knew how much she owed him, and almost any price he might extract from her seemed worthwhile.

But the third reason was the most important. Quite simply, she knew what Gordon was capable of. She'd seen the way he could treat people who crossed him, from the women she'd once worked with through to the men he dealt with in his business. He was a ruthless and violent man. It wasn't even that he might lash out at her in a moment of fierce anger – though he was more than capable of that. It was that, if it suited him, he might take a much more ruthless and absolute revenge. He'd destroy her, destroy the new life he'd enabled her to build, strip away her legal status, leave her penniless and homeless, and with no choice but to return to the world he'd chosen to drag her out of.

So, repulsive as she found Gordon's demands, she continued to meet them. She knew she'd continue to do so, until he became bored with her. She didn't even want to think about what might happen at that point. He'd cast her aside, but she hoped that, if it was his own choice, he might simply leave her be. Once he lost interest in her, that would be it. She wouldn't even be worthy of his attention. She could easily live with that.

She drew up her car next to his huge vehicle. She assumed the size of his car was intended to compensate for his shortcomings in other areas, but that wasn't a thought she could afford to share with anyone.

The previous day, she'd thought she would have to cancel this visit to Gordon. The roads had all been snow-covered and many of the back roads had been closed. She'd contemplated phoning Gordon to postpone, but had failed to work up the necessary courage. Even though there'd been nothing she could do, he would have blamed her. It probably wouldn't have been sufficient to end their arrangement, but it would have been enough to make him extract some suitable retribution when they next met.

Overnight, the temperatures had risen and much of the snow had thawed. The main roads were now largely clear and even the back roads had mostly been opened up. Although she never really came here willingly, she was mostly relieved. She hadn't wanted to try to offer Gordon her excuses, legitimate as they might be.

As she always did, she'd been sitting in the car for several minutes preparing for the moment when she'd have to face Gordon again. He'd be as pleasant as he always was when he was getting what he wanted. Even then, he made her skin crawl and she had to conceal her disgust at his touch.

And there was always the possibility he might already have drunk too much. That seemed to be happening with increasing frequency in recent months. Gordon wasn't a pleasant drunk, and he was prone to losing his temper over nothing at all, taking offence at some passing comment or accusing her of disrespecting him. He'd been violent with her more than once, although his mood could change in a moment and he'd turn remorseful and self-pitying. Those days were not ones she enjoyed.

She climbed out of the car into the cold afternoon air. Despite the partial thaw, the landscape was still largely white, the land before her falling away down towards the firth. The day had brightened, and the sky was a clear blue. For most people, it would be a day to stop and admire the view, but that wasn't an option for her.

She'd asked Gordon if she could have her own set of keys so that she could avoid disturbing him when she arrived. She'd thought it was an innocent enough request – many of her cleaning clients were only too happy to trust her with a set of keys – but it had been another moment when Gordon had become unexpectedly furious, accusing her of wanting to undermine his safety and security. She'd never mentioned it again.

It struck her that Gordon was taking an unusually long time to answer the door. Usually he was only too keen to get his hands on her. He'd be at the door in seconds, almost dragging her inside, desperate to satisfy his own unpleasant appetites. It was only when he'd done that to his own satisfaction that she'd be allowed to get on with her cleaning and other domestic duties.

She pressed the bell again, gazing around her as she did so. There were the marks of tyres in the remaining snow on the driveway. It looked as if the marks had been made since the overnight thaw, which suggested that Gordon had already had a visitor. That wasn't too surprising, even though her impression was that very few people came to see Gordon up here. Other than the needs that Sacha satisfied, he claimed he had little desire for other company, and could conduct the bulk of his business remotely.

It was another aspect of his personality that Sacha could barely comprehend. She lived alone, but not through choice. She'd gradually been able to make friends in the village she lived in, even if it had taken them some time to grow accustomed to this odd foreign woman in their neighbourhood. Most of them were decent people who'd shown her increasing friendship and hospitality as they'd grown to know her. She needed company, companionship. It was what she remembered from her early life and, though she knew she'd never find that sense of community here, she did at least now feel she was welcomed.

Impatient now, she pressed the bell again. Much as she might feel relieved at delaying her encounter with Gordon, she wanted to get on with it, get it over and done with so she could return to her own form of normality. Even so, she didn't want to sound impatient, even in the urgency with which she pressed the bell. That would just give Gordon another excuse.

There was still no sign of any response from inside the

house. Where could Gordon be? Had something happened to him?

She reached out to press the bell again, but hesitated. If Gordon was involved in some important phone call or trying to finish some complex business task, he wasn't going to thank her for incessantly ringing the doorbell. Her hand dropped nervously to the large brass door handle.

To her surprise, it turned. She twisted it and pushed at the door. It stuck for a moment then opened fully. That was unheard of. She knew Gordon always kept the front door firmly locked, with a series of deadlocks and bolts, which he painstakingly drew back and reset whenever he had a visitor. He was almost obsessive about security.

She stepped uneasily forward into the hall. Gordon would be angry if she came into the house without permission, however honest and honourable her motives. 'Gordon?' she called tremulously.

There was no reply. The house was eerily silent. She took another step forward, listening hard for any sound, ready to jump back outside the door if Gordon should appear.

'Gordon?' Her voice was louder this time though she was still unsure whether it would penetrate to other parts of the house.

Still no response. She walked forward another few steps, beginning to feel uneasy. Gordon had known to expect her today, and she couldn't imagine that wouldn't have been higher priority to him than anything else. She knew his appetites too well. 'Gordon? Is everything okay?'

The silence seemed almost oppressive now. It was the silence of a deserted house. She took a few more steps forward and drew level with the door of the living room. There was something else now. A scent or smell she couldn't identify. Something rich, cloying and unpleasant. Something that felt like a warning.

She moved towards the living room door and stopped. It felt as if she'd been physically struck, as if all the breath had been knocked from her body. She could no longer move, could only stare in horror at what she was seeing.

The living room had always been expensively but anonymously furnished. Two solid leather sofas, a glass-topped coffee table, an unnoticeable beige carpet, landscapes on the walls chosen by some paid designer. She'd never detected a trace of Gordon in there.

There was plenty now, though. The carpet was thick with blood, a wide congealing patch spread below the coffee table. There were more splashes of blood on the walls and – well, everywhere.

There was no doubt about the cause, and no question that the blood was Gordon's. His body lay prone across the coffee table, his head hanging across the far edge. He was dressed in a pale blue shirt also soaked with blood.

She wanted to turn and run. But she knew she couldn't do that. She didn't even know for sure whether Gordon was dead. She had to check that and then decide what to do. She told herself she had to call the police and perhaps an ambulance. She had nothing to fear in doing that. Her legal status was sound. She had nothing to hide. She had no reason to be afraid.

Except, of course, she would never not be afraid of dealing with the authorities. Because of what she had experienced in her early life, and because of what she had experienced here.

Even so, she had to do what was right. She took a breath and then walked another couple of steps forward.

She saw immediately that she'd been wrong. Gordon's head was not hanging over the far side of the coffee table.

Gordon's head was not there at all.

28

'You didn't need to come. Or is it that you don't trust me?'

Helena Grant gazed at the snow-covered landscape surrounding them. 'I've worked with you for a long time, Alec. Of course I don't trust you. But that's not why I came.'

'No?'

'Alec, we've had three brutal and shocking murders here in less than a week. The Christmas break has enabled us to keep the detail out of the media so far but all hell's going to break loose shortly. And someone's bound to notice I've been conspicuous by my absence.'

'I suppose you have a point. Hope it's not wrecked your romantic weekend too much.'

'A decapitated corpse does tend to put a dampener on things. But, no, it's fine. I've said I'll go back there tonight and I was planning to head home tomorrow anyway. So I'll do that and then come in.'

'You still don't need to. I think you're right about showing your face here, but nobody but me and the team will know you're still on holiday tomorrow. We're not going to grass you up.'

'That's a less reassuring thought than you imagine. But I can't let something like this happen and stay away.'

They were standing outside Gordon Prebble's house. His driveway was filled with police and other vehicles, and the site was being fully sealed off. 'At least we've got a proper crime scene,' McKay said. 'Doesn't seem much doubt that the killing happened *in situ*.'

'There's no delicate way of asking this,' Grant said. 'But did they find the head?'

'It wasn't exactly lost. The force of the blow or blows had knocked it into the corner of the room. But our witness wasn't exactly in a state to register that.'

'How is she?'

'Recovering, I think. I left Ginny looking after her. Thought that might be more effective than trying to do it myself.'

'Sound thinking, Alec. So who is this woman?'

'Claims she was here as his cleaner. Though I'm a little unclear what sort of cleaner comes on Christmas Sunday or whatever we're supposed to call today.'

'What's she like?'

'Young. Well, young by my standards, anyway, and even younger by Gordon Prebble's standards. Attractive.'

'You think she was doing more than cleaning?'

'She might just be a dab hand with a mop and feather duster. Just seems an odd time to come. But that's a question for later.'

'We don't think she's a suspect?'

'I can't see it. For a start, there's no blood on her. I've left the scene to the examiners for the moment, but by all accounts there's not much of the room left untouched by blood splatters. It's hard to imagine that whoever did the deed wouldn't have been similarly covered. In any case, she seems genuinely traumatised by it.'

'So what do we know about Gordon Prebble? The name rings a bell.'

'So it should. He's another of our legitimate businessmen. Similar to Hamish Forres, though even murkier. He's another who's managed to avoid any formal dealings with us, but he's come into our sights more than once. Including when we were looking into Donaldson's associates at the start of the year.'

'So very like Forres, then?'

'Very. Which means that we're starting to see a pattern developing.'

'Middle-ranking dodgy businessmen being bumped off?'

'Middle-ranking is right. These aren't big players. Mind you, neither was Donaldson, really. He'd just carved out his own little niche up here in the backwoods. These were people who did all right for themselves without ever troubling the big boys too much.'

Grant gestured towards the house. 'Must've been doing okay, though? It's a decent place.'

'Aye, it's not bad. It would have cost a bob or two with that view. But it's not exactly a mansion. Same as Forres's place. Although I think both of them probably also had cash stashed safely away offshore somewhere. Looks like neither he nor Prebble really got to enjoy their ill-gotten gains.'

'My heart bleeds.' Grant had been watching the activity around the house. There was plenty going on, including a team searching the moorlands surrounding the house. 'What about the murder weapon?'

'According to Jock Henderson, it was most probably an axe. Would probably have taken several blows to actually sever the head.' He gestured towards the far side of the house. 'There's a log store over there and no sign of an axe so that might be the source. We've not found any sign of it. That's why I asked them to look at the moorland. It might have just been tossed away.'

'How many people have you been able to get up here?'

'Not enough. I recalled the team who'd been doing the door-to-doors in Cromarty because I thought this was a higher priority, but it's robbing Peter to pay Paul. I hate bloody Christmas.'

'This one seems to be becoming bloodier than most. Why the hell would you decapitate someone? There are much easier ways to kill.'

'I bow to your expert opinion,' McKay said. 'But yes. And Prebble was a big man. I can't imagine he'd have leaned over for the haircut very willingly.'

'Any sign of a struggle in there?'

'A little, according to Jock. A chair knocked over, the table at an angle. It looks as if Gordon Prebble probably didn't go quietly.' McKay shrugged. 'Which wouldn't be surprising. Prebble was a nasty piece of work. I mean physically nasty. The closest we got to him was a couple of times on assault and GBH charges, but in both cases the victims were – well, let's say less than co-operative.'

'You think they'd been got at?'

'I'm sure of it. But we could never prove it, and they were pretty small-beer charges. Not even like getting Al Capone for tax dodging. Not worth the effort. But he had a reputation for violence. He wouldn't have been easy to subdue, especially if someone was coming for him with a bloody great axe. I don't imagine anybody's going to miss him too much, except for maybe young Sacha in the car over there.' He paused. 'I should go and see if she's up to a chat.'

'I'll leave you to it, then.' Grant smiled. 'And, Alec, thanks for not dragging me back into work.'

'You came anyway,' McKay said. 'Despite everything I said.'

'It may have escaped your attention, Alec, but I'm the senior officer here. It's not up to you to tell me what to do.'

'As if I'd dare.'

'But thanks again for trying to respect my holiday. It was appreciated.'

'Aye. It's the thought that counts.'

29

McKay opened the rear passenger door and slid inside the car.

The woman they so far knew only as Sacha was huddled at the far end of the seat, her face white, her eyes apprehensive. She was a striking figure, McKay thought. Perhaps in her late twenties with a face that wouldn't have embarrassed a supermodel. At the moment, she mainly looked terrified. McKay couldn't immediately work out whether she was more terrified by what she'd seen or by the prospect of dealing with a police officer. He exchanged a glance with Ginny Horton in the front passenger seat.

'Sacha?' McKay had spoken softly but her response suggested he might almost have punched her in the stomach. Eventually she nodded.

'Do you have a surname?'

She hesitated. 'I call myself Barnett now.'

'But that's not your real name?'

'It is now. I wanted to leave my past behind.'

'Are you in the country illegally?'

'All legal. I was granted asylum. This is years ago. Gordon –

Mr Prebble – he helped me to gain citizenship. He's a good man.'

McKay wasn't about to argue the toss. He could imagine why Prebble had helped this attractive young woman, and what he might have demanded in return. They could check in due course, but McKay's instinct was that Sacha's claims were on the level. She must have known any lies would be quickly exposed.

'Tell us exactly what happened today, if you feel up to it.'

'I had an arrangement to do work for Gordon – Mr Prebble...'

'What sort of work?'

'I do various things for him.' She stopped. 'I did, I mean. Cleaning, tidying up. I cook him meals till my next visit. Stuff that can be frozen. He's not very domesticated–' She halted again. 'He wasn't.'

'You arrived here at the appointed time? You weren't put off by the snow?'

'I hate to let Gordon down.'

Not as much as he'd have hated being let down, McKay thought. 'So you let yourself in. Mr Prebble had given you a set of keys?'

'No, he won't give me any keys. I thought at first it was because he didn't trust me, but I don't think he trusted anyone.'

'How did you get in?'

'I rang the bell but there was no answer. The door was unlocked so I came inside. I thought Gordon might be angry if I came in but I was worried. I came into the living room and I saw... that...'

'It must have been a shock.'

'It was horrible. There was blood everywhere and...'

'I'm sorry,' McKay said. 'What did you do then?'

'I didn't do anything at first. I was too shocked. I was scared because I thought... whoever had done it might be in the house.'

She shook her head, as if remonstrating with herself for her own foolishness. 'I went to my car and I called 999.'

'You did the right thing,' McKay said. 'It was best that you left the house. You didn't disturb the scene which makes it easier for us to gather evidence.' He spoke slowly, unsure how much Sacha was taking in.

'You said the front door was unlocked,' Horton said. 'Was that unusual?'

Sacha looked up as if baffled by the question. 'He wouldn't have left it unlocked. He didn't do that.'

'He was concerned about his security?'

'He said it was very isolated up here and he didn't take any chances.'

'Did he have any specific concerns?' McKay asked. 'Did he talk about any particular threats?'

'He was a wealthy man. I guess he was afraid of being burgled. He'd always been like that. But he seemed to have got worse recently.'

'In what way?'

'I don't know. More worried, I suppose. He always wanted to make sure the doors were properly locked, the alarms were on...'

'This had become more extreme recently?'

'I think so. He wanted to check the doors even after I'd come in.'

'When do you think the change occurred?'

'The last month or so, maybe?'

'Was there anything that prompted the change? Anything you saw?'

'Nothing I saw. But Gordon didn't share much with me.'

'You've known him for some time?'

'A few years, yes.'

'How did you meet him?'

'I can't remember exactly...'

McKay had no doubt she was lying, but he knew if he pushed harder she'd probably clam up entirely. He suspected there was plenty of interest in Sacha's past. She spoke good English, but there was an accent he couldn't immediately identify. Eastern European or further east?

'How long have you worked for Mr Prebble like this?' McKay asked Sacha.

'Like this? Three, four years.' McKay could see she was weighing up what more to say. 'He helped me. But I am doing okay. I have other jobs too now. Cleaning jobs,' she added, as if expecting McKay to offer some alternative suggestion. 'I work hard now.'

'I'm sure you do. Where do you live?'

'Dingwall. Your colleague has my address.'

'Quite a drive for you here,' McKay said. 'Especially on a day like today. You're clearly very conscientious.'

'Mr Prebble expects me to come,' Sacha said before correcting herself. 'Expected, I mean.'

'Did you see any other vehicles near the house?'

She thought for a moment. 'I passed a few other cars. Had to stop on the single-track road to let them pass.' She closed her eyes, as if trying to summon up the images of the cars she'd seen. 'There was one with a man and a woman in it. I remember them because I stopped in one of the passing places so they could pass, but they didn't wave to thank me. It seemed rude in conditions like that.'

It was normal practice in the area, as in most rural areas, to behave courteously towards other drivers on the narrow back roads, and that generally included an exchanged wave of acknowledgement when someone was good enough to wait for you to pass. 'Can you recall anything about them or about the car?'

'Not really. I was focusing on the road once they'd passed. It was a big car, I think.'

'Big like a people carrier? One of those cars you can fit a family into?' McKay asked.

'I think so. Something like that.'

'What about the couple? Any impression of them? Young, old? Anything about their faces? Glasses, facial hair?' He stopped, wanting to prompt but not lead her memories.

She thought again. 'Young, I think. I mean, perhaps my age.'

'If it's not too rude, can I ask how old you are?'

'Twenty-eight,' Sacha said.

'So late twenties or something like that?'

'I think so. Not teenagers but not–'

'An old wrinkly like me,' McKay said. 'Or my colleague over there.' Ginny Horton was in her mid-thirties. She stuck her tongue out at him, hidden from Sacha by the headrest on her seat.

'Younger than you, yes,' Sacha said. 'A little younger than your colleague, perhaps.' Horton offered him a smug grin.

'That's helpful. Anything else?'

'Glasses,' Sacha said. 'The woman. She was wearing glasses, I think. Big ones with thick frames. She looked clever.' She frowned. 'It's hard to be sure. I think I remember things but I don't know.'

As far as McKay was concerned, that was preferable to witnesses who related their recollections with absolute certainty. Witnesses were unreliable, their memories always fallible. The best were those, like Sacha, who recognised that fact. 'Just give me your impressions. Don't try to overthink it. What about the man?'

She closed her eyes again. 'I'm not sure. No facial hair, I think. I've an impression of him being tall...'

'But you only saw him in the car? Was he driving?'

'He was driving. He was nearer to me. His head just looked higher than the woman's. Notably so. That's what made me think he was tall...' She tailed off, and McKay decided he'd extracted as much as he was likely to from her.

'Thank you, Sacha. That's very helpful.'

'I want you to catch them. The people who did this.'

'You must have been very fond of Mr Prebble,' McKay said.

There was a prolonged silence, and McKay was unsure how Sacha was going to respond. Finally, she just gave a slight shake of the head, which might or might not have been an answer to his question. 'He was a good man,' she said, after another moment.

30

Helena Grant finally arrived back at Bill's at around 8pm. McKay had kept insisting she should head off, but she'd felt obliged to remain at the crime scene until they'd had a debrief with Jock Henderson. Not that Henderson had had much to tell them beyond what they already knew – that Prebble had been decapitated by several blows from a sharp instrument, most probably an axe. The killing would have required some significant physical strength, especially if Prebble was also being physically restrained. However, there were also signs of a substantial head trauma so Henderson speculated Prebble might already have been unconscious.

'Aye,' McKay said. 'I'd have hated for Prebble to have suffered unduly.'

'Makes sense, though,' Grant said. 'Prebble was no youngster but I'm guessing he'd have resisted strongly if someone was trying to cut his head off.'

'Hell of a way to go, though,' Henderson commented. 'There are simpler and easier ways to kill someone.'

'I'll take your word for that, Jock.' McKay had been chewing on his trademark gum. 'But complicated and high effort seem to be the fashion these days. Christ knows why.'

Beyond that, there was little new. There were traces of blood in the hallway, presumably left by the killers on their departure, but fewer and less obvious than Henderson might have expected. They'd found a number of fingerprints in the house, the majority of which belonged to Prebble. The remainder would be collated and checked, with Sacha's also to be eliminated. 'Early days,' Henderson concluded cheerfully. 'There's plenty to go at. Nice to have a proper crime scene to work on for a change.'

'As long as we keep you happy, Jock,' McKay said. 'It's my only goal in life.'

'Well, there's a very simple way you could do that just now. Let me get on with my work.'

Grant had left them to it, deciding there was little more she could contribute. She'd been unsure whether she should stay with Bill again tonight, or just return home so she could head into work from there in the morning. But Bill had been keen for her to stay, and she'd wanted to stick with their original plan as far as possible. She would go into the office in the morning, but McKay had made it clear that nobody would expect her early.

Bill had insisted on giving her a set of house keys so she was able to let herself in. She'd called Bill during the return journey to let him know she was on her way, and as she entered the hallway she could smell the pleasant aromas of dinner being prepared. 'Bill! I'm back.' *Christ*, she thought, *I sound like the wife in a cosy sitcom.*

She walked down the hall and peered into the kitchen. There was a pot boiling on the stove, but no sign of Bill. She made her way to the living room.

He was standing by the uncurtained window with his phone in his hand. He'd clearly just ended a call and was looked distracted. But as he turned towards her, his face broke into a smile. 'Glad you're back. I missed you.'

She immediately felt reassured by the warmth of his expression. 'I've only been gone a few hours. You'll have to get used to that.'

'I suppose so. I'm sorry our weekend's been interrupted, though.'

'Me too. But you'll need to get used to that too. It goes with the job.' It occurred to her that, although neither of them had openly acknowledged it, they were already talking as if they were in it for the long haul.

'I should know. I've written about it often enough. Isn't that what usually drives the grizzled cynical cop to drink? Speaking of which...' He gestured towards the coffee table which held an open, expensive-looking bottle of French red and two wine glasses.

'Do I look that grizzled and cynical?'

'We can grow grizzled and cynical together.' He crossed to the table, slipping his phone into his pocket, and poured the wine. He lowered himself onto the sofa, and she moved to sit beside him.

'All okay?' she said.

'Think so. Especially now you're back.'

'You seemed to be on the phone when I came in.' She wasn't sure whether it was even appropriate to mention this, given he hadn't acknowledged it. She didn't want to seem to be prying. On the other hand, she thought, if they were getting really serious about the relationship, surely anything he did ought to concern her.

'Nothing important. Just more publishing stuff. There's always something.'

'Nothing bad, I hope.'

'Nothing that won't get sorted. It's always the little things that are trickiest to resolve. Now, I should tell you about supper.'

'You should.'

'I've made a bouillabaisse. Or maybe a zarzuela. A fish stew, anyway. With all the trimmings, including roast potatoes. And then a creme caramel. Or maybe a Spanish flan. So very French, or possibly Spanish.'

'It sounds very cosmopolitan.'

'My cooking tends to be good but geographically imprecise.'

'I can live with that. It sounds delicious either way.'

'Won't be long, anyway. How was your day? As grisly as it sounded?'

She'd told Bill only the barest minimum about why she'd decided to go to the murder scene, but she'd felt she had to tell him enough to justify her unplanned departure. 'Fairly grisly, yes.'

'God, this is... what, the third of these now?'

'We don't know if they're connected. They're all very different.'

'But all bizarre. That can't be coincidence, surely?'

'We just don't know yet. It's important we don't jump to conclusions. It's been a challenge for us to make any progress at all over Christmas.'

'I guess that might not be accidental. Perhaps the killer's all too aware of how under-resourced you are over Christmas.'

'That sort of stuff appeals to you crime writers, Bill, but it's usually not that sophisticated.' She was keen to move the conversation on, but she wondered if Bill did actually have a point. The killings they usually dealt with were far from sophisticated, but these seemed in a different category. Whatever the motives behind them, the murders had been meticulously planned. That planning might well have included timing the killings to coincide with one of the most challenging times of year for the police.

He smiled at her. 'I can take a hint. You don't want to talk shop.'

'It's been a hell of an afternoon and I'd rather just put it behind me.'

'I know. My professional curiosity keeps getting the better of me. Sorry.'

'No worries. But it would be nice to talk about something else tonight. Anything else, really. Anything that doesn't remind me that I've got to throw myself back into it tomorrow.'

'Don't you enjoy it?'

'Enjoy isn't quite the word. I always thought it was what I was born for. But this weekend's made me wonder if there's more to life.'

'There's always more to life,' Bill said. 'Though I'd hate to see you give up the day job. I was hoping to gain some inspiration from you.'

'I hope that's not all you see in me.'

'No, that's just a very small bonus.'

'I hope so, or you might find yourself disappointed.'

Bill had clearly got the message. 'No expectations at all, except that you're suitably appreciative of my food.'

'No problems there, then.'

'In that case, I'd better go and get it ready to serve.'

He departed for the kitchen and she sat sipping her wine. She'd noticed Bill had left his mobile on the table. She was momentarily tempted to pick it up, see if it was locked, perhaps check who he'd been talking to earlier before she entered the room. It wasn't nosiness, she told herself. It was just wanting to know everything she could about him. She wanted to know him as fully as possible.

But she resisted the temptation. It would be wrong. It would suggest she didn't trust him. And in any case, she smiled to herself, the phone was sure to be locked.

31

Gary Forres drove back up to the Highlands early on Monday morning, even though the police had advised that he was unlikely to be allowed immediate access to his father's house. He knew the examiners had been going over the place seeking evidence about what had happened on the day of his father's disappearance.

He was planning to stay overnight, as he'd arranged with the police to visit their offices in Inverness the following day to give a statement and, more painfully, to provide formal confirmation of his father's identity. All the local hotels were closed in the new lockdown, but the police had arranged for him to stay at a small hotel in Inverness as an essential traveller. Even if the house had been accessible, he wouldn't have wanted to spend the night there. Not yet. It was all too raw.

His wife had tried to persuade him not to return just yet. 'Give it a few days to sink in,' she'd said. 'You'll be able to cope with it better then.' But she'd clearly known she was wasting her time. He'd done his best to ensure the kids had a more or less normal Christmas, even after he'd received the news. The children had known something was wrong and had guessed it was something involving their granddad. But Gary had maintained the pretence that everything was okay while in their presence. It was only after they'd finally gone to bed on Christmas Night that he'd allowed his true feelings to show.

Even now though, he was unsure what those feelings actually were. Grief, certainly. Loss and bereavement, obviously. But also bafflement that this should have happened to his father. And, behind all that, something else he hadn't initially been able to identify. It had taken him some time to realise what he was feeling was something close to resentment. Resentment that his father had allowed this to happen.

In Gary's eyes, even as a child, Hamish had always seemed a rather mundane figure. A businessman engaged in unfathomable work that dragged him away from home too often, and left him tired and uncommunicative when he was there. Worse still, from Gary's perspective, Hamish didn't even try to make his work sound glamorous or interesting. He was just a 'pen-pusher', he'd told Gary, a 'desk-wallah'. Gary hadn't even understood the phrases, but he'd known they weren't something you could boast about at school.

As he'd grown older, though, he'd begun to resent Hamish's work for almost the opposite reason. He couldn't recall when or how he'd first picked up the idea that his father's business activities weren't entirely kosher. Maybe it was a comment from one of his school friends – at least one had been the son of a police officer. Or maybe it had been something Hamish himself had said in an unguarded moment. Maybe it was just the way his father had behaved. He was ultra-cautious, always wanting to know what Gary was up to, who he was mixing with. He never wanted to go on holiday, insisting he had to be at home to keep an eye on the business. There were times when he seemed wary, almost fearful, as if expecting retribution.

Gary had never wanted to delve any more deeply into his

father's work. He'd remained curious, but a wiser part of his brain told Gary to keep his distance, not to risk opening a Pandora's box that could never be closed.

He set off early and it was only lunchtime when he arrived at the hotel, but he was able to check in and drop his luggage in his room. Although the hotel was otherwise closed, the landlady had offered to prepare a sandwich for him as there'd been nowhere open for food on the journey. The hotel overlooked the river, and as he sat eating by the window, he gazed out at the water and the road beyond. The weather had improved and the snow was slowly thawing, the sky a clear blue. A stiff breeze was blowing, the surface of the water ruffled by the wind. It was still a few days till Hogmanay, but it felt as if the year was turning, a new season beginning.

As he finished eating, his phone rang.

'Mr Forres?'

Gary had already recognised the distinctive voice of the caller. 'DI McKay.'

'You're still on your way up?'

'I'm already here. Sitting in the hotel.'

'I'm calling with some good news. The examiners have finished with your father's house so you can go in whenever you want.'

'Did they find anything?'

'Nothing very conclusive. We'll need to take your finger-prints tomorrow for exclusion purposes. No signs of any strug-gle, but you'd probably have noticed if there had been. We've also searched the house and taken away a couple of large boxes of documentation. I assume you've no objection to that?'

'I assume you'll keep me informed if you find anything significant in there?'

'As far as we can,' McKay said.

'I can go to the house now, though?' he said.

'You're free to go in and out as you please. I presume it belongs to you now?'

'As far as I'm aware. I'm the only heir. But we haven't even started thinking about the legal side yet. That's a treat in store.'

'I don't envy you that. Been through it myself a good few years back.'

'One of the many tasks for next week. Not exactly the Christmas I'd envisaged. Speaking of which, what time do you want me tomorrow?'

They confirmed the arrangements for Gary's visit to police HQ, including arrangements for Gary to provide a DNA sample to confirm that the victim was indeed his father. 'Not that there's really any doubt,' McKay said.

That prompted a thought that had been nagging, so far unarticulated even to himself, in Gary's head. 'You said you identified my father. How did you know him?'

'I had a few dealings with him over the years,' McKay responded vaguely.

'He wasn't involved in anything criminal.'

'We do talk to people who aren't criminals,' McKay said. 'Your father was a prominent businessman in the area. I spoke to him over the years in relation to various enquiries.'

McKay clearly had no intention of saying more. As they finished the call, the landlady came over to collect Gary's empty plate. She was regarding him with only partially disguised curiosity. He didn't know how much the police had told her, and he half-expected she might broach the question of why he was here. Instead she said, 'Will you be needing some food tonight? Obviously the kitchen's closed, but we can rustle something up for you.'

Gary gazed at her for a moment as if unsure what she was

talking about. 'Yes, thank you. That would be good.' He smiled and gestured towards the Cromarty Ales pump at the bar. 'I'm only sorry I won't be able to get a pint of Happy Chappy. It sounds just what I need.'

32

The silence in the house had a different quality even from the last time he'd been here. There was something distinctive about the silence of an empty house, but this felt different even from that. The last time he was here, there'd still been a chance his father would be found safe and sound.

Now Hamish was dead. He'd never return to this house, and that made the place feel different again, the silence somehow even more complete.

Gary supposed McKay was right and that the house was now his. He was intending to contact Hamish's solicitor to find out what would be happening next. The house itself must be worth a bob or two, and there was no mortgage on it as far as he was aware.

He'd half-expected that the police would have left the place a mess, but it looked little different from when he'd last been here. Various items belonging to his father had been left apparently untouched – a newspaper and a book on the table, a pair of glasses on the dresser at the side. The mobile phone had been taken for examination, but that was the only change that Gary could immediately see.

In the fridge there was a bottle of milk that was still in date, along with a few other food items – an unopened packet of mature cheddar, a half-used tub of butter, some vegetables. Gary guessed his father had been trying to use up the perishable foodstuffs prior to his going away for Christmas.

For a moment, that thought was almost unbearably poignant. Gary filled the kettle with the intention of making a coffee, partly simply because he was thirsty and partly because he wanted to make a toast to the old man. Hamish would have preferred a fine single malt, but for the moment coffee would have to do.

He was still making the coffee when the doorbell rang. Most probably one of the neighbours who'd seen Gary come in and was here to offer condolences. That was the last thing Gary really wanted at the moment. He'd hoped to be able just to sit here in silence, thinking some suitably valedictory thoughts. Sighing, he made his way to the front door.

The visitor was a young woman. She was smiling as if preparing a cheery greeting but as she saw Gary her expression changed to one of bewilderment. 'I'm sorry. I was hoping to see Hamish. My name's Kelly. I'm a friend of his.'

For a moment, Gary stared at her in silence, unsure what to say.

'You must be Gary,' she went on. 'He talks about you sometimes. I'm one of the local volunteers. I've been doing shopping for Hamish during the lockdown. Kelly Armstrong.'

Gary remembered his father mentioning the name during one of their regular phone conversations during the pandemic lockdown. 'Look, you'd better come in,' Gary said. 'I'm afraid I've some bad news.' He wasn't sure that he ought to invite her inside, but it wasn't a conversation he wanted to have on the doorstep.

'Bad news? Has something happened to Hamish?'

He led her into the kitchen. 'You'd better sit down.' He waited until she'd sat facing him at the kitchen table and then said, 'There's no easy way to say this. I'm afraid Hamish is dead.'

Her expression was one of bewilderment. 'Dead? Was he taken ill?'

'Not exactly. I'm surprised you haven't seen it on the news.' He turned from her and began to refill the kettle. The British response to any tragedy, he supposed.

'I haven't seen the news for days. Been with my mum and dad. But I don't understand. What's happened to Hamish?'

Gary took a breath, steeling himself to tell the story. 'I came to pick him up on Christmas Eve. He wasn't here. None of the neighbours had seen him. Eventually I called the police and reported him missing.'

'But he'd barely left the house since the pandemic. Where would he have gone?'

'That was why I was concerned. One of the neighbours had seen a car outside earlier that morning, so the most likely explanation is that he went out with whoever that was.'

'Who were they?'

'Your guess is as good as mine. In the end, I had to leave it in the hands of the police. There was nothing else I could do. Then on Christmas Day, I had a visit from two police officers to inform me he'd been found dead.'

'What happened to him? You said he wasn't taken ill so how else...?'

'He was murdered.' The police had asked him not to reveal any details of Hamish's killing.

'But who'd want to kill Hamish? He was just an old man–' She stopped. 'I didn't mean...'

'I know what you mean. He was just an ordinary person like me.'

'He had his wallet stolen the other day. Could that be connected somehow?'

'It doesn't look as if the motive was robbery. There's nothing missing from the house as far as I can judge, and Hamish wouldn't have had anything of significant value on him. It's baffling. But I reminded the police about the stolen wallet, so they're aware of it.' The kettle had finished boiling. 'Let me get you a tea or coffee.'

'If it's no trouble. Tea's fine. Hamish used to make a cup of tea for us both, once I was allowed to come inside.' She was silent for a moment. 'I still can't believe it.'

He brought the tea over to the table. 'I'm the same. I'd spoken to him the night before and he seemed the same old Hamish. A bit cantankerous, but that was just the way he was. You must have seen him earlier that day. How did he seem to you?'

'The same as ever, really. He was a bit annoyed about the wallet, but he didn't seem worried about anything else as far as I could tell.'

'I imagine the police might want to talk to you.'

'I'm not sure how much I can tell them.' She paused. 'Although, thinking about it, I'm probably one of the last people to see him alive.'

'I suppose it's some sort of blessing that it was someone like you.'

'I'm not sure everyone will agree with that.'

Gary had been sitting with his back to the kitchen door. While Kelly had been speaking those last words, he'd half-registered a sound behind him.

He was turning to look when he felt a shove to the side of his head. Startled, he fell sideways from his chair, stumbling onto the floor. Something was thrown over his face, and he felt hands forcibly holding his head down on the ground. He struggled to regain his equilibrium, lashed out with his hand, but someone seized his wrist, roughly pulling back his shirt sleeve, breaking the buttons at the cuff.

A moment later, he felt a prick in his inner arm, then a sharp pain as a needle entered his flesh. He struggled for a minute longer and then, quite suddenly, he was aware of nothing else.

33

The call had come into the control room at 2.12pm. An anonymous 999 call from a mobile number reporting the finding of a body at a house in Cromarty. The caller had refused to provide more information, other than insisting the police should attend as a matter of urgency. The dispatcher had identified PC Billy McCann as currently patrolling the area. 'It sounds like a hoax,' the dispatcher had said, 'but we'd better check it out.'

'It is a hoax,' McCann had responded. 'And a pretty sick one. Do you know whose house that is?'

'Not offhand. I don't share your encyclopaedic knowledge of the residents of Cromarty.'

'No, but you should keep an eye on the logs. That house belongs to Hamish Forres, murder victim of this parish.'

'Oh, right. Does sound like someone's idea of a joke then. But you'd still better check it out. Just in case.'

As it happened, he was already on the outskirts of the town so the inconvenience was minimal. As far as he knew Forres's house was uninhabited, and he knew that until very recently, it had been sealed off as a potential crime scene. Even so, there were lights showing inside the house.

He pressed the bell. There was no immediate response. He waited a few moments and then, as he was about to press the bell again, he noticed the door wasn't quite closed. He cautiously pushed it open and peered inside.

It had occurred to McCann that he might be being set up in some way, whether for a joke or for more sinister purposes. 'Hello! Anybody in there?'

He stepped into the hallway and looked around him. The house would be gloomy even on the brightest of days, and most of the lights were on. McCann had the sense that, even if the house was unoccupied now, someone had been here very recently.

He walked down the hall and peered into the sitting room. The lights were on here, too, but the room was deserted, with no sign of recent occupancy. He continued towards the kitchen.

He pushed open the kitchen door. It was only as he took another step forward that he finally saw it. A body on the floor on the far side of the table. It was lying face down but McCann had no doubt of its identity. Gary Forres.

McCann kneeled beside Forres and checked his pulse, realising to his enormous relief that Forres was still alive. He moved Forres into the recovery position, recalling what he'd been taught in his first-aid training. His first act was to summon an ambulance, spelling out the urgency of the call. Then, hesitating just for a second, he dialled Ginny Horton's number.

'Forres?' McKay said. 'You're joking.'

'Billy McCann just phoned to update me.'

'What does he reckon?'

'Billy's first thought was an attempted suicide.'

'I spoke to him on the phone a bit earlier. He didn't sound suicidal, but I suppose people sometimes don't.'

'Billy reckoned there were no obvious signs of foul play. There was a chair on its side, but Forres probably just pulled that over when he fell. No signs of injury. He might have just keeled over. He must have been under a lot of stress.'

'He looked the fit and healthy type, but they're often the first to fall off the perch.'

'You keep telling yourself that, Alec. I'll keep on running.' Horton was a serious runner, a practice that was frequently and roundly mocked by McKay, although mainly because he didn't want to acknowledge how much he respected the commitment and effort she put into it.

'It's all a bit of a coincidence, though, isn't it?' McKay went on thoughtfully. 'What do we know about Forres's condition?'

'Billy told me that the paramedics thought it was serious, but they wouldn't commit any further than that.'

'Can we keep tabs on how he's doing?' McKay said. He was staring out of the window as if the Inverness cityscape might offer him some enlightenment.

'Is this just your innate compassion for your fellow man, or do you really think he might be part of all this?'

'Ach, you know me. Mr Compassion. As for the other question, I don't know. Just copper's gut.'

'You can take something for that, you know,' Horton said. 'But, yes, I'll make sure we get updates. Billy's going to contact Forres's wife to break the news.'

'Not been a great Christmas for them.'

'You might say that. How are we doing otherwise?'

'Not much new. Young Ben Connor's continued his work on the cameras in the area. We've found one more relevant sighting of the car on the A82, heading west. No sightings further out, so most likely heading into Inverness. But nothing to help us pin it down any further. The examiners are still working up at Prebble's. Plenty to work on, but nothing significant yet, or at least nothing Jock Henderson's deigned to share with me. Meanwhile tracking down anyone who might have known Prebble. That's looking as if it's a fairly short list. He wasn't the sociable type.'

'Have the media started connecting the dots yet?'

'Not yet. Comms have issued a couple of bland statements on the deaths so no one can accuse us of not being transparent–'

'Heaven forbid.'

'But we've not released any of the detail, and so far no one's made a big deal of it. But that's only because they're all still hung-over from Christmas. As soon as anyone looks at it properly, it'll all hit the fan. One of Helena's tasks for this afternoon: sitting down with the comms team to work out how we're going to handle it.'

'It'll take some handling. Three bizarre murders in a week.'

'We need to start making some progress. How are you doing with Forres's business stuff?'

One of Ginny Horton's designated tasks was to lead an investigation into Hamish Forres's business dealings. McKay's view was that the key to Forres's killing was likely to lie there, rather than in any more personal vendetta. 'I've really only been able to follow up what's in the public domain so far. Interesting reading, though. Quite the little network of companies he had. Most of them either wound-up or dormant now, but the kind of spider's web that's designed to enable maximum flexibility and deter anyone from delving too closely.'

'And these are just the ones he had registered in the UK,' McKay pointed out. 'I imagine the real core of his business would have been registered somewhere more tax efficient.'

'That's one of the things that struck me,' Horton said. 'Most of the businesses had substantial turnover but very low or non-existent profitability. He wouldn't have got rich from any of these.'

'I don't pretend to understand business, but I guess it depends how much he was able to siphon off in other ways. Don't think it's that unusual for businesses to have low profitability. Minimises the corporation tax. I've really no idea how wealthy Forres really was. Word was that he lived fairly frugally to help keep the revenue off his back but that there was a lot more stashed away. Maybe that was true or maybe it was just business bullshit. If it was true, I wonder how accessible that money is now.'

'I was having a look at the directors of these various companies. A lot of them are basically just Forres, though there are a few other names scattered about.'

'Something for us to follow up.'

'One other thing. As far as I could see, there's just one live company in there.'

'Really? Thought he'd retired to a life of leisure.'

'Except for this one company.'

'Still trading?'

'The last accounts are nearly a year ago. But it clearly was then. It's like the others. Substantial turnover but overall it made a small loss. Same in previous years. Sometimes a marginal profit, sometimes a marginal loss. From the published accounts, there's no way of telling where the money's coming from or going to.'

'Something for us to look at, then. Is this another solo venture of Forres's?'

'Actually, no. There are two directors listed. Forres and someone called Simon Crawford.'

'Crawford? That's another name that rings a bell.'

'I looked him up. Accountant, apparently.'

McKay sat down, dropping his head into his hands.

'You okay?' Horton said.

'I'm thinking.'

'Ah, no wonder you look so stressed. I imagine it's been a while.'

'He's another one.'

'Another what?'

'Another one who drifted into our sights during the Donaldson enquiry.'

'I don't remember him.'

'The rumour was that he was basically the accountant to the stars. Or at least to the dodgy business types round here. He's got a legitimate practice over the other side of Inverness somewhere, but the rumour is he's also got a shadow practice helping his clients clean up their sometimes rather grubby earnings, as well as finding them lucrative places to stash the money.' McKay had remained sitting uncharacteristically still, his eyes fixed on the ground. 'I wonder whether Gordon Prebble was one of his clients.'

'You think he might have been?'

'I think it's likely. Prebble is exactly the kind of client Crawford would have been interested in. Perhaps we should go and pay him a visit.'

'You just don't want to be here when Helena comes back from comms.'

'Sometimes, Ginny,' McKay said, 'I think you know me too well.'

34

'Our local business types may be small fry in the bigger scheme of things,' Ginny Horton said. 'But they seem to know how to live.'

They had turned off the main road and were heading up the narrow track to Simon Crawford's house. Horton was beginning to have her doubts. They'd driven a good quarter of a mile since leaving the main road, and Horton was beginning to suspect they'd taken a wrong turning.

'That looks like the place.' McKay pointed ahead of them to where two white towers had loomed into view.

'Blimey. Looks like a castle.'

It turned out to be a large and imposing house, if not quite a castle. Horton pulled up in front of it. 'Not bad.' She turned and looked behind them. 'Nice view.'

'You sound like the world's least enthusiastic estate agent.' McKay climbed out of the car and looked around. 'No one's here to greet us. I'd have thought they'd have seen us coming.'

'Assuming anyone's in,' Horton said.

Much of the snow had thawed as the temperature had gradually risen, but there was still a coating on the hillsides around them. 'You're right about the view, though. "The house benefits from spectacular views of Loch Ness, home of the famous Loch Ness Monster." That's how you do it.'

McKay led them up the path from the gravelled parking area. The house and garden were well maintained, and McKay suspected that some significant money had been spent on the place in the not-too-distant past. Crawford clearly wasn't short of dosh.

The front of the house was dominated by a substantial porch at the top of a short flight of steps. McKay pressed the bell, waited for a few moments, then pressed again, holding it down for longer.

'Looks like there's no one home,' Horton said from behind him.

'Looks like it.' McKay trotted back down the steps and made his way around the house, occasionally stopping to peer in one of the windows. 'No sign of life,' he said. 'Though there are a few lights on.' He continued around the house till he arrived back at the front door.

'The question is,' McKay said, 'if he's out, why is his car in the garage out there?'

'Is it?'

'Maybe he's got more than one car. He's obviously not short of a few quid.'

'Maybe.' McKay had climbed up to the front door again. He pressed his finger on the bell and held it down for another minute. Eventually he released his finger and stepped back. Then he tried the handle of the imposing front door.

To his surprise, the door opened. McKay glanced back at Horton, then peered inside. The wide hallway was empty. McKay pushed open the door and walked in.

'You can't just walk in,' Horton protested. 'He's obviously just out somewhere.'

'We're police officers, Ginny. Here to keep an eye on the place as a civic duty. I'm sure he'd want that.'

'I'll leave you to do the explaining.'

'In the meantime, we might as well have a look around.' McKay peered around the hallway. 'Nice place, isn't it?'

'Too nice for the likes of us to be wandering round in.'

Ignoring her, McKay peered into what was clearly the main living room. It was tidy, filled with what to McKay's inexpert eye looked like expensive furniture. 'Very tasteful,' he muttered to no one in particular.

He left the living room and pushed open the door of what turned out to be the kitchen. 'Ah.' His tone was that of Sherlock Holmes finally finding the clue that he'd known would be there all along.

'What is it?'

'I'm no culinary expert,' McKay said, 'but I think that pan will need throwing out.'

Acrid smoke hung in the air, and the room was unnaturally warm. McKay had already spotted the cause – a saucepan set on a lit but thankfully low electric ring. He pulled a plastic disposable glove from his pocket, slipped it on and carefully turned off the ring. Then he turned back to Horton who was standing in the kitchen doorway watching him with curiosity.

'I think it was soup,' he said, 'though I wouldn't like to guess what sort. Now, it's mainly charcoal.'

Horton was looking at the workplace next to the cooker. 'That looks like it's on its way to being a cheese and pickle sandwich.' There was a loaf of bread from which two slices had been cut. Some cheese had been similarly sliced, with the open packet sitting next to the plate. An opened jar of pickle sat beside that.

McKay frowned. 'From the state of this soup, I'd say it's been here at least overnight. What sort of person gets halfway through making a meal, leaves the soup simmering on the cooker, and then buggers off for a day?'

'Someone very forgetful?'

'How old's Crawford?'

'His date of birth was on the Companies' House site. Late thirties, from what I remember.'

'Even I'm not this forgetful. Let's check the rest of the house.'

It took them only a few minutes to complete a cursory initial search of the remaining rooms. There was no sign of Simon Crawford, and no obvious explanation for his absence.

'It does happen,' Horton pointed out. 'You get interrupted in the middle of something, end up rushing out to deal with some crisis, and forget you've left something on the stove. It doesn't necessarily imply foul play.'

'Not necessarily,' McKay agreed. 'But it's not the first mysterious absence we've had to deal with in recent days. This is uncannily like Hamish Forres's disappearance.'

'Except that Gary Forres had good reason to expect his father to be there. We've no particular reason to expect Crawford to be here, except that he appears to have been halfway through preparing a meal.'

'I've a bad feeling about it, that's all.'

'That's why we're here, isn't it? Because you had a bad feeling about this.'

'Let's go and check outside again.'

As they approached the front door, McKay stopped to check a range of outdoor coats hanging on a rack beside the doorway. There were several coats there, but there was no way of knowing if any was missing. Similarly, there was a selection of shoes and boots on the floor below, including a pair of walking boots, but it was impossible to tell if any had been removed. McKay didn't even know whether Crawford lived alone, although he thought the house had a distinctly male feel.

He stepped back out into the bright afternoon and walked across to the garage he'd noticed on the previous circuit of the house. It was a single garage, largely filled by the bulk of a recently registered Land Rover Discovery. The car was locked, and there was no sign it had been driven recently. McKay peered in through the passenger window, but the interior of the car was deserted.

There were no other outbuildings at the rear of the house, other than a small shed at the edge of the garden. McKay walked across the snow-covered lawn and tried the shed door. The handle was stiff but eventually he forced open the door. There was nothing inside but a collection of garden tools and large lawnmower.

'Anything?' Horton was still standing by the steps to the front door.

He closed the shed door and walked back over to her, shaking his head. 'Nothing.'

'What do you think?'

'I don't know. We don't have enough to call it in as a missing person. All we've got is an unlocked front door and a half-prepared meal.'

'So what do we do?'

'It doesn't feel right to me. But I think all we can do for the moment is keep an eye on the place.' He climbed back up the steps to the front door. He stopped at the top of the steps and pulled out a notebook. He scribbled a short note, tore out and folded the sheet, and then left it in a conspicuous spot on the floor just inside the front door. He'd already checked the lock on the door. There was a deadlock, but also a simpler latch which he could use to secure the door, without preventing him from gaining access later if he needed to.

'I've asked him to call me urgently when he gets back.'

'I had a look at his website. It's fairly basic, but there's a number for him on there.'

'Even better.'

'You're serious about this, aren't you?'

'We've had three deaths in a week. I'm not keen to have another one.'

'We might have four already,' she reminded him. 'Depending on what's happened to Gary Forres.'

'You always know how to brighten my day, Ginny. I suppose we'd better check.' He pulled out his phone, flicked through his contacts and found the number for the hospital at Raigmore. 'The last time I used this number, it was you lying in hospital.'

'Don't remind me,' Horton said. 'That all came much too close to home.'

It took McKay a few minutes to be transferred to the ward where Forres was staying. 'DI Alec McKay,' he said. 'I'm just trying to get an update on Gary Forres's condition.'

'His condition's improved over night. Quite considerably so, in fact. He's still in the ICU for the moment, but we're hoping to be able to release him to a general ward if there are no further problems.'

'We'd like to speak to him,' McKay said. 'When do you think he'll be up to that?'

'Not today,' the nurse said firmly. 'He's still unconscious.'

'Do we have any more clues as to the cause of his illness?'

There was another pause while presumably the nurse weighed up the ethics involved in answering his question. 'Nothing definite,' she said finally, 'and you'll really have to talk to the consultant. But we don't think it's natural causes.'

McKay did his best to keep his voice neutral, while signalling to Horton that he was hearing something potentially significant. 'Really?'

'That's what the consultant said. They did some initial checks, There's no sign of any heart problems or similar. He hasn't had a stroke. He appears to have simply collapsed. It was touch and go for a short while, but then he rallied and has been improving. They're still trying to work out what the problem might be.'

'So what diagnosis do they think it's likely to be.'

'Well, that's the point,' the nurse said. 'They think the cause is something he's consumed or which has somehow entered his body...'

'You mean drugs?'

'I couldn't really say.' The nurse's tone was that of someone who fears she might have already said more than was wise. 'But that was one of the explanations being talked about. Apparently there are several drugs that could cause this effect.'

'Are we talking about something self-administered?'

'Again, it's really not for me to say. But the consultant seemed to think not. He thought that because of the timescales involved it was more likely to be something administered intravenously by a third party.'

'Would it be possible for me to speak to the consultant?'

'I'll track him down and get him to call you back.'

'Please make sure he understands it's urgent.' McKay glanced at his watch. 'In fact, I'm currently heading back to police HQ at Raigmore. It'll probably take me about twenty-five minutes. If he hasn't phoned me back by then, I'll pop into the hospital and come in to speak to him directly.'

'He is very busy–'

'I appreciate that. But I've a hunch that at least one more life might depend on finding out what actually happened to Gary Forres.'

35

McKay and Horton were five minutes from police HQ when McKay's phone rang. Horton was driving, allowing McKay to check the screen before answering. He nodded to Horton and smiled.

'DI McKay? This is Mark Livingstone from Raigmore.'

'Ah, Dr Livingston, I presume.'

'You can call me Mark. And, yes, I have heard that joke before.'

McKay smiled. 'Thanks for getting back to me.'

'I was given the impression I didn't have much choice. But I'm only too happy to help. In fact, if it's not inconvenient to you, I was going to suggest you pop into the hospital anyway. It's probably easier than trying to talk on the phone. You shouldn't have any difficulty parking today.'

'We'll be there in a couple of minutes.'

Livingstone told them where to find him, and Horton diverted from their route to turn into the Raigmore site. A few minutes later they'd found their way to the ward that he'd indicated. A nurse directed them to a consulting room along the corridor.

Livingstone looked up as they appeared at the door. 'DI McKay, I presume?'

'Good to meet you. This is my colleague, DS Horton.'

'Not a room to encourage social distancing, I'm afraid.' He sat down opposite them. 'So you're interested in Gary Forres.'

'How is he?' McKay asked.

'He'll survive,' Livingstone said. 'But he was lucky.'

'The nurse I spoke to suggested he might have been drugged.'

Livingstone paused for a moment. 'Can I ask why you're interested in Mr Forres's condition? You'll appreciate that, while I'm happy to be as co-operative as possible, I also have to take account of patient confidentiality.'

'Partly I'm just concerned about Mr Forres's well-being. As you may be aware from the media, we're investigating the death of Mr Forres's father.'

'I wondered if there was a connection. Is Gary Forres involved in the investigation?'

'We have our own code of confidentiality, Mr Livingstone. But, no, not directly. I was due to interview him tomorrow though only as a potential witness. But I'm intrigued by what's happened to him. He was found by one of our officers whose first thought was that Gary Forres had tried to take his own life. I have to say that I'd spoken to him only shortly before he was found and he hadn't sounded suicidal.'

'To be honest,' Livingstone said, 'that doesn't prove very much. It's often difficult to tell much about someone's state of mind from the way they talk. But I think it's very unlikely that this was a suicide attempt. That's why I was keen to talk to you. I think this was attempted murder.'

McKay glanced at Horton. 'I think you'd better explain what you mean.'

'I don't have much doubt that Forres was drugged. We don't

know yet exactly what drug. We've taken blood samples that we're getting analysed but my money's on something like sodium thiopental.'

'Isn't that the truth drug?' Horton asked.

'Historically, it was used for that. It's a quick-acting barbiturate, used mainly for anaesthetic purposes these days. It's also part of the cocktail of drugs used for execution by lethal injection in the US, and some states have developed protocols using only sodium thiopental.'

'Forres was injected with this sodium whatever-it-is?'

'Thiopental. Yes, or something of that kind. That's why I don't think this is a suicide attempt. There's some bruising on the arm where it looks as if the injection was carried out, and I don't think it would be possible for someone to inject themselves in that position. So the injection was carried out by a third-party.'

Horton said, 'Would it be possible to inject someone against their will? I mean, I know it's something that happens in films but could you do it in real life?'

'It depends. But if the victim was being restrained in some way, it would be possible. This looks like it was done hurriedly but quite skilfully.'

'When we catch up with them, I'll remember to congratulate them on their nursing skills,' McKay said. 'So if Forres was injected with this sodium thingummy, why isn't he dead?'

'Whoever did it must have slightly misjudged the dose. As I say, it's used as an anaesthetic, and in the end that's basically how it affected Forres. But I suspect it wouldn't have taken a much stronger dose to have done the job properly, assuming that was their intention. And if they didn't intend to kill him, they were taking a hell of a risk because they came very close.' Livingstone had been staring at the desk, his expression suggesting bafflement that anyone would behave in this way.

Now he looked up at McKay. 'Do you know why anyone would want to kill him?'

'I can't say we do. But then we still don't know why anyone wanted to kill his father either.'

'Is he likely to be in danger in hospital?'

'I'm afraid I can't say, Mr Livingstone. I suppose your next question is whether there's any danger to you or your colleagues?'

'I'm more concerned for my nursing colleagues than for myself,' Livingstone said. 'They're the ones who are on duty overnight. There's good security here, but it's not designed to keep out a killer. I think it's a reasonable question for me to ask.'

'I can't argue with that. We don't yet know what's behind this. In the short term, we can assume that whoever did this probably thinks they've been successful. We discovered Forres because we received an anonymous call informing us about the presence of a body at his father's address. So whoever made that call either wanted us to find Forres dead or, if they knew he wasn't dead, wanted us to get there in time. At the moment, I'm more inclined to think the former.'

'How long do you expect to keep Gary Forres in here?'

'It's difficult to say. We won't really know what condition he's in till he regains consciousness. Even then we'll need to carry out a range of tests to check what the impact's been.'

'I'll see if I can organise some police protection,' McKay said. 'Though it's not the best time of year to get the resources.'

'Tell me about it,' Livingstone said. 'Anything else I can tell you?'

'Where could they have acquired sodium thiopental?' Horton asked.

'Nowhere legally. But you can get anything on the dark net, I guess.'

'When do you think Mr Forres might be in a condition to talk to us?' McKay asked.

'I really can't say. I'm not being difficult. Until he recovers consciousness, we won't know if he's in a condition to talk to you or anyone else. But we'll let you know as soon as we think he's ready to talk.'

McKay slid a business card across the desk towards Livingstone. 'You do that. But as soon as possible. Forres is likely to have some very interesting things to tell us.'

'I understand. On that basis it's presumably in your interests as well as ours to organise some protection for him.'

McKay smiled. 'I can see why you've got all those letters after your name. I'll do what I can. We'll leave you to it. How can we contact you if we need to?'

Livingstone extracted a business card and handed it to McKay. 'I'm not sure which is stranger. The police carrying business cards or doctors carrying business cards.'

'One day I'll get used to it,' McKay said. 'But today's not the day. Thanks for your time, Mr Livingstone. It's been very useful.'

'I'm glad to hear it,' Livingstone said. 'And the next time you want to speak to me, call the mobile number on my card. It's probably easier than hassling the nurses.'

36

They arrived back at police HQ to discover that Helena Grant was about to kick off a briefing meeting in the large room on the floor below. 'You go and join it,' McKay said. 'Tell Helena I'll be along in a few minutes. I'll organise some uniformed protection for Forres.'

'That's the surest way to get you to do something, isn't it?'

'What is?'

'Organising a meeting. You'll do anything rather than attend.'

'Just prioritising, that's all.' McKay paused. 'Actually, I do think it's important we keep Forres as safe as possible. If whoever did this really did want to kill him, they might just have made their first mistake. Forres should have some interesting things to tell us.'

'I hope he's in a state to talk to us,' Horton said. 'Livingstone didn't seem too certain. I was thinking about Forres's wife and children if he doesn't make a full recovery.'

'I was thinking more about the lost evidence,' McKay said. 'But, aye, I suppose you're right.'

'You're all heart, Alec. I'll go and let Helena know you've found a good excuse to delay coming to the meeting.'

It took all of McKay's persuasive skills to extract some uniformed resource to provide protection for Forres. But eventually, with a little arm-twisting and some low-key blackmail, he succeeded. Once he'd achieved his objective, he made himself a coffee and strolled down the stairs and entered the meeting room.

'Afternoon, Alec. See you've finally deigned to join us. Why don't you come up here and keep me company.' Grant gestured to the seat beside her at the front of the room.

'Apologies,' McKay said, easing his way down the side of the room, carefully nurturing his coffee mug. 'I was delayed doing some proper work.'

'There's a first time for everything, then,' Grant said. A murmur of laughter ran round the room. 'You'd be completely forgiven if you'd thought to bring me a coffee too.'

'Ach, there's no chance of me ever being completely forgiven. What have I missed?'

'Mainly my warning that the excrement is about to hit the fan. The comms team's view is that we can't sit on this any longer. All we've done so far is issue a fairly bland statement about the bonfire death: "Police are investigating the discovery of human remains" and so on – and a similar statement about Forres's death. But there are enough witnesses to both that the rumours are beginning to leak out, and probably in more lurid form even than the truth. We've not yet made any statement on Gordon Prebble's killing. But comms are already being pestered by journalists who are adding two and two together and making some random number of their own choosing...'

'They'll do that whatever we say to them,' McKay growled.

'No doubt. But the comms view is that we need to be more transparent now.'

'What do they have in mind?'

'They're suggesting we issue a statement saying that we're now investigating potential links between the two deaths on the Black Isle. We also need to make some sort of statement about the Prebble killing, but they're advising that at this stage we don't imply any link between that and the Black Isle deaths.'

'Interesting definition of transparency,' McKay muttered.

'They're trying to keep it under control,' Grant pressed on, 'but they think the media are going to become more persistent in their questioning and more devious in how they try to get information. So if any of you receive any approaches which seem suspicious, just be careful what you say. If in doubt, refer them to comms.'

'What about public safety?' Josh Carlisle asked. 'That's going to be the hook they hang this on, isn't it? If we have two potentially linked murders, are the public in danger?'

'You're right, Josh. I've discussed that with comms. We've no reason at this stage to believe there's any risk to the wider public.'

'Can we really say that, though?' Ginny Horton asked. 'We still don't know who the first victim is. We're assuming that the murders are targeted in some way, but we can't be certain.'

'It's a fair point,' Grant said, 'but equally it doesn't look as if these are simply random killings, especially if we factor in Prebble's death. Neither Forres nor Prebble appears to have been robbed, even though both were apparently targeted in their own homes. I don't think it's in anybody's interest to stir up public anxiety about this unless and until we've reason to believe there's a wider danger. The main lesson, as always, is that we need to make some progress, and take account of each new development as it occurs.'

'Speaking of which,' McKay said quietly, 'we have a new development.'

Grant turned to him. 'I'm guessing this isn't good news.'

'It's not as bad as it might have been. And with a bit of luck, it might give us our first breakthrough. As some of you will be aware, Gary Forres, the son of Hamish Forres, was found unconscious in his father's house this morning.' He paused, holding back the punchline. 'Turns out he was drugged. Looks as if he was restrained by person or persons unknown and then injected. The good news is that it looks like the dosage wasn't sufficient to kill and he's pulled through, though the consultant's being cautious about what state he might be in and when he'll be fit to talk to us. But when he does, he should be worth talking to.'

McKay could almost feel the surge of renewed energy around the table. He knew how much the team had been frustrated by their lack of progress and the challenges of operating over the Christmas break. Those problems hadn't gone away. They'd have three days of relatively normal working, then they'd be back into the Hogmanay break, scraping together whatever resource they could while their uniformed colleagues battled with all the challenges of a Scottish New Year's Eve. But the prospect of a breakthrough, however minor, would re-energise them, at least for the present.

'None of this makes much sense,' Ginny Horton commented. 'Why would anyone want to kill Gary Forres? As far as we know, he had no links to his father's businesses.'

'Maybe that's not true,' Grant said. 'Or maybe this isn't about his father's business interests, after all.'

'Maybe not,' McKay said. 'But I do have one other bit of news that may also be pertinent. The reason why Ginny and I were unforgivably late for this meeting was because we went out to see Simon Crawford.'

'Crawford.' Grant frowned. 'Why does that name ring a bell?'

'He's another one who's been in our sights in the past. Dodgy accountant, although we've never found a way to make that stick. We came across him – or rather Ginny did – because he's a joint director of what was Hamish Forres's only live company.'

'So what did he have to say for himself?'

'He didn't. He wasn't there.'

'I think you need to work on this anecdote, Alec. It doesn't seem to have a punchline.'

'We need to work on the punchline. The point is Crawford wasn't there, but his front door was unlocked–'

Grant nodded. 'So naturally you went inside.'

'I was concerned about his welfare. No sign of him in the house, but a saucepan of soup burnt out on the cooker and a half-prepared cheese sandwich on the table. Also, his car was still there.'

'What are you saying? That he's been snatched?'

'There's no easy way of knowing, is there? Maybe he had to rush away at very short notice to deal with some emergency. Maybe he has a second car. Maybe somebody gave him a lift. All we know is that he wasn't there and the circumstances seemed – well, unusual. But not dissimilar to what happened to Hamish Forres.'

'So we can expect his body to turn up in some equally unusual circumstances in the next day or two? Is that what you're saying?' Grant asked.

'I'm just telling you the facts. I'm not even sure there's enough there for us to intervene at the moment. But it's something else to bear in mind.'

'You always know how to make life more complicated, Alec.'

'I try my best. So when's this comms statement going to be issued?'

'The plan is to issue a statement on Prebble's death tonight. No real detail except that we're investigating an apparent unlawful killing in the Inverness area. The plan is to hit the broadcast and online media this evening, and it'll be in the print media in the morning, along with the usual requests for anyone with any information to contact us. Then they'll issue a fairly low-key update on the Black Isle deaths tomorrow.'

'So we might get a flurry of calls from the public tonight?' McKay asked.

'I've geared up the control room for that, though Prebble seems to have been a bit of a loner, business aside, so not sure how much we'll actually get.'

'What about the car that Sacha Barnett saw? The people carrier. Have we found any more sightings of that?' Horton asked.

'I've been checking the cameras in the surrounding area,' Ben Connor answered from the back of the room. 'Trouble is, there are no cameras on the back roads up there, so there's really no chance of getting anything until you get back onto the A-roads around Dingwall. Even then, there's not much. We've identified a couple of VW Sharans of the right colour, but both have legitimate local licence plates. I'll follow them up, but it would seem odd for them to use a false plate for the previous killings but not this. So if the same car was involved, it looks as if they probably just managed to dodge the cameras. I'll try further afield.'

Grant nodded. 'Okay, Ben, you plug on with that. It's probably one of the most useful things we can do at present. Tomorrow's a different matter. The holidays are briefly over so we should have a bit more resource to play with. We need to get working on the door-to-doors in Cromarty and start following up as many of Forres's and Prebble's business contacts as we can. I've asked for the files on the Donaldson case earlier in the year because we looked at a lot of these people during that. We're also going through all the papers that were taken from Forres's house, though I'm guessing he was too smart to commit anything significant to paper. Right, everybody clear what they're doing? If not, come and talk to me and Alec afterwards. Any other questions?'

There were a few questions on points of detail before the meeting finally broke up and the team dispersed back to their various tasks. Grant, McKay and Horton remained seated at the head of the table.

'You really think Gary Forres might give us a breakthrough?' Grant asked.

'Seemed to be a tonic for the troops, didn't it?' McKay said. 'I hope so. The first question is if and when he'll be in a condition to talk to us. But he must have an idea who attacked him and what the circumstances were.'

'And we're assuming this must be linked to his father's murder?'

'Unless the family's managed somehow to attract the attention of two separate killers, I'd have said so.'

'I'm just surprised, given how much care and effort they put into Hamish Forres's killing, that they should have gone into this one half-cocked with the dosage.'

McKay nodded thoughtfully. 'Aye, I was wondering about that. This sodium doodah–'

'Thiopental,' Horton said.

'Aye, that one. It's used for a variety of purposes, from an anaesthetic to execution by lethal injection in the US.'

'Versatile,' Grant said.

'Well, exactly. If they'd wanted to be sure about killing him, why not give him a bigger dose so there was no margin for error. There could be many reasons for that. Maybe they could only get a limited amount. Maybe they didn't get the full dose into him for some reason. Maybe they didn't want to kill him.'

'But that makes no sense,' Grant said. 'As you say, if he recovers then he'll be able to give us information about his attackers. Why do it, if they weren't going to take it the whole way?'

'I've no idea,' McKay said. 'I'm just outlining the possibilities. But, while I was mulling on that, something else occurred to me.'

'No wonder you're looking tired, Alec. You've obviously been doing a lot of thinking.'

'Aye, I don't know what's come over me. Anyway, what occurred to me was that all the killings to date involved forms of execution.'

'That tends to be the case with killings.'

'Yes, but I mean state executions, historically at least. We've had burning, hanging, beheading and now an attempt at death by lethal injection.'

'I suppose,' Grant said doubtfully.

'Someone went to a lot of trouble to commit the murders in that way,' McKay said. 'It may be coincidence or I might be overthinking it, but it strikes me these methods were chosen deliberately.'

'To what end?' Ginny Horton said.

McKay shrugged. 'To make some kind of point? Perhaps that these are punishments?'

'But even if that gives us an explanation for Hamish Forres or Gordon Prebble, it doesn't explain Gary Forres. As far as we know, he's not been involved in anything criminal.'

'Maybe that's something for us to explore when we're able to speak to him,' McKay said.

'And we still don't have an identity for the first victim,' Grant reminded them. 'If we were able to put a name to him, it might help us pull the jigsaw together. It feels as if we're a long way from that. No fingerprints, no DNA matches. According to Jacquie Green, there's nothing distinctive about the remains – no breaks to the bones or implants or anything of that nature.

All we've got is the possibility of matching with dental records, but unless he's locally based that could be needle in a haystack stuff.'

'Feels as if we're more likely to generate leads if we focus on the other deaths for the moment,' McKay said. 'Though we don't even know for sure if all the deaths are connected.'

Grant leaned back in her seat and gave a deep sigh. 'You know, I had a very restful Christmas. First time in years. But it already feels as if the benefits are melting away.'

37

Tuesday morning dawned dull and mild. McKay drove into the office before the sun was up, but as he crossed the Kessock Bridge the sky was a deep red over the Moray Firth to the east. Some snow still lingered, but the thaw was setting in, and it felt as if Christmas was well and truly over. There was still the bacchanalia of Hogmanay to come, of course, and that had traditionally been the bigger deal up here, even if this year's celebrations were likely to be more muted.

The relative optimism he'd felt after his conversation with Mark Livingstone had faded overnight, replaced with an increasing fatalism. He'd called Raigmore first thing to check on Gary Forres's condition, and had been told that there was little change. Forres remained 'stable', whatever that might mean, but was not yet in a condition to talk. Perhaps, McKay thought, he never would be.

The nurse had told McKay that Forres's wife and children had arrived at the hospital but had been able to do nothing but sit and wait. McKay had wondered if he should go and talk to them, but had been able to think of nothing he might say that wouldn't sound either intrusive or patronising. That stuff was probably better left to people who were good at it.

He was unsurprised to see Helena Grant in the office before him. McKay thought of himself as conscientious, but Grant was in a different league. She'd still be feeling guilty about having taken time off over Christmas, however much she might have needed it. He stopped by her door and peered in. 'You're in early.'

Grant gestured vaguely towards her computer. 'No shortage of things to do.'

'I take it you didn't stay over with your fancy man last night?'

'Fancy man? Not that it's any of your business, but no I didn't.'

'Not had a falling out, I hope?'

'On the contrary. I just knew if I stayed over there I'd struggle to get into the office early.'

'Too much information. As long as it's going well.'

'I think it is,' she said. 'I had a great Christmas, and I'm going to spend Hogmanay there as well. I'm just a bit worried that I'm getting cold feet.'

'You need thicker socks,' McKay said. 'It's that time of year. But you're not really, are you?'

'It's just that it went so well it's now beginning to feel real. That makes me feel nervous.'

'Understandable,' McKay said. 'It doesn't mean it's the wrong decision. If you can get on with someone over Christmas, everything else will be a cinch.'

'Fair point. But I do need to get to know him better. I feel as if at the moment it's all a bit superficial.'

'He's a writer,' McKay said. 'Surely he talks about himself all the time?'

'He doesn't, though. I don't mean he's secretive. But he's clearly uncomfortable talking about himself.'

'You're sure he's a writer?'

'He claims so. I think he's just reserved, really. And I probably don't let him get a word in edgeways. I'm not sure he's used to dealing with someone like me.'

'You never get used to it,' McKay said. 'Most of us have just learned to defer to you.'

'I'm living for the day when you do what you're told.'

'I'm buggering off now. Just like you told me to.'

'I never told you to.'

'No, but you're thinking it.' He grinned and left her to whatever thoughts she might really have been thinking. He dumped his bag by his desk and then headed for the kitchen to make himself a coffee. Josh Carlisle was already in there, waiting for the kettle to boil.

'Morning, guv. Perfectly timed. What can I get you?'

'That's very public spirited of you, Josh. As you seem to be all out of the single malts, I'll have a coffee. Milk, no sugar.'

'I was waiting for you to come in, actually.'

McKay raised an eyebrow. 'Hope you've not been waiting long. At your age, you still need your beauty sleep. What's the trouble?'

'Not trouble exactly, but a bit of a puzzle. Got a message this morning from one of the uniforms who's been working on the door-to-doors over in Cromarty. Apparently, this guy had been delegated to go and take statements from the two who originally found Forres's body.'

'Can't imagine they'd have had much more to tell us.'

'That was what we expected.'

'Don't tell me they surprised us.'

'In a manner of speaking. They weren't there.'

'Weren't where?'

The kettle had boiled and Carlisle spent a moment pouring the water into the mugs. 'At the address they'd given us.'

'You mean they'd left?'

'They were never there.'

'Go on.'

'There was no one who matched the names we had. Alastair Farlowe and Becky Delaney. The residents of the house were an elderly couple who claimed they'd never heard of them. They'd lived in the house for twenty or more years.'

'Maybe they got the address wrong. Or we transcribed it wrong.'

'You don't normally get your own address wrong.'

'You do when you get to my age, son. Maybe we misheard.'

'It's possible,' Carlisle conceded. 'But the officer in question checked with other neighbours on the street. No one had even heard of Farlowe or Delaney. Delaney maybe not be surprising as she was only visiting. But Farlowe claimed to live there.'

McKay picked up the coffee mug which Carlisle had pushed towards him and thought back to that chilly morning on the snow-covered waterfront. A man and a woman. The man tall, thin. The woman shorter with thick heavy spectacles. 'Christ.'

Carlisle nodded. 'That's what I was thinking. But surely they wouldn't...'

'If they did, they're playing with us. They even had a bloody dog with them, for Christ's sake.' He paused, trying to come to grips with what this might imply. 'You really don't think we could have just somehow made a mistake with the street name or the number?'

'The street name, no. There's nothing else in the village that's similar, as far as I can tell. Obviously, it's possible we might have somehow made a mistake with the number, but it's a fairly short street. We've tried most of the houses, and no one had any idea who they might be. We'll check with the rest, but I suspect we're going to get the same result.'

'It would take a hell of a lot of bottle to commit a murder, tell the police you've found the body and then still be on the scene when they arrived.' He took a breath. 'But then we know they've a fair bit of bottle from the way the murder was committed.'

'It's unbelievable,' Carlisle said. 'When I first took the message, I thought the idea was insane.'

'Maybe we're both losing it,' McKay said. 'Do we know who else talked to them apart from me?' McKay felt a spasm of irritation with his own gullibility. He told himself he'd had no reason not to take the two supposed witnesses at face value, but he felt he should have scented something wrong, something that rang false.

'I'll check which of the uniforms dealt with them.'

'Thanks. And let's do a proper search on Farlowe and Delaney. I don't want to set too many hares running until we're absolutely certain they weren't who they claimed to be. This could be embarrassing enough. It'll be even more so if it turns out they're living in the next street all along.'

Carlisle nodded. 'Guv.'

'If it looks as if they don't exist, or if they weren't the couple we met that morning, then there's other stuff we need to check. Like whether there are any other sightings of the famous VW Sharan that morning. We've got it on camera heading away from Cromarty in the small hours. So did it return carrying our two friends just so they could have a laugh at our expense? Or did they return in some other vehicle? We can get Ben Connor to check that. He seems to love the camera work. And make sure we add this to the house-to-house questioning. Any sightings of either the couple or the car on Christmas Day morning.'

'Will do, guv. Anything else?'

'Do we still employ sketch artists?'

'As far as I know. Though I think they're called forensic artists now,' Carlisle said. 'Use computers, these days.'

'Of course they are and of course they do. Can you see if we can get hold of one? I've no idea what the drill is now. But, if it turns out that Farlowe and Delaney don't exist, I'd like to sit down with someone and get down what I can remember about those two. If we can do the same with the uniformed officers who spoke to them we might get something half-accurate.' He shook his head. 'Jesus, Helena's going to love this.'

By the time he'd returned to his desk, McKay had regained something of his equilibrium. Whatever his own embarrassment, it felt as if, finally, they might be starting to make progress. Tiny steps, for sure, but McKay was long enough in the tooth to know that in most investigations you needed the tiny steps before you had any chance of making the large strides. He could probably live with Helena's mockery if it meant they started to get somewhere.

The most encouraging, if also disturbing, part of this was what it said about the killers. If it really had been the murderers that he'd spoken to, only metres from the still dangling body, it suggested they were capable of taking the most extraordinary risks. That had been evident in the nature of the killings themselves. From McKay's perspective, that was encouraging because it meant that, sooner or later, they'd take one risk too many. They would make a mistake.

But it was also disturbing.

Because if they really were prepared to take these kinds of risks, he had no idea what else they might be willing to do.

38

Simon Crawford wasn't sure what had wakened him. Perhaps the first daylight creeping through the grimy window above him. The rustling in the far corner of the room behind a pile of apparently random junk. Or something else, a noise from beyond the door at the top of the stone steps.

He had no idea where he was or how he'd been brought here. He was lying on a rickety and uncomfortable camp bed. He didn't know how long he'd been here, but the aches in his body suggested a considerable time.

What the bloody hell had happened? He forced himself to sit up, ignoring the pain as he tried to clear his foggy brain. A large bottle of what looked to be clean water had been left by the side of the bed. He opened the bottle and took a large mouthful.

It was only as he tasted the water that he realised how thirsty he was. He swallowed more, gulping it down with relief. With each mouthful, he felt his mind was growing clearer. He drank a third of the bottle and then replaced the lid, conscious he had no idea how long the water might need to last.

He pushed himself to his feet, aware of a numbness in his limbs alongside the dull aches in his back and shoulders. Once upright, he forced himself to walk the length of the room several times until he felt more like his usual physical self.

Some of it was coming back to him now. The ringing of the doorbell. The woman who had claimed to be someone called Jo. Who had claimed to know him. He recalled opening the door, and then being forced backwards. Something over his face. Then nothing at all.

He looked around the room, trying to make sense of what he was seeing. It was little more than a bare cell, furnished with nothing other than the old camp bed, with a thin bare mattress and a worn old duvet. There was a single window, high in one wall, suggesting this was a cellar or basement room with the window at ground level. The window allowed in some daylight, but was too high for him to reach and there was nothing he could use to climb on.

The walls were bare plaster and the floor was concrete. Apart from the bed, there was only the pile of junk in the corner – old paint cans, some unidentifiable electrical device, a bundle of cloth he didn't want to speculate about. It was from behind there that he'd heard the scratching. Something else he didn't want to speculate about.

The entrance to the room was a single wooden door at the top of a flight of unrailed stone stairs. He climbed the stairs cautiously and tried the door. As he'd expected, it was locked with no sign of a handle on the inside. He examined the door carefully but, short of stumbling across a crowbar among the junk, he couldn't see any way he was likely to open it.

From the top of the stairs he could see through the window on the far side of the room. The view told him very little. The window looked out over an overgrown garden, but there was no way of knowing whether this building was located in the middle of a town or miles from anywhere.

Was this connected with whatever Gordon Prebble had been

worried about? Crawford had never thought of Prebble as a fearful man, even though much of the man's bluster had been little more than hot air. But he'd been deeply rattled by something, and perhaps he'd had reason to be.

But Crawford himself had received no threats, nothing to warn him this might happen.

Still standing on the stairs, he looked down at himself. He was wearing the clothes he'd been wearing when he'd been taken – just a shirt and trousers, even the slippers he'd been wearing when he'd answered the door. The room he was in was already chilly, and he could see no obvious source of heating. If he was left in here for long, in late December, he could envisage it becoming very cold indeed.

That again raised the question of how long he'd already been in here. He'd been woken in part by the grey daylight coming through the window, which would indicate he'd been unconscious overnight. His last memories were of the previous lunchtime, so that suggested he'd been here for the best part of twenty-four hours. That would be consistent with his thirst on waking, and with the fact that, as his brain finally resettled into some kind of normality, he was feeling extremely hungry. He could assume only that he'd been drugged.

It also occurred to him that, for all his bafflement, he didn't yet actually feel afraid. In part, that was because he had no idea what threat he might be facing. He had to take it seriously. People didn't go to these lengths for no reason. But he still couldn't bring himself to envisage what might be about to happen to him.

Even as he was thinking these still shapeless thoughts, he heard a noise at the top of the stairs. Moving as quietly as he could, Crawford descended the steps and lowered himself back onto the camp bed, hearing it squeak in protest beneath him. He pulled the thin duvet back over his body and lay motionless, his eyes half open, pretending still to be unconscious.

From the top of the stairs, there was the sound of a bolt being withdrawn and the clunk of a turning lock. Crawford held his breath and listened harder as the door slowly creaked open.

39

'You're kidding.'

'I don't hear anybody laughing,' McKay said.

'You actually stood and had a chat with our killers? Who were taking their dog for a walk?' Helena Grant said.

'It's looking that way.'

'Did you ask if they'd committed any good murders lately? Offer to hold the dog for them so they could kill again?'

'Aye, aye. Make the most of it.'

'In any other circumstances, it would be one of the funniest things I've ever heard. Alec McKay, eagle-eyed detective, has a cosy chat with the killers and then allows them to go on their merry way.'

'Feel free to laugh–'

'Oh, I will, Alec. So will a few other people round here.' Grant decided she'd pushed her taunting far enough. It had been hard to resist, given McKay's usual behaviour towards everyone else, but this was a serious development. Maybe, alongside whatever Gary Forres might be able to tell them, the beginnings of a real breakthrough. 'But you're serious about this. You really think it was them?'

'You think I've exposed myself to widespread public ridicule just for the hell of it?' McKay shook his head. 'Josh has been checking it out. There's no mention of this Farlowe on the electoral roll or any other local records we've been able to check. We can't find any evidence that he lives in Cromarty or has ever done so. He seems to be entirely fictitious. The address for Becky Delaney is a fake, too, and we've no evidence so far that she's real. We've checked with the immediate neighbours and nobody has any recollection of seeing anyone who matches the description we gave them.' McKay had commenced his familiar patrolling of the room, furiously chewing on a stick of gum. It was as if he had to match the churning of his brain with an equivalent physical restlessness, Grant thought.

'So these two committed the murder and then returned to report the death to us?'

'I can't think of any other reason anyone should assume a fake identity to report the finding of a body.'

'But why would they take that risk?'

'In the immediate term, it wasn't much of a risk,' McKay said. 'Why would anyone assume two boring dog walkers were actually the murderers?'

'I don't know. Because he was a razor-sharp detective with decades of experience?'

'Oh, bugger off. I didn't have any reason to suspect them. There was nothing suspicious about their behaviour.'

'I'm winding you up, Alec.'

'It's not a joke, though, is it? They were standing there, right in front of me. And I didn't even notice. Maybe I am getting too old for this lark.'

'Don't beat yourself up, Alec. There are plenty of people round here who'd happily do that for you. Whoever these people are, they're good. They know what they're doing.'

'They're playing with us, that's what they're doing.'

'That's what really infuriates you, isn't it?'

'That and three deaths. Four, if Gary Forres doesn't pull through. And Crawford missing–'

'We don't know for sure he's missing.'

'I've just tried his number. Still no reply.'

'It doesn't mean he's missing.'

'I've asked a squad car to pull by there when they're passing to check if anything's changed. It doesn't smell right to me.'

'If you say so, Alec. I'm not rushing to seek out more victims than we already have.' She watched him still pacing up and down the room. 'So what are we doing about our two friends?'

'Josh's organising for a sketch artist to help us put together a likeness of them. A couple of the uniforms also spoke to them, so between us we ought to be able to come up with a likeness.'

'That'll give us something we can use on the media appeals at least.'

'We're also checking for any sightings of the Sharan around the time Forres's body was found. They might have returned in a different vehicle, but taking the risk of coming back in the same car sounds more their style.'

'They might be playing with us, but they've managed to give us more of a lead than we had before.'

'That's what's nagging at me,' McKay said. 'Why make it easier for us?'

'Because they think they can get away with it? Why go to such lengths with the murders? Because they think they're invulnerable. Because they're addicted to the risk. If so, that should play in our favour.'

'I keep telling myself that. If they're this reckless, they'll make a mistake. Maybe they don't care about that. But there's also part of my head saying that so far they've managed not to put a foot wrong. That makes me wonder whether there's something more behind this. Whether we're being set up in some way.'

'In what way?'

McKay stopped pacing and shrugged. 'If I knew that, I wouldn't be their patsy, would I?'

'Fair point.'

'There's just something about the whole thing that feels – what's that fancy word they all use these days? Performative. As if we're being led somewhere.'

'Bit fanciful for you, isn't it, Alec?'

'It's just the usual gut thing. Something doesn't feel right.' He stopped again, looking dejected. 'Mind you, the old gut thing didn't do me much good when I met those two, so who knows?'

McKay was about to say something more when he was interrupted by the buzzing of his mobile phone. He checked the screen. 'Raigmore, I think. I'll put it on the speaker so you can listen.'

'DI McKay. It's Mark Livingstone from the hospital.'

'Good to hear from you, Mr Livingstone. I've just put you on speaker as I'm sitting here with my DCI.'

'Morning, Mr Livingstone,' Grant said. 'Helena Grant here.'

'I'm being as good as my word, and calling you as soon as we had some news.'

McKay exchanged a glance with Grant. 'And?'

'It's good news, I'm pleased to say. Mr Forres recovered consciousness this morning. He feels a bit groggy and has a headache, but otherwise seems none the worse for his experience.'

'That's good to hear. Pass on our good wishes. When will we be able to talk to him?'

'As soon as you like as far as I'm concerned,' Livingstone said. 'We'll probably keep him in overnight to complete some more tests on him. Just make sure that whatever was put into him didn't do more harm than it seems to have. It looks like I was right about that, incidentally. Sodium thiopental.' Livingstone was silent for a moment. 'I said I thought Forres had been lucky,' he said, finally. 'I'm not so sure about that.'

'If he's recovering, it sounds as if you were right,' McKay commented.

'That's not what I meant. I meant that his survival might not have been luck. Well, not entirely, anyway.'

'Go on.'

'It was a substantial dose. More than you'd normally give someone for anaesthetic purposes. But short of what you'd give someone if you wanted to kill them. If you wanted to be sure of killing them. You can never be certain with that kind of thing–'

'I'll take your word for that, Mr Livingstone.'

Livingstone laughed. 'I've not tried to kill anyone. Been tempted once or twice, given some of the management I've had to deal with. What I mean is that drugs can affect people in different ways. Someone with an underlying health condition, for example, might have reacted differently to the dosage Forres was given. Or if he'd been left for longer without receiving medical treatment. But for a youngish, healthy man like him, the dose was almost certainly too small to kill him.'

'So you're suggesting whoever did this didn't actually intend to kill him?'

'I can't say that with any certainty, obviously. Maybe they didn't know what they were doing or just got it wrong. But, whether by accident or design, it was well calibrated. My feeling is that they achieved the outcome they wanted.'

'Does this suggest to you that we're dealing with an expert in the medical field?' Grant asked.

'Hard to say. If it was as well calibrated as I'm suggesting, that would require some knowledge. But you could acquire that from a variety of sources. Administering the injection would require some expertise but not at a particularly high level.'

'And you're okay for us to come and talk to Forres straight away?' McKay asked.

'I think he's up to it. He seemed keen to talk to you. We're getting him something to eat, but other than that he's ready when you are.'

'In that case, we'll be over very shortly. Thanks again for letting us know so promptly.'

'To be honest, I'm as intrigued by this as you are. It's not like anything I've ever encountered before.'

'No,' McKay said. 'I think that's true of all of us.' He ended the call then sat for a moment staring at the phone. Finally, he looked up at Grant. 'Well.'

'Well,' she repeated. 'It sounds as if you might have been right. Performative.'

'And we're the audience. I'll get over there. If she's available, I'll take Ginny with me. I feel as if I could do with her clear head on this one.'

'You're judgement's fine, Alec. But Ginny might be a bit more detached from it.'

'You think I'm chasing shadows, don't you?'

'I don't, actually. I think your instincts are right. There's a game going on here. You may well be right about the detail, too.' She hesitated, wondering how to phrase her reservations. 'I just think you need to retain your objectivity. Don't get too sucked into this. It does look as if they're playing games with us, and it looks as if they're doing so very skilfully. If we are being played, we need to keep our wits about us. We need to be one step ahead of them, not the other way round.'

'We've not done too well with that so far,' McKay agreed morosely.

'That's my point. If this is a cat-and-mouse game, we don't want to end up being the mouse.'

'I'm not a numpty. And I've got you and Ginny to keep me on the straight and narrow.'

'Aye, like we've always managed to do that, Alec. And I'm not sure my head's entirely where it ought to be at the moment.'

'Love's young dream, and all that?'

'Not very young, and I don't know about love, not yet. But it does feel a bit dreamlike.'

'Make the most of it. You deserve it.'

'People keep saying that,' Grant said. 'Makes me nervous. Makes me wonder what it is I deserve.'

'Good things.' McKay was heading to the door. 'I'll go and round up Ginny, and we'll get over to Raigmore. Fingers crossed for a breakthrough.'

'Aye,' Grant said. 'Fingers crossed.'

40

Gary Forres had been moved to a room of his own. A uniformed PC was sitting by the door, idly playing with his phone.

'Hope you're keeping alert, Andy?'

The officer looked up and nodded to McKay and Horton. 'Afternoon, Alec. Ginny. This one of yours then?' PC Andy Anderson was middle-aged but looked much fitter than McKay felt. McKay didn't know how long Anderson had been with the force, but he'd become something of a fixture, one of those solid coppers you could rely on always to do a decent job.

'Seems so,' McKay said. 'Anything we should know?'

'Been very quiet. Docs and nurses in and out. Doc's in there with him at the moment.'

McKay peered through the window into the room. Livingstone was standing by the bed talking to Forres, who was sitting up, looking healthy enough. 'No sign of any trouble, then?'

'Nothing.'

'What about his wife?' Horton asked.

'She's on her way back over. She's been here most of the

morning, but has gone with the kids to sort out somewhere to stay in Inverness. Sod's law, he woke up after she'd gone.'

'Thanks, Andy, you're doing your usual grand job.'

'Aye, sitting on my arse. One of my finely-honed skills.'

McKay laughed and tapped on the window. Livingstone beckoned them in.

'Back in the land of the living, Mr Forres?'

Forres smiled and glanced at Livingstone. 'Mark here seems to think so. I'll keep an open mind till I've shaken off this headache.'

'We'll try not to make it worse. Do you feel up to talking to us?'

'I want to find out what's behind this as much as you do.'

McKay and Ginny Horton took seats by the bed. 'We'll try to be gentle with you.'

'I'll leave you to it,' Livingstone said. 'You should be fine, Mr Forres, but if you do start to feel too tired, just let them know.'

McKay waited until Livingstone had closed the door behind him. 'Tell us what happened, as best you can recall it.'

'It is all a bit hazy. I'd gone to my dad's house a short while after I spoke to you on the phone.'

'How long after?' McKay had already checked the time of his phone conversation with Forres.

'Not long at all. Ten, fifteen minutes at most. I hadn't been expecting to be able to get inside, so when you gave me the all-clear, I thought I might as well seize the moment.'

'Talk us through what happened. You went into the house, and then what?'

'I was at a bit of a loss at first, to be honest. As far as I can recall, I just wandered through into the kitchen and started to make myself a cup of coffee. I'd just sat down to drink it when the doorbell rang.'

'Go on.'

'I thought it would be one of the neighbours wanting to offer condolences. But it was the student.'

'Student?'

'The one who was part of the volunteer group who brought him shopping during lockdown. He'd mentioned her to me. The one who spotted that his wallet was missing. She told me her name. Kelly something. Kelly Armstrong.'

'Kelly Armstrong? You're sure?'

'Pretty sure. That was why I was happy to let her in. My dad had mentioned her to me, and she'd obviously been good to him during the lockdown. Does the name mean something to you?'

'We've come across Kelly once or twice. Not in any criminal capacity, though she does seem to have an extraordinary ability for being in the vicinity of trouble.'

'She certainly was in this case. She said she'd come to call on my dad. She seemed to be unaware of what had happened to him. So I invited her in and broke the news to her. She seemed shocked, as you'd expect.' He paused, clearly struggling to get his thoughts in order. 'I offered to make her a drink. I suppose I was trying to give her a chance to take in what I'd said. Anyway, she sat down at the kitchen table. I finished making her drink, then sat opposite her, with my back to the kitchen door. We were talking. About Dad, I suppose, though I can't remember exactly what. Then I heard a noise behind me. I thought it was the front door being blown open, that I'd maybe not quite shut it properly when she'd followed me in. It was blowing a gale off the firth.'

'Then what happened?'

'I'm not exactly sure. I was turning to look at the front door, to see if I needed to go and close it. Then I was hit by something across the side of my head. Not enough to knock me out, but enough to stun me and knock me off my chair. Something was thrown over my head. I'm not sure what – a coat or a blanket. Something fairly heavy. I was being held down, didn't know what the hell was happening. Then I felt my sleeve being pulled up and something jabbed into my arm, like an injection.'

'Exactly like an injection, it seems,' McKay said. 'Apparently you were injected with a drug.'

'So the doctor told me. I can't remember anything after that till I recovered consciousness here.' He paused. 'So what happened to Kelly Armstrong?'

'That's the question,' McKay said. 'Or it's one question among many. All we can tell you is that shortly after that, we received an anonymous emergency call informing us that a body had been found at your father's house. We almost dismissed it as a hoax given the address, but luckily for you PC Billy McCann took it seriously.'

'It seems to be one of his qualities,' Forres said. 'It's stood me in good stead so far.'

'As for what happened to Kelly Armstrong, that's a mystery at the moment. She wasn't mentioned in the call and there was no sign of her at the house. We can check with Billy McCann but I think he'd have reported her presence.'

McKay looked thoughtful. 'You say you were held down after you were struck. How many people do you think were holding you?'

'It's difficult to say. The blow had left me disorientated, and I couldn't see. But probably only one person. Someone who was holding my shoulders and arms. I remember trying to kick out with my feet, so they were still free.'

'What about the injection?' Horton asked. 'Could that have been administered by the person holding you?'

'I don't think so. They were pressing down on my upper arms with both of theirs. I don't think they could have got a hand free to inject me as well.'

'So it sounds as if at least two people were involved in the assault.'

'Are you suggesting that this Kelly Armstrong might have been involved?' Forres said.

'I'm suggesting nothing at the moment. But either she was involved or she's in trouble.'

'But why would they drug me but then kidnap her?' Forres asked. 'It makes no kind of sense.'

'None of this seems to make much sense, Mr Forres. That's why we need as much information as you can provide.'

'I'll get someone onto tracking down Kelly Armstrong,' Horton said. 'We should still have her details on file. As far as I'm aware she still lives in Cromarty with her parents.' She rose and left the room.

'Whatever the precise circumstances,' McKay said to Forres, 'someone attacked and drugged you. Have you any idea why anyone would want to do that, Mr Forres?'

'No idea at all.'

'Sometimes we make enemies without even realising we've done it. One of my own qualities, to be honest.' McKay paused for a moment. 'How much do you know about your father's business.'

'Not much, really. He never really talked about it.'

'But you must have had an idea what his work involved.'

'To be honest, not much.' Forres was silent for a moment. 'I suppose, as I got older I began to suspect it was something not entirely kosher.'

'What gave you that idea?'

'I honestly can't remember. Something he said to me, or something someone else said about it. It was one of those things that starts as the germ of a thought and gradually expands to fill your head.'

'You were maybe a bit excited by the idea and proud of him at the time?' McKay suggested. 'That sort of thing can seem a thrill when you're a teenager.'

'It never really felt like that. I remember mostly being scared by the idea.'

'But you never talked to him about it?'

'It just made me want to know less about what he might be up to. It almost became a superstitious thing. As long as I didn't know about any of it, it couldn't harm me. Or him.'

'Did you remain on good terms with your father?'

'We had the usual teenage son/father fallouts, but never anything that lasted or was serious. He was a fairly reserved individual, but there was no bad blood between us.'

'You didn't think you ought to report your father for his business activities?'

'Report what? I'd no information, no evidence of anything. Nothing but gossip and hearsay. Even if I'd felt any inclination to do something, you wouldn't have taken any notice of me.'

'What if I told you his business activities included human trafficking and modern slavery?'

'I'd say you were lying. I don't know what kind of business Dad was involved in, but it wasn't anything like that.'

'Probably not directly, no. From what we know of your father's business, he never really dirtied his hands with that sort of activity. But we think that he knowingly dealt with people who did.'

'I can't believe it. I'd envisaged a lot of things, but nothing like that.'

'Something a little more romantic, maybe.' McKay sat back in his seat, watching Forres's reaction. Unless he was a very skilled actor, it was clear that he was genuinely shocked by what McKay had said. 'I'm sorry. I'm being more blunt than I'd intended. But we have three deaths, not to mention the assault on you, so I think it's time for me to be straight.'

'If he did deal with people like that, Dad wouldn't have

known what they were up to. Anyway, if there is anything in this, why didn't you ever take action against him?'

'Plenty of people slip through the net, for good or ill. We looked at your father's businesses a few times, but, to be honest, there were always bigger fish to fry. If we'd have arrested your father, it would have been as a route to some of the more significant players, but the right combination of circumstances never arose.'

'So you've no real evidence for what you're saying?'

'Not enough for a case that would satisfy the Fiscal, let's put it that way. But enough for me. I'm sorry if this is a shock.'

'So you think this is what's behind his death?'

'I honestly don't know. Whatever the nature of his business, your father was retired. If this was connected to his past, I don't know why someone would have acted now. But we can't ignore what we know of his background.'

'What you claim to know of his background.' Forres was beginning to sound defeated now, his initial bravado fading in the face of McKay's assertions. McKay wondered whether Forres had known or suspected more about his father's business dealings than he was prepared to admit.

'I'm not going to push it,' McKay said. 'Let's just say there are some secrets in your father's past that could provide a motive for his death. The same's maybe true of the other killings we're dealing with.'

'You said three deaths,' Forres said. 'I'm assuming one is the body that was found just before Christmas. Has there been another?'

'Another that we think might be linked, yes. The victim had a similar background to your father's.'

'What about me, though? I was attacked too. Whatever you might claim about my father, I can tell you none of that applies to me.'

'You're still living and breathing. Which strikes me as interesting.'

'I don't understand.'

'Neither do I. Someone attacks you, injects you with a potentially fatal drug, leaves you apparently for dead. But calls us anonymously so we find your comatose body. According to the doc, the dose you were given, although substantial, seems to have been carefully calibrated not to kill you.'

Before McKay could say anything more, the door opened and Horton peered in. 'The good news is we've tracked down Kelly Armstrong. The bad news is that what she's saying just seems to raise more questions.'

McKay looked back at Forres. 'Looks like we may have to leave you for the moment. I understand your wife and children should be here very shortly.' He paused. 'I'm sorry if this has all been a shock. All I can tell you is that what I've said is the truth.' He wasn't sure what else to say. Finally, he simply repeated, 'I'm sorry.'

41

'I honestly don't know what you're talking about.'

They were sitting in the living room of Kelly Armstrong's parents' house, an attractive residence converted from a couple of smaller cottages in the centre of Cromarty. As in many of the houses in the town there was a maritime theme to the décor and pictures of local seascapes dominating the walls.

'You didn't visit Hamish Forres yesterday?'

'Hamish Forres. But I thought he was– I mean, I saw on the news...'

McKay glanced at Horton, who shrugged. 'That's right, Kelly. Unfortunately, he was found dead on Christmas Day.'

'So I don't understand. How could I have visited him?'

'We're not sure we understand either, Kelly. The facts are these. Hamish Forres's son, Gary, visited his father's house yesterday. While he was there in the early afternoon, he received a visit from a young woman who claimed to be visiting Hamish, apparently unaware of what had happened to him. The woman gave her name as Kelly Armstrong.'

'But that's not possible. I was here all day yesterday. My mum and dad can confirm that.'

'You didn't leave the house?'

'I had some work to do for uni. I've been putting it off over Christmas, so I thought I should get on with it. I spent the day on my laptop.'

'You say your parents can vouch for that?' McKay asked.

'I think my dad might have gone out briefly but my mum was in all day. I couldn't have left the house without her knowing.' She paused, her eyes still fixed on McKay. 'You're not accusing me of something, are you?'

'We're just trying to make sense of what we've been told.'

'Why would anyone claim to be me?'

'No offence, Kelly,' McKay said, 'but that's the question we're asking ourselves. We'll need to get confirmation from your parents, but I'm happy to accept it wasn't you who was at Forres's house yesterday. So who was it?'

'He had a fake visitor before, you know,' Kelly said.

'So we understand,' Horton said. 'You were there that day?'

'I was delivering some shopping for Hamish. We'd been doing it throughout the lockdown.'

'Did he seem at all different in the last few weeks? More nervous? Worried?'

'Maybe. He seemed a bit more – fearful, I suppose. I just put it down to isolation. People got out of the habit of going out. But he did seem to become more nervous. He tried to hide it, but I had the sense he was thrown by his wallet being stolen. Not by the wallet itself. But by the fact that he'd allowed himself to be fooled. That he'd let someone like that into his house.'

'Do you have any idea who this woman was?'

'No idea. She obviously knew something about the volunteer group, though that wouldn't have been difficult. We'd been promoting what we were doing locally, so most people would have been aware of us. I just assumed she was a chancer, an opportunist thief.' She paused. 'So what happened at Hamish's house yesterday? You two wouldn't be here about another wallet theft.'

'Gary Forres was attacked.'

'By this woman?'

'We think there were at least two people involved.'

'It wouldn't have been difficult to get my name. I was mentioned in a couple of the features about the volunteer groups.'

'But how would they have known you were the volunteer visiting Hamish?' Horton asked.

'I don't know. I guess Hamish might have mentioned me by name to the woman who took the wallet.'

'Who was involved in the volunteer group?' McKay asked.

'It ended up with a core group of about half a dozen of us. It was the usual story. We had a fairly large group of people interested initially, then a smaller group who came to the first meetings. By the time we'd really got going it had whittled down to the people who were willing and able to put the time in.'

'Do you have a list of the people involved?'

'I've got some information on my laptop.' She left the room and returned a few moments later carrying the computer, setting it up on the coffee table between McKay and Horton. 'This is the file. There's the list of names and addresses. Those are all the people who came to the first meeting.'

'Can you email those to me?' McKay asked.

'I've got photos, too, if that's any help. We had to apply for DBS checks and all that, but we also had the idea that we could provide the people we were visiting with photos of all the volunteers so they could double-check the identity if it wasn't the usual volunteer visiting them. It never really came to anything because we ended up with a pretty small core group anyway.' She opened another file and showed them a series of full-face images.

'Do you know all these individuals, Kelly?' McKay asked.

'Most of them, one way or another. Obviously, I've got to know the core group pretty well. The others were a mixed bunch. There are a couple I know well, and a few I've seen around town, though I didn't really know them. And there were some I didn't recognise at all. It's surprising. You'd think this was a pretty small place – and it is, especially when you've had to spend months here when you expected to be at university. But there are still people you don't know at all. I suppose because they work somewhere else and don't spend much time here.'

McKay was idly flicking through the images. As Kelly had said, they appeared to be a very diverse group – mostly middle-aged or older, a scattering of younger people like Kelly. He scanned through a few more then stopped, peering closely at the screen. 'Do you know who this is?'

Kelly peered at the screen. 'No, that's one of the people I didn't know at all. No idea who he is. His name and address should be underneath.'

McKay scrolled down and then looked up at Ginny Horton. 'Well.'

'Go on,' Horton said.

'This man gave his name as Alastair Farlowe. The address is the one he gave to us previously.'

'The address where no one called Alastair Farlowe actually lives,' Horton agreed. 'And is it him? The man you met?'

'I think so. That's why it caught my eye.' He turned the screen towards Horton. 'It's not a great picture, but it might save us the cost of a sketch artist.'

The man on the screen was relatively young, probably mid-twenties, with a thin, slightly gaunt face and pale brown hair swept back from his forehead.

'Is there anything you can tell us about this Alastair Farlowe?' McKay asked Kelly.

'I don't really even remember him. He must have come to that first meeting, but he didn't make any impression. We had quite a lot of people there – well, you can see from the photographs – and there were a few who dominated the discussion. I don't recall this guy saying anything.'

'I'm surprised he allowed himself to be photographed,' Horton said.

Kelly grinned. 'I'm not sure he had a lot of choice. We've a couple of people who tend to take charge. You need people like that if this kind of thing is going to work. Anyway, they more or less insisted that everyone took part in the photo session. They thought people would then feel obliged to commit, but it didn't really work like that. But no one was allowed to escape without being photographed.'

McKay was still staring at the image on the screen. 'I'm not sure they really care, to be honest. They seem to be enjoying flaunting themselves in front of us like this. Maybe assuming we'll never spot it. Maybe not caring much if we do. We're still a long way from knowing who they are.'

'Not as far as we were,' Horton said. 'At least we've got an image we can share.'

'Are you saying this person was involved in Hamish's death?' Kelly asked.

McKay reminded himself that Kelly Armstrong had a tendency to get more involved in their enquiries than was necessarily good for her. 'We don't even know that, Kelly,' he said, cautiously. 'We just know that we have some questions we'd like him to answer.'

42

Helena Grant had agreed to drive over to Bill Emsworth's house for dinner. She'd hesitated when he'd first asked her, feeling that, now the Christmas break was finished, it might be better to revert to her old routine for the moment. She'd already made a tentative arrangement to spend New Year's Eve with him, and she'd wondered whether it might be better to use the intervening time to give herself some space to think about their burgeoning relationship.

But Emsworth had been keen to continue where they'd left off over Christmas, and she could see the sense in what he was saying. Yes, she didn't want to rush headlong into something she might regret. But neither of them was getting any younger, and maybe they shouldn't risk wasting even a single night.

Anyway, she told herself, *it was only dinner.* She'd told Bill she'd prefer to drive home at the end of the evening, so she could be in the office early in the morning. Even there, though, she hedged her bets by sticking an overnight bag in the back of the car. She could feel herself drifting further and faster into this than she'd perhaps intended, but she wasn't sure she really cared.

In the days since Christmas, the temperatures had risen and the snow was largely gone, though traces lingered in the edges of the fields and other sheltered places, and the bulk of Ben Wyvis, looming over the Black Isle, was still thickly covered.

Grant had been later leaving the office than she'd intended, catching up first on a debrief from Alec McKay and Ginny Horton about their conversation with Kelly Armstrong and then a further discussion with the head of comms about to use the image of the so-called 'Alastair Farlowe' as part of an appeal in the following day's media. She called Bill to warn him she was running late. He'd told her not to worry. He was cooking a casserole that would keep until she arrived.

It was past seven when she crossed the Kessock Bridge, the lights of Inverness glittering behind her. She took the Munlochy turn and following the coast road through Avoch and Fortrose to Rosemarkie. As she pulled up outside Bill's house, the front door opened. It looked as though he'd been awaiting her arrival.

'Sorry I'm late,' she said, as she approached the door. 'You know how it is.'

'I remember how it was,' he said. 'It's a while since I worked in an office.'

She followed him inside, closing the front door behind her. By contrast with the chilly night, the house felt warm and welcoming. 'How's the food going?'

'Fine. It'll happily just sit there and be ready when we are. Thought that would allow us to spend maximum time together, rather than me bobbing up and down all the time. Glass of wine?'

She hesitated. 'Why not? But I'd better stick to just the one if I'm driving home tonight.'

'Are you driving home tonight?'

'That was the plan. I do need to be in early in the morning.'

'It's not much further from here.' Bill smiled. 'And I bet you brought an overnight bag in the car.'

She laughed. 'That's probably exactly why I shouldn't stay. You're getting to know me too well.'

'Well, let's see how the evening goes, shall we? Whether I can tempt you. To a few more glasses of wine, I mean.'

A bottle of red wine and two glasses were already waiting in the living room. He poured one for her and they sat together on the sofa.

'How's your day been?' he asked.

'Not so bad. Slow progress, you know. But that's how it is.'

Bill smiled. 'Don't worry, I won't press you for more information. Just making conversation.'

'So how's your day been? Lots of words?'

'Not yet. Still at the plotting stage.'

'I thought you didn't do much plotting, usually, just threw yourself into it.' This was what he'd told her at one of their early meetings when they'd still been largely discussing matters of police procedure.

'It varies. Mostly I just write. But this one felt like it needed some more upfront thought to make sure I got it right.'

'What's it about?'

His expression was one of mock horror. 'You can't expect me to tell you that. Any more than you'd tell me about your ongoing investigation.' He laughed. 'It's a bit of a superstition, actually. I don't like to talk about it till I've finished.'

'Fair enough. Hope it's going well, anyway.'

'Like you say, slow progress.'

'You still haven't shown me your office or whatever you call it.'

'I suppose I haven't.'

'Is that another superstition. Don't you show people where you work, either?'

'To be honest, no one's ever really been very interested before.'

'Well, I'm interested. I'd love to see it.'

'There's not much to see. Just a desk and a computer.'

'I'd still be interested. It's a big part of you. It's what you do.'

'Well, if you insist. Just don't set your expectations too high. I'll give you the grand tour, if you've thirty seconds.'

He led her up the stairs to the first floor. Bill's bedroom, the only room she'd been inside up here, was ahead of them. The writing room was to its right, although also at the front of the house, presumably with a similar view out over the bay. He ushered her inside, turning on the light as he did so. 'Here we go.'

As he'd said, there wasn't actually much to see. There was a solid antique desk by the window with an Apple Mac desktop on it. Next to the computer sat an apparently random pile of papers. There was an office chair, and rows of bookshelves lining the walls.

'Not much to it, I'm afraid,' he said. 'I did warn you.'

'It's where you work your magic, though.'

'It's where I mostly drink coffee and stare out of the window.'

'Must have an impressive view.' In the dark, Grant could see little other than a scattering of lights on the far side of the firth.

'That's one of the problems,' Bill said. 'I should go back to living in the London flat I had with nothing but a view of someone else's back wall. I'm sure I got more work done.'

'It must be inspiring, though.'

'It certainly makes me conscious how far I've come.'

She was examining the bookshelf next to the desk. 'These are all your books?'

'A selection of them. Various editions. A few foreign editions and suchlike. I've a lot more in boxes scattered around the house.'

'I hadn't realised you'd written so much.'

'Well, I've been at it for a long time.'

She was scanning through the titles. Since she'd met him, she'd been trying to catch up on his work, more or less in chronological order, though she'd only scratched the surface. 'I've enjoyed the ones I've read.'

He laughed. 'You have to say that, though, don't you?'

'It's still true.' She turned back towards him. 'If I'd read the books before I met you, I think I'd have been surprised.'

'In what way?'

'I'm not sure exactly. I'd have expected someone – I don't know, darker, maybe, more intense. Also the author's biogs imply you're something of a recluse. Can't say that's something I've noticed.'

'That stuff's just generated by the publicity people. Truth was, I was always a bit shy. Wasn't keen on doing interviews or attending conventions. All that stuff writers are supposed to do to promote their books. So they decided to make a virtue of it, paint me as Mr Mysterious. No photographs on the books, that kind of thing. It was always nonsense, but it gave the media a hook, I suppose.' He smiled. 'Mind you, I think people up here thought it was true when I first moved here. My move coincided with writing a book I was struggling with against a tight deadline, so I had a good few months of head-down writing. Then of course we all went into lockdown, so none of us saw anybody. I'm sure there were all kinds of rumours circulating about me, particularly if people had seen the stuff about me being a recluse. Everyone was surprised when lockdown was loosened and I started getting active in the local community.'

As he was talking, he'd taken her into his arms and kissed her softly on the lips. 'Then of course I met you, so it's not been a bad year, all told.'

'It's been a strange year,' she said. 'But, yes, it's not turned out too badly.' She kissed him back and then turned back to the bookshelf. 'What's this one?' She held up a paperback which had been sitting face down on the shelf in front of the other books. The author was credited as Brian Ellis and it looked very different from Emsworth's books. It was called *Bad Justice.* For some reason, it rang a bell in her mind.

Emsworth looked awkward. 'Oh, God, that. That goes a long way back.'

'Who's Brian Ellis?'

'The initials are a giveaway, It's a pseudonym.'

'You mean it's one of yours?'

'It's rather different from my other books. My one foray into true crime. All the rage now, of course. I must have been ahead of my time. Load of crap, though.'

'I'm sure it isn't.'

'I wouldn't advise you to read it. It wasn't my idea in the first place. Someone approached me about a supposed miscarriage of justice.' He paused, as if unsure how to explain himself. 'Actually, it was what first brought me back up into this part of the world.'

'It was a local case?'

'Inverness. Got a lot of coverage at the time. Youngish accountant killed in a drive-by shooting.'

She was gazing at him with an odd expression. 'The Bruce Dennis case?'

'You know about it? Well, I suppose you would.'

'I don't just know about it. I worked on it. One of my first jobs as a very inexperienced DC.'

'Oh, God, this is even more embarrassing.'

She was staring at him. '*Bad Justice.* I'd completely forgotten that. I hadn't realised it was you.'

He'd reddened with apparent embarrassment. 'There's no

reason why you should have. God, I wish I hadn't brought you up here now.'

'No, it's fine. I never read the book – it was all a bit too raw for me – but I read various reviews and articles at the time of the retrial. From what I read, you weren't entirely wrong. And I'm sure your motives were good, even if it was the wrong outcome.'

'I'm sorry,' he said. 'This really has put a damper on the evening, hasn't it? All I can say is that it was twenty-odd years ago.'

'Actually, I thought the issues you raised in the book were spot on. The DCI in charge of the investigation was – well, let's say, prone to cutting corners when it suited him. Jackie Galloway. He got his comeuppance later, in more ways than one, but he was king of the hill in those days. The evidential issues you identified were all real. I don't know exactly what Galloway did, but some of the evidence was decidedly dodgy.' She paused. 'I still think we got the right man, though. It was a kick in the teeth when Kenny Rogan was eventually acquitted.'

'If it's any consolation,' Bill said, 'I've come round to the same conclusion. That's one reason I'm embarrassed by the book now.'

'You shouldn't be,' she said. 'You uncovered some real anomalies. I'm sure what happened in the Dennis case was one of the factors that ultimately helped end Jackie Galloway's career.'

'I was too zealous, though. I was adamant Kenny Rogan didn't kill Dennis, and I used the inconsistencies in the evidence to push through that conclusion. That's why he was acquitted.'

'You highlighted the issues with the prosecution case, and the jury decided his guilt couldn't be proved beyond reasonable doubt. That's how justice works. It doesn't mean he didn't do it.'

'I've sometimes wondered about doing a sequel or an updated version. But the interest wouldn't be there. I'm just glad it's out of print.' He was silent for a moment. 'What do you think now? Do you still think Kenny Rogan was guilty?'

'I do, actually. We didn't have much doubt at the time. But the whole thing was very political. With a small "p", though possibly with a large one too for all I know. It was one of those turf wars – small-time mobsters squabbling over their territory. Dennis was far from squeaky clean himself, as you probably pointed out in the book–'

'Something else I've regretted since. You can't libel the dead, but I should have been more considerate to his family.'

'You've a duty to the truth, surely. Dennis was far from an innocent party. He was involved in money laundering and a load of other stuff. His killing was a warning to the people who employed him.'

Bill had turned away. 'I'm not so sure about any of it any more. If Dennis really was guilty of that stuff, that was a matter for you to deal with. It doesn't justify him being shot.'

'I'm not saying that for a moment. I'm just saying the whole thing was tangled. We didn't have much doubt Kenny Rogan was behind the killing, though we didn't believe he'd done the deed himself. Rogan had some influential backers, and we knew we'd struggle to build a case the Fiscal would support. That was what led Jackie Galloway into his corner-cutting. If in doubt, create and plant the evidence. That was Jackie's way.'

'Noble corruption. That's what you call it, isn't it?'

'I'm not sure there was much noble in Jackie's case. I wouldn't be surprised if he was receiving backhanders from the other side. Jackie wasn't averse to boosting his own conviction rate, but he'd be even more inclined to take the risk if there were a few quid involved.'

'The rest of you let him get away with it?'

'I was the lowest of the low,' she said. 'There were rumours about what Galloway was up to, but I wasn't in a position to prove or disprove them. As for the others in the team – well, you'd have to ask them. One or two were in Galloway's pocket. That emerged later. But I imagine others were in the same position I was.'

Bill was still turned away from her, so she had no idea how he was reacting to what she was saying. He clearly had regrets about the book and its outcome, but that was hardly her fault. Finally he turned back towards her, his expression still unreadable. 'He's dead now, isn't he?'

'Galloway? He came to a sad end. Pigeons coming home to roost, and all that.'

'I remember reading about it in the papers. It was one of the things that made me think about the book again after all these years. I suppose Galloway was as responsible for Rogan's acquittal as anyone. If he'd played by the book, Rogan would still be paying the price.'

'In fairness,' Grant said, 'if Galloway had played by the book, we might never have laid a finger on Kenny Rogan in the first place. But, yes, you're right.'

'You said it's how justice works,' Bill said. 'But justice doesn't work, does it? Bruce Dennis and his family never got justice.'

'Nothing else could have been done,' Grant pointed out. 'Once Rogan was acquitted, we had nowhere else to go. We weren't looking for anyone else. We were unlikely to gather any more substantive evidence against him. As far as I know, the case is still officially open, but everyone knew it was going nowhere.'

'I'm sorry. I shouldn't have opened this all up. I'd only got the book out because I wanted to check some details about the trial that are relevant to the project I'm working on at the moment. I'm thinking of kicking it off around the same time as the Rogan trial. It never occurred to me you might have been involved in the original enquiry.'

'It's mainly a historic curiosity for me now. A reminder of how policing used to be, back in the days when beasts like Galloway were in charge.'

'I take it it's different now.'

'It's not perfect, but we've made progress.'

'That's good to hear. Right, enough wallowing in the past. We should get downstairs to the casserole before it turns into a cinder. It's a tolerant recipe but we shouldn't test its patience too much.'

She smiled. 'I'm sorry for drawing attention to the book. I hadn't realised I was touching a nerve.'

'It's just something I've been thinking a lot about recently, for one reason or another.'

'You say you're working on something set around the same time?'

'Kicking off around the same time, anyway. It'll probably come to a conclusion in the present day.'

'Sounds intriguing.'

'It's probably too soon to say how exactly it'll pan out.' He led her back out of the office, turning off the light as he left. 'Let's get back downstairs.'

He left her in the living room while he went to tend to the food in the kitchen. She sat back down on the sofa, sipping her wine. She still wasn't entirely sure what had happened upstairs. She'd clearly touched a nerve, though she wasn't sure why Bill was so bothered by a twenty-year-old book. On the other hand, though she hadn't thought about the case for years, it continued to bother her. Not because she thought herself culpable for what had happened. She'd only been the tiniest cog in the wheel, and nothing she'd said or done would have made any difference.

But she was like all half-decent coppers. She hated to see justice not done, or in this case justice being undone. Yes, it was right that Rogan was ultimately acquitted. There was sufficient doubt about the evidence to undermine the prosecution case. But equally she'd had no doubt he was guilty, and that he was being protected by others who, in their various ways, were no doubt equally guilty. It had pained her to see Rogan walk free. It was a common frustration of the job, but that didn't make it easier to deal with.

She took another sip of the wine. Now that the case had come back into her mind, there was something nagging at her. Something she'd forgotten about the detail of the case. She couldn't remember too much about the specifics of the case. She'd just been a foot-soldier doing what she was told to do, focusing mainly on not screwing up in a way that might have attracted Galloway's legendary wrath.

Maybe in the morning, if she had a moment, she might get hold of the file, refresh her memory. There was something troubling her, some itch she couldn't quite scratch. Maybe Alec would remember. He'd have been around at the time, though hadn't worked on the case for some reason.

She was still mulling this over when Bill reappeared. 'I've just put the veg on,' he said. 'Another few minutes and we'll be there.' He took a seat beside her. 'Wine top-up?'

She hesitated. For a few moments upstairs, she'd really thought that, between them, they'd managed to bring the evening to a dead stop. She'd been certain then that she'd stick to her original intention and head home at the end of the evening. But already she was relaxing again, and returning to her empty house was the last thing she wanted to do.

'Go on then,' she said. 'Why not?'

43

Crawford lay on the camp bed, scarcely breathing, listening to the footsteps descending the stone steps. Whoever had entered the room was moving slowly, as if with caution. Crawford heard something being placed on the ground, then there was an extended silence.

He opened his eyes slightly, hoping to gain some idea of what was happening. There was nothing in his line of sight that provided any insights, and, for the moment, he preferred not to reveal that he was conscious.

He heard footsteps again, this time moving away from him. A voice said, 'You awake yet?'

Crawford remained motionless, then stirred on the creaking bed, making what he hoped was the sound of someone recovering consciousness. 'What–?'

'You awake yet? Looks as if you probably are.'

Crawford felt a judder as something struck the bed. He made more noises and rolled over. The bed shook from another blow. It felt as if the bed was being kicked.

'That ought to wake you. You've been out long enough.'

It was a man's voice. He rolled over again and sat up, blinking as if he'd only just been exposed to daylight. 'I don't–'

'That's more like it.' The man was at the foot of the steps. If he had kicked the bed a few seconds before, he'd clearly moved back as Crawford had stirred. His face was covered by a balaclava-type mask, only his eyes visible. His stance was calm and confident, but Crawford thought he could detect an underlying tension. 'We need you to be ready.'

Crawford looked around him, as if seeing the room for the first time. 'What the hell's going on? Where am I?'

'It doesn't matter where you are,' the man said. 'And you'll find out soon enough what's going on.'

Crawford moved himself into a sitting position. 'Who the hell are you? You can't just snatch someone from their own home.'

'That's exactly what we've done. Scandalous, isn't it? But there isn't a lot you can do about it.'

Crawford pushed himself to his feet, trying to look as if he was having difficulty standing. He noticed that the man had taken an involuntary step backwards.

For a moment, Crawford contemplated whether he'd be able to take on the man if that was the only way of forcing his way out of here. The man looked substantially younger than Crawford, but he was relatively slight and Crawford kept himself in decent shape. On the other hand, he didn't know what steps the man might have taken to protect himself. He didn't even know if the man was alone, or if there might be others waiting upstairs.

If it came to it, Crawford might have to take the risk. For the moment, he decided he was better taking stock and trying to learn as much as he could about what was going on here. He'd always seen himself as good in a crisis, and he was surprised by how calm he was still feeling. The use of the mask was a positive sign. It meant the man was concerned about Crawford being able to recognise or describe him subsequently. And that, he told himself, meant they were at some point intending to release him from here.

'Food,' the man said, pointing towards the end of the camp bed. On the floor was a plate containing half a baguette, a lump of pallid cheese and an apple. Before Crawford could offer any response, the man turned and climbed hurriedly up the steps.

As the door closed and locked above him, Crawford sat down on the bed and reached over to pick up the plate. The food looked far from appetising, but there was little point in starving himself in the face of whatever might be coming his way. He broke off pieces of bread and cheese and began to eat.

Crawford had little doubt his kidnappers knew exactly who he was. He wasn't a particularly wealthy man in his own right, but he had access to very considerable amounts of other people's money. He had a reputation for utter trustworthiness in his handling of those assets, and that was something he wouldn't sacrifice without a real fight.

The problem was that he had no idea what kind of fight he might be facing.

44

Helena Grant had set an early alarm on her phone, and the room was still pitch-black when she was woken by the rhythmic buzzing. It took her a moment to recall where she was.

She turned on the bedside light and slowly eased herself out of bed. Beside her, Bill stirred. 'What time is it?'

'Just gone six.' She'd warned him the previous evening she had to be up early. 'You can go back to sleep. I'll get showered and then dress in the bathroom.'

He rolled over onto his back, stretching out his arms. 'It'll do me good to get up early. I've got plenty to do today. Tell you what, you get dressed and I'll make us some coffee.'

'If you're sure.'

'I'm more of a lark than an owl.' He pulled his dressing gown around him. 'Heating's not on yet. I'll put it on when I go down.'

She still hadn't been quite sure she'd made the right decision in staying over. She hadn't regretted it, but she'd been conscious it wasn't what she'd intended. Even so, there was a particular pleasure in waking up beside someone. And an even greater pleasure in having that person take care of you at this time in the morning.

She finished showering and dressing, pulling on the set of clothes she'd brought in the overnight bag. At least that would stop Alec McKay making acerbic comments. By the time she emerged from the bathroom, the heating was on and the morning was beginning to feel less bleak and more welcoming.

Something was still nagging at her brain following her discussion with Bill the previous evening. Something to do with the Bruce Dennis case. She'd been hoping the elusive thought might have popped into her head, unbidden, while she was sleeping. It was often the way. But not this time. This time, the thought, whatever it might be, remained tantalisingly out of reach.

She entered the kitchen to the smell of coffee and frying bacon, Bill busy at the cooker. 'Coffee on the table,' he said. 'Bacon roll in a minute or two. Assume you've got time?'

'I'll make time,' she said. 'You really are spoiling me. I assume you don't do this every morning.'

'Writer's perks. But, no, it's usually toast or granola. I thought you deserved something better if you were having to slog into work at this unholy hour.'

'I don't know about deserve,' she said. 'But I certainly welcome it. Thank you.' She sat at the table and poured herself a cup of coffee. 'Even the smell of it's making me feel better.'

'Quite right.' He deposited two rashers of bacon onto a sliced and buttered morning roll and handed it to her. 'There we go. Anyway, it gives me an excuse to have one myself. There's ketchup and various relishes in the fridge if you want them.'

'It's fine like this. I'm really not used to this kind of treatment.'

He sat beside her. 'I can do us the full Scottish on New Year's

Day, if you like. Haggis, Stornoway black pudding, tattie scones, the lot. See the new year in properly.'

She looked at her watch. 'I'd better not delay too much. Otherwise it'll defeat the purpose of getting up so early.'

'Busy day ahead?'

'They're all busy. But especially at the moment. We need to take advantage of these few work days to get as much done as we can before everything closes down again for Hogmanay.'

'You lot must really hate public holidays.'

'They're not exactly flavour of the month in the middle of a large enquiry.'

'Hope it goes well today, then. Any chance of seeing you this evening?'

She felt herself yielding yet again. 'I'd better not. I'm going to be working late again, and I've got loads I need to do at home. But I'll come over for Hogmanay as we agreed. I don't know if I'll need to go in on New Year's Day yet. Depends how things are going.'

'I understand. Maybe you'll have a bit more time when you finally get this investigation out of the way.'

'I wouldn't bet on it.' She pushed herself to her feet. 'But, really, Bill, thanks for last night. And for the bacon roll. And, well, for everything else. Don't think that I don't appreciate it, or that it doesn't mean a lot to me.'

'You've a job to do. I realise that.'

'If we do make something of this, Bill – I mean, if it really does become something permanent – it's something you're going to get used to. It's the job. Not all the time, but a lot of the time.'

'I realise that. My job's largely the opposite. I have deadlines, but mostly I work as I please. That means I'll be able to fit around your schedule and take proper care of you.'

'That sounds like a very attractive idea. Right, out into the cold.'

He followed her to the front door. It was still dark outside, the clear sky thick with stars, with only a faint crimson blur out across the day to indicate morning was coming. 'Looks like it's going to be decent day,' he said. 'Even if it is bloody cold.'

'It's certainly that. You'd better get back inside.' She pulled her coat more tightly around her and climbed into the car. She'd half-expected she might have to scrape frost from the windows, but the cold dry night had left them clear. She started the engine, waved to Bill as he stood watching her from the doorway, and pulled out into the road.

She had no regrets now about having stayed over. Every minute she spent with Bill felt like another test of their relationship, and so far he was passing with flying colours. She was experienced enough to realise this blissful period wouldn't last. But that was fine. She wouldn't want him getting up and making her bacon sandwiches at 6am every day, even though it had definitely brightened this dark morning. But there was enough there to make her feel this was likely to be all right.

The traffic was almost non-existent at that time of the morning. Many people would still be on holiday, enjoying an extended break over Christmas and the New Year, and those who were still in work wouldn't be busting a gut to get in early. She had the car radio playing softly as she crossed the Kessock Bridge, some rock tune she half-recognised teasing gently at her ears.

She was still trying to come up with whatever had been troubling her about the Bruce Dennis case. She could barely remember anything beyond the main events. Dennis had been an accountant with a growing practice supporting small local businesses. His killing had initially been mystifying. He was in his forties, happily married with two small children, a supposedly respectable pillar of the local community. His shooting had been shocking and initially inexplicable, the subject of 'shock horror' headlines and coverage in the local and national press.

Gradually, the police investigation had uncovered some less comfortable truths about Dennis's practice. He was much less squeaky clean than his public image had indicated. Alongside his more reputable clients, he had a number who were familiar to the police. Many of them weren't exactly criminals, or at least had never been convicted as such, but had reputations for enhancing their legitimate incomes with more dubious practices. The suspicion was that it was Dennis who helped them to clean up the proceeds.

The police's conclusion, enthusiastically endorsed by Jackie Galloway, was that Dennis's killing had been intended as a warning. Some of his clients had been expanding rapidly, and were treading on the toes of some of the established interests in the area. Galloway himself had decided – at an early point in the investigation, as she recalled – that the primary suspect was a small-time businessman called Kenny Rogan. That seemed plausible enough. Rogan had a record for crimes ranging from fraud to GBH, and was widely perceived as a nasty piece of work.

At the time, Grant had felt that Rogan was unlikely to be the brains behind the killing. He had plenty of associates who were smarter and more successful than he was, and it was their interests that were really affected by Dennis's clients. But, along with most of her colleagues, she hadn't had much doubt he was guilty of the killing, and that the chances of bringing his associates to justice were relatively small. Galloway had prioritised building a case against Rogan, and that had been the focus of their efforts.

Later, when Galloway's questionable track record became more evident, she'd wondered about Galloway's motives for pursuing Rogan so determinedly. At the time, she'd seen Galloway as an unpleasant misogynist bully, but not necessarily as corrupt. But she suspected now that he'd been incentivised to focus on Rogan as payback for Dennis's death.

She'd probably never know for sure whether that was true, but certainly Galloway had driven the case zealously. There'd been a suspicion that Rogan was being protected. Witnesses were reluctant to testify. Rogan had alibis that seemed questionable but which appeared to hold water. Galloway had become increasingly frustrated, and had been determined to bring Rogan to court. In the end, he'd managed to muster sufficient evidence to satisfy the Fiscal, but much of that evidence was subsequently thrown into doubt at the retrial, prompted at least in part by Bill's book.

In short, it had been a mess. By the time it really hit the fan, Galloway had already been thrown out of the force in disgrace and without a pension. His close colleagues had mostly also been subject to disciplinary sanctions, reflecting their relative seniority and level of involvement in Galloway's corruption. Grant had been concerned that she and other junior officers might end up carrying the can. But, although there'd been an enquiry, there'd been little scope to take action against the key individuals involved, and the case had been largely written off as history. Rogan had walked free and had his moment in the sun, threatening to sue the police for his wrongful arrest. In the event, he'd died only a few months later in a car crash on the A9 and, in the absence of any next of kin the case was quietly buried with him.

That was really as much as she could recall. Her own role had been largely routine, although she'd been thrilled at the chance to be involved in her first major enquiry. But something continued to bother her, some connection she was still failing to make.

The police car park was largely deserted and she pulled in beside Alec McKay's car. This was going to be a long day for all of them, and Alec had clearly also decided to make an early start.

It was as she was climbing out of the car that the memory came to her. It was something McKay had said, just recently, about Simon Crawford. He'd called him, jokingly, the 'accountant to the stars'.

They weren't stars in any real sense. Just middle-ranking business types engaged in dodgy practices. But she'd known what McKay meant. Crawford's clients were big fish in a very small pond. That was the way it was up here. It was too remote to interest the big players, and the business tended to be too fragmented for any one operator to gain dominance, although some were more influential than others.

But that was the world in which Crawford operated. Just as, at the time, it had been the world in which Bruce Dennis had operated.

And then she realised what had been nagging at her brain.

45

McKay was deep in conversation with Ginny Horton. Grant had been preoccupied as she'd climbed up the stairs, racking her brains to recall more details from twenty years before, trying to be sure her half-memory was correct.

'I see the gang's all here,' McKay said as she approached. 'Thought you'd be enjoying a bit of a lie-in this morning.'

'Forget it, Alec,' Grant said. 'I've been through every possible jibe that you might throw at me, and I've got a response for all of them.'

'Is that right?'

'Aye. A universal bugger off.'

'I'll keep my mouth shut then.'

'There's a first time for everything.' She sat down beside the two of them. 'How's it going?'

'We're just planning out the schedule for the day. The image of Farlowe, or whoever he really is, should be hitting the media in the course of the morning so we can hope for a response.'

Grant nodded. 'Comms' view was that we should get it out there as soon as possible. We've got a media conference this afternoon to present it formally and to give more background. At this stage, we're describing him as an individual we wish to talk to in connection with Hamish Forres's death.'

'We're going to speak to the others in Kelly Armstrong's volunteer group,' Horton said, 'just in case any of them can shed any more light on who he is and where he's from. And we'll do the same with Forres's neighbours.'

'We're still a long way from anything substantial,' Grant said. 'But it does feel as if we've got some movement.'

'I'm hoping so,' McKay said. 'As long as Farlowe doesn't turn out to be another dead end. We're making a lot of assumptions.'

'I've got one other small thing to throw into the pot which may or may not be useful,' Grant said.

'Anything you throw into the pot's bound to improve the taste,' McKay said.

'Do you remember the Bruce Dennis case?'

'Vaguely. One of Jackie Galloway's, wasn't it? Another one that went tits up.'

'That's the one. You weren't involved, were you?'

'From what I recall, I was seconded doing missionary work down south somewhere for a bit. I'd probably got up the nose of the wrong person, not for the first time.'

'Or the last. Anyway, it became a bit of a cause célèbre. Miscarriage of justice and all that.'

'Even though we all knew that the guy we nailed was guilty as hell? What was his name? Logan?'

'Rogan. Kenny Rogan. And, yes, we all knew he'd done it, but Galloway fitted him up.'

'Typical bloody Galloway. If he hadn't already royally screwed up his career, that would've have done it for him. Got a lot of coverage at the time, as I recall.'

'There was a book,' Grant said. 'Written, under a pseudonym, by none other than Bill Emsworth. I came across it at his house. He's a bit embarrassed about it now.'

'He shouldn't be,' McKay said. 'He was right.'

'Aye, but he feels he was too evangelical. Too ready to attack the police and give Rogan the benefit of the doubt.'

'But that's always the way, isn't it? Has to be black or white. I assume that's what sells books. So what does this have to do with our current case?'

'Maybe nothing. But there was something nagging at me about the Dennis case. Some half-recollection that seemed pertinent. Then I finally remembered what it was. Simon Crawford.'

'Crawford?'

'It came to me when I thought about you referring to Crawford as the accountant to the stars. Dennis played much the same role twenty-odd years ago.'

'And?'

'And he had a very junior assistant – trainee, I suppose – called Simon Crawford.'

'Really?'

'I'm pretty sure so. I was going to check the file to make sure I wasn't misremembering.'

'Doesn't mean much, though, does it?' Ginny Horton said. 'Even it is the same Simon Crawford, all it tells us is that he's a chip off the old block. We've only got a tenuous connection between Crawford and Forres – the one joint directorship.'

'I'm not sure,' Grant said. 'It set me thinking. Some of the people Dennis was involved with are familiar to us. Gordon Prebble was. As was Donaldson from our investigation at the start of the year. Not sure about Forres but it wouldn't surprise me.'

'So Crawford effectively took over Dennis's business?' Horton said.

'I imagine it didn't happen immediately. Crawford was young and only part-qualified. But he might have mopped up

Dennis's former clients.' Grant turned to McKay. 'Any news on Crawford?'

'I tried his landline again a couple of times yesterday afternoon. No reply. And I had a patrol car go by the house. No new sign of life. Maybe he's just gone away over the holiday, leaving his front door open and his lunch half-prepared. We've all done it.'

'I'm quite capable of doing it,' Grant said. 'But I take your point. Perhaps we should start taking Crawford's disappearance more seriously.'

'Could we include him in your media briefing today?' Horton asked. 'Just as someone we'd like to talk to in connection with our enquiry. If anyone knows his whereabouts, etc. After all, he is someone we want to talk to about Forres.'

'I'll see what the chief super thinks.' She paused, thinking. 'I'm going to get the files on the Dennis case pulled out of the archive. I want to make sure I'm right about Crawford's involvement. I'd like to know who else Dennis worked for and whether any of them might give us a lead on the current case.'

'You think the two cases are linked?' Horton asked.

'It's a long shot, I know, but just humour an old lady, eh?'

'You're younger than me,' McKay said.

'Thanks for that, Alec. You've no idea how much better it makes me feel.' She climbed to her feet. 'And on that cheery note, I'll leave you both to it.'

46

It was a busy morning. The picture of the man calling himself Alastair Farlowe was issued to the media in time to make the local lunchtime news and the later editions of the dailies. The call handlers were ready.

For the first time it felt as if they were getting somewhere, and McKay could feel the heightened energy in the team. Some had cancelled or postponed leave to be in, and for the moment McKay was keen to harness the renewed enthusiasm. At the morning's briefing, new tasks were allocated, priorities determined, and for the first time it felt as if the team had a real sense of purpose.

McKay was working his way through a further set of notes from the door-to-door interviews when Ginny Horton, who'd been talking earnestly on the phone, strode across the office towards his desk.

'What have I done wrong this time?'

'Nothing,' Ginny said. 'Or nothing more than usual. But I've just had a call from Billy McCann.'

'I've told you no good will come from consorting below stairs.'

'He's just seen our picture of the so-called Alastair Farlowe. He's met him.'

'Met him?'

'That's right. The first day Forres went missing. Billy went off to talk to a couple of the neighbours. He's fairly sure the first one he spoke to was the man calling himself Alastair Farlowe.'

'I'm being a bit slow here, Ginny. Are we saying that our elusive Farlowe has been one of Forres's neighbours all along?'

'That's where it gets more puzzling. McCann reckons it was Gary Forres who'd first spoken to this neighbour when he'd initially been trying to track his father down. He'd tried a couple of the neighbours' houses, and this young man was the first he went to. According to McCann he wasn't able to help but suggested he try some of the other neighbours who knew Forres better.'

'When did McCann talk to him?'

'Later the same day, when he was seeing if he could find out anything more from the neighbours. McCann caught the man we know as Farlowe as he was leaving the house. Was in a hurry and said there wasn't anything he could add so McCann didn't push it. I've checked the door-to-door notes and there's been no response from that house since we've been carrying out the interviews. We assumed it was someone who was away for Christmas.' She paused, clearly building up to the punchline. 'But McCann, being the conscientious young man he is, decided to do some online searching before he called me. The house in question is a holiday let. He found it on Airbnb and a couple of other sites – two-bedroomed cottage, short walk from the sea. According to the online calendar, it's booked for a couple of weeks over the Christmas period. McCann's already been over there. No sign of life from the outside, and, as far as he could see through the window, the place looked deserted.'

McKay lowered his head into his hands. 'They really are playing with us, aren't they?'

'It feels that way, doesn't it? I've got someone following up with the house owners to get info on who booked it, but I suspect we won't get far. No doubt a fake ID, money transferred from some third-party account that'll be a nightmare to track down. We'll get access to the house and I'll get the examiners to give it a good going-over. But again...'

'They'll be a step ahead of us. But why did they even need the house? We know the vehicle they were using left the Black Isle and then brought Forres back here on the night of his killing.'

'We know the vehicle did,' Horton pointed out. 'We don't know that Forres went with it.'

McKay sighed. 'You mean that all the time Forres was missing he might have been being held just a few metres from this own home? Please no.'

'It's possible, isn't it? According to Billy McCann, there's even a back entrance to the house only a short distance from Forres's gate. Just a couple of metres further than taking him to the parked vehicle. They might have thought that was lower risk than transporting a reluctant passenger any distance.'

'And the proximity to the site of Forres's killing would have allowed them to scope that out in advance, and not have to take Forres very far to do the deed. It would also have allowed them to keep watch on Forres's house so they'd know when Gary Forres returned. Still seems risky, though.'

'Not if they were careful. Even in a murder enquiry, we're not going to search random houses without good reason. If Forres was restrained upstairs, there's no way we or the neighbours would have known. But I agree it would have taken some cool nerves.'

McKay was silent for a moment, thinking. 'You know right at

the start of all this, when we were focusing on the bonfire killing, we speculated on a gangland murder or some internecine war over what was left of Archie Donaldson's business.'

'Those halcyon days when we only had one corpse to deal with?'

'Seems like yesterday. But you remember I mentioned the mysterious Ruby Jewell?'

Jewell had been Donaldson's estranged daughter. They'd concluded after the event that she'd been the manipulating force behind the destruction of Donaldson's business empire and his own eventual arrest. Jewell herself, a cool-headed apparent shape-shifter, had vanished into the ether.

'You seriously think she might be behind this?'

'I'm beginning to give the idea more weight,' McKay said. 'We know how nerveless she can be. We know how ruthless she is. We know how skilled she is at hiding in plain sight.' He stopped. 'And we know we're dealing with a relatively young man and woman.'

'If it is her, you must have spoken to her on the morning after Forres's death?'

'That's exactly what I'm thinking.'

'Wouldn't you have recognised her?'

'I doubt it. Last time I saw her, she was a larger-than-life character with the dyed hair and earrings working in Donaldson's offices. The person I met in Cromarty was plain, quiet, self-effacing. The exact opposite. But she was roughly the right size and the right build. Beyond that, who knows?'

'If you're right – and you have to admit that it's a big if – does that mean that it might have been Jewell who visited Gary Forres? The woman who claimed to be Kelly Armstrong.'

'It seems likely it was the same person, doesn't it? Looks like we're going to need that sketch artist after all.'

'We issued a likeness of Jewell when we were trying to track her down in connection with Donaldson's murder, but that was based on the way she'd looked then.'

'It's not difficult to change your appearance. Putting on or losing a pair of glasses. Different hairstyle. If you're a man, growing or shaving a beard. Different style of clothing. It might not fool someone who really knew you, but it would throw off most witnesses.'

'So what do we have? Serious-looking studenty type. Heavy glasses. I'm envisaging Velma in *Scooby Doo*.'

'Definitely something of that vibe about her.'

'So that's another task,' Horton said. 'Create an image of her based on your description and those of the other officers who encountered her that morning. We can test that out with Gary Forres, and see if it resembles the woman who visited him.'

'Although,' McKay commented gloomily, 'she may well look different again by now. Who knows?'

'It's worth a shot. It's another image we can release to the media. Every step gets us closer.'

'I wish I was sure of that,' McKay said. 'I can't shake off the feeling that they're playing with us. Dropping us a clue when it suits them. Waiting until some idea penetrates our thick skulls and moving on before we can do anything with it. Even what happened to Gary Forres seems designed to pull us in.'

'Jewell can't be that smart,' Horton pointed out. 'She's just a young kid.'

'She was one step ahead of us on the Donaldson case. And we've not got close to her since.'

'She doesn't have supernatural powers.'

'She has nerves of steel, which is maybe more important,' McKay said. 'But if this is her, what's she after? We thought her motive with Donaldson was a mix of personal revenge and a desire to take over his business. There's no question she siphoned off some of his money, but she's shown no moves in that direction since. It's been the usual suspects jockeying for their share of what Donaldson left behind.'

'Including Gordon Prebble, presumably?'

'He was one of the names in the frame, certainly. But that wouldn't explain why Jewell would have him in her sights particularly. And it certainly wouldn't explain Forres.'

'And we still don't have an ID for the first victim,' Horton reminded him.

'That's the most frustrating one of all,' McKay said. 'It really feels like we're getting nowhere with that. If it turns out not be connected to the other killings, we've got almost nothing.'

'We've just got to keep plugging on. I'll get Josh Carlisle to chase up the sketch artist again, and I'll see what we can get on the holiday cottage. And we don't know what response we'll get to the release of the picture of Mr so-called Farlowe. There's plenty going on.'

'Aye,' McKay said, 'I'm sure you're right. It's just that none of it seems to hang together. It feels as if we're missing something. One thing that would just pull all this together, and give it focus.'

'Such as?'

'I've no idea. I've just a hunch that it's right in front of us. We're looking right at it and not seeing it.' He shook his head. 'And if Jewell is behind this, that's just the way she likes it.'

47

Simon Crawford lay on the camp bed, straining his ears for any movement. But there was nothing. He'd hadn't even heard a repeat of the rustling sound from the junk-filled corner. Perhaps whatever made that noise came out only when it was dark, and that that was probably still some hours away.

He had no real idea how long he'd been lying there. His mobile phone was back at the house and his Rolex had been removed. Whether it had been taken for its value or simply to prevent him keeping track of time he had no idea. For the present it seemed the least of his worries.

The single window in the room was too high for him to reach, and he'd found no other exit other than the door at the top of the steps. The door itself was solid and firmly locked and bolted.

His only option was to take advantage of any visit to the room to try to force an exit. He regretted now he'd not seized the chance when the man had brought him food earlier, though at the time it had seemed prudent to bide his time. Since then, there'd been no further visits and no other signs of life outside the room. He had no idea how long he might have to wait till anyone appeared.

And, when they did, it might of course be too late.

He'd lain for what felt like hours thinking these and related thoughts, when he finally heard a sound from the door above him. The sound of bolts being drawn back and a key turning in the lock.

Crawford tensed for what might follow. He'd been contemplating whether there was anywhere he could hide in the room, or whether he could pretend to be ill or use some other ruse to wrong-foot whoever might enter. But that play-acting only worked in films. All he could do was wait and try to grab his moment.

In the event, the moment never came. The second visit proved to be an anti-climax. The door opened briefly, and a hand deposited a further plate of food on the upper landing. Before Crawford could even move, the door closed and the key was turned and the bolts slid back into place.

Gloomily, he ascended the stairs to pick up the plate. He'd finished the initial food they'd provided very quickly, and was conscious he was growing hungry again. He felt it was important to get whatever sustenance he could.

They'd gone to more trouble this time. There was some sliced bread, some slices of cold ham, an apple and a banana, and a small plastic bottle of orange juice. He carried the plate down the stairs and sat on the edge of the camp bed to eat. It was surprising how even a slice of plastic ham could seem tasty when there was nothing else available. He shook his head, his brain still working unceasingly through potential options for escape, and opened the bottle of orange juice. He was thirsty again, and he swallowed half the bottle almost in one mouthful. It was only as he removed it from his mouth that it occurred him the juice had left an odd aftertaste.

He sniffed at the contents, but could detect nothing strange about the aroma. He took another cautious sip, wondering if the juice was past its best or had begun to ferment. He took another careful swallow, now unsure whether he'd merely imagined the taste at the back of his throat.

It was only a few moments later, as he felt increasingly drowsy, that he realised he'd been right.

48

Helena Grant knew she was too busy to waste time on something likely to lead nowhere. If it had been Alec McKay doing this, she'd probably be subjecting him to one of her polite but lacerating tongue-lashings. She'd allowed her curiosity to get the better of her.

The files had turned up from the archive more quickly than she'd expected, probably because the staff there were under-utilised over the Christmas break. There were no doubt mountains of documents but she'd asked only for the core files, wanting just to remind herself of the basics of the Bruce Dennis case.

The basic facts were pretty much as she'd remembered them. She skimmed hurriedly through the documents, searching for the records of interviews with Dennis's family and contacts. There was an interview with Dennis's wife which told Grant little except that the woman had either had little idea what her husband was involved with, or had chosen to feign ignorance.

Dennis had had a couple of staff working for him. The first was an administrator and receptionist, whose job had been to organise Dennis's office but who clearly had no knowledge of the content or substance of his work.

The second, as she'd thought, was Simon Crawford.

At the time of Dennis's killing, Crawford had been only nineteen. He was still working on a part-time basis towards his accountancy qualifications and had been taken on by Dennis as an apprentice. Given the nature of Crawford's work, Grant wondered what had motivated him to involve a third-party. It seemed a relatively generous arrangement, with Crawford being given significant time off to complete his studies.

It took her another few minutes to find an interview with Crawford himself, which threw a little more light on Dennis's reason for taking on the young man. Crawford was the son of Martyn Crawford, one of Dennis's clients. Martyn Crawford was long dead now, but Grant remembered him from the Dennis investigation. A fairly big player locally, and another who operated on the borders of legitimacy. That probably explained why Dennis had been prepared to take on the son. There'd have been some business quid pro quo, and Dennis would have assumed he had enough potential dirt on the father to provide leverage if the son stepped out of line.

Grant's impression was that Dennis had been looking for a protégé to develop the business and ensure it outlived him. Presumably, he hadn't envisaged that would become an issue quite as quickly as it did. It seemed that Dennis also had a son, Thomas, who was a little older than Simon Crawford. Dennis's original hope had been that Thomas would succeed him in the business, but Thomas's ambitions had apparently lain elsewhere. He'd had no interest in accountancy and no desire to spend the rest of his life in what he'd seen as the parochial culture of the Highlands.

Grant eventually found an interview with Dennis's wife which, at least in passing, added a little more flesh to these narrative bones. It seemed that, although Dennis had resented his son's decision, there'd been no great falling out. Dennis had been happy for Thomas to undertake a degree in English literature at Aberdeen, and father and son had remained on good terms. Grant vaguely recalled the son from the investigation. She hadn't met him face-to-face as far as she could remember, but she'd heard stories about him haranguing her colleagues about their initial failure to make progress. He'd obviously cared deeply about his father and, like Dennis's wife, had claimed to have no knowledge of the business Dennis had been involved in. Quite possibly that had been true, or perhaps Thomas hadn't allowed himself to acknowledge the real nature of his father's work. Very like Gary Forres, it occurred to her.

She pushed aside the file and walked through into the small kitchen area to make herself a coffee. She'd spent the best part of an hour working through the files, and she wasn't sure she had much to show for it. She'd merely confirmed her half-recollection that Simon Crawford had been part of the Dennis investigation all those years before.

That took her nowhere. Other than the tenuous corporate link between Crawford and Forres, and McKay's still-unconfirmed concerns about Crawford's well-being, there was no evidence that Crawford had any connection with their current investigation.

Even so, Crawford's involvement in that previous case troubled her. Perhaps it was the sense of patterns being repeated between that case and this. The parallel between Gary Forres and Thomas Dennis. The way the same personalities popped up in both enquiries. Among those the police had interviewed at the time were both Hamish Forres and Gordon Prebble. Neither was seen as a suspect in the killing itself, but both, along with various others, were business associates of Kenny Rogan, and both had been among a small group who'd initially helped provide an alibi for Rogan – some so-called sportsman's dinner at a club in Inverness at which all were supposedly present. Under pressure from Galloway, the alibi had gradually crumbled as those present admitted that they couldn't recall with any certainty whether Rogan had been there all evening or, in some cases, whether he was there at all, although he'd been on the guest list. Grant's impression was that, once it became evident which way the case was going, Rogan's associates had thrown him to the wolves rather than risking their own not-always-pristine reputations.

'Penny for them.' Alec McKay had entered the kitchen without her noticing and was looking at her with some curiosity. 'I was wondering how long I'd be standing here before you noticed me.'

'Sorry, Alec. Miles away. Well, twenty years away.'

'The Dennis case?'

'Just been skimming through the file.'

'And?'

'And I'm probably wasting time I can ill afford to waste.'

'Trust your instincts,' McKay said. 'Isn't that what you always tell me?'

'In your case, I usually tell you *not* to trust your instincts.'

'Ah, I knew it was something like that. But you've found nothing?'

'Not nothing exactly. I confirmed my memory that Simon Crawford was involved in the case.'

'Was he now?'

'Nineteen years old. Working for Dennis. Sort of apprentice, doing his accountancy exams part-time.'

McKay raised an eyebrow. 'I'm surprised Dennis would have risked an apprentice given the shady nature of his business.'

'He wanted his son to join him in the business, but the son wasn't interested–'

'Smart kid.'

'Aye, except that he claimed not to know anything about what Dennis was up to. He was more interested in reading books or some such, so Dennis brought in young Crawford. Son of Martyn Crawford.'

McKay gave a low whistle. 'Now there's a name from the past.'

'You ever had any dealings with him?'

'Not close at hand. Nasty piece of work by all accounts. Top dog locally in his day. Screwed over a lot of the competition. Was he one of Dennis's clients?'

'Looks like it.'

'So not much risk for Dennis in taking on Crawford Junior then. That makes sense.'

'I was just musing about how we keep stumbling across the same personalities in both investigations,' Grant said.

'It's a small ecosystem up here. You're bound to see the same unprepossessing creatures circling around.'

'Forres and Prebble were among those who provided Rogan with a supposed alibi initially.'

'They were all part of the same clique,' McKay said. 'Rogan was presumably the smallest fry among them. That's why he became the fall guy.'

'What about Crawford? Any news on him?'

'Nothing. I got his place checked out again, but still no sign of life. But, if he's away, he's likely to be away till after New Year. We've really no grounds for taking any further action.'

'Except your gut feel.'

'Except my gut feel. And apparently I'm not supposed to trust my instincts.' McKay paused. 'You really think this might be linked to the Dennis case?'

'It's a stretch,' Grant acknowledged. 'I'm probably only making the connection because of the paucity of other leads.'

McKay was still thinking, taking her musings more seriously than they probably deserved. 'What was the nature of this alibi that Rogan supposedly had?' he asked.

'Some kind of... sportsman's dinner, whatever that might be.'

'Probably as grisly as it sounds if that bunch were involved. Some black-tie do with a bunch of pissed arseholes listening to some guy blethering on about his glory days with Ross County. All of them patting themselves on the back because they're pretending to raise money for some dodgy charity.'

'The original claim was that Rogan was there all evening, but they'd all backtracked by the time it came to court.'

'I bet they had,' McKay said. 'Jackie Galloway could be very persuasive.' He shrugged. 'I imagine a smart lawyer would have pulled it apart anyway. From my very limited experience of that kind of do, everyone's half-cut if not fully-cut, and I bet none of them could swear under oath whether Kenny Rogan was there or not. Do we know who else initially contributed to this alibi?'

'There were few names I recognised. One or two I didn't.' She reeled off a selection of those she could recall.

'Most of those are dead,' McKay said. 'Shockingly low life expectancy among the Scottish criminal glasses.'

'A lot of them would have been getting on a bit even then, and we're talking twenty plus years ago.'

'Gordon Prebble was probably the youngest in that generation,' McKay said. 'Bit of an infant prodigy was Gordon by all accounts. He'd acquired a fair bit of wealth and power by the time he was in his early thirties. Forres was older but I'd guess still younger than most of the others. Not surprising they should be the two who'd survived.'

'Until now.'

'Which is interesting in itself, I guess.'

'You're coming round to my point of view, aren't you?' Grant said. 'That there's a link between the two cases.'

'That's a point of view, is it? I thought it was just gut feel.'

'So what's your gut telling you?'

'At the moment, it's telling me to get you away from the kettle so I can make myself a coffee.'

She stood aside and gestured for him to help himself. 'And beyond that profound insight...?'

'I think you're right. It feels as if there's something there.'

'I've got the list of the others who were supposedly at this sportman's thingie. Maybe the names will give us some other ideas. You know the underworld scene better than I do.'

'Flatterer. I just keep my ears to the ground. It's worth a shot, anyway.'

She waited till McKay had made his desired coffee, knowing he'd be more than usually insufferable without it, and led him back to her office. She picked up one of the files and flicked through till she found what she was looking for. 'There.' She pushed the file across the desk towards him. 'The supposed guest list for the dinner.'

McKay looked at the list, printed on the letterheading of some now-defunct Inverness nightclub. 'A real rogues' gallery.'

'The list's not necessarily an accurate reflection of who was actually there on the night,' Grant said. 'For a start, Rogan's name's on there. These were the people who'd paid and were expected to attend. Club reckoned they always had one or two people missing on the night. People who'd changed their plans, or who reckoned they'd made their charitable contribution by buying a ticket.'

'Or people with better taste,' McKay commented. 'Not that I'd imagine many of these would fall into that category.' He ran his finger slowly down the list. 'There are a couple I don't know or at least can't remember, but most of these were stalwarts of the legitimate business community at the time.'

'By which you mean...?'

'Dodgy as fuck. To varying degrees, you understand. A few were out-and-out crooks. But most of them were like Forres and Prebble – some legit stuff supplemented by a lot that was anything but. Ah–'

'You've spotted Archie Donaldson's name there?'

'Among others, but yes. Not particularly surprising, though again he must have been pretty young at the time. Similar to Prebble.' He shook his head. 'Took us twenty years to finally catch up with Donaldson, and we never managed it with Prebble and Forres.'

'Interesting that we keep coming back to Donaldson.'

'He can't be involved directly,' McKay pointed out. 'He's still very firmly behind bars.' Donaldson had been tried and convicted a few months earlier, having pleaded guilty to a range of serious charges including people trafficking, modern-day slavery and money laundering. He'd received some leniency in his sentence because he'd been relatively co-operative with the police, although McKay suspected he'd only revealed what suited him. Even so, he was expected to be inside for a long time.

'It also brings us back to his daughter, though. The enigmatic Ruby Jewell. Not her father's greatest admirer.'

'That's one way of putting it,' McKay said. 'You think she might be bumping off her father's former associates?'

'Not personally, I guess. But we know what she's capable of.'

'But why would she do it?'

'I don't know. More proxy revenge against her father?'

'I can't imagine Donaldson giving that much of a bugger about Forres or Prebble,' McKay said. 'Though it's interesting that they weren't among the names he gave us.' Donaldson had been prepared to shop some of his former associates in his attempts to demonstrate his co-operation, but those involved had been relatively small fry. 'If Jewell really is involved, it feels to me as if something else is going on here, but I've no idea what.'

'You think I'm just chasing ghosts with this, don't you, Alec?'

'That's usually my territory. But, to be honest, I don't know.' He was still looking down the list. 'Most of these are no longer with us. Gone to meet their maker, upstairs or downstairs. In fact, the only one that I'm certain is still alive is Archie Donaldson.'

'What about the rest?' Grant said. 'Are we talking suspicious deaths?'

'A mix, from what I remember. Some were definitely just old age. A couple were victims of the famous Caledonian diet. Heart attacks and the like. There were one or two more suspicious deaths. There are a few names on there I don't recognise, so I can't vouch for everyone.'

'So where does this get us? Anywhere?'

'I've no idea. It does suggest there might be benefit in speaking to Simon Crawford.'

'We still don't have any basis for intervening, though. He's not been reported missing. Apart from an unlocked door and an unfinished lunch, there's nothing particularly suspicious about his absence. You've already pushed it by entering his house without good reason.'

McKay held up his hands. 'I was just concerned for his security and well-being. And I still have concerns.'

'So you're going to go back?'

'Are you telling me not to?'

'I'm just saying that if Crawford comes back and makes a complaint, I'll deny this conversation ever happened.'

McKay smiled. 'Forgotten it already.'

49

McKay returned to Simon Crawford's by himself. He was conscious that, however good his intentions, entering and searching Crawford's house without authority or even particularly good reason would be difficult to defend.

He hoped that, if it came to it, he'd be able to talk his way out of trouble. There had been no answer at the door and the house was unlocked, so he'd entered to check on the security of the house and Crawford's own well-being. That, along with a flash of his warrant card, would be enough to satisfy most law-abiding citizens. But Crawford was less law-abiding than most, and might well be suspicious of a police officer's motives for entering his house, particularly when that officer was a plain-clothes detective.

McKay wasn't even sure what he thought he was going to find. He and Ginny Horton had checked the house on their previous visit, though they'd hardly conducted a full-scale search. Their aim had been to confirm that Crawford wasn't in the house, either unwell or in difficulty.

Crawford's imposing house looked unchanged from McKay's previous visit. He parked his car in a spot where it would be invisible from the road – the last thing he wanted was to attract the attention of one of the patrol cars he'd asked to check out the house periodically. Before approaching the house, he checked that Crawford's car was still sitting in the garage. Donning disposable gloves, he tried the doors but they remained locked. He peered in through the windows, but there was nothing out of the ordinary.

He walked back towards the house. On leaving after their previous visit, he'd used only the basic lock, having first checked he'd be able to access it by sliding a bank card down the edge of the door. It took him only a couple of minutes to regain entry. He stepped inside, closing the door behind him.

The house felt as silent and empty as on their previous visit. He looked around the hallway, seeking any clue as to what had happened to Crawford. There was nothing. No sign of any disturbance or struggle.

He continued through to the kitchen. The burnt saucepan still sat on the cooker, although the smell of burning had dissipated. The cheese, bread and pickle still sat on the table, now attracting the attention of an unseasonal fly. Again, there was no sign of disturbance. The likely explanation was that Crawford's food preparation had been interrupted either by a call or by the front doorbell.

A call. It occurred to McKay for the first time to wonder what had happened to Crawford's mobile phone. If he'd left the house voluntarily, he'd have taken it with him. If it was still sitting around the house somewhere, that would suggest he hadn't left the house of his own accord. Something to look out for.

He left the kitchen and checked out the other downstairs rooms, without finding anything of interest. The whole place was pristine, with the air of a showhouse. McKay was the opposite of an expert in such matters, but he assumed that the décor was the work of an interior designer. He could detect little of

Crawford's own personality. There were a couple of old photographs in the living room depicting a couple arm-in-arm. McKay leaned closer and recognised the man as Martyn Crawford, Simon's father. There were no photographs of Simon himself or of any other relatives or friends.

The only other signs of Crawford's past presence here were a couple of magazines on the coffee table in the centre of the room – one devoted to sports cars, the other to photography. McKay wondered what sort of life Crawford actually led here. As far as McKay had been able to discover, Crawford lived alone, and McKay couldn't imagine that he'd received many passing visitors. It looked as if he might have a cleaner visiting periodically, although McKay also suspected that there might not be much that needed cleaning.

He made his way upstairs and entered the room he recalled identifying as Crawford's bedroom. Again, there was no sign of anything untoward. The duvet had been pulled back neatly over the bed, and there were no clothes lying around the room. Crawford was clearly a man who believed in tidiness. McKay pulled open the doors of the built-in wardrobe but the interiors revealed nothing further – carefully hung rows of clothes including a selection of expensive-looking suits.

McKay checked out the remaining upstairs rooms. A couple were apparently used as guest bedrooms, although there was no sign that either had been used recently. There was a bathroom that looked as pristine as the rest of the house.

Finally, McKay turned his attention to the room at the front of the house which Crawford obviously used as an office. It was well chosen – a light, airy room with large windows providing a striking view out over the loch. On a clear winter's day, the view was spectacular.

Crawford had positioned his desk in front of the window. The desk itself was for the most part as tidy as the rest of the house, holding only an Apple Mac desktop, a landline phone and a notepad which had been left in a position perfectly parallel to the edge of the desk. McKay flicked open the notebook. In a crime novel, this would be where he found a significant phone number. But the book was blank and unused. McKay wondered whether it was there more for appearance than any practical purpose.

Finally, he spotted what he assumed was Crawford's mobile phone sitting beneath the screen of the computer. McKay picked up the phone and turned it on. As he'd expected, it was locked, openable only by either a thumbprint or a PIN. He tried a couple of obvious numbers on the off-chance but was unable to access the phone. Something for the experts, if they needed it.

He surveyed the rest of the room. There were a couple of filing cabinets, and another table at the rear of the room. The table held a printer, a scanner and, beside them, a relatively disordered pile of papers. McKay couldn't recall noticing the papers on his previous visit, though their comparative untidiness seemed out of place with the order of the rest of the house.

McKay tried the two filing cabinets, but both were locked. They were heavy-duty and McKay knew they'd resist any attempts he might make to break into them, even if he'd been inclined to take that risk. Again, a job for the experts if necessary.

He turned his attention to the table. The papers looked as if they'd been hurriedly dumped there. Perhaps Crawford had been planning to do something with them after his interrupted lunch. McKay peered at the sheet lying on top. It looked like a printout of a bank statement, though the bank name and logo meant nothing to him. He picked it up and looked more closely. An offshore bank based in what he assumed was a tax haven. McKay took a closer look at the sums involved and gave a quiet whistle.

It was only then that he registered the names of the account holders. It was a joint account, and the two account holders were Crawford himself and Hamish Forres. The statement was relatively recent, only a couple of months before.

McKay skimmed through the upper part of the pile. More statements from the same account, with substantial amounts of money being moved in and out. Below that, statements from other offshore accounts also in the names of Crawford and Forres, with similar substantial sums being deposited and withdrawn. All were relatively recent, within the past nine months. McKay was no expert, but the statements suggested Forres was a wealthier man than anyone had suspected.

Pulling the papers towards him, McKay delved further down the stack. Below the statements from accounts belonging to Crawford and Forres, there were more, this time relating to accounts in the names of Crawford and Gordon Prebble. The sums involved here were even larger.

McKay hesitated, unsure what to do. His own status in the house was already uncertain, and he had no justification for appropriating the documents in front of him. The statements could well be evidence of illegal activity of interest to his colleagues and quite probably also to the Revenue, but he lacked the expertise to be certain. Would someone like Crawford really be reckless enough to leave incriminating material lying around even in his own home?

In the end, McKay contented himself with using his personal phone to take photographs of a sample of the statements. He skimmed down through the pile of papers selecting examples that he felt were broadly representative of the total. He'd initially assumed all the statements related to accounts in the name of either Forres or Prebble, but as he reached the lower papers he realised he was wrong.

At the very bottom of the papers was a slightly thinner stack relating to accounts held in the name of Crawford and a third name. The pattern was similar to the Forres and Prebble accounts, although there were fewer statements and the amounts of money involved were generally less, although still substantial by McKay's standards.

He separated out the statements and carefully photographed each page, still unable to believe what he was seeing.

It was the name of the joint account holder that had caught McKay's attention.

Bill Emsworth.

50

For the second time in less than twelve hours, Simon Crawford woke from a drug-induced sleep, his brain confused, his mouth dry, his head throbbing with pain. The first time he'd woken uncomfortably on a rickety camp bed. This time, he had no idea where he might be, except that it felt a thousand times worse.

He forced himself to open his eyes, his body desperately wanting to drop back into unconsciousness. He was feeling a physical discomfort that extended far beyond the aching in his head, though he was still struggling to make sense of the sensations that stretched through his body.

At first, even when he'd managed to open his eyes, he could see nothing. It was only as his eyes gradually adjusted that he realised he was still in the cellar room, but it was now dark outside. He could just about discern, as a slightly paler rectangle of darkness, the roof-level window which had previously allowed some daylight into the room.

But he couldn't make sense of his own perspective. He was on his feet, but seemed to be higher than floor level. He was upright, held in position by restraints on his wrists, his feet only just making contact with the surface beneath them. His whole body felt numb, though he was unsure whether this was an after-effect of the drugs or because of the unnaturalness of his stance.

What the hell was going on now?

He pulled against the restraints but they remained firm. There was no way he could move his body more than a few centimetres in any direction. There was nothing he could do but wait, and he had no idea what he might be waiting for.

He didn't know how much time had passed before he finally heard something. Somewhere above him he heard the bolts being drawn back and the door being unlocked. Then, unexpectedly, the room was flooded with light.

At first, he was utterly blinded by the two spotlights shining directly at him. He closed his eyes, trying to give them time to readjust. He could hear footsteps descending the stairs. More than one set, he thought, though it was difficult to be certain.

Although his eyes were gradually adjusting to the light, the strength of the glare was still dazzling. His eyes were streaming from tears, and he could barely see through the haze and the after-glare. Finally, though, he made out two semi-silhouetted figures standing in front of him.

One was the man who had visited the room earlier – he was similarly tall, with the same slight angular figure. This time, though, he was wearing no mask. Crawford could only partially make out the man's face, but he looked no more than early-twenties. The expression on his face was one of amusement. 'Perfect,' he said.

The second figure was a woman. She was also gazing at him with what looked like amusement. She was shorter than the man and had the air of a serious student, with neatly bobbed dark hair and a pair of thick-framed glasses. It took him a moment to realise she was the woman who had rung his doorbell, the woman who had claimed to be called Jo.

'What the hell's this all about?' As he spoke, Crawford looked to his left and right, trying to work out how he'd been restrained. His back was set against a solid upright beam of wood, perhaps half a metre wide. A crosspiece had been fixed to the upright, and his outstretched arms had been tied to the crosspiece with plastic ties.

It was another second or two before he realised what the set up resembled, and then he felt a sickening chill in the pit of his stomach.

It was a crucifixion.

He looked down. He was standing on a table, which was preventing him from simply hanging from the crosspiece. If the platform was removed, the pain in his limbs would be unbearable.

There had been no response to his question. The two observers continued to watch him.

'What is it you want from me?'

Crawford had thought he'd be able to hold out, at least for a short while, before handing over the information that these people presumably wanted. The codes and usernames and passwords that would enable them to access the network of accounts he maintained on behalf of his clients.

He realised now he'd been fooling himself. He'd told himself that, if he gave away this information, he'd be destroying his reputation forever. That was true but he no longer cared. He was happy to give these people anything they wanted, if only they'd release him from this.

'Whatever it is you want, just tell me. I'm sure we can come to some arrangement. There's no need for anything drastic.'

The woman laughed. 'What do you think we might want from you, Simon?'

'Who are you? How you do know me? How do you know my name?'

'We know everything about you, Simon. We know all about your business, about the services you provide. About your clients.'

'I can give you anything you want.' He was conscious he was sounding desperate now. 'Just tell me.'

'We don't want anything from you. We have everything.'

'I don't understand. What do you mean?'

'What do you think we might want from you, Simon?'

'I don't know. Passwords, access codes. I can give you all that. I can tell you how to get to the money. To whatever you want.'

'Why would we need any of that, Simon? I already have it all.'

'You can't–'

'You thought you were being very careful. You'd obviously taken some good security advice. But not the very best. It took me a little while, but in the end it wasn't that difficult to access it. All those clients. Hamish Forres. Gordon Prebble. Bill Emsworth. To name just three who were of particular interest to me. But there are plenty more.'

'You're bluffing.'

'It doesn't really matter to you any more. I've left a pile of documents in your house ready to be found after you've gone, and there'll be others making their way to the authorities in due course.'

'This doesn't make any sense,' Crawford said. 'I can give you access to all that. You'd be wealthy.'

'If I wanted to be wealthy, I could achieve that easily enough, Simon. I could simply have taken the money and you'd never have realised until it was too late. That's not what I want.'

'So what is it you do want?'

'That's very simple, Simon.' She laughed again. 'Simple

Simon. That seems appropriate enough. You all think you're smart, equating your wealth with some measure of self-worth. All you're doing is living off the backs of others. Exploiting the poorest, the weakest, the most vulnerable.' She paused, her expression suggesting she'd perhaps said more than she intended. 'As for what I want, that's very simple. I want retribution.'

'I don't–'

'There's nothing else you can give us, Simon. We don't need your passwords or your access codes. We don't need your money. All we need is your life.'

As she spoke, she and the man stepped forward and, between them, took hold of the two ends of the table beneath Crawford's feet. He tried to kick out at them, but they evaded his flailing legs without difficulty.

They pulled the table forward, leaving him hanging only from the plastic ties around his wrists. He was still a good metre from the floor and the pain in his joints was agonising. He struggled for a moment, but every movement made the pain worse. He screamed, beyond knowing or caring whether his voice might be heard outside the room.

The woman was still watching him with what looked like amusement. 'That must be painful. Don't worry, Simon. We won't leave you in that kind of agony for long.'

The man had bent over and was picking up a backpack. He reached inside and pulled out a large hammer and a handful of substantial nails, which he held out in Crawford's direction with the air of a salesman demonstrating his wares.

'First, we'll introduce you to a whole new level of agony,' the woman said. 'And then, very soon, it'll all be over.'

51

McKay found nothing else of significance in Crawford's house. He was conscious it was already growing dark. Crawford had left a couple of lights burning around the house on his mysterious departure, but McKay was reluctant to turn on more in case he attracted external attention. With a final check in each of the rooms, he left the house and returned to his car.

For several minutes he sat thinking, trying to decide what to do next. He looked again at the photographs he'd taken, squinting at the bank statements on the tiny screen of his phone. He really had no idea of their significance. He had little doubt that Forres and Prebble had been involved in criminality, but he was reluctant to say the same about Bill Emsworth without much more unequivocal evidence. The more immediate question was what, if anything, he should say to Helena Grant.

After a few minutes, having reached no conclusion, he dialled Ginny Horton's number.

'I've just finished at Crawford's house.'

'Anything?'

'Still no sign of Crawford, and no more real clue as to what might have happened to him. But I have found one interesting thing.' He explained to her what he'd found and its possible significance.

Horton was silent for a moment. 'That's very convenient, though, isn't it? I mean, that those documents should be there waiting for you.'

'That's why I'm wondering how it got there. Whether Crawford left it behind accidentally or deliberately, or whether someone else put it there. Do you recall noticing it when we were in there before?'

'We didn't spend a lot of time looking round upstairs. Just checked that Crawford wasn't there. I don't recall noticing anything like that, but that doesn't prove much.'

'I'm in the same position,' McKay said. 'Crawford normally seems a stickler for tidiness, so it stood out to me today. But it was on a table behind the door. I could easily not have registered it the first time. But, as you say, it's convenient that the material relates to Forres and Prebble.'

'Not to mention Bill Emsworth. What are you planning to say to Helena?'

'That's the question, isn't it?'

'You've got to tell her, Alec.'

'Aye, I know. But tell her what? I don't have a clue what these statements actually mean. I've no grounds to accuse Emsworth of anything. This might just be an attempt to smear him by association with Forres and Prebble.'

'But that's not the only consideration, is it? Forres and Prebble are both dead.'

'You mean Emsworth is in danger?' It was a thought which McKay had been trying to push to the back of his mind.

'There's no way of knowing, is there?' Horton said. 'But if we do think there's a possible risk, we've an obligation to let her know, surely?'

'I don't think I've got a choice,' McKay agreed. 'It won't be the most comfortable conversation, though.'

'What about Emsworth? Do we tell him directly?'

'That's a trickier one,' McKay said. 'If there's something here we need to be investigating, then we don't want to tip him off about that. But it's all conjecture.' He sighed. 'Okay, I'll head back in. Is Helena about?'

'I've seen her around. Shall I tell her you want to talk to her?'

'I'm not sure "want" is the word,' McKay said. '"Need" might be more accurate. See you shortly.' He ended the call. The darkness had thickened around him while he'd been talking, and the location suddenly felt very isolated. He looked back over at Crawford's house which, apart from a couple of rooms at the rear, sat in darkness.

He started the engine and turned to pull back out onto the road.

'What's this all about, Alec? Ginny was being very enigmatic, and now you've dragged me all the way over here.' Grant and McKay were in one of the small meeting rooms away from the main office of the serious crimes team.

'It's about Bill Emsworth.'

'Bill? What about him?'

McKay slid his phone across the table. Grant picked it up and studied the image on the screen, then looked up at him in bafflement. 'What's this?'

'It was among a pile of papers I found at Crawford's house. They were all printouts of bank statements from offshore banks. Most of the statements related to accounts held jointly between Crawford and a small selection of his clients. Or people I assume are his clients. Three people, to be precise. Hamish Forres. Gordon Prebble. And Bill Emsworth.'

'Is this some kind of pre-Hogmanay wind-up, Alec?'

'I know I've a crap sense of humour,' McKay said. 'But even I wouldn't pull that kind of stunt. It's genuine enough. That I found them, I mean. I can't vouch for the documents themselves.'

'Crawford just left these documents lying around?'

'That's another question. It's possible he did. But it's also possible that someone left it there for us to find.'

'Whoever was responsible for his departure, you mean?'

'I've no real answers. Only a lot of questions.'

Grant was still staring at the image on the screen. 'And these statements for Bill's accounts are similar to those for the accounts for Forres and Prebble?'

'Look, Helena, I'm no expert in any of this. They look similar. Even some of the same banks. The amounts here are smaller than in Forres's and Prebble's accounts, but the movement of funds is the same.'

'Still pretty substantial amounts, though,' she said. 'By my standards, anyway.'

She was looking slightly shell-shocked, McKay thought, as if she had no idea how to respond to what he was showing her. 'I'm not drawing any conclusions, Hel. I just felt I couldn't not tell you.'

'Shit,' she said. 'I mean, yes, you're obviously right. Thanks.'

'I need to get them checked out. See if we can find out what they're telling us.' He paused. 'I thought I'd get an informal view first, before we set too many hares running.'

'We've got to do things by the book, Alec. I'm already far too close to this.'

'Until now, we've had no reason to have any concerns about Emsworth. Nobody can criticise you for that.'

'But now we do have.'

'It's still very tenuous. We don't know the provenance of these documents. We don't know if they're genuine. Even if they are, we don't – or at least I don't – have a clue about their significance.'

'You don't sound as if you're even convincing yourself, Alec. But, aye, I suppose you have a point.'

'There's something else. The main reason why I felt I needed to tell you about this straight away. Whatever the provenance and meaning of these documents, we can't ignore the fact that Forres and Prebble are both dead. That both were murdered.'

'You mean Bill might be in danger?'

'I've no idea. I've no more idea about that than about any of the rest of this. But we can't ignore the possibility.'

'Who'd want to harm Bill? He's a writer. Nobody cares about them.'

'If those documents are genuine, he's a very wealthy writer. We don't know why Forres and Prebble were killed. We don't know what's behind any of this. We can't assume that Emsworth isn't at risk.'

Grant was holding her head in her hands. 'So do we tell him he's at risk?'

'That's another question, isn't it? If we do have any reason to investigate Emsworth's finances, we don't want to tip him off that we're interested. I don't know how we'd tell him he might be at risk without explaining why we think that's the case.'

'So what do we do?'

McKay had never heard Grant sounding quite so lost. She'd been through numerous tribulations over the years, but even in the most difficult periods she'd always sounded in control, decisive. Now she seemed to have no idea how to respond.

'I'm so sorry about this, Hel–'

'I don't need your sympathy, Alec. I need your help. I've only just realised – I mean, now, literally this minute – how much I've really invested in this. In Bill, I mean. I really thought...' She trailed off.

'We still don't know there's any problem with him, Helena. This is all just precautionary.'

'I still need to recuse myself from all this. I can't be involved from here on.'

'Look, Hel. Give me till tomorrow to see what I can find out. If it goes tits up, I'll take the hit for it. If necessary, I'll deny I ever told you any of this–'

'I won't let you do that, Alec.'

'If you contradict me, they'll just think you're trying to protect me. Who are they going to believe? A lifelong pain in the arse like me or a fine upstanding cop like you? Seriously, Helena, I just want to help. And if it turns out that Emsworth really is a wrong 'un, then there's not much I can do about that. But I don't want you sacrificing yourself for no good reason.'

'So what are you proposing?'

'First, that you let me look into these bank statements. I know a man who owes me a favour who can give a view as to what these documents tell us. There's no point in jumping to conclusions before we need to.'

'What about Bill?'

'When have you arranged to see him again?'

'I was due to go over tomorrow for Hogmanay.'

'My instinct is you just carry on as planned, if you feel able to do that.'

He could sense her hesitating, thinking about the implications of her position. 'I don't want to jeopardise what I've had with Bill unless I really need to. As you say, if it turns out that he really is involved in something criminal, that's obviously a different matter. But I can't just throw all this away for nothing.'

'That's the right answer, Hel.' He hesitated. 'I know how

much this means to you. The truth is we don't know what's going on here. Whether Emsworth is culpable in some way, whether he's a potential victim, or whether he's really got nothing to do with any of this. Give me a chance to see if I can find out anything definitive about the significance of the bank statements.'

'What about Bill? What if he is in danger?'

'I can probably talk the neighbourhood team into keeping his place under observation without giving too much away. But that's hardly high security. Other than that, I don't know.'

'Maybe I should go over there tonight. I'd know to keep alert and call it in if there's any sign of any problems.'

'Do you think that's wise?'

'I've no idea what's wise any more, Alec. I feel torn in two. But if Bill's innocent and I were to allow something to happen to him...'

'It's got to be your judgement,' McKay said. 'I'll do as much as I can. And if you need me, just call. Any time.' He rose to his feet. 'I'll see what I can do with the documents.'

She was still staring blankly. 'Thanks, Alec. I appreciate your being straight with me.'

'I'm not sure I'd appreciate it in your shoes.'

'Well, you know what I mean. I'm not sure I'm exactly feeling grateful. But I appreciate it was the right thing to do.'

McKay smiled. 'You'll forgive me eventually.'

She smiled back, though he could tell it was a struggle. 'You've done worse.'

52

She'd hesitated for a long time before finally forcing herself to make the call. It rang for so long that she thought it would ring out to voicemail. But finally it was answered.

'Helena?' He sounded slightly flustered, as if she'd interrupted something.

'Sorry, Bill. Is this a bad time?'

'No, that's fine. I'd left the phone in my office and popped downstairs, that was all. Heard it ringing from the kitchen.'

'I was just wondering if you'd mind me coming round tonight?'

There was a slightly extended silence that made her think she'd taken him by surprise. Whether the surprise was a welcome one, she wasn't entirely sure. 'That would be brilliant, if you're able to.'

'I've some things to finish off, but I don't think I'm going to be as late as I thought.' She paused. 'Assuming it's convenient for me to come, of course. I don't want to assume.'

'It'll be lovely to see you. I'll start thinking about what to cook.'

'Don't go to any trouble. I'm sorry it's all a bit short notice.'

'Don't be silly,' he said. 'You could have just turned up.'

He's protesting too much, she thought. *I've caught him on the hop. He didn't want to say yes and he's regretting it. Or am I projecting my own feelings onto him?*

She did feel as if there'd already been a shift in her own feelings. It wasn't that she didn't want to see Bill or that she wanted to end their relationship. But she felt more wary, less immediately trusting. More inclined to ask questions, rather than taking what he said at face value.

Part of her was inclined to curse Alec McKay. After all these years, after everything she'd been through, just when she'd thought everything was coming right. But she knew McKay had done the right thing, and she'd have found it much harder to forgive him if he'd kept silent. But that didn't lessen her unhappiness.

'About 7.30, then?'

'That would be great.' He was silent for a second. 'Are you planning to stay over?'

She hadn't expected him to ask explicitly, and, stupidly, she'd had no answer prepared. Different impulses were wrestling in her head. Part of her wanted to stay, part knew that for the moment it was anything but wise. And another part was aware that, if she was concerned about Bill's safety, it might be risky to leave him alone overnight.

'Do you want me to?'

'Don't be daft.'

'I'll have to be off fairly early. I've a lot to do tomorrow, and I assume we're still on for tomorrow evening?'

'I'll be preparing the Hogmanay steak pie specially, so we'd better be.'

Even in her current state of anxiety, she couldn't deny he was good company. All she could do was pray there was nothing in what McKay had found, that the documents were indicative of nothing criminal. A lot of people invested offshore. She might disapprove of it, but it wasn't necessarily illegal. If Bill had some money to invest, from whatever source, he might well simply trust it to advisers such as Simon Crawford. She knew from their past investigations that much of Crawford's business was legitimate. Most likely, Bill's involvement was firmly in that category.

'See you later, then,' she said.

'I'll look forward to it.'

She ended the call and sat for a further moment staring down at the meeting room table. It was too late now to make any changes, but she didn't really know what she'd just done or what its implications might be.

~

'Wally. Long time, no speak and all that.'

There was a moment's silence at the other end of the line. 'Bloody hell, is that Alec McKay?'

'Aye, Wally. Still here. Still living and breathing, or so they assure me, anyway.'

'Well, well. Can't remember the last time we spoke. You're after something, obviously.'

'I'm hurt, Wally. I'm cut to the quick.'

'Aye, right. So what is it you're after?'

McKay had worked with Wally Kincraig on a number of cases over the years. He was one of a small team of highly specialised forensic accountants who went wherever they were sent by Police Scotland. Kincraig had retired a couple of years earlier and was enjoying a life of relative leisure in some small village in the East Neuk. But his skills were still much in demand, and he supplemented his pension with consultancy work for the force and other organisations. 'There's always a need for people who can literally follow the money,' he'd told McKay.

Without going into any more of the background detail than was necessary, McKay explained what he needed. 'At this stage, all I really want to know is whether the documents provide any *prima facie* evidence of criminality.'

'*Prima facie*? Is that what they teach you in cop school these days? I learned all my Latin from going to mass.'

'That's where I'm going wrong,' McKay acknowledged.

'So you say these documents are bank statements? If that's all there is, I don't know how much I'll be able to help you. I can tell you about the various jurisdictions of the different banks. Obviously, some countries are more likely to be indicative of criminality than others, whether it's tax-dodging or something even more serious. But that wouldn't be definitive. At the end of the day, a bank statement doesn't tell you much except that an account exists and that there's money moving in and out of it. Of course, the bank itself might be dodgy, and there are plenty of those, but otherwise it's difficult unless you've more information about the sources and destination of the transfers.'

McKay could tell that Kincraig was already clambering aboard a hobby-horse. That was fair enough. It was that kind of enthusiasm that would encourage him to help. 'There were various other documents in each group,' McKay added, 'but they meant nothing to me. I'm hoping they might mean more to you.'

'You're not looking for anything formal? In evidential terms, I mean.'

'Not at all. Like I say, just a view as to the likely illegality or otherwise of the activities behind the documentation. I don't want to go around trying to drum up support and resources to launch an investigation, and then discover there's nothing to investigate. I don't even want to spend money on people like yourself without being sure we're not wasting anyone's time.' McKay hoped that Kincraig could recognise a carrot being dangled.

'No, well, that's understandable. As long as you decide to spend some in due course.' Kincraig had clearly taken the bait.

'You'll be the first person on our minds,' McKay said.

'I'll be happy just to be on your tender list. Have you got these docs in electronic form?'

'That's another long story, I've got photos of a sample of them.'

'This is something you've acquired in your usual idiosyncratic way then, Alec?'

'That's another reason I need to know if there's anything significant in them before I take it any further.'

'Message understood. And when do you want this for, taking for granted that I'm not going to be happy with whatever timescale you request?'

'I was thinking of tomorrow morning?'

'Ach, you're a hard taskmaster, Alec McKay. I'll see what I can do. I'm supposed to be entertaining the in-laws tonight. Mainly so I can avoid having to spend Hogmanay with them. But I'll get back to you as quickly as I can in the morning.'

'That's much appreciated, Wally. I'll buy you a pint next time you're up in these parts.'

'I'll look forward to it. You can buy me supper too.'

'Don't push it, Wally. But, seriously, thanks. This could be an important one, for various reasons.'

'I'm not making any promises, but I'll see what I can do.'

McKay ended the call, and then emailed the images directly to Kincraig from his personal phone. He wasn't even sure about the legitimacy of what he was doing. He'd photographed what were presumably confidential documents without permission, and he was now sending them to someone who, although entirely trustworthy, was no longer a member of the force. Maybe not the smartest of moves. But, then, no one had ever accused McKay of being smart. Not in that way, anyway. When people used the word about him, it tended to be suffixed with '-arse'.

Too late now, anyway. He knew that, whatever the procedures might say, morally he was doing the right thing. At least this way he was doing his best to protect Helena from suffering more than she needed to.

The only question was whether his best would be good enough.

53

As on Grant's previous visits, Bill Emsworth was standing at the doorway waiting for her as she climbed out of the car. He looked no less welcoming than before, but Grant was already feeling as if there was an invisible barrier between them. It was her own fault, no doubt, but that didn't make it any easier to deal with.

And actually, she thought as she drew closer, he didn't look entirely himself either. She couldn't pin down what felt different, and she wasn't sure if she was imagining it, projecting her own anxieties onto him. But he seemed less relaxed, a little on edge. He had the air of someone who was waiting for something, and that something wasn't simply her own arrival.

She followed him into the house. As always, there was the pleasant aroma of cooking in the air, this time something spicy and fragrant. 'Smells good.'

'Thought I'd do a curry for a change,' he said. 'I've been busy grinding spices.'

'You shouldn't have gone to any trouble,' she said. 'I've just sprung myself on you.'

'I'm always happy to be sprung on by you.' He paused. 'But,

actually, I already had this on the go.' He seemed nervous now, with the air of someone about to break some possibly unwelcome news. 'I've actually got a small confession to make. I haven't been entirely honest with you.'

Here it comes, she thought. The inevitable confession. The heartbreaking news she should have been expecting from the first time she'd come here. The only question was what form the confession would take. The usual 'I'm afraid I'm married' or the even more disturbing 'I'm actually a money launderer and tax dodger'.

He held up his hands, having clearly read her expression. 'I'm sorry. I'm doing this really badly. I haven't lied to you. It's just that I haven't filled in all the gaps.'

'I'm not sure I'm following you, Bill.' Her voice sounded frostier than she'd intended.

'Look, come through. I need to introduce you to someone.'

'Introduce me to who?'

He opened the living room door. As he did so, a young man rose from the sofa and turned to face them. 'Matt, this is Helena. Helena, this is Matt.' Another pause. 'My son.'

She looked in bafflement from Bill to the young man. 'Your son? But I thought...'

'That I didn't have a son. I know.' Bill at least had the grace to look shamefaced. 'It's a long story.'

The young man – Matt, she reminded herself – was shaking his head. 'I'm really sorry. This is my fault.'

'It's not your fault, Matt. If it's anybody's, it's mine,' Bill said.

Grant was wondering whether to just turn on her heel and leave. 'Perhaps someone would be good enough to explain what's going on.'

'Let's sit down and have a drink,' Bill said. 'There's no sinister agenda here, Helena. Just me being an idiot as always.' He ushered them to take seats on the sofa and began pouring glasses of wine. Grant took one, feeling she probably deserved it. If she decided to leave, half a glass of wine shouldn't cause her any problems.

Once he'd distributed the glasses, Bill said, 'Matt's my son from my former marriage. We've always had a distant relationship. My ex-wife didn't want me to have contact with him, I think mainly just because she wanted to get at me. I fought it initially and tried to seek access – which wouldn't have been an issue as she didn't have any grounds to deny me it, whatever she might have tried to claim. But in the end I decided that the fighting was doing Matt more harm than good.'

The young man smiled. 'And of course, egged on by Mum, I blamed Dad for abandoning me. So we had no contact for years.'

'It was agonising for me,' Bill said. 'I mean, I got used to it, but I missed him dreadfully at first. But I thought I was doing what was right for him.'

'Why didn't you tell me any of this?' Grant said. 'I wouldn't have minded.'

'I don't know. It just seemed a bit complicated and, in a way, a bit irrelevant. Matt and I didn't really make contact again until a year or so back. He's twenty-five now–'

'Twenty-six, Dad.'

'Twenty-six, yes. I lose count. The point is that he's more than capable of making his own decisions. He contacted me against his mother's wishes.'

'She'd always poisoned me against him,' Matt said. 'Painted him as the devil in the story. Ironically, maybe, that made me want to meet him. See what this evil man might be like. And I realised he was okay.'

'Does your mother know you're here now?' Grant said.

'Not specifically now, no,' Matt admitted. 'But she knows I'm back in touch with Dad. She doesn't like it, but there's not much she can do about it.' He paused, looking slightly awkward. 'Dad says you're a police officer. I know I'm not really supposed to be here.'

Matt's possible transgression of the lockdown regulations was the least of Grant's concerns. 'Not really my department,' she said.

'I came up to stay with some friends before Christmas. We'd been planning to come up to Aviemore for Hogmanay, but obviously that was all cancelled. So I thought I'd take the opportunity to see Dad. And here I am.'

'I still don't understand why you didn't tell me any of this,' Grant said to Bill.

'I just didn't think it mattered. Everything I told you is true. I was on my own for Christmas. Matt's got his own circle of friends now. I just assumed that eventually I'd be able to introduce you to him, and it wouldn't be any big deal.'

It made sense in a way, Grant thought. The existence of Matt didn't make any material difference to her relationship with Bill. It wasn't as if he was a dependent child who she'd need to take responsibility for. On the other hand, she found it odd that, while she and Bill had been sharing the intimacies of their past lives, he'd chosen to omit this particular nugget of information. It made her wonder what else he might not have told her. 'I'm just a bit gobsmacked.'

'I never expected to break the news like this. It was just that Matt phoned me after you'd contacted me about coming over. It was out of the blue, but obviously I couldn't say no to him. And I wouldn't have wanted to. I wondered about phoning you to tell you, but I was worried you might insist on cancelling and I didn't want that. I thought this would be the perfect place to introduce you to each other. Which in retrospect was probably pretty naïve of me.'

'That's why I say it's my fault,' Matt said. 'I shouldn't have just turned up.'

'You're welcome to turn up any time you want, Matt. But I'm sorry, Helena, I shouldn't have handled it like this.'

Grant didn't really care about Matt himself. It was more that Bill had held something back. That, coupled with everything else she'd learned today, continued to raise her doubts. 'I'm just – surprised,' she said. 'I mean, it's good news. I don't want to seem unwelcoming, Matt.'

'No, no, of course. I ought to just go. Find somewhere else to stay.'

'You can't do that,' she said. 'Not at this time in the evening. And in any case I don't mean that. I'm really pleased to meet you, Matt. If anyone ought to go, it's me. I should leave you to spend time with your dad.'

'That's not what I want,' Bill said. 'I'm always glad of time with Matt. It feels as if we're making up for what we've missed. But we'll have plenty of time to do that tomorrow when you're at work. I wanted this to be an opportunity for you and Matt to get to know each other. It seems – important, in the circumstances.'

She could feel her initial resolve crumbling. Bill had handled this badly, but he seemed genuinely unhappy at the mess he'd created. Matt seemed a pleasant enough young man, his tall, slightly ungainly body shifting awkwardly as he tried to say and do the right thing. If she and Bill were serious about the future, despite her new-found reservations, she'd need to build a relationship with this young man. On top of all that, her original reasons for coming over here tonight – her concerns about Bill's safety – remained unchanged. 'I can understand that. I'm really not trying to be difficult, and I'm not angry or resentful or anything like that. I'm just trying to absorb it all.'

'I've made a total mess of this,' Bill said. 'But I really didn't mean to make anything difficult for you. On the contrary.'

'Yes, of course.' She finally allowed him a smile, and then

turned to Matt. 'I'm sorry, Matt, I've been dreadfully rude. I'm delighted to meet you, and I'm really looking forward to getting to know you.'

'Likewise,' Matt said. 'Dad's told me a lot about you. He can't talk about anything else.'

'Oh, God,' she said. 'I can only apologise for that.'

'It's all good, though.'

Bill stood up, a relieved expression on his face. 'Why don't I leave you two to it for a few minutes while I go and tend to the food? Give you a chance to get to know each other. And if nothing else I can promise you some decent rotis.'

The remainder of the evening went more smoothly than Grant had feared. Even once she'd accepted she was staying, she'd feared the night would be hard work. But Matt turned out to be charming and very enjoyable company, and Bill was clearly working hard to ensure everything went smoothly. The food was as excellent as he'd promised, and the conversation was surprisingly relaxed.

She'd succumbed to more wine, partly because she'd initially feared that the evening would be a challenge without it, and she'd accepted that this meant she'd be staying the night. She didn't know whether that in itself might be awkward given Matt's presence, but she guessed that Matt was old and experienced enough not to be unduly fazed by it.

All in all, though, everything had gone well, and she'd once again found her concerns about Bill fading into the background. They hadn't entirely vanished. That would depend on what Alec McKay came up with in the morning. But for the moment she felt prepared to give Bill the benefit of the doubt until she knew more.

She'd warmed to Matt more quickly than she'd expected. She wasn't entirely surprised to discover he worked in telesales, and she imagined he was good at it. She could envisage his engaging warm manner would be perfect for gently drawing clients into a deal. As the night went on, she could feel herself being mildly seduced in the same way, and she found she didn't resent it.

With the evening growing late, Bill poured the dregs of the wine from the third – or was it fourth? – bottle of wine. Grant was feeling mildly woozy, but they'd drunk the wine over a long period with an extended supper. She was fairly sure she'd drunk less than the men, and she remained relatively sober.

'Should I crack open another bottle?' Bill asked.

'Not for me,' Helena said. 'I still want to be up fairly early in the morning.'

'If you're sure.'

'Certain, thanks. I might risk a glass of water.'

'Fancy a wee dram as a nightcap, Matt?'

'Why not?'

Bill gestured towards a cabinet in the corner of the room. 'I've a decent selection over there. Pick whatever suits you. I'll go and get the glasses and some ice and water.'

He vanished into the kitchen, while Matt crouched in front of the cabinet, peering at the selection of bottles. 'Didn't know Dad was such a collector.' There was an edge of something in his voice, Grant thought, but she couldn't interpret the tone. He selected a bottle, apparently at random, and brought it over to the table. 'This looks as good as any.'

Bill returned carrying a tray holding two whisky glasses, a tumbler full of ice and a large glass of water for Grant. He placed the tray on the table and peered at the bottle. 'Good choice. You've got expensive tastes.'

'Bet you'd have said that whatever I picked,' Matt said.

'Probably.' Bill poured a glass of water and handed it to Grant. 'Sure we can't tempt you?'

'I could easily be tempted,' she said. 'But I better not.' She took a large mouthful of the water and frowned. 'You haven't put something in this, have you? Tastes a bit odd.'

'Straight from the tap,' Bill said. 'Maybe something in the glass, though it looked clean as far as I could see. Do you want me to get you another?'

She took another mouthful. 'No, I'm sure it's okay. Probably just my palate suffering from the wine.'

She watched as Bill poured a dram of whisky for Matt and himself. She was feeling slightly more drunk than she'd realised, as if the effects of the wine were creeping up on her belatedly. She closed her eyes, suddenly feeling tired.

'There you go, Matt,' Bill said. 'Help yourself to ice and water as you want to.' He held up his glass. '*Slàinte.* Which I suppose is appropriate in its way. To the new year. An end and a new beginning.'

Grant was struggling to keep awake, her clouded mind baffled by the oddly poetic tone of Bill's toast. Perhaps it was some private father and son joke. 'I think I'd better get up to bed,' she said, conscious her voice seemed slurred.

'Are you all right?' Bill was looking at her with what she took to be concern.

'I'm fine,' she said, not knowing whether she was telling the truth. 'Just a bit more drunk than I'd thought.' She pushed herself to her feet, aware of her own unsteadiness.

'Hang on.' Bill rose and took her arm. 'I'll give you a hand.' He steered her slowly towards the door, then helped her climb the stairs towards the bedroom. 'Back in a sec, Matt.'

From behind her in the living room, she heard Matt's voice calling after them. '*Slàinte.*'

54

PC Drew McBride hated the early morning shift, especially at this time of the year. He started it in the dark and it was barely light by the time he finished. On top of that, he was scheduled to be on duty for the whole Hogmanay holiday. He hoped it would be relatively quiet this year, with the pubs and bars all shut. But no doubt a few bampots would still find a way to wreak havoc, and tomorrow he'd have to deal with the aftermath.

Still, it wasn't as cold as it might have been. Temperatures had gradually risen since the Christmas snows, and the morning felt almost mild. So far, too, it had been relatively quiet. There'd been a couple of call-outs but both had turned out to be false alarms. No doubt everyone was saving their energies for tonight.

He was driving through the city centre when the call came in from the dispatcher. 'We've had an anonymous report of a body in a cellar room...' The address was in a backstreet not too far from his current location.

'A body? You mean, a human body?'

'It's most likely a hoax. Refused to give a name, cut off very quickly. Mobile number they called from now unavailable. So, no, quite possibly not a human body, or even a body at all. Just someone wasting our time, but you'd better check it out.'

'Aye, I suppose,' McBride said wearily. *What sort of person gets a laugh out of pulling this sort of stroke at this time of day*, he thought. The answer, he supposed, was someone still well and truly stoshied from last night.

He pulled up in front of the address he'd been given. A lot of the local shops, particularly those off the main drag, had suffered as a result of the lockdown, but this one looked as if its closure long pre-dated this year's troubles. He couldn't even work out what sort of shop it had once been, and the grimy signage told him nothing. He climbed out of the car and approached the door. This was the last thing he wanted to be bothered with on a miserable midwinter morning.

There was no doorbell. He peered into the shop through the window but it was impossible to make out anything inside, even when he shone his torch through the glass. He banged loudly on the door and pushed against it.

To his surprise, it opened. The door had been left unlocked, though there was no way of knowing how long it had been like that. He cautiously pushed it open and shone his torch through the gap.

The interior had been stripped back to an empty shell. There were a few items of junk mail inside the door, but even those looked months' old. He hesitated for a moment, almost tempted just to turn back, then stepped inside. The air smelt damp and musty.

He made his way into the rear of the building. There was little else here. A storeroom, a small and now filthy kitchenette. There was an office upstairs, also now apparently unoccupied, but that was accessed through a separate entrance.

Finally, he looked around for the cellar. At first, he thought this might also be part of the hoax but he finally spotted a door in the corner of the storeroom. The door had bolts and what looked to be a sturdy and relatively new lock, but the bolts had been drawn back and, when he tried the door, he found that it was unlocked. Beyond it, a flight of stone steps led down into darkness.

For the first time, he found himself feeling nervous. He wasn't seriously expecting to find human remains here, but it was possible some joker had left a dead animal for him to find. Given the general state of this place, he couldn't imagine that the cellar was in any better condition.

He shone his torch down the stairs, but that revealed nothing. Finally, almost holding his breath, he began to descend. For the first few steps he kept his torch aimed squarely on the steps beneath him, not wanting either to slip or to step in anything unpleasant. It was only when he was finally fully below ground level, standing just a few steps up from the bottom, that he was able to shine the torchlight around the remainder of the cellar.

At first, he thought it was as deserted as the room upstairs. There was an ancient camp bed, with a couple of blankets tossed across it. At the far end of the room, there was a pile of unidentifiable junk.

He moved the beam slowly round the room to ensure he'd not missed anything. He had no desire to step further inside if he could help it. At last the torch beam reached the wall to his right, and he saw it. What had been placed against the bare brick of the wall, and what was hanging from it.

'Holy shit,' he said.

55

McKay stood in the doorway, chewing pensively on a stick of gum. The sun was up by now, but it did little to improve the appearance of his surroundings. A desolate decaying backstreet in a city he'd come to love, even if, like most of the country, it was going through tough times.

The street had been sealed off at both ends, the boundaries protected by uniformed officers. That didn't prevent groups of rubberneckers from gathering to peer curiously in his direction. He was tempted to wave to them, but decided it would be undignified.

From behind him, he heard Jock Henderson's less-than-dulcet tones. 'Christ almighty, Alec, I don't for the life of me know where you find them.'

'It's a gift,' McKay said without turning. 'And years of training. How's it going?'

'Ach, we're having a whale of a time.'

'Aye, you and a crucified corpse, Jock. That has all the makings of a party. What can you tell me?'

'White male. Forties, probably. Looks fit and healthy–'

'Apart from the whole being dead thing.'

'Looks as if he'd been fit and healthy. Until some bugger started hammering nails into him, aye. Cause of death – well, my guess would be simply loss of blood. There are no signs of any other major traumas as far as a I can see, though the doc may spot something.'

'Which would mean a fairly slow death, I'm assuming.'

'I'd have thought so. He'd have been in a lot of pain generally. Not just the nails but also the pull on his joints from hanging like that. I imagine he'd have lost consciousness at some point.'

'Aye, always look on the bright side, eh, Jock? What sort of bastard does something like that?'

'A pretty sick one.' Henderson stepped past McKay out into the open air and produced a cigarette packet from somewhere. He held it out to McKay. This had been Henderson's idea of a running joke since McKay had finally given up a few years before. 'We have an ID, by the way.'

'Simon Crawford,' McKay said.

Henderson raised an eyebrow. 'You psychic or actually the murderer?'

'Just a wild shot in the dark,' McKay said. 'He's been missing. Someone wanted us to find him. Just as they wanted us to find Gary Forres.'

'You're right, anyway. There's a wallet in his pocket. Including a driving licence with his likeness on it. So looks pretty definite.'

'Crucifixion,' McKay said.

'Not something I come across every day,' Henderson said. 'You think this is some religious nutjob?'

'Anything's possible,' McKay said. 'But putting aside the Christian connotations, crucifixion was just a form of execution, wasn't it?'

'I suppose so,' Henderson agreed. 'It's not an area where I'd claim expert knowledge.'

'Me neither,' McKay said. 'But it fits the pattern. Burning. Hanging. Decapitation. Death by lethal injection. And now crucifixion.'

'Can't be much else left.'

'Whoever's behind this seems to be full of surprises,' McKay said. 'So who knows?'

'So what's the message, then? That these people deserve to be punished?'

'That would be my reading. In fairness, from what we know of most of the victims, that's probably a fair judgement. Anything else?'

'It looks as if Crawford spent some time in that room before the killing. We've found his fingerprints around the room. Mainly on the frame of the camp bed, but also in a couple of other places. So it looks as if he might have been held there until–'

'He was nailed to the cross. That would make sense. We know he's been absent from his home for a few days. No other prints?'

'Nothing useful. Whoever did this must have worn gloves. Forensics may come up with something more, but that'll take a while.' Henderson finished his cigarette and ground the stub out under his heel. 'We found some papers too.'

'Papers?'

'Aye. Quite a mishmash of stuff. What look like copies of bank statements, company accounts.'

'What sort of names on them?'

'Some of the names we know. Forres and Prebble, for example. Others didn't mean much to me. William Emsworth?'

'Emsworth? Can you show me?'

'Hang on a sec. We've got them all bagged up in what seemed like sensible groups.' Henderson disappeared back into the shop, and then reappeared a moment later with a selection of large evidence bags, each filled with a stack of papers. He carried them over to one of the marked cars lined up along the street, and spread the bags out across the bonnet. 'These ones look to be bank statements. Those seem to be company accounts with Emsworth as a named director. I didn't know what to make of these ones, though.'

McKay picked up the bag and peered at the document inside. It was very different in nature from the other material. A copy of an article from what McKay initially thought was an old copy of *Private Eye*. The layout and font didn't look quite right, but McKay wasn't sure if that was simply because the piece dated back some years or because it was from some other source.

It was a piece that had clearly been written shortly after the publication of Emsworth's first book, and was headed: 'William Emsworth: Too Much of an Insider?' The gist of the article was that Emsworth's book drew heavily on his own dubious business background. Much of the content seemed to be little more than innuendo, but the implication was that Emsworth had had gangland connections and had acquired a non-inconsiderable fortune through a range of criminal activities. Again, the detail of the activities wasn't spelled out, but there were hints at money laundering, people trafficking and enforced sex work. Nasty stuff, if there was any truth in it.

The article implied that Emsworth's supposed reclusiveness primarily stemmed from a desire to conceal his real background, and concluded by querying whether Emsworth's publishers were aware of his history and the sources both of his insider knowledge and his personal wealth.

McKay's view was that Emsworth's publishers probably wouldn't have given a flying one about Emsworth's history, and had probably been disappointed only that he wouldn't allow them to use it for promotional purposes. But McKay tended to be cynical about things like that.

The article was relatively thin on convincing detail, but, along with the bank statements he'd already seen, it began to confirm the picture that was already coalescing in McKay's head. It would be interesting to hear what Wally Kincraig had made of the statements.

'There's more on the other side,' Henderson said, gesturing towards the bag in McKay's hands. 'There were two pages. I put them back-to-back so you'd be able to read them in the bag.'

'Very smart, Jock.' McKay turned the bag over and continued reading. The article ran for another half page, the content adding little other than more innuendo. But next to the article was a picture, apparently of Bill Emsworth.

It was an old picture, McKay knew. But he still couldn't make sense of what he was seeing. He looked up at Henderson. 'Can I hang on to these, Jock? I need to check something. I'll make sure they're booked in properly.'

'Too right you bloody will,' Henderson said. 'I'll make sure it's all recorded by the book, with your name firmly against it. But, aye, if you think they're going to be useful.'

McKay was still staring at the picture. 'I think they're more than useful, Jock. I think they're bloody terrifying.'

56

Helena Grant slowly opened her eyes. The process felt painful even though the room was only dimly lit. *Christ,* she thought. *Never again.* She couldn't remember how many times she'd thought that over the years.

But she'd thought now that she'd put that time behind her. She couldn't remember the last time she'd been drunk, and she certainly couldn't recall the last time she'd had a serious hangover. But that was what she seemed to have now. A pounding headache. Nausea. A mouth that felt as though a selection of particularly unhealthy animals had spent the night there.

It took her another few moments to realise that a hangover, however substantial, was the least of her problems.

What the hell happened?

She was in Bill's bedroom, and she was lying supine on his bed. But she also seemed to be fully clothed and her arms and ankles had been secured in some way to the frame of the bed itself.

What the fuck?

She twisted her head, trying to make sense of her predicament. The bed had an ornate Victorian-style metal frame. Her arms had been secured to the upper bedposts with plastic ties. She could only partially see her ankles, but the arrangements there seemed more complicated, with some extension attaching the ties round her ankles to the lower bedposts.

Why the hell had this been done to her? Her first thought had been that Bill himself must be responsible, either as some grotesquely ill-conceived joke or for some more sinister reason. But then she had a second, perhaps even more chilling thought. That she and Bill might both be victims in this, and that she'd been restrained while they'd done whatever they wanted to with him. She wondered again about the unexpected presence of Matt the previous evening.

She struggled with the ties, trying to see if she could loosen them, but it was futile. She was firmly secured and there was nothing she could do that was likely to loosen the hold. That in turn meant that she was unable to do anything else. She looked around again, hoping to see something, anything, that might help free or loosen her restraints, but there was nothing.

Finally, in the absence of any other options, she began simply to scream, as loudly and forcefully and angrily as she could. It might well achieve nothing. It might even make her circumstances even more unpleasant, depending on who responded to her screaming and how. But at least it helped relieve her feelings.

She continued for as long as she was able, then fell silent, concerned not to damage her throat. She'd be better to pace herself, hope that somehow someone would come into earshot who might actually help her.

Finally, after she'd been silent for several minutes, she heard the bedroom door opening. She angled her head to try to see who was entering but before she could do so she heard Bill Emsworth speaking. He spoke softly, as if he'd come to wake her with coffee and toast. 'Good morning, dear. I hope you're feeling a little better now.'

'What the fuck is this, Bill? What have you done?'

He moved to stand in her range of vision. 'I'm sorry about this. I appreciate it may be uncomfortable. Unfortunately, it is necessary until we reach the appropriate time and that may be some hours yet.'

'Is this some kind of joke, Bill? If it is, it's not bloody funny.'

'No joke. Unless it's some kind of cosmic one. Which I suppose is only too possible.' He was silent for a moment, watching her. 'I'd have preferred to wait until this evening so you wouldn't have had to suffer for quite so long. Matt persuaded me we should take advantage of your unexpected early arrival. It reduced the risk of something going wrong, he said, and I suppose he's right. Though of course there is the risk that you'll be missed today. But I hope I've taken care of that.'

'I don't know what the hell you're talking about, Bill. But if you don't release me from this immediately, I swear–'

'I'm afraid there really is nothing you can do, Helena. I'm sorry about that. I'd like to say that I'm sorry it had to end this way, but that was always the plan.'

'Plan? What plan?'

'I may try to explain some of it a little later. It probably won't make much sense to you, but I think you deserve an explanation. I do appreciate you're not personally to blame. Not as much as many others, at least. But you were left holding the baton, as it were.'

'Have you gone completely mad, Bill? I've no idea what you're raving about. There's still time to stop this, whatever the hell it is. Time to end the joke.'

'That may be true,' Emsworth said. 'Though not in the way you mean. That's the whole point of this, I suppose. To put an end to all this.'

Grant had no idea what was happening. Her first thought was that Emsworth had suffered a mental breakdown, was suffering from psychosis, but this was like no form of mental illness she'd ever heard about. He seemed relaxed, calculating. As if he was reaching the conclusion of some carefully constructed plot. Perhaps that was it, she thought. Perhaps he was somehow trying to enact the plot of one of his novels. But none of this made any sense.

'I'm afraid I'm just going to have to leave you lying here,' he went on. 'There's not even much I can do to make your experience more palatable. I don't imagine you're feeling too well in any case, given the dosage we gave you.'

Dosage. So she'd been drugged the previous evening. There had been something in the water, as she'd initially thought. That was why the apparent drunkenness had overcome her so quickly and unexpectedly. It was hardly a surprise, given her current predicament, but it left her even more baffled. 'You'd been intending that all evening?'

'As I say, it was really Matt's idea. It probably wouldn't have occurred to me to be quite so… opportunistic. I tend to develop a plan and stick to it. Matt's a little more creative. Probably one of the benefits of being young. As soon as he knew you were coming over last night, he suggested it. I was unsure at first, but as so often he was right.'

'You mean, through that whole evening, while we were laughing and joking, this was always how you intended it to end.' Somehow, absurdly, that seemed even more of a betrayal than what he'd actually done.

'I'm afraid that's true. I'd rather have done this some other way, but sadly no other way was available to us.'

'I don't begin to understand this. Who's us? You and Matt? What's this all about?'

'It's about all of us, I suppose.' He turned and picked up a large plastic bottle of water which had been standing on the cabinet beside the bedroom door. 'You may need a drink now.'

'You think I'm going to drink anything you give me after what you did last night?'

'It's your choice. This is just water. I am going to put you back to sleep, but I have other means to do that now you're secured.'

'I don't want anything from you.'

'As I say, your choice. Now...'

She saw now that there was a small bag, similar to a wash-bag, sitting on the cabinet. Emsworth picked it up, unzipped the bag and extracted a syringe.

She was staring at him, her eyes wide. 'You can't–'

'I'm afraid I have to.'

57

McKay arrived back at his desk to find a message from Wally Kincraig waiting for him. He hesitated for a moment, keen to confirm the disturbing realisation that had struck him when Jock Henderson had shown him the documents. But what Kincraig might have to tell him might also contribute to that confirmation, so he sat down at his desk and made the return call.

'What have you got to tell me, Wally?'

'Interesting set of documents you've sent me here, Alec.'

'Interesting good or interesting bad?'

'Well, all of this is couched in the usual caveats. There's only so much I can conclude from what you've given me, and a smart lawyer would probably be able to come up with suitable defences without a lot more evidence.'

'But?'

'But I'd be treating these as the start of an investigation. There'd be enough here to justify an enquiry, I think. All the banks are in countries on the tax haven blacklist, and some of them are known to us as dubious practitioners. There are huge sums of money coming in and out of these accounts, often staying in the account only for very short periods. Obviously, the next question would be where those sums are coming from and going to. It would be interesting to see the accounts of the associated companies.'

'We may now have some of those,' McKay said. 'We've just come into possession of a whole new stack of documents.'

'Interesting. This kind of investigation is often like completing a jigsaw. Trying to put together the different pieces in ways that fit together in the hope that you'll be able to start making sense of the picture. You very rarely get to complete the whole thing, but if you can put together enough you can potentially make the case stand up.'

'Very poetic, Wally. But I get the point.'

'Of course, the other issue is always the provenance of the documentation. Whether it's genuine, whether it's admissible as evidence, all that stuff. It's never straightforward.'

'I don't know how much that's going to matter in this case, given that most of the key players are now dead. At this stage, I'm more interested in trying to discover who killed them.'

'Ah, I see. You think their deaths might be linked to what these documents seem to be telling us.'

'It seems likely. What about Emsworth's accounts? How do they look?'

'There are fewer of them. And the sums involved are a little smaller, though still not inconsiderable. But on the face of it, I'd say they show the same sort of pattern. So, yes, dubious practices. Probably money laundering.'

'I was afraid you were going to say that.'

'Not what you wanted to hear?' Kincraig sounded surprised. 'Not like you to be giving a potential villain the benefit of the doubt.'

'It's a long story, Wally. I'll tell it to you when we get together for that pint. It looks as if Emsworth isn't what he seems to be.'

'Which of us is, Alec? Hope my input's been useful anyway.'

'Definitely, Wally. It's helped to confirm what I thought, or in Emsworth's case what I feared. And it looks as if we've now got a whole new stack of documents to work with, so I hope we can start putting together your jigsaw.'

'Good to hear, Alec. And if you lot need expert support, I'm always out here.'

'I'll pass the word on, Wally. Thanks again.'

'I'll look forward to that pint.'

McKay ended the call and sat back, thinking about what he'd just heard. None of it had been a surprise, but that wouldn't make it any easier to break the news to Helena. And even now none of it was definitive.

He walked over to Ginny Horton's desk, carrying the evidence bags that Henderson had given him. She'd been on the phone, co-ordinating the various activities still continuing over in Cromarty. He sat down opposite her and waited until she'd finished.

'It sounds like you've had a grisly morning,' she said.

'That's one way of describing it. I don't know what's going on here, but it's certainly giving us some new experiences. Though I'll happily forego witnessing another crucifixion.'

'It's unbelievable. What sort of person is capable of doing something like that?'

'The same sort of person who's capable of burning, hanging or decapitating someone, it seems.' He gave a theatrical shudder. 'I've never thought of myself as the squeamish type, but this is giving me the creeps.'

'You and me both.'

'Have you seen Helena this morning? She wasn't in her office when I came past.'

'Didn't you hear? She's not feeling well, apparently.'

'Not well?'

'Yes, we apparently had a call earlier saying she'd woken up feeling under the weather this morning.'

McKay frowned. 'When was the last time Helena stayed off work because she was feeling under the weather? Unless she thinks she's got the dreaded virus?'

'I don't know any more. Just that she wouldn't be in today.'

McKay was silent for a moment. Then he took the evidence bag containing the magazine article and pushed it across the desk towards Horton. 'You interviewed Bill Emsworth, didn't you?'

'Yes, for what it was worth.'

McKay tapped the photograph in the article. 'What do you think of that picture?'

She picked up the bag and peered at the image. 'I don't understand. That's not Emsworth.'

'You're sure? It's an old picture.'

'It looks nothing like him. I'm good at faces. His face is a completely different shape. This looks nothing like him.'

'He'd have been much younger then,' McKay persisted. 'People change.'

'They don't change that much,' Horton said. 'If he'd grown or shaved a beard, or started wearing glasses, or radically changed his hair, it might be harder to be sure. But this is someone who's clean shaven with short hair and no glasses, just like Emsworth. It's just not the same person. Is this some sort of joke?'

'If so, it's not all that funny. Sorry for pushing you like that, but I wanted to be sure. You've just confirmed what I thought. As soon as I looked at the photo, I realised it wasn't Emsworth. Or at least not the man we know as Emsworth.'

'Where did this come from?'

'It was left with Crawford's body, along with a further stack of financial documents like the ones I found in Crawford's house.'

'Somebody trying to tell us something?'

'It looks that way, doesn't it?'

'What does it mean, though?'

'There are two possibilities, aren't there? Either this isn't a picture of Emsworth – which is possible, given we don't know where this article was published or how reliable it is – or the man we've met isn't Bill Emsworth.'

'But how could that be possible? You can't just replace someone.'

'Can't you?' McKay said. 'I mean, normally it would be difficult, but maybe less so in Emsworth's case. We know he had a reputation as a recluse – perhaps because he didn't want to risk encouraging any more articles like this. Helena told me there are no pictures on any of his books, and he avoids his picture being used in reviews or articles.'

While he'd been talking, Horton had been tapping on her computer, carrying out an internet search for Emsworth's image. 'You're right,' she said. 'All that comes up are pictures of his book covers. Nothing of him at all.'

'So he's someone who's always avoided being photographed, at least publicly, probably because he has plenty of skeletons in his cupboard. Moves to live in the Black Isle, presumably again because it's a remote spot where he won't be recognised. We've been in lockdown for much of the year anyway, so he's unlikely to have been seen.' McKay stopped. 'Then when lockdown's lifted, he suddenly breaks the habits of a lifetime and emerges as a pillar of the local community, fronting a major local event. Even had his picture on the poster. That was how I recognised him in the first place.'

'You're seriously suggesting that someone replaced the real Emsworth?'

'And then stepped forward to occupy his place very publicly to ensure that no one would think to question it.'

'It would need a hell of a lot of nerve.'

'Which is the one thing we know our killers have.'

'Christ. But if there's any truth in this, what happened to the real Bill Emsworth.'

McKay was silent for a moment. 'We still haven't identified our first victim. The man in the bonfire.'

Horton was staring at him, her eyes wide. 'You think that was Emsworth?'

'If you wanted to make sure the body was unidentifiable, that would have been an effective way to do it.'

'If you're right, when the fake Emsworth lit the bonfire–'

The same thought had occurred to McKay. 'He knew exactly what he was doing. Burning a man alive.'

'That would have been a huge risk.'

'But that's been true of everything they've done. It's almost as if that's part of what motivates them. Even down to contacting the local police supposedly for help with Emsworth's research. Which made it even less likely we'd suspect anything was wrong.'

'And Helena...'

'I know. That's why I hope I'm wrong.'

Horton was still staring at him, her expression suggesting she was still struggling to process what she'd been hearing. 'So if the man we've met isn't Bill Emsworth, who the hell is he?'

'I've a theory,' McKay said. 'But at the moment it's nothing more than that–' He suddenly stopped. 'You said there was a call saying Helena wouldn't be in?'

'Yes, that's right. I'm not sure who took it.'

'But it was Helena herself who called?'

'I've no idea. I can try to find out.'

'Bugger,' McKay said. 'I'd forgotten. She was planning to go over to Emsworth's last night.' He pulled out his phone and dialled Grant's home number. The phone rang out to voicemail. He tried once more with the same result, and he then tried her mobile. Still no answer.

'She's not at home.'

'Shit.'

'Quite. Just as all this seems to be coming to some sort of climax. I think we'd better get over to the Black Isle. And we'd better get some backup over there as well, just in case. We can do that on the way.'

58

Helena Grant woke feeling even worse than before. Worse in almost every single way. Physically, emotionally, and in terms of any hope she might still have been harbouring.

She was in the same position. Still secured to Emsworth's bed, her wrists and ankles held as tightly as ever. The room seemed unchanged, and it took her another minute to realise that Emsworth was standing at the foot of the bed.

'Ah, you finally seem to be waking. I was thinking we might have to wake you. Things seem to be becoming more hurried than we'd anticipated.'

The son, Matt, was standing just behind Emsworth, watching her with what looked like amusement. 'This has gone far enough, Bill. I've no idea what this is all about or what sort of game you're playing, but it can't go any further.' She tried to force her voice to remain calm, but she was conscious it carried a tremor she couldn't entirely conceal. 'I'm not feeling well, Bill. Just stop this and let me go.'

'I'm sorry, Helena. We are nearly at the end, but I can't let you go.'

'I don't understand–'

'No, well, I'll try to give you an explanation. But time is short. We've just had word from our associate that things are moving a little faster than we'd hoped. I'd hoped to time this for midnight. The end of the year. That seemed fitting. But then time – in that sense at least – is really just a construct, isn't it?'

'What the hell are you talking about?'

'The year's ending all over the world. We're all starting again. Or they are. The precise time doesn't matter. The solstice passed a few days ago anyway, and that's probably a better marker of the end of the old year. That was why I started then.'

'Started what?' She strained against the bonds holding her wrists, sensing now that something was coming to a head.

Emsworth looked at Matt, as if seeking his view. 'I'm not sure what we should call it. The sacrifice. The punishment. The reckoning. Some grandiose name like that. The cleansing, perhaps. That's really what it was. Ridding the world of some of those who've been responsible for our mounting sin. There are countless more, of course, but we can only deal with those that mean most to us.'

Grant offered no response, sensing that Emsworth was now talking only to himself. There was an odd evangelical tone to his voice, something she'd never detected before. It was as if he'd slipped loose of reason, his mind now somewhere she couldn't imagine.

'There are some things you need to know, Helena. The first is that I'm not Bill Emsworth.'

He really is mad, she thought. *He's inhabiting some alternative reality, losing contact even with his own identity.*

'I wonder if you'd have liked Bill,' he said. 'The real Bill, I mean. I don't think you would have, to be honest. He had none of my charm. He was a bit of an old thug, to be honest, though he had talent. He could tell a story. Or at least he could when it had been suitably polished by his editors. He told his own story, mainly, or versions of it. Highly sanitised versions, of course. No, I don't think you'd have liked him.'

'What the hell are you talking about, Bill?'

'Helena,' he said patiently, 'I've just explained. I'm not Bill. I'm Thomas. You might as well know that now. Thomas Dennis.'

Grant had finally begun to realise that, whatever this man's mental state might be, these were something more than the incoherent ravings of a madman. Thomas Dennis. The son of Bruce Dennis. The son who hadn't wanted to go into his father's business.

'You're claiming to be Bruce Dennis's son?'

The man brought his hands together in mock applause. 'Well remembered. That's me. And just in case you were wondering, this isn't really my son. Just someone who's helped me with this. He's only here to say his farewells.' He turned to the younger man. 'You'd better get off while you've still time.'

Matt nodded. 'Go well, Dad.' There was a note of mockery in the last word. 'If this is really what you want, I'm not going to stand in your way.' He was smiling, his expression one of detached amusement. His coldness seemed almost more chilling than the older man's mania.

'My time's almost gone anyway,' the man said. 'At least this way I can do something useful with it.'

Matt looked as if he was about to say something more, but then, without another word, turned and left the room, closing the door behind him.

'I needed help to complete this,' the man said. 'Matt understands these things. And now he and his friend will finally reap the rewards.'

'His friend?' Grant felt she needed to keep the man talking, buy herself as much time as she could, though to what end she had no idea. She only knew that the man kept talking about time running out, which perhaps meant the possibility of an intervention.

'She gave me the focus, really. I've been contemplating this – something like this – for a long time. But she knew what to do, how to handle it. She knew this world, the personalities involved. She helped us plan it.'

It had taken Grant a few moments to realise who he must be talking about. 'Archie Donaldson's daughter?' The woman they'd known only as Ruby Jewell.

The man looked surprised. 'Yes, you're right. That was why I was reluctant to trust her at first. But then I learned what she'd done to her father and his business. She wanted us to get the same kind of revenge.'

'She and Matt...?'

'Partners. Though not in that sense. Not yet, anyway.'

Grant was still trying to process everything she was hearing. 'So if you're not Emsworth, what happened to him?'

'He was our first sacrifice.'

'Your first–'

'On the night of the solstice. Our fire sacrifice, if you will. Our first execution.'

Christ. The significance of what he was saying struck her immediately. 'So when you lit the fire...?'

'It was no accident. It was partly just Matt's little Wicker Man joke, but it served its purpose. It meant Emsworth's corpse was essentially unidentifiable.'

Grant was beginning to realise what this meant for her. That her brief, apparently idyllic relationship with this man had never been anything other than a sham. It was a minor point in the context, she tried to tell herself, but for her it was devastating. 'You bastard,' she said. 'You utter fucking bastard.'

'I'm sorry,' the man said. 'I wanted you here. I needed you to complete the cycle.'

'Why me? What the hell do I have to do with any of this?'

'I'm afraid you're just the last one standing. The last of that corrupt police team who failed to obtain justice for my father. The last of the ones who betrayed him.'

'That's insane. I was just a new DC. There was nothing I could have done.'

'You could have exposed Galloway. You could have told the truth. You could have ensured the investigation was carried out properly. Of course I'd rather have had Galloway or one of the others here, but you'll just have to bear the responsibility instead.' He laughed. 'And Matt rather liked the idea. Another of his Wicker Man jokes. An officer of the law came here of her own free will. Hardly a virgin, of course, but you can't have everything.'

Grant had finally lost patience with this madness. 'Fuck you,' she said, calmer now. 'Fuck you and everything you stand for. I don't know what you think you're doing or what messianic mission you think you're on, but this is nothing more than mindless savage killing.'

'It's a necessary sacrifice. This year has been a dark one. The darkest I can recall. Removing these people, exercising the justice that people like you have failed to deliver, all of that may just help the world return to the light.'

There was little point in arguing with such insanity. There was nothing Grant could do except hope. 'So what are you going to do?'

'The last of my executions. Including myself. I don't pretend I'm any better, and my future is constrained in any case. I had planned on using gas as the final execution method, but I'm afraid that will be too slow. There are two large canisters releasing butane downstairs. There should be substantial release of gas by now in what's essentially a sealed room. When I leave you here in a few minutes, my intention is to ignite it.' He paused, smiling. 'I imagine you'll hear the result.'

59

McKay heard the explosion even inside the car. A moment later, he saw the billow of a cloud of smoke rise above the village. Even though the darkness was falling, the significance of what they were seeing was unmistakeable. Horton pressed the accelerator to the floor as they pulled off the main road towards the house.

They'd called for backup as they were leaving the office, but it looked as if they were first on the scene. By the time they reached Emsworth's house, there were already flames licking at the now broken downstairs windows from within.

'Christ.'

Horton pulled up the car as close as she dared and McKay tumbled out, heading immediately for the front door. He tried the handle but the door was locked. It looked a solid piece of work, and McKay couldn't envisage that his own relatively slight frame would make much of an impact on it. He turned his attention to the windows, but the flames already visible behind the only potentially accessible window were likely to impede any attempt at entry.

Finally, short of any other ideas, he hurried round to the rear of the house. Here, there was a solid rear door leading into the kitchen, and a pair of patio doors into a living room. Those looked to be the most promising entry point.

McKay looked around him. Large boulders had been set decoratively in the flower bedding. He freed the largest that he judged he'd be able to lift easily and then, praying that the doors weren't constructed of toughened glass, he threw it hard at the pane.

To his relief it shattered. He picked up a second stone and used it to knock away the remaining glass and then slipped carefully into the room. Not for the first time, he gave thanks for his slender figure.

Even in this room, with the door closed, he could smell the acrid stench of smoke. He pulled off his coat and held it across the lower half of his face before cautiously pulling open the door. In the hallway, the heat and the smoke were less bad than he'd feared, although he could see the orange flickering of flames from a room opposite.

Still holding the coat to his mouth, he crossed the hall and peered into the room. It was already filling with flames and smoke, the room itself badly damaged by the explosion. There was a figure lying at the far end of the room, but from the state and angle of the limbs McKay guessed that it was beyond any help. Whoever it was, it wasn't Helena.

He closed the door, hoping to buy himself more time, then quickly checked that the remaining rooms on the ground floor were unoccupied. Finally, he raced up the stairs and entered the room immediately ahead of him.

Helena Grant was lying on the bed, obviously terrified, her arms and ankles secured to the bed frame with plastic ties.

'Jesus, Hel. This is no time for your sex games.'

He hesitated for a moment, wondering how to free her. Then he remembered Fiona's Christmas present, which he'd slipped into his pocket mainly out of politeness. *You said it would come in useful, Fiona*, he thought as he pulled out the knife. *You didn't know how right you were.*

Forcing himself to keep calm, he cut carefully through each of the ties before helping Grant off the bed. She seemed unharmed but distressed and she struggled to walk. Supporting her as best he could, McKay brought her down the stairs.

Flames were already licking around the door he'd closed only minutes before.

He led Grant back into the room through which he'd entered the house, and then slipping through the broken window, he helped her to follow him, taking care that she wasn't further injured by the remaining shards. Finally they were out in the cold evening air, and he was able to lead her back around the house to the road where Ginny Horton was waiting.

Behind them, the fire was now well-established.

As they reached the car, McKay looked down the road to their right. He could see a convoy of blue lights heading in their direction.

'Right,' he said. 'So *now* you bother to turn up.'

60

Helena Grant was lying on the hospital bed, now fully asleep. She'd been sedated and it was likely to be a while before she woke, but McKay wanted to be there when she did. He didn't want her to have to come to grips with all this alone. And the truth was, he thought, that she had no one else she could really turn to. She had friends, of course, and some very close ones, such as Jacquie Green, the pathologist. They'd give her the support she needed later on, but McKay guessed that, in the short term, she'd need the company of someone who knew this job the way she did.

Ginny Horton had insisted on staying with him, and he'd been glad of that, knowing Ginny could offer a sensitivity that he'd no doubt lack. She'd gone to get herself a cup of water, and now returned, sitting herself down beside McKay. 'Any sign of life yet?'

'Not yet. Nurse reckoned it shouldn't be long but who knows?'

'She's okay otherwise, though.'

'Looks like it. They're still doing tests which is why they're keeping her in. But I think she was mainly suffering from shock.'

'Can't say I blame her.' Horton took a sip of the chilled water. 'So the man we knew as Bill Emsworth was really Thomas Dennis?'

'That's what Helena said in the few minutes we had to talk before the ambulance arrived. She was in a bad way, but I don't think she was delirious. And it would make sense. Thomas was always obsessive about what had happened to his father. Insisted it was only police corruption that had prevented him getting justice.'

'He wasn't wrong about that.'

'No. Though ironically my guess is that if Jackie Galloway was receiving backhanders it was more likely to be from Bruce Dennis's associates. Galloway's aim was to get Kenny Rogan convicted for the killing, not to get him off. Rogan was only released because Galloway fabricated evidence. But that wasn't how young Thomas saw it.'

'So this was all revenge for his father's death? Killing people like Forres and Prebble because they'd helped protect Rogan.'

'And because they were part of the consortium that commissioned Dennis's killing, I imagine, though we'll never prove that now.'

'What about Simon Crawford?'

'My guess is that Thomas thought Crawford had been a spy in the camp, that he was leaking information to the other side. As I recall, there was some thought at the time that Rogan was suspiciously well-informed about Dennis's movements and habits. And ultimately Crawford took over a lot of what had been Dennis's business. That was another thing that Thomas always used to claim when he was supposedly campaigning for justice – that somehow Dennis's killers had robbed the family of their rightful inheritance.'

'But I thought Thomas had already walked away from the business?'

'These things aren't always logical, are they? And I'm not sure that it was even about greed or desire for the money. I suspect Thomas felt guilty that he'd not supported his father, that in walking away he'd let his father down in some way, allowing Crawford to become a surrogate son. I think that's why he was so obsessive about not letting his father down again.'

'Freud would have had a field day,' Horton commented. 'But why do it in such a convoluted way?'

'I'm only piecing this together from what Helena told me, but it all sounds very murky. It seems as if Thomas had persuaded himself, or had been persuaded, that this wasn't just a matter of sordid revenge but an act of salvation.'

'Salvation?' Horton said. 'Okay. Go on.'

'These weren't just executions. They were sacrifices.'

'Sacrifices.' Horton's face was deadpan.

'At the turning of the year. Starting with a fire sacrifice on the solstice, and ending with the sacrifice of an officer of the law on New Year's Eve.'

'This was supposed to achieve what exactly?'

'According to Helena, it was the return of the light. That this has been one of the darkest years in memory, and that it needed an act like this to start everything anew and lead us back into the light.' McKay held up his hands. 'Hey, I'm only the messenger.'

'It sounds – what's the phrase? – batshit crazy.'

'It sounds to me,' McKay said, 'like the kind of sick psychotic joke our friend Ruby Jewell might have come up with. Thomas apparently confirmed that she was involved. He reckoned she'd given them focus, or something like that, and that she was the one who'd come up with the ideas. It wouldn't surprise me if she wasn't the one who'd wound up Thomas's obsessions to get to this point, and it sounds as if this mysterious Matt is just as dangerously psychopathic as the rest of them. Whoever he is, my guess is that he's doing her dirty work for her now. We know she's skilled at manipulating people like that to get what she wants.' He paused. 'I still can't fathom her motives. She's left behind evidence which might well help the National Crime Agency to recover a lot of the money that the various victims had squirrelled away. No doubt she's already siphoned off some for herself, as she did with her father's business, but it doesn't all seem to be about personal greed. There's something weirdly altruistic in there as well.'

'If you say so. But for the moment she's slipped away from us yet again.'

'For the moment. We've got bulletins out for the two of them. They can't evade us forever.'

'Can't they?' Horton asked. 'I don't know about this so-called Matt but my guess is that Jewell will yet again do her chameleon act and disappear.'

'We'll see. I'm hoping her fatal flaw is her love of risk. That she'll play one game too many.'

'We can only hope,' Horton said. She was still looking at Grant, asleep between them. 'God, I don't know how Helena's going to come to terms with all this. Not just the end of a relationship, but the knowledge that it was never real to begin with.'

'I don't know,' McKay agreed. 'I'm just glad she's survived.'

'Me too. If losing Helena really was the price of returning to the light, I think I'd rather stay in the darkness,' Horton said.

McKay was still gazing at Grant, his expression unreadable. 'Aye, it's bollocks. Helena's one of the good ones. If things are ever going to get better, it'll be because of people like her. And there aren't many of them around. We can't afford to lose one.'

THE END

ACKNOWLEDGEMENTS

This was a tricky book to write. I started it in the summer of 2020, and, as the book was to be set around Christmas, my initial instinct was to set it in 2019 to avoid any mention of the coronavirus pandemic. At that point there was little clarity about how events would develop, and I was concerned about creating hostages to fortune. But as I began writing I realised that the pandemic would provide an ideal backdrop for both the tone and the plot of the book. So I decided to take a risk and set it around the forthcoming Christmas period instead.

That meant that, although on publication the book would be set in the recent past, I was writing a book set in the very near, but still uncertain, future. In the event, I was fortunate in that the Highlands stayed under only relatively minor constraints for most of the rest of 2020, so little changed in the intervening period. However in mid-December, just as I was congratulating myself on my good luck and prescience, the Scottish Government announced that the whole country would move to the highest level of regulations from Boxing Day – that is, right in the middle of the timeframe of the book.

Of course, many people were affected by this decision in

ways that were far more significant than my very minor inconvenience but it did mean I had to make some last-minute changes. Luckily I was still in the middle of responding to the ever-excellent input from my editor, Clare Law, so I had an opportunity to revise the book to reflect the new regulations. In the end, I hope that the book accurately reflects the way life was in this corner of the UK at the conclusion of one of the strangest years in living memory. There is one inaccuracy, though. Sadly, the white Christmas described in the book turned out to be wishful thinking (though we did have a sprinkling of snow on Christmas Eve and more afterwards). I hope readers will forgive that small piece of artistic licence.

The creation of an army of scarecrows across the Black Isle did actually happen and, as the book says, was promoted by the wonderful Groam House Museum in Rosemarkie. Groam House is devoted largely to Pictish life, art and culture, and is well worth supporting and visiting. You can find more information at https://groamhouse.org.uk/

Finally, as always thanks to Clare, Tara Lyons and everyone else at Bloodhound Books – and especially to Betsy and Fred for their continuing support for Alec McKay and his colleagues. And, of course and as ever, thanks to Helen, my first and best critic.